C000313101

# flying

*Also by Henry Sutton*

Gorleston
Bank Holiday Monday
The Househunter

# henry sutton
# flying

First published in 2000 by Hodder and Stoughton
A division of Hodder Headline
A Sceptre Book

A CIP catalogue record for this title
is available from the British Library.

ISBN 0 340 71732 7

Typeset by Hewer Text Ltd, Edinburgh
Printed and bound in Great Britain by
Clays Ltd, St Ives plc

Hodder and Stoughton
A division of Hodder Headline
338 Euston Road
London NW1 3BH

to jane and holly

✈ LHR–JFK

# london

It's completely normal, she thinks, shutting her eyes, letting the seat take the weight of her body, giving in to the pressure, collapsing a little inside herself. Feeling the vibration in the seat, in the floor, change from a shuddering rickety-rick to a chilling, seemingly electrically charged buzzing, hearing the rising whine of the engines, a sound that suddenly seems to be pouring through her. It's completely normal, she tells herself again, realising it's not quite so normal, nothing like, as if, in a flash, she's been blessed with extrasensory insight. As if she can see beyond the horizon for once to a place where everything doesn't go according to the flight plan, where routine take-offs and happy landings don't always occur every ninety seconds or so. Somewhere apocalyptic – where they are headed, the aircraft's, and her destiny. This startling idea fills her head, which is already stuffed with noise and jarring. She opens her eyes, seeing not the dark hair and pale faces of a row of businessmen directly in front of her and the neatly groomed heads of other business people behind them, but the back of the plane folding up, like a wave breaking on top of them. As if something's shunted the plane from behind, or it's ploughed into the side of a mountain and she's witnessing the back catching up with the front. Except she's somehow not feeling it, she's not getting hurt and is still strapped to her seat whole.

She finds her hands are clasped rigid around the edge of her seat and that they're making the grey vinyl coating sticky with sweat. She can feel the uneven surface of the vinyl, how it's been moulded to appear like leather. The sweaty imprint she's made. She looks down at her knees half uncovered by the uncompromising cotton and polyester mix cloth of her regulation skirt. It's a bland, darkish colour (nearer a maroon than anything else) which she's always hated because it doesn't go with her skin tone, or anyone else's for that matter. She tries to take comfort in the bits of her knees she can see – two knobbly caps oddly poking away from each other, like they've turned their backs. She latches onto their familiarity, despite their inelegance, the particular oddity of how they're appearing now, wrapped in the navy tights they have to wear. She wants to unclasp her fingers from the shaky seat rim and squeeze herself just to make sure she's still alive, to relish her own flesh and blood which she's never been wholly enamoured of but knows it's all she's got, that it's what she is, her. As if this confirmation of herself will somehow steady everything, make her feel all right. Make her feel less scared.

Her feet are a foot or so apart and turned in at the toes with the soles pressing firmly onto the floor and the inch-high heels just glancing the carpet, which is another indistinguishable colour, reflecting her uniform but a few shades lighter. She can sense the engines in the soles of her feet, like an echo of what she's experiencing in her bottom, of what's shifting up her spine. Of what's in her ears channelling deeper into her mind. She wonders whether it's because she's so used to the sensation that for some reason she's feeling it afresh. As if she's being made to start again. There's a dryness in her throat and, still tipped forward in her seat, she lets her head droop for a moment, feeling the creases in her neck like a lump until she thinks her windpipe is being blocked and she cannot breathe and she quickly lifts up her head, fighting the pitch of the plane, the steady acceleration, the mild

G-force – letting her eyes be sucked in by the overhead locker lighting leading down the cabin and bathing the distant rows of cramped Economy seats, interrupted every so often by the galleys and the toilets, with what is she decides (for the first time) a deeply claustrophobic orange light, a sickly light – determined to shake this anxiety, this fear, however. She's felt anxious about things before but they have mostly been understandable, obvious. What's troubling her now is she doesn't know where this anxiety is coming from.

At home she's currently redecorating the living room and she's not sure she's picked the best colour for the walls. She recently woke up in the middle of the night worrying about this. She tries to fix her mind on the colour, which she realises is perhaps too similar to the light at the back of the plane, seeing the smoked-glass mirror above the mantelpiece with its thick black frame and this sickly orange colour on the surrounding wall. She's not convinced the colour goes with the tint of the glass or the frame and she's certainly not going to change the mirror, which she loves. But her mind soon fills with anxiousness as it drifts back to her current predicament with her eyes unable to take in any more of the aircraft, the full scale of it, or linger for long on the flashes of daylight beaming through the nearby windows which are making her wish more than anything she was on the outside. She'd rather not contemplate the outside, however, the ground, home, as if this might bring bad luck and they really will crash. She can look only at her dull skirt and her odd knees. For a second her stomach leaves her completely and she feels the straps dig into her shoulders as she's being lifted off her seat a fraction into weightlessness, into bottomlessness, followed by the plane making this sideways movement, at least that's what it feels like, and she lets go of the vinyl trying to be leather with both hands, bringing them up to her mouth to stifle a scream.

Yet the plane continues climbing at an impossibly slow speed, her heart and mind racing ahead, urging the plane on and up. She folds her arms on her lap thinking if she looks casual, if she adopts a casual demeanour, maybe it'll rub off on her state of mind, her breathlessness and she'll start to calm down. Besides, she's beginning to worry that some of the passengers might have noticed something's wrong with her. She tries to worry about her make-up. She feels hot and cold at the same time and is too tense, too confused to tell whether her face, her brow in particular, is perspiring and the foundation is beginning to smudge and crease. She carefully crosses her legs, letting her right leg slide over the left, leaving no room for any of the men immediately facing her to catch a glimpse of her knickers, which she thinks she remembers are her black satin ones (recently bought in a pack of three from Knickerbox, Terminal One). She finds her mind unfolding to this morning – her bedroom in faint winter light, herself naked and cold as she searches for her robe – only to be sharply brought back to the present because it occurs to her that she's dwelling on something outside the plane, something solid and earthy, and that they'll crash. She uncrosses her legs not even conscious of who might be trying to look up her skirt, wanting to make firmer contact with the structure that's flinging her through the air – as it has done so countless times before, she points out to herself. But never like this. Or rather with her never feeling quite like this. She shivers, wondering whether it can possibly be true that the harder you concentrate on your worst fears the less likely they are to materialise. She pictures again this wave of crumpled plane coming at her, urges it forward with all her might, just so they can keep flying through the thinning, choppy air over southern England. This is what praying really is, she decides. How you can only begin to get close to it when your life's on the line. She has a sudden, overwhelming sense of the precariousness of life, the temporariness. And how unattached she seems to have become.

She braces herself for the impact, seeing her life flash past her, all these bright colours, thinking why me, what have I done wrong? She knows she might not have grabbed every opportunity, but she doesn't think she's been too lazy. Plus she's never been one of these people who try to be more than they are, at least she hopes she hasn't. And she knows she can look pretty. Perhaps, she thinks, she's never been appreciated enough. In a way she wants to feel an earth-shattering jolt, the completeness of death, so she won't have to contemplate further why things haven't gone better for her. Peering towards the tipped-down back of the plane once more, into the eerie yellow gloom, peopled with hundreds of restless souls, she suddenly realises she feels quite alone. Quite helpless.

Get a grip, Selina, she says to herself, placing a hand on the seat belt buckle, the strikingly cold metal. Get a grip girl. Because she knows any moment now the ping's going to go and she'll have to stand up with all the other cabin crew on board as if everything is as it always is.

*Greg watches the cloud slam into the electrically heated windscreen panels, bursts of it. But in the short breaks when the air is clear and he imagines the aircraft pulling away unhindered there is a view below of tiny buildings and fields and a reservoir and further to the left a thick black road split by a faint line. He quickly realises it's a motorway and that as usual they are powering out of London parallel to the M4. The cars are bright swishes of colour against the smooth dark surface, and the background drabness of the fields and coppices and the dull, unreflecting reservoir, which all look so weighed upon by the low and mid-level cloud cover (strato and altocumulus) the aircraft is flying through, trying to break clear. Greg finds he's good at taking in broad sweeps of land in an instant, as if it's the last piece of earth he might ever see. There is always this feeling of grasping a moment that might never be seized again, a transitoriness. How it is with flying, he thinks. The windscreen is being hit hard once more with shattering cloud while daylight's playing on the top of the glare shield – this gentle slope of dark grey vinyl layered with dust and static – creating a strobe effect. Light is tumbling over the rolled border in stand alone shards, or waves, greatly diminishing the AFDS mode control panel lighting, what should be an amber glow, making it hard to read the digital settings, especially the IAS/Mach, heading and altitude windows, and not so much dimming the CRTs as smoking them – cutting the sheen off the PFD, which contains the attitude indicator complete with flight director bars and the airspeed and altitude tapes, with the small radio altimeter at the top of the screen and a compass arc, currently displaying the magnetic heading, at the bottom. It's the most colourful screen on the forward instrument panel, with land being beige and the sky a perfect, unblemished blue and the aircraft a thick T of magenta. And this image is surrounded with numerals and letters, telling how quickly and at exactly what angle to the earth the aircraft is making headway in greens and whites and more magentas. Everything is clear enough but not as clear as it can be, Greg thinks, because of this flickering daylight which is gaining strength, as if the windscreen has shattered and pure light is shafting over the forward instrument panel and the central control panel, and just aft of that the thrust levers looking like they come from another time, an earlier, mechanical age, with the speed brake, on the left of the throttles, set to detent and the flap lever on the right having just been pushed to the up position, and on over the fuel cut-off knobs and the radio and the audio select panels, the transponder, the weather radar controls, the cabins interphone, the evacuation signal button, until it's just glancing – Greg notices because he's reaching that way – the passenger and cabin crew seat belt sign switches and the one they no longer have to use for no smoking because every flight is now no smoking.*

Nigel flips open the buckle and pushes the straps off his shoulders. He stands, letting his legs adjust to the pitch of the plane and a sudden but gentle buffeting, before crouching a little almost instinctively so he can glance out of the window set deep in passenger door D1R just on his left as he's facing aft. He makes for the windows at every opportunity. He especially loves to see the land disappearing behind cloud and the plane lifting into the vastness of the sky, that moment when he feels they're no longer connected to the earth but another world with its own rules and regulations, ways of communicating and conventions. After all these years he still feels a thrill. A few feet away and at this angle he can see rushing cloud, wisps bouncing along the fuselage. Leaving the window, he turns and straightens himself, his large body now attuned to the motion, at one with it, as if he's just another part of the plane, and surveys his cabin – the calmness of First with its fourteen giant sleeper seats, eleven of which are occupied today. There are eight men and three women, all of whom Nigel regards as his personal guests. He knows each of their names and titles and how they wish to be addressed, their particular likes and dislikes, even who'll be taking an afternoon nap. Sometimes he doesn't think he's on an airliner at all but that he's presiding over a small but sumptuous hotel, an exclusive retreat. He has always been keenly aware of the responsibility of his job. He briefly dwells on the fact that he's been stationed in First yet again – where he knows he belongs on board, his rightful place. Not only does he understand the finer aspects of customer service but believes he can relate to the passengers on their level. He sees it as a matter of balance, meeting people's demands with just the right degree of charm and confidence. That to be over friendly is as bad as being incompetent. He brushes his shirt front, flattening his clip-on tie over his stomach, which protrudes much further than he'd like, and glances quickly over his shoulder to the window once more. He no longer sees wisps of cloud but a magnesium flash of brilliance, a porthole of pure white, and he smiles to himself as he swiftly steps across the aisle and straight into the galley, the thick, fire-resistant galley curtains still pinned back for take-off.

The galley is empty which surprises Nigel because he didn't exactly rush here after the cabin crew unfasten seat belt chime went. Wondering where the other two are, he looks at his watch, a fake Rolex he picked up on Canal Street almost a year ago and which remarkably not only still works but keeps almost perfect time, though he did pay $30 for it, about $20 too much in his opinion. It's a chronograph, gold-braceleted, encased and faced, with the outer dial, which Nigel swivels when he's nervous, in a dark metallic blue – a blue that reminds him for some reason of sports cars (he's never had one, he can't even drive). He has no idea what the dial is for but it makes a soft clicking sound. He bought the watch to impress his mother, it's what all the pilots wear, and many of the passengers he sees in First, especially the Americans. However, he doesn't think his mother has noticed it. She's certainly never commented on it despite the hints he's dropped and the short-sleeved shirts and T-shirts he usually wears around the house, and the way he always takes it off and places it on the window ledge, propped against the glass, so he can still tell the time whenever he does the washing up. In the evening, if he places it carefully, the sun can catch the edge of the case and send shivers of gold light around the room. He thinks it's unavoidable but knows his mum's eyesight is bad – getting worse than ever. He taps the watch the way he's seen countless pilots tap their watches (usually while waiting to pass through crew immigration), with a quick one two of the forefinger, the edge of his nail striking the glass with a slightly tinny ring – as if this action might square up the time somehow. It's 14.28 and as he lifts his head the other two people working with him today out of Galley 1 – Carlo the galley chef and Wendy a senior cabin crew – enter from both sides at exactly the same time, sweeping through the curtained-back doorless doorways as if their entrance has been strangely choreographed. He immediately feels sandwiched, threatened even.

I'm sorry, Nigel says nervously, looking at his watch again, stretching his arm in front of him and slowly bringing his wrist up to his face for maximum effect, but did we get a little lost on the way to work? He watches the chef, Carlo, say nothing as he unclips one of the curtains on the left side of the plane, letting it drop into place with a faint disturbance of the already warm and stale-smelling galley air. It blows away a thick beam of sunlight which was striking the buffed aluminium counter and seemingly leaking into a pool of liquid light about the size of an entrée plate. Nigel only noticed it was there by its sudden absence, realising he hasn't seen any sun since he was last at this altitude, the weather in England over the last few days having been continuously overcast. He looks for an imprint, a shadow of the sun's brief presence in the galley, this strong light, but sees no trace in the now dimmer pinkish hue gently slipping over all the aluminium work surfaces, and the chrome beverage makers and water spouts and catches and paddle blades dotted around the dry and wet lockers and the grey and beige wall and ceiling panels (there is no discernible pattern). A fat, almost graspable wedge of tainted air.

It's a big plane, Wendy says.

Nigel doesn't like the sound of Wendy's voice, realising he probably shouldn't have been quite so sarcastic. He's done the job long enough to know that if you set the wrong tone at the beginning of a flight, if you piss off the members of your team this early on, you're going to have to live with it or worse for the duration. In the hot, confined space of the galley he knows that moods can only get more fractious. The delicacy of cabin crews' egos in the airline business never ceases to amaze him. He's normally meticulous with the atmosphere he attempts to create (as he is with everything connected to the job). Of course, he believes people should be able to have a laugh and time to chat but the passengers obviously come first, particularly up this end of the plane, and one's prime duty is to run an efficient, tidy galley that produces the required food and drink when requested with the minimum of fuss, as well as ensuring that the cabin is always as comfortable and relaxed as possible. He has to be able to operate in a calm atmosphere so he can clearly see everything he's doing and has lined up to do. He's come to rely upon routines, on order. He also wants to be respected. He's no longer young and not everyone becomes a purser. He has status. He thinks carefully before he says, Wendy, let's just get cracking, shall we? They must be gasping for a drink by now.

Who isn't? Wendy says. She mimes someone knocking back a cocktail – Nigel can tell it's a cocktail because of the shape of the imaginary glass she's holding. Phew, she says, after she's finished it and staggers a little, reaching for the counter.

Nigel shuts his eyes for a moment, seeing a crazy, panicky swirl of bright orange particles. He can't bear clowns. He reaches for the dial on his watch which he slowly turns, sensing trouble. He wonders why he's been singled out, why he should have been put in charge of her, why they should both be on this flight after things had been going so smoothly for him, so trouble-free, for so long. He feels it personally, as if some greater being has planted her here on purpose to ruin everything. He wonders whether he's run out of luck. He can supervise a galley, knows exactly how it should be run, but he's never been able to cope with dissension. He's pathetic when it comes to exerting his authority. Which is probably why he's never risen beyond the rank of purser, a fact he doesn't like to contemplate often. He knows he's too fragile to go all the way, to become a cabin manager.

Are you sure we haven't worked together before? says Wendy.

Oh yes, says Nigel. I'd have remembered. And at the age of forty-six he knows his chances for promotion in the future are slim. Most of the cabin managers he comes across nowadays are in their early thirties, like the one on board today, Selina. He doesn't know how they can possibly have the necessary experience. Feeling sorry for himself, he lets his mind linger on the thought that his career is going nowhere, that he's stuck with Wendy for the next seven hours, and a mute chef who's clearly not English, that his mother is seriously ill – that she's dying. Yet oddly, he doesn't feel as depressed as he should, not about his mum anyway. He looks at Wendy afresh, her heavily made-up eyes, her scrawny frame – she must be almost his age and she's not even a purser. Perhaps, he thinks, she was only trying to be friendly but doesn't yet know how to react to him, how he is. Few people do. He says, But that doesn't mean, darling, we're not going to get along just fine. He can't believe he said darling, it's so unlike him.

*Greg dials 28000, seeing the figure come up in the small altitude window just to the right of the centre of the glare shield control panel. He presses the altitude button below it, then selects Brecon on the FMS before he activates the LNAV switch. The change in engine tone is immediately audible in the cockpit, despite the heavy sound-proofing and the constant rushing noise the air conditioning makes – like a car going very fast with the window open a crack, he's often thought. He coughs, trying to get comfortable, as the aircraft slowly banks to the right. He removes his shoulder straps, leaving just the lap belt digging into his soft, gassy stomach and puts his left hand out, reaching for the corner of the glare shield, just above the clock. He begins to tap lightly on the dark grey dusty vinyl — little finger to thumb again and again — feeling the warmth the sun has made on the surface already despite the cool draught specifically fed there so the heat doesn't build up too much. He watches the aircraft slowly right itself.*

There's always a time early on when you suddenly know what the rest of the flight's going to be like, whether it'll be a laugh or complete drudgery, thinks Becky. She's just had one of these moments, having spent the last few minutes checking out exactly who's working from the main Economy galley, Galley 5, with her — the first proper chance she's had. Okay, she's not always correct, sometimes she can be surprised half way in. People are always putting on these acts, just as sometimes they might show you a glimpse of what they're really like. It's not that everyone is pretentious, she thinks, though some people can be, more they like to exaggerate a little, they like to embellish stuff to make their lives sound interesting. But mostly she finds flights fall into a set pattern with people behaving pretty much as they first appear. She doesn't think there are any big secrets in this business.

She catches herself in the galley mirror, which is just to the right of the beverage maker so it's a bit steamed-up already. She likes the way her features appear softened in it and her hair thicker and darker than normal. She thinks of one of those fashion shots you see everywhere nowadays, where nothing is in focus and you can't tell what on earth is going on, no more than the most striking colours and shapes anyway. She's always in two minds about her hair. On the one hand she wishes she were blonde and that it were straight so she could do what she liked with it. On the other she's usually the only brunette on board, so at least she sticks out and people aren't always muddling up her name with someone else's. Her hair's been really short now for some time. She knows it's not exactly elegant, more boyish if anything, but she finds it easy to get ready — she likes to sleep in as late as possible. She flicks the palm of her hand across the top of her head, from left to right, something she does a lot, feeling the way the styling moose has turned her hair crunchy. She's often thought about dyeing it blonde but believes her complexion's too dark and that it would look ridiculously fake — which she doesn't think is her at all. She has huge brown eyes. At least people are always telling her they are huge, so she's sort of grown accustomed to thinking of them this way — as these huge, smudgy ovals, quite out of proportion. But looking into the steamy mirror she doesn't see her eyes, she sees her nose and her forehead and her chin — the bits of her face she hates most.

Excuse me, Valerie says. She's trying to release a trolley from its stowage position.

Sorry, Becky says, backing out of Valerie's way and shifting along from the mirror so at least she doesn't have to be reminded of her awful appearance. Valerie, she decided a few moments ago, is like this perfect vision of a hostie, almost too good to be true — she sees them occasionally. Her hair, streaked blonde, is pinned up on one side of her head only with a few strands purposefully left free to fall over her right ear. On the other side it appears to have been cut shorter and left unpinned but the whole effect, amazingly Becky thinks, looks balanced, exactly how it should be. She has one of these delicate noses, not too stubby or drawn out but perfectly in proportion to the rest of her face. Her eyes are a grey blue and deep-set, making her seem curious and distant at the same time. And perhaps most impressively of all to Becky is the fact she's tall with a great figure, not too busty, or flat and skinny, just really graceful and sexy. Watching Valerie assemble the bar top — she's managed to pull the trolley clear — particularly the way she's placing the glasses, with all this nonchalance, as if she should obviously be doing something a little more important, Becky decides she's like dead sophisticated. Quite un-English. Exactly how she'd like to be. Sometimes she simply hates being herself.

She pushes herself off the counter, which her back seems to have sunk against, and steps across the sticky galley floor (it's always sticky, even at the beginning of a flight) feeling awkward and clumsy. And too short and too fat, and too dark, and that everybody else has noticed this and is trying not to look at her out of pity but can't help themselves. As she crouches towards her trolley and the paddle blades that hold it in place for take-off she catches Valerie's eye. She smiles but turns away before Valerie has a chance to acknowledge her – just in case she doesn't. She twists the paddle blades clear, unlocks the trolley wheels, stands and pulls the trolley out with all her might because she's pulling against the pitch of the plane and the plane suddenly seems to be climbing again and the trolley weighs a ton. It's already loaded, so she only has to fix on and arrange the top, which is meant to be the enjoyable bit, where, according to the company guidelines, you can add a little individuality, some flair – it makes her weep. She thinks at least she's got muscles, she doesn't know how girls like Valerie manage it. She gets the trolley into the middle of the galley without bumping it into anybody else's trolley and upsetting their displays – which is a miracle, she usually manages to mess up someone's. She stamps on the brake, locates a spare trolley top, spends a few moments trying to attach it. This is something she's always had a problem with, too. There's a knack and after three and half years she still doesn't have it.

Here, says Valerie, let me.

Thanks, says Becky. She stands aside while Valerie effortlessly clips the thing into place. I can never do that, she says.

There's a knack, Valerie says, shrugging. You pick it up after a while.

How long do you think I've been doing this job? Becky says.

Not as long as me, baby, Valerie says.

Becky decides Valerie is foreign but she can't place the accent. I wouldn't bet on it, she says. It's not as if she feels she's been doing it forever, she can remember being at school and when she was unemployed, though it's the only job she's had.

Nine years, says Valerie, shrugging again.

You're joking? says Becky. She can't believe Valerie's been a hostie for nine years, she doesn't think she can be that much older than her.

You know how it is, Valerie says, you start thinking you're only going to be in the job for a couple of years so you can do some travelling, then you think perhaps I'll give it a year or two more because it's not so bad, right. Maybe you get involved with someone, a pilot, and it sort of makes sense to carry on for a bit longer as you're both leading this crazy life, one minute in New York and the next in LA, that nobody else would put up with you, and somehow you're still here nearly ten years later, without the guy – who's replaced you with someone younger. Baby, I say for a couple of years, three max, it's fine then you've gotta quit.

Too late, says Becky, I'm in the deep end already.

You're in the what? says Valerie.

For a start I've been here for three and a half years, she says. Secondly my boyfriend's a first officer – in fact we've just got engaged. Becky feels she's blushing and that it's obvious despite her skin tone and the amount of make-up she's wearing and has to keep touching up every ten minutes or so. She's paranoid about her make-up being messy.

Oh baby, that's fantastic, says Valerie.

For a moment she thinks Valerie's going to hug her, which wouldn't be out of the ordinary because everybody hugs each other all the time in the galleys, whether they've known each other for ten years or ten minutes (which is more often the case), but she suddenly turns back towards her trolley, so Becky concentrates on arranging hers – the miniatures and the mixers, the drip mats and the serviettes, the nuts and the swizzle sticks – feeling slightly snubbed and this odd ache in her stomach, as if there's a hole there. Her stomach always feels the same when she's worried about something and she's suddenly not sure she wants to be engaged. She's not sure about anything any longer, except perhaps that this flight's going to be a real fucking drag.

# shannon

Suddenly all Nigel can feel is complete stillness, as if, he imagines, they are at the very point of stalling. A long split second of going nowhere. He's sure he can hear the engines idling. Even Carlo appears to have stopped arranging a plate of canapés and is poised, serving slice in hand. Nigel breaks the stillness at last and moves towards the left curtain just as the plane seems to accelerate, making him take larger steps than he'd intended so he's sweeping aside the curtain before he knows it. He waits until the curtain has fallen back into place shutting out the glaring galley lights, making sure it fits snugly (he knows how stray light can annoy the guests), sensing the plane gathering pace, the engines grabbing more and more air – he wonders why he's feeling the movement of the aircraft so sensitively today, whether it has anything to do with his strangely, seemingly not suppressible good mood, the way he so uncharacteristically blurted out darling – before he glances across the cabin, seeing unperturbed calm, except perhaps for Wendy who's chatting to a passenger, Mr McPhee, an aging American. (She's crouching in front of him so her knees and a sizeable portion of her skinny thighs are showing, the way he's seen so many of the female cabin crew address the gentlemen in First.) When he's unsure about anything, particularly how he's behaving, he looks at what else he currently doesn't understand and tries to make it all add up – the loosest of connections.

Feeling the plane levelling out and seeing no one's looking at him, Nigel skips across to the window in passenger door D1L, a surprising sprightliness to his step. Putting a hand on the bulge in the door made by the emergency escape chute, exactly where you are not meant to put any weight except everyone does, almost by the very sign of a person sitting with a red cross through them, he leans towards the deeply recessed porthole, his weight making it hard for him not to actually sit down. So hovering uncomfortably, with the strain in his legs and back building up almost immediately, he quickly looks over his shoulder to check he's not being observed before he lets his nose nudge the inner Perspex (or whatever material it's made of) shield, the surface of which is cold and slightly sticky, and his eyes fall on the sky. It takes a moment or two for them to adjust to the intense brightness, this being the sunny side of the plane, but slowly a bank of cloud becomes discernible and a soft blue rising from the horizon and deepening into crystalline indigo space. Nigel knows the names of the basic cloud formations (because his mother once gave him a Meteorological Office book about the sky for a Christmas present, under the impression he was studying to be a pilot) – cirriform (fibrous), cumuliform (lumpy), stratiform (layered) and nimbus (rain-bearing) – and that they are further divided according to their height so you can have, for instance, altocumulus, which is a middle-level lumpy cloud – alto meaning middle-level, cumulus being lumpy. He knows it can get much more complicated than that with numerous special features, each given distinct Latin names, and that you can get formations consisting of several types of clouds. He has seen clouds over every continent and ocean of the world, structures he thinks defy description, but what he sees now is simply dazzling altocumulus stretching all the way to the horizon. Waves of it, broken in places.

Something, a flash in the corner of his eye or perhaps a further manifestation of this strange sensitivity that he seems to be infused with today, makes him press closer against the window. With his leg resting on the emergency chute and his cheek rubbing against the sticky inner windowpane picking up the thrilling vibration of the engines shifting through the airframe, which in turn is passing through the thinning atmosphere, he looks down and through a clearing in the lumpy cloud he sees earth. Specifically he sees a wavy coastline running away to the west of the sun and beyond some smallish mountains becoming bumps and dips and eventually dreary rolling countryside. He finds he's turned and, now facing aft, succumbed to his weight and is half sitting on the chute, and that the coastline is rapidly diminishing and the cloud is filling in the gap – or maybe it's an illusion because the plane has moved on and he's looking from a much more acute angle, but his view of the earth, of the Welsh coastline and perhaps a smattering of Somerset, his last glimpse of England, is being completely swallowed by the altocumulus. He always thinks the last view of England, of home, is like the ultimate release, a sort of throwing away of your past, your history – the way you can watch it shrink to nothing or, as in the case today, see it suddenly wiped out by a layer of pure, untainted cloud. However he realises he feels different about it today. He feels an uncertainty mixed with nervous excitement.

For a split second he pictures his mother propped up in bed with her eiderdown puffed around her, then the curtain separating First and Business, which is just in front of him, rustles and parts and while he attempts to stand and look as if he hasn't been sitting on the door and just staring into space for the last few minutes but making his way into the galley, he sees the cabin manager, Selina, sort of fall through the half-parted curtain, reaching for something to hold on to, for something to steady her. She settles for the toilet door. He's never seen anyone, certainly any crew member, move from one section of the aircraft to another quite so inelegantly. He immediately forgets to worry about the fact that she might have noticed what he was doing and thinks of his passengers and what they are going to make of it. Happily, though, it appears no one has noticed. But that doesn't stop him thinking, as he's always thought, the company shouldn't be promoting women into positions they don't have the necessary experience for just because they are attractive. Are you all right? he says.

Fine, thanks, Selina says. She lets go of the wall and, still feeling slightly dizzy, brushes some imaginary dust from the front of her blouse and her skirt – something she does when she's nervous, a habit really. I seem to be a bit unsteady on my feet today, she says. She feels a complete fool in front of this man, the First purser. She instantly knows his type – someone who looks down on women, particularly women in superior positions, because they think they know everything there is to know themselves. Someone who will never get as far as they believe they deserve and who resents people like her for being nearly half their age and promoted way above them. Sorry, mate, she thinks.

Focus on something outside for a while, Nigel says. I find it can help you to get your balance. He moves further away from D1L, as if to let her step into his place.

Oh God, no, she says, I hate looking out of the windows. I get vertigo. She's not sure she really does get vertigo but she knows she definitely can't look out of the window at the moment and see quite how far away from land they are. She feels even more embarrassed for herself having just said this thing about vertigo so she says, Well, we can't stand here any longer, people will start thinking we don't have anything to do.

Nigel says, quietly, to himself, You don't. He's always thought the cabin manager's post is largely redundant – an excuse to just walk up and down the plane, nosing in on everyone else's business. At least he, as the First purser, actually has a proper job to do. He looks at Selina, her highlighted hair scooped into a ponytail that sits almost on the crown of her head, like she's got a spout – he wonders whether it's to make her look taller – her green blue eyes encased in large smears of a similar-toned eye shadow and dark brown eyeliner, with her eyelashes heavily mascara-ed and elongated – he can see globs of mascara hanging on the ends – her cheekbones brushed with a great sweep of bronzing powder and her lips, coated in a bright pink and edged with a darker liner. Nigel knows his make-up – over the years he's watched it being applied in every conceivable fashion. Not often, though, has he seen it been done quite so badly, which is a shame, he thinks, because he can tell underneath the mess Selina is very attractive, that she has good bone structure, pretty eyes and a kind mouth. He realises he would normally feel a great deal of animosity towards this woman – being someone who's probably half his age but who has been put in charge of him because of her sex, someone who's clearly incompetent – but he feels drawn to her. Perhaps due to her incompetence, her obvious nervousness. Maybe he even feels sorry for her. Deep in the back of his mind, in a place he barely registers, a thought flickers through that it's not often he comes across someone who appears as disconnected, as fragile as himself. He follows her into his galley, wondering why he's giving everyone the benefit of the doubt today. He decides he should try to act like the fussy, pompous know-all people usually seem to take him for. Carlo, he says, looking at a plate of smoked salmon he appears to have finished preparing and has set aside with a couple of other dishes ready for Wendy to take through, haven't you forgotten something?

Yeah? Carlo says.

The chervil? Its omission glares at Nigel. He hates it when a galley chef can't even prepare a starter properly. Nigel is only too aware of the importance of presentation, and what his guests expect. And how in many ways presentation matters so much more than the content – that the illusion is what's important. He can't think why else anyone would pay what they do for First.

Carlo swivels the plate round revealing a few shrivelled, browning sprigs of chervil. No, he says. I don't think so.

Selina says to no one in particular, Everything okay? She smiles, catching Wendy's eye. She knows it will take her a while to get over this awkwardness she feels towards the other cabin crew. She supposes it's all wrapped up with her recent promotion, how, as even her best mates have questioned, she managed to land the job when she had neither the experience nor quite the necessary people skills. Just a pretty face and long legs – as even Mike said in one of his kinder moments. She knows everyone thinks being a cabin manager is a non-job, that all you have to do is wander up and down the plane sticking your nose into other people's business. But she finds it truly hard work, particularly because of the responsibility and the stress this induces. She's in charge of not just one galley and one cabin, but five. She's accountable for the comfort, and to a certain extent the safety, of nearly 400 people. At least, she suddenly realises, she'd rather be worrying about this, to have her mind focused on whether the in-flight entertainment systems are working correctly or whether there's enough water for the toilets, if the temperature is okay in each of the controlled zones, that the kids' packs have been distributed in Economy and the second cocktail round in Business has begun on time, anything but let her mind settle on the anxiousness that swept through her the moment they took off – so abruptly and surprisingly, so strongly she felt she was never going to be able to stand up when the ping went. An anxiousness that frightened her with its very intensity, the way it seemed to attack her grasp on reality, on her very being – because she's never felt these things before, because she had no idea such force, such depth of feeling was in her.

What's beginning to dawn on her is the fact that what you do, the job you've grown fully accustomed to, maybe even to love a bit, can suddenly seem completely hostile and stuffed with danger. Brilliant, she thinks, a cabin manager who's afraid of flying. Don't forget, she says, again to no one in particular, that the plates must be warmed for the hot entrées. What do we have today – the char-grilled chicken pieces and the goats cheese?

Shannon says, 'Cleared direct to five two north, one five west, level three seven zero.'

Greg says, Cleared direct to track Charlie, five two north, one five *west, level three seven zero. He cross-checks the coordinates and the flight level which has already been fed into the FMS before the new heading and altitude are dialled and executed on the AFDS mode control panel. He senses the thrust levers advancing automatically to cruise climb the aircraft at some 500 feet per minute to its target height of 37,000 feet, hearing the corresponding increase in whine from the engines, and sees the aircraft begin to bank once more, revealing, down on his right between the co-pilot's head and the last visored windscreen pane, thick altocumulus cloud showing shear zones and the beginnings of a north south wave pattern and, like you might spot an island in the middle of an ocean or an oasis sprung deep in a desert, a patch of comparatively bright, welcoming land, a patch of Ireland the size of a coin if you were to hold out your hand. As if this land, this tiny fragment of earth is an after-thought, a final reminder of what you are leaving behind and shouldn't really be there at all, he thinks. The clock says 15.11, giving a TSD of fifty-one minutes. He feels a surge of electricity sweeping through him, as if he's just coming alive.*

Becky thinks, I'm last again, surveying the empty galley while hauling her trolley through the curtain and over the bump, or the strip of rubber that lies between the ever sticky galley flooring and the dull, scuffed cabin carpet, which always catches crew out and now sends the glasses and bottles on her trolley top crashing into each other. Some of the girls, Becky has noticed, seem to be able to get their trolleys over it without so much as a jangle, but of course she's never learnt this particular knack. Once in the aisle, she manages to turn the thing around, keeping her head down – she hates letting the passengers see her struggling with a trolley and is already aware that she'll have alerted them to her incompetence and that they'll be staring at her, hoping she makes another mistake.

She doesn't look up until she's level with row 42, seeing the gradually tapering end of the aircraft and the three columns of seats – three by four by three until you get to the very end when they become two by four by two. Sun is beaming across the tops of the headrests from right to left because most people in the window seats on the sunny side of the plane either haven't thought about or worked out how to pull their visors down, yet she can still make out the amber glow of the side wall and overhead locker lighting which, similar to street lighting, she thinks, keeps dragging your vision further into the distance. Almost everyone is facing their seat-back video screens, hooked-up to their headsets, but a few passengers are looking up expectantly, searching out the cabin crew and any sign of their free drinks and food, perhaps waiting for Becky to make another mistake. Becky senses an impatience, knowing she should have been out here much quicker. The plane is three-quarters full and the back section, Zone E, is probably the emptiest, though it contains a number of families with small children and a few leery single men and the odd grim-looking couple, plus the usual crowd of smokers who aren't allowed to smoke but still ask for the rear seats out of habit, or because they know that's where their fellow sufferers will be − drinking heavily to make up for the lack of nicotine. It's the worst section to work and Becky always seems to get it. She lets her trolley pick up momentum because of the pitch of the plane − even in mid-flight the aircraft slopes a degree or two aft − and roll on its own the last few packed rows to the toilets and the service door, D5R, at the very rear where she'll stamp on the brake, catch her breath and release it a few moments later to begin the first (late) drinks service by slowly dragging the bloody thing the twenty-five rows up to the galley. You're meant to go this way so you can face the passengers as you serve them, and if for some reason the brake fails you don't get knocked over. Fully loaded, she thinks, it could kill you.

Sun is glancing people's faces, most now being pointed her way and, with headsets still in place, mouthing orders quite out of turn. Sorry, madam, you'll have to wait a second, Becky says. She smiles questioningly at the man in seat 53J. Can I get you anything to drink, sir? (In Economy, unlike Business, women aren't served first. It's strictly by seat location, whatever anyone expects.)

Beer and a couple of whiskies, please, he says, struggling to uncross his legs and fold down his table.

He reminds Becky slightly of her dad. How stocky he is. There's always at least one passenger per flight who reminds her of someone. She crouches – carefully, so as not to let anyone have the opportunity to look up her skirt (they all have a go) – to open the drawer containing the beer. She retrieves a can and places it on the man's table along with a glass, a drip mat and a packet of nuts, the while trying not to lean on the woman in 53H. She repeats the process with the whiskies, except not bothering to give the man – who maybe looks even more like her dad than she first thought – a second packet of nuts. Standing, feeling mildly dizzy, she glimpses the narrow passageway beyond the emergency door, off which are a couple of toilets and the crew rest area. She'd love to just slip into there for a couple of hours (Becky, as crew number 10 and the person in charge of D5R, also holds the key to the crew rest area, not that it's normally used on an East Coast run). She reckons she's got brain ache from trying not to think about Ben and her engagement for the last five minutes or so. Madam, she says, can I get you anything to drink?

I thought you were never going to ask, the woman says.

# shanwick

Halfway between Galley 1 and Galley 2, averting her eyes from
the windows by keeping just the aisle seats and their subdued
occupants and the plain dark aisle carpet, this worn track of it, in
focus but failing to keep her mind in one place, Selina pictures
the tree outside her bedroom window. It's an acacia which has
been flowering since the middle of January. Her flat's on the
second floor and the top of the tree is almost level with the
bottom of her window. It's in the garden of the large house next
to her block of flats. The yellow is so intense it appears to have
stained the bare concrete yard which runs around the back of the
flats, making the space look inviting for once. In the eight years
she's lived there she's never sat in the yard, though some people
do. She can't believe it hasn't occurred to her before but she now
knows why she picked such a particular yellow for the living
room – beyond hoping a bright colour would make the place
more habitable. That it would help her to feel more at home.

Approaching the Business galley, barely aware of where she
really is, or that the Business purser, David, has stepped out from
behind the curtain with a couple of opened wine bottles and is
bang in the middle of her path, a feeling comes over her – how

she gets when she's spent too long in the flat on her own. She thinks it's like being completely stuck. As if she's weighed down, the atmosphere having become leaden. And she pictures the living room not in its bright new colour but how it was, a sort of dull peachy orange which had been there when she moved in and over the years had assumed a distinctly greyish tone. She sees the soft brown settee pushed up against the radiator, the TV and video in its stand to the left of the fireplace which contains the gas fire made to look like a real log fire, the dining table with the vase her mum gave her for her thirtieth birthday standing on it empty (her mum's always giving her useless presents). She feels something brush hard against her arm so she instinctively jumps sideways.

Shit, David says, can you look where you're going?

God, sorry, darling, Selina says, finding herself pressed against a toilet door, I was miles away. She pulls aside the curtain and walks into the galley smelling not the usual stale galley air – a cloying mixture of burnt food, old coffee, cheap perfume, expensive aftershave and aviation fuel – but her flat smell, a smoky, slightly rancid odour. She's always forgetting to open the windows or take the rubbish out when she goes to work – the minimum she's away is three days. And even if Mike hasn't been over for weeks she can still smell his fags. She gave up trying to make him smoke outside ages ago – he smokes so much she'd never see him. Though she's not sure why she does still see him anyway. She's known for a long while that their relationship is not going anywhere. Sometimes she wonders whether she can really call it a relationship. He just rings her up when he feels like it and comes over to screw her. That's how it seems. Okay, she calls him occasionally, she calls him if she hasn't heard from him for a particularly long while because she thinks that if she didn't she'd feel totally used and that the years they have know each other would have been a complete sham. In a way she believes it's a duty to that time. Plus he does have something of an excuse for not always contacting her. Her schedule is different every month and she's never exactly sure how long she'll be away, if say a plane goes tech and she gets stuck in San Fran or Miami or Boston for an extra couple of days. Or if she's on standby and doesn't know whether she'll be gone for four hours or four days. He's always saying, 'What the hell am I meant to do? Keep calling you every ten minutes? I can't keep everything on hold. I've got a life to lead as well.' She hears his voice, croaky from smoking too much, the bitterness in it. How he can make her feel so guilty, as if she's the problem, the reason why the relationship's the way it is.

The Business galley's hot and rushed and, trying to not get in anyone's way, Selina backs into the corner by the waste compactor, finding its metal lid is already warm to touch. She listens to David ordering about – perhaps a little too bossily in her mind – the Business cabin crew, Angela and Karen. Selina's good with names, finding it easy to memorise the duty list, who's working where, though she's terrible with faces, and shrunk in the corner wishing she were invisible, wishing she weren't in charge and didn't have to assume this responsibility, she's not sure which one's Angela and which one's Karen, though they do both look pretty similar. The marginally taller of the two turns to her and smiles, so Selina says, pushing herself out from the corner and picking up a copy of the chef's notes for the Business galley, I wouldn't rush the meal. I'd probably do another cocktail round before you clear in. I can give you a hand if you're feeling stretched.

We've already been round twice, the girl says. It's not too busy. They're not exactly drinking like mad out there.

We have been going for just over an hour, David says.

Selina catches him making a point of looking at his watch, a big chunky thing, a chronometer, the kind only pilots used to wear but now everyone seems to. Whatever you say, she says. Opening the chef's notes and flicking through a couple of pages, she says, Isn't it about time they changed the menu?

They won't until the middle of March now, David says.

How many pan-fried salmons with a saffron and caper tartar sauce, she says reading from the notes, can there be in the world?

Wow, have you seen what goes into this sauce? She closes the roughly stapled together booklet and returns it to the counter. She looks back towards David as if she has another question but quickly turns away again. He was still looking at her and in that split second she realised there's something oddly familiar about him, at least there's something disconcerting. Perhaps it's just that she finds him attractive, and that despite the watch and the very short hair, and his tight, muscular body and full, rather feminine lips she can tell he's not gay. Well, she says, feeling this tingle deep inside her, if you're sure you don't need a hand with anything I'm going to pop along to Economy. She suddenly feels more self-conscious than ever and a need to escape this galley and David's presence.

We're fine for the moment, says David slotting a tray of bread rolls into the warming oven. Good luck, he says, laughing, not looking at her.

Okay, darlings, love you and leave you, Selina says, hurrying out of the galley and turning right. There are things she says on board that she doesn't have any control over. She finds they just come out, particularly when she's feeling on edge, as if she has that disease where you can't stop swearing. It has occurred to her that having spent the last twelve years working for the company she's become so embroiled in her job, this way of life, she's like the sum of everyone she works with – the voice of 5000 cabin crew. When she says these things it makes her feel she's been taken over. Darling, she says to herself, sweetie – as if to emphasise the fact. She shrugs and shakes her head but not too vigorously because she doesn't want to catch even the slimmest glimmer of bare daylight coming from a window that hasn't had its blind pulled all the way down – the idea that there's life outside the plane, some reminder of earth, even if it is just sky. She knows she has to keep her focus clearly on board to keep the plane in the air, to keep it from crashing. She thinks she probably needs blinkers. Plus she doesn't want to upset her hairdo.

She squeezes against a seat so a passenger can pass. He takes longer about it than she reckons is necessary, casually letting his arm brush against her breasts – quite on purpose she's sure – but to her amazement she finds the sensation almost arousing. Normally it really pisses her off when someone tries to rub up against her in the aisle – it happens on every flight. The man's not bad looking, dark-haired, well built, an inch or so taller than her. But it's not him who she realises she's thinking about, why she's feeling aroused. She's still got David clearly on her mind, with part of her thinking it was him who brushed so provocatively against her, and not some stranger. She sees his chunky chronometer on the end of his arm, the massing of dark hairs that always seem to congregate around men's wrists. And again she feels this tingle, this itch of desire deep inside her (she knows it's not a muscle spasm) like a distant echo from a former self. When, perhaps, she still believed in men and love and the possibility of a fulfilling sex life. A time before Mike spoiled all that, or rather she let Mike spoil it. It was probably her fault.

Still going gently downhill (going aft) she sucks in as she passes a long queue for Toilet J and parts another curtain and moves from the relative calm of Business into frenetic, disturbed Economy. She finds even the air smells differently in Economy. So much less of the perfumes and aftershaves and expensive soaps people in Business seem so keen on using so liberally, coupled with the distinctive whiff of dry-cleaning, and so much more of what people usually smell of most of the time – sweat and old socks, body odour and bad breath, and sometimes vomit too (but usually later on in a flight). She smiles at a mother struggling to bottle feed her baby in the first row of Economy, seat 26D. The baby is trying to wriggle out of it and the mother is looking up for help, as if Selina knows what to do. She loves babies but she doesn't know the first thing about them. She has no nieces or nephews and none of her close friends has kids. She always seems to lose touch with colleagues who go off to have children. They all say they'll be back in six months or a year but they hardly ever return. The crew she knows who have children tend to be much older and she finds these women, with two or three teenage kids and usually a stable marriage, intimidating. They're not like everyone else, they have organised, fulfilling lives with routines and schedules which don't just revolve around the airline.

She can't help noticing most of the blinds in Economy have been pulled down, though a few have been left open a fraction and thick wedges of light are cascading across the cabin, making people's hair transparent and foreheads glossy. Selina wades through this light, seeing it turn hoops of her uniform almost luminous. It reminds her of a Lycra dress she used to have and which she always wore clubbing. She used to love clubbing, even the dingiest of crew hotels' basement nightclubs. In fact she probably preferred those places because it was easier to stand out in them – she's never been into the really hardcore stuff anyway. Her favourite was probably the Mexican-style one attached to the LA crew hotel, with its open air courtyard and great-looking waiters who always gave them free drinks. She's not sure why she doesn't go dancing anymore, there's always someone who's up for it. She supposes it has something to do with Mike and how he's simply wearing her down, destroying her sense of fun, her sense of herself.

Walking deeper into Economy towards Galley 5, the natural wedges of light giving way to the gloomy orange hue of the low wattage side wall and overhead locker strips – as if, she's often thought, the lighting in the back of the plane is purposely kept dim in a bid to try to dampen the spirits of the heavy drinkers and non-smoking smokers – she sees the odd reflection of the seat-back video screens in people's glasses and a flickering of colour on their absorbed faces. Suddenly she is worrying that no one is thinking about the present, the aircraft, or where they are and have drifted off into worlds of make-believe, into fantasy, or simply mindlessness. She wishes she could somehow make them all concentrate on the aircraft, their current predicament – the trilling, whining engines, the buzzy air conditioning, the fact that they are at 37,000 feet above the earth or whatever it is today (she doesn't think the captain's made any route announcement yet), hurtling through the sky in a fat tube of aluminium – to keep the bloody thing flying. If they all realised quite how unnatural, how extraordinary this sort of travelling is surely they'd make an effort to maintain some element of collective faith. As it is she feels she's the only person on board who's keeping the plane aloft, and that she might run out of will power. She's getting knackered.

Aware she's smiling stupidly (she always smiles as she walks through the cabins – it's part of the job), feeling the tautness of her lipstick, she wonders whether in fact Mike might be partly responsible for her sudden anxiousness, the way her mind keeps digging away at things when she used to just let them go, when they never even bothered her in the first place. She wonders what part he might have played because she has a sense – she doesn't know why – that it has more to do with her life on the ground than in the air. (She knows she's becoming more insightful as she gets older, though it takes her a while to put everything into context.) Sinking even deeper into the gloomy back of the plane where, incongruously, she can see a number of passengers are beginning to rev up on whisky and vodka and a vast array of mixers plus loads of Swan Light and the 1998 Chevalière Reserve Chardonnay (which according to the Economy menu is silky smooth with flavours reminiscent of peaches, apricots and exotic fruit, though she thinks it tastes more like soap), passengers whom she smiles sweetly, extravagantly at but also tries to ignore individually – she finds that if anyone catches your eye for longer than a second they suddenly find all manner of things to start complaining about – she can't help feeling that part of her still wants to be with Mike, even though she knows it's not going to lead anywhere. Perhaps it's because she can't bear the thought of being totally on her own. She needs to have someone in the background, however useless they are. Which makes her think – as she parts yet another drab curtain and moves from the scuffed and worn carpet onto the sticky lino squares of G5, stepping out of the yellowed-gloom into the wickedly unflattering artificial brightness of the galley, with the chrome catches and scratched aluminium madly reflecting the square ceiling lights – that the yellow, the particular tone of paint she chose for her living room to match the acacia she thinks is so bright and full of life, so full of vitality, hasn't made her flat any more friendly or habitable for a (basically) single thirty-two-year-old female cabin crew who's recently been promoted to the rank of cabin manager not because she's particularly good at her job but because she's got decent legs and a pretty face and she's been doing it for just about long enough, though which to her seems like forever. Her mother always refers to her as an air hostess (Selina feels her mother's never accepted what she does) despite her protestations that the term is completely defunct nowadays and viewed by her and her colleagues as derisory, even though they spend a large amount of time on board referring to each other as hosties, or even hosties with the mosties – those with the larger tits anyway.

Hi, says Becky.

Hi, says Selina – Becky. She's not sure why she's managed to put this name with this face but she's certain they go together.

Becky feels both a tinge of pride at having been recognised and named by the cabin manager so early on and also a sense of inevitability because it's not unusual. Cabin managers don't normally forget her from the pre-flight briefing room. How could they with her distinctively misshapen face and dark hair and thick demonic eyebrows, and fat dumpy body she can only just squeeze into the largest skirt the company has manufactured? (Any bigger, goes the unwritten rule, and you're too large to be a cabin crew.) Yeah, Becky says, that's me. She can never think of anything to say to the cabin manager at first. She always feels intimidated until she gets to know them a bit and has worked out whether they're human or not. Mostly she just tries to avoid even saying hi.

Wow, it's busy back here, Selina says.

As ever, Becky says. Though she feels chattier than normal today. There's too much on her mind for her to completely clam up. This is her first flight as an engaged hostie, as someone's fiancée (she doesn't think she'll ever be able to get used to the idea, it's as if she's become someone else). And though she's dying to talk about it – she knows that cabin crew like nothing more than discussing other people's relationships (herself included) and that there's this general understanding whereby you're meant to reveal everything, that there must be no secrets in the galley (not that this stops people making stuff up) – she's also afraid to mention it she realises, to admit it to herself even because it suddenly seems such a big step. She wishes she could just relax about it, at least for the flight. Indeed, the first thought she had after Ben quite unexpectedly asked her to marry him was how great it would be telling her colleagues. She imagined herself in a galley, exactly as she is now, slowly, excitedly telling everyone, perhaps shedding a couple of tears, with maybe someone saying, Bless, and fetching her a tissue. She imagined she'd be the centre of attention for once, that no one would believe dark, dumpy little Becky with her out of proportion features had managed to hook a pilot, who's actually not at all bad looking. She thought all this before she'd even had time to consider her reply (though she was never going to say no, despite her mum always telling her to do so the first time she was asked, at least to hold out for a while). Yet so far she's only told Valerie. She can't help thinking this should be her one big moment on board. Hardly anyone ever gets married, despite most people being desperate to do so. She wishes she wasn't suddenly so confused, so uncertain about everything. She knows she needs reassuring, at least to talk to a few more people about it, even though she won't be able to be as enthusiastic as she'd like to be in front of her fellow crew – the people she spends more time with than anyone else in her life, who've quickly come to mean so much. She thinks if she doesn't get a little more off her chest soon she'll suffocate standing up. Besides, she's always relied on what other people think.

The cabin manager has moved to the other end of the galley and is talking to Debbie, the Economy purser. Becky can see Selina's got this great figure, legs that go on forever, even longer than Valerie's, legs she'd die for, and has a really pretty face, even though she's done something weird with her make-up. She can also tell that she's not married (unlike Debbie), even though she hasn't yet looked for the lack of a ring. She quickly does so to back up her instinct, her foresight and, as she knew she would, she sees the third finger of her left hand – this hand propped on a slender but shapely hip – is glaringly empty. (Of course she knows some hosties wear wedding rings anyway so they at least appear married, or, as someone once told her though she's not convinced, because it attracts the pilots, and the Business passengers like nothing else. She doesn't have her engagement ring yet, however Ben has promised to have one ready for when she gets back.) Becky thinks the fact Selina's not married is written all over her, her face, her poise, and while wondering quite what sort of message she's giving out herself, she realises she feels less intimidated by the cabin manager. That she's not an alien.

An oven-ready buzzer sounds and Tim, the only boy working in Economy, opens the oven which is showing a green light and at once the galley is overwhelmed by the stench of twenty-five hot meals. The smell used to remind Becky of school, particularly this squeaky, bustling corridor that led to the dining room – as if she were heading that way on a conveyor belt she couldn't get off, a conveyor belt taking her deeper into her childhood. Now it just reminds her of past flights, one after the other, three and a half years' worth. This smell that's become a part of her uniform, however much she has it dry-cleaned, a smell that clings to her hair and skin after countless showers in distant crew hotels, so the job's always with her like she's wandering around in a cloud that says airline on it. She watches Tim take out the two trays of foil-packaged meals and load them onto the top of his trolley, completing the cargo for his first hot run. Still watching she sees him search for a spong and, once armed with the tong-like instrument (a cabin crew's most vital piece of equipment), start to pull his trolley through the curtain, crashing it over the bump and out into the cabin – the curtain swiftly falling back into place shutting out any trace of direct daylight and oddly, she thinks, any sense that there might be 315 Economy passengers sitting there, with many becoming increasingly agitated because their food is taking forever to turn up. Once curtained off she finds it easy to forget about the passengers and what she's meant to be doing – she could easily spend the entire flight propped against the counter daydreaming. Except Tim has reminded her of exactly what she should be doing and she's bracing herself for her oven buzzer to go, hers being the last as usual. She particularly hates handling the hots, it's not just the smell, she's not very adept with the spongs and always manages to spill something scorching on her hands and arms because the foil lids never fit properly. She has scars to show for it. A patchwork of them, as if she's into self-mutilation. Or has tried to top herself tons of times. (In fact she's only attempted it once, though she wasn't being serious. She was only seeking some attention, some help. She remembers feeling it was like she had come to this dead end, with everything pressing down on her, and couldn't see her way out. How her life could carry on. Why she would want to let it.)

Just from the smell that's still lingering in the galley (and which will continue to do so for the entire flight – once the hots have been warmed up there's no getting away from it) Becky knows the menu inside out – beef in green peppercorn sauce and chicken korma, with pasta in a mushroom and cream sauce being the vegetarian. It's the same as last week's and the week before that, in fact it hasn't changed since Christmas. And even though she finds the smell nauseous and the food revolting, she knows she'll pick at the opened but untouched meals when the trolleys come back after clear-in and help herself to the crew sandwiches, which aren't much more palatable, and perhaps a piece of someone's homemade cake, Debbie's probably – the purser having had the good sense to bring her own food to nibble on. There's always someone who does, usually one of the older hosties. Becky loves snacking, she always feels hungry and with her body clock being continually out she never knows when she's meant to eat or not. And because of her tummy ache, which feels more like a hole than anything else of course and which seems to come on more strongly every time she thinks about her engagement, she knows she won't be able to control herself today. She's always found eating comforting, knowing how it helps her when she's missing home and her music and Misty curled on her lap and, she supposes, Vicky and Kate – not that she's seen much of her flatmates since she's been going out with Ben. And when anything's particularly troubling her her appetite goes haywire, it's like she has to stuff herself completely – even though she's often made herself sick. She doesn't think she's bulimic, she doesn't force herself to be sick – not often – it's just that she simply eats too much. She gets carried away.

She recognises she has a complicated relationship with food, how she goes through love-hate phases (at the moment she's into Thai, anything hot and spicy) and eats until she's sick, and yet she can't cook a thing. She has no feel for different tastes and ingredients, what you can blend. She's even worse at it than Ben. But with their schedules there never seems much point in learning how to do it properly. If she gets stocked up with food things only go off. She finds it easier to buy ready-made meals from M&S she can stick in the freezer or get takeaways. Maybe, it occurs to her, she really despises food and continually stuffing herself is all about self-loathing and this is why she's so confused about Ben's proposal. He asked her to marry him shortly after they had finished a Thai from this brilliant new place in Staines called Ku. They had shared three or four 25 cl bottles of the Chevalière Reserve Chardonnay and despite being full Becky was beginning to feel warm and tingly in all the right places, how she gets when she's anticipating going to bed with someone she really fancies (and she really fancies Ben). She got up and walked round to his side of the table, plonking herself teasingly on his lap as she's always doing, moving her bum a bit so she could feel whether she was arousing him at all, letting the hem of her skirt ride up her thighs which were squashed wide by the angle she was sitting on him (she hates the way they do that). She draped her arms over his shoulders and started kissing his left ear, dipping her tongue into its waxy cavity (she's tasted worse things), shifting her bum some more, picking up an edge of his desire.

The oven-ready buzzer goes making her jump – as if someone had set it off to spoil her reminiscing. Dead on cue.

*Greg turns his gaze to the ND just in time to catch the waypoint five two north one five west flick from magenta to white – from the future to the past – and the next waypoint, at five two north two zero west, start to glow magenta beside the permanently magenta track line. On the PFD the Mach indicator at the bottom of the airspeed tape is hovering between 0.858 and 0.86. The bug on the altitude tape is steady at 37000. Greg checks their amended New York arrival time, hearing in his left ear only – because he has slipped the headset off his right ear – the first officer confirming their position with Shanwick. He glances over to the upper EICAS display and scans the strip of digits detailing the engine pressure ratios, the fan speeds and exhaust gas temperatures, registering their normality in seconds. He hears Dan setting up a Selcal check with Shanwick and the resulting chime, a sort of dong. He looks down at the centre console to see the Selcal sign on the radio panel illuminated but he finds his head soon swings back up and his mind, like his focus, begins to drift away from the cockpit and the aircraft, across the thinning atmosphere. Slotted into their oceanic, which happens to be track Charlie today, it's the first proper moment he's had to relax since take-off. He usually makes an announcement to the passengers about now but knows it can wait, so he completely removes the headset, hanging it on a special hook just above his left shoulder.*

*Settling back into his seat – he can never get comfortable – he lets his gaze be sucked further and further away from the aircraft, following the brilliant cloud blanket all the way to the horizon, feeling no longer the rush of time but a gripping fatality. How easy it is to be swallowed up by forces beyond your control, to feel that life ultimately shapes you, not you it. The intrusions and temptations – whatever's put in your way. He doesn't believe he's guilty, weak maybe, but not guilty.*

*Shafts of sunlight begin to flicker in elongated stars across Greg's tinted vision. (He's wearing the shades he bought on his last trip to the States from the old lady who runs this sunglasses place just off Venice beach, where all the pilots go.) He suddenly feels calmer, almost religious, as if he's expunged something. And senses, strangely, the beginning of a conclusion, a drawing to a close, an ending. He toys with the notion of death for a moment. Finality. It begins to scare him, making him want something real, something concrete to hang on to. Searching, he focuses on the horizon, where the cloud band puffs and arcs, slowly dissolving into a deep spacey blue. A blue that used to make Greg ache, though for what exactly he was never sure, except perhaps more of it.*

*Greg, Dan says. Greg.*

Becky finds it odd how she can so easily think about sex while handing out the meal trays and sponging on the hots – trying to be mindful of any scorching spillage – how she can think about sex, particularly in-flight sex, at all on board. Because whatever anyone says, whatever she might once have thought, being a hostie is not a sexy occupation. She doesn't think planes are exactly conducive to experiencing multiple orgasms. Running through the safety routine, working in the galley, waiting on the passengers, telling people not to smoke in the toilets, clearing away half-eaten meals, soiled tissues and projectile vomit that's splattered half an aisle, she thinks, should not inspire what she spends at least half of every flight thinking about. She has a recurring fantasy, for instance, about Ben running his hands all over her naked body while she's lying on the galley floor. He quickly starts using his tongue to caress her nipples, letting it trail down her stomach, this sharp wetness, while his whole body seems to slip between her legs parting them until his tongue suddenly hits the spot that always makes her shiver at first, the lightest pressure, and makes her forget about her lumpy, mis-shapen body, her wobbly figure, her shortcomings, as if she's simply become a vehicle, a receptacle for pleasure, a ball of nerve endings. Maybe this is why she loves sex so much, because it seems to transcend her physical being, because it takes her out of herself. And she doesn't understand how the worse the condi-tions are on board – say, when there's a school party, or an outbreak of food poisoning – the more fertile her imagination becomes. She's fantasised about having sex with various captains while they're coming in to land, with a particular purser (who admittedly she had a crush on) bent over a trolley in the middle of an aisle, group sex with the non-smoking smokers at the back (she starts off being passed naked from row to row), going down on a female cabin crew, using the sponge as a dildo. Sometimes she wonders whether she's more like a man than a woman because of the sheer amount of time sex seems to be on her brain. Ben thinks she's obsessed. She thinks perhaps she just gets bored. None of it comes to anything. She has only masturbated once on board, on a bunk in an empty crew rest area during a break on a West Coast run – unlike the guys who are apparently always doing it, in the toilets, even the galleys (if a couple of them are in on it), especially G1, because the First class passengers don't have a habit of wandering in for a glass of water and a good nose, they just press their call buttons. Excuse me, madam, Becky says, is it the chicken or the beef?

The vegetarian, please, says the woman in 49H.

Certainly, madam, says Becky. Can you just pop your table down. That's it. Mind your sleeve, thanks. Any wine?

The white, the Chardonnay, please, the woman says.

I hope you enjoy the meal, Becky says, placing the Chevalière on the woman's tray. Returning to her trolley she releases the brake and hauls it a row forward, thinking back to two days ago, in the midst of this Chardonnay blur, how they didn't even make it out of her stuffy kitchen. She unbuckled and unzipped him where he was, still sitting at the table full of empty Thai takeaway cartons, the Formica smeared with coagulating green curry sauce. She went down on him first, tasting the salty dryness of his stiffening cock, her fingers digging in his trousers for his scrumpled balls. She loves flicking her tongue across the very end of his cock, the tiny slit, sensing him flinch as she does so. The chicken or the beef, sir? she says.

*Greg says, knowing he's going to sound both authoritative yet non-chalant, even slightly lazy, how he always speaks to the passengers, he says, Urrgh, good afternoon ladies and gentlemen, this is the captain. We've reached today's cruising height of thirty-seven thousand feet and* are currently some three hundred miles west of Ireland. The weather en route is looking good though it might get a little bumpy as we approach the Newfoundland coast. The forecast for New York I'm afraid is not quite so good — it's overcast with a steady breeze and the possibility of snow showers later. I'll tell you more when I have the information. However, despite our late departure, we're making good time and should arrive at Kennedy on schedule at four thirty in the afternoon local time. For those of you who would like to reset your watches the current time in New York is five to eleven in the morning. I trust our very experienced and capable team of cabin crew are doing everything they can to make your flight as comfortable as possible. If you need anything do of course let them know. Please sit back and enjoy the rest of the flight .

Replacing the headset on its hook, Greg smiles to himself at the thought of the cabin crew doing everything possible for the passengers' comfort. He wasn't particularly impressed with the way the cabin manager was taking the crew briefing session when he popped in. She seemed incredibly nervous to him. He thinks she looks a bit odd, too — great figure though there's something wrong with her face. He wonders whether it's just the way she's done her hair and make-up. Had she not been on standby he might have said something to the duty roster manager, not that they'd have been able to do anything. Greg regards it as yet another indication that the airline's not what it used to be. He's always now coming across girls who in his mind have been put in positions they're not experienced enough for, some who probably shouldn't have been employed in the first place, and countless doddering old queens who can barely push a trolley up an aisle and who should have been retired ages ago. He knows the food's even more disgusting than ever, that standards everywhere seem to be slipping. Until really quite recently he remembers there being this far greater level of integrity, this competitiveness, an edge their rivals didn't have.

But he doesn't care about the falling standards (he wouldn't really have reported what's her name — Selina? — to the duty roster manager — he presumes she's just having an off day), the fact that the airline's beginning to appear tired and more than a little scruffy, that it's resting on its past reputation. He's no longer so proud of the airline, or his job for that matter. He's beginning to realise it doesn't mean to him quite what it did.

42

*And again he picks up on this idea of an ending, a closure, as if a curtain is about to be drawn across the windscreen and he's going to be shut off from the view – the brilliant tumbling cloud, the patterns and irregularities, how cloud can rise up like a mountain in the middle of an ocean (the Atlantic say, in his case it's almost always the Atlantic), or just as dramatically shimmer from solid cirrocumulus into nothing in a blink, as if you're tipping over the edge of the world and find yourself suddenly falling through a field of blue photons. But he doesn't feel so calm, so peaceful about it now. It's as if he's about to be denied forever such a pure, unhindered view of the almost painfully endless sky. That all this light and space will no longer be available to him. That it's no longer something he can take for granted, part of the everyday, the norm. And he realises for the first time – why it's taken him so long to come to this conclusion he has no idea – that of course it's coming to an end. He's fifty-three and has to retire in two years' time, presuming he passes all his medicals until then – which is something he is no longer certain of. Recently he's been getting odd twinges in his chest and feelings of numbness in his arms and legs. He's worried about his prostate – he needs to pee all the time. He knows he's overweight and very unfit, that his blood pressure is not as low as it used to be. He's stressed – the job can be stressful, but he doesn't help himself. The tangles he gets himself into. No, he doesn't feel guilty, but perhaps he's no longer as good at handling certain situations as he used to be. He just seems to make more of a mess of things. He gets too involved. Shit, he says to himself, he's suddenly, glaringly aware of his age, how he obviously can't keep operating in the same way. For the first time, he thinks, he's really aware of the coming to an end of his working life, his flying years – of his own mortality. And it all seems to have gone so quickly.*

*Why he's thinking like this now, why this idea of his imminent retirement has just hit him, he doesn't know. Perhaps, as with so many things, he'd simply managed to push it to the back of his mind, but his mind not being quite what it used to be, not being quite so agile, like the rest of him, couldn't contain it any longer. He shifts uncomfortably in his seat wondering how much longer he can go without having to have a pee, like it's some sort of test. If he can last another five minutes then there's nothing particularly wrong with him, nothing imminently fatal. Another ten and he's fit enough to stay the course. He looks at his watch, a Rolex chronometer Jeanette bought him when he first became a captain. He remembers how proud he once was. And how proud of him his wife was. He feels a chunk of warmth rush through his body, not some feeling of love but guilt (perhaps he is guilty), and the need to pee even stronger. There's this stinging sensation, as if he's wetting himself already.*

What time did he say we're going to arrive? says the man sitting in 46J.

On time I think, says Becky, turning away from him and letting her mind quickly revert to what it can't help but fix on, with images and feelings and confusion coming at her from all angles. She's gone over it again and again, each time trying to register the exact level of sincerity in Ben's voice and his subsequent actions. He was still breathing hard. She could feel his thumping heart and his shrivelling cock at the same time, this incongruity. How stuff was beginning to leak out of her and onto his lap. And just as she was wondering whether she should climb off him and kick start the process again with her tongue – Ben comes so quickly she normally tries to make him do it twice, at least to go down on her or use his hands the way she's taught him – he said it, quite out of the blue. 'Becky,' he said, croaky and faint because he was still catching his breath and his heart was thumping of course, 'I've been thinking, perhaps we should get married.' Perhaps we should get married, she thinks – what does perhaps mean? And then he said, 'You're too good to let go. I think you're fucking dynamite.' She puts her foot on the brake and bends down to reach for a meal tray feeling her own heart thumping, sensing just how shaky she is today, how on edge. She's suddenly acutely aware of the trill of the engines, their exact pitch, the dim lighting and complete lack of fresh air – just how safe and secure it all really is. Flying has never worried Becky but there are times when she's more aware of it than others, like now. How there's a sort of rhythm to it, a pulse, and how this rhythm can be broken by something quite unconnected to the actual process of flying, making you much more sensitive to your environment. Bollocks, she thinks, fully aware that she's standing in the middle of Zone E facing aft with tons more meals to hand out and God knows how many hours to go, even if the captain says they've made up some time and the plane's still going to land on schedule.

*Fuck it, he thinks, when at last there's time to relax, with only the sky to stare at, to soothe you, there's this bloody thing pressing between your legs, halfway up your arse, like a ball of cramp with pins stuck in it, reminding you of not so much where you are but who you are. This bloody nagging. So he releases the lap belt, saying to Dan, You have control. He shifts the seat back electronically – it takes forever – and climbs out. He feels blood fall to his feet, feeling seep into his legs, the slow full weight of him. This tremendous pressure on his prostate. Stiffness everywhere. Pain in the small of his back, as if his kidneys are about to explode. He half stretches, rolling his shoulders and stumbles across to the toilet door.*

*The cockpit toilet, so far unused this flight, smells of cleaning fluid. He pulls the door closed behind him, shutting himself into the warmly lit, stinking clean cubicle, thinking at least the contract cleaners still know how to do a proper job. He flips open the lid with his foot, unzips himself and gets out his hot, semi-swollen penis. It takes a moment or two before he can actually pee and when it comes it burns at first and the jet stutters, spraying onto the toilet lid and the surrounding wall. He tries to ease the flow and aim more accurately, wondering why it is that he can never pee straight at first. Eventually he gets it under control and aims onto the metal flap at the bottom of the toilet seeing how far open he can force the flap with the strength of his amber pee. It's something he always does. As if somehow he'll be able to get the flap entirely out of the way so he can piss directly down the tube. But he can't as usual and the tiny cubicle fills with this sharp acidic smell as the urine vapour mixes with the cleaning fluid. Sensing the pressure easing he glances at himself in the large tinted mirror covering much of the wall above the sink. The first thing he focuses on are the bags under his eyes, the fact he's worn out. Looking more closely, he sees the numerous thick dark hairs which protrude from his nostrils and some stubble he missed this morning on his chin and the way his cheeks have become so jowly lately. The grey pallor to his skin. And for a moment he has this overwhelming idea that he's not looking at himself at all, that he's somehow lost sight of himself. He turns away from the mirror shaking his prick vigorously. However hard he shakes himself he always ends up dribbling a little inside his underpants. He kicks the flush and waits for the roar and that damp feeling.*

Nigel glances at one of the few windows remaining clear of a blind or someone's head and shoulders and which happens to be situated halfway along Zone A, looking very naked. He sees this oval of baby blue light. A solid sheet of it, as if it leads nowhere, as if there is suddenly no depth to the sky. He's tempted to rush over to check there actually is an outside that goes on a bit further, that goes on forever, but for once a sense of duty, a sense that he hasn't pulled his weight so far, that he hasn't exerted his authority or even particularly made his presence felt stops him. He turns – still seeing for a moment this perfect oval, its image burned on his mind – reaches for the curtain, parts it and enters the steaming galley (the true reality of his working environment). He says, in a mock Italian accent, Carlo, chop chop, we've got some hungry guests out there – the chef seems to be taking ages to do anything. Carlo doesn't answer or even look up and Nigel moves over to the counter feeling embarrassed – he doesn't know why he put on the silly accent (again it's so unlike him) – and insignificant and useless, and fat. He always feels fat when he feels useless. He desperately, hopelessly looks over the galley, wondering where Wendy is because she acknowledges him at least. She might not be on his wave length exactly but she's not hostile – he thinks they might even become friends. Over the years Nigel has found that there is no middle way with cabin crew – people either make an effort to get on or they don't. The ones that don't usually think they're too good for the job and that by just talking to the other crew they're accepting their role, they are complicit with it. He thinks Carlo probably wishes he were a chef in some fancy Italian restaurant, or running a textile business or whatever else Italians do. On further reflection Nigel doesn't think he looks cut out for working at all, like so many of the youngsters he sees today. The Italians he has to crew with aren't usually as arrogant as the French but he's never found them easy going, not like the Spanish, or the Scandinavians, though he finds the Scandinavians aren't always as clean and well turned out as he would expect, coming from such neat and well organised countries. That it's almost as if personally they have to be the opposite.

Nigel remembers the time when there weren't any foreigners working for the company at all, before the company became part of this worldwide alliance. Not that he really minds the foreigners (he has always found Mediterranean types awfully attractive — those lovely olive complexions and brown eyes), he just wishes they would pay a little more respect to how things should be, to what fronts all the company literature, to the company's motto, pleasure in service, for instance. And the very Britishness of the operation, or so he's always felt. He's been aware for some time of the erosion of the company's identity, its individuality. He used to feel something of a thrill wandering through crew customs and strange terminal buildings in his uniform. It used to mean something. He now might as well be working for any major transatlantic airline — same customers, same planes, same service (if not worse). Virtually the same uniform, not that the girls would agree. They think they've got the worst deal in the world — a set of drab corporate colours, which they say don't go with any skin tone or hair colour. He acknowledges the uniform, particularly the girls', is a bit tacky and cheap-looking — especially the skirt — but he doesn't think the darker girls look too bad in it, as long as they're not at all overweight. Nigel doesn't think he's a snob. He knows he can be fussy and might occasionally seem a bit pompous, but this is because he cares passionately about service and manners. He knows how things should be. He'll admit to being a traditionalist but there's no way he'll admit to being a snob. How could he be and happily continue doing this job? Or live where he does with his mum?

A sudden overwhelming sense of home comes over him. He can even smell the reek that greets him every time he opens the front door after he's been away, a smell that despite being ingrained in his mind, that despite him expecting it, is so powerful it always makes him stand back for a moment to regain his composure, to get his breath. He thinks it's like someone died a long time ago yet years of air freshener and every conceivable cleaning agent still haven't been able to erase the odour of decaying flesh. He can taste it now too, this thick cloying air that hangs in the hallway and that he has to struggle through with both his soft and hard flight cases – it doesn't take long before it gets the back of his throat. His mother never opens the windows and always leaves the heating on full blast whether it's winter or summer. Yet it always surprises him how quickly he becomes used to it, as if he's never been away. Quite how soon he can sink back into a way of being he thinks he's only ever wanted to escape from (in a matter of seconds he doesn't notice the smell or the airlessness or the heat or even his mother's soft, persistent banter) but he rarely contemplates this because he knows it's easier to carry on. He's always been afraid of con-frontation, upheaval, change. He has long recognised he's a coward. 'It's me, Mum,' he always says. 'Back already.' There are other reasons why he's stayed, too. He knows he can't leave his mother after everyone else has deserted her. He's the only person she has. And as much as he wants to get away there's a part of him that wants to feel needed, that wants to feel loved and cherished. 'I'm so glad you're here safely,' she always says. Except things have now changed. He wonders quite what her welcoming will be like when he gets home on Sunday morning, whether she'll be able to talk, whether she'll even recognise him. Maybe he's being over-dramatic but he doesn't think she'll be shuffling out of the kitchen to meet him in the hallway or appear at the top of the stairs in her cleaning things – this old green cardigan and brown tweed skirt – a cloth in one hand and a can of Mr Muscle in the other, as she usually does, saying, 'Nigel, is that you?' She'll probably be in bed, where she's already spent most of the week, unless she's been transferred to hospital. For a moment he tries to imagine what it will be like going home to find her not there and the house empty – whether the smell would still be as pervasive. Whether it will feel roomier, less claustrophobic, less stifling. But he doesn't dare contemplate this for long because whenever he does (over the last few years there have been two or three times when he's been sufficiently worried about his mother's health for him to think she might not be there when he gets back from a trip) his imagination ignites and strange, ugly thoughts seep into his head – like how free he'll be without her. How he'll be able to live and express himself exactly how he wants to. And quite how powerful the pressure she's exerted on him over all these years – to be the sort of person she's wanted and expected as a son – has been.

Standing in the hot bright galley stinking of warmed meals (straight out of the oven the food in First smells no better than that in Business or Economy) he feels the weight of that time he's spent living with her, under her gaze, her rules and prejudices, pressing in on him from every angle. The more he concentrates on it the worse it becomes, the heavier. It's like the sky – the only place he's ever really been able to lose himself – is collapsing in on him. But strangely he also senses a rising excitement behind this oppression, an opposing lightness, almost a frivolity. He feels these two forces acting on him, one seemingly coming from the outside and the other beginning to explode within. He realises it must have something to do with this odd sensitivity that's been pulsing through him since he left home this morning (after saying goodbye to his bedridden mother, after kissing her wrinkly, dry cheek), this extraordinary energy. In a way he feels it's like he's able to catch hold of air at last, to get a measure of its weight, to actually balance it – to grasp onto life, like he's suddenly attained a new gift. And perhaps it's this gift – of perception, of hindsight? – which is making him dwell on aspects of his past he'd normally rather not confront. And also which is possibly making him act out of character, or at least not be quite himself. Darling, he says quietly, trying to sound Italian, dar-ling. He lets the word dribble off his tongue until his old clumpy self catches up with him and stops him.

But thoughts are coming too quickly. He feels he's stumbling over himself in his mind. Wendy has still not appeared and he sees Carlo has lined up on the counter a roast loin of English lamb stuffed with apricots, almonds and morel mushrooms and a pan-seared seabass (though pan-seared long before it got onto the plane). Nigel always studies the chef's notes to prepare himself for any question a guest might have about the food, though he will never admit to a passenger that the galley chef doesn't really cook the food so much as just reheat it. He doesn't think he would even like to press this point with Carlo. He sees steam drifting up from the plates and sprinkling the nearby stowage lockers with irregular shapes of dull condensation, shapes like countries or, he supposes, shadows of countries. The left curtain's a small step away and Nigel leans across and quickly pokes his head out hanging onto the last dry locker for support, but keeping the rest of his large body out of sight. As he realises he expected he sees Wendy talking to Mr McPhee, facing aft, crouching subserviently, but also revealingly, again. He releases his hold on the locker and lets more of his body slip out of the galley into the cabin and begins to try to attract her attention by flapping the fingers of his upheld right hand, like a small child might wave. Nigel knows how guests hate to be cornered by cabin crew, how they expect to be left in peace. Wendy appears not to notice or is choosing to ignore him and doesn't budge. He spots her knickers, a small patch of white between her thighs, and he feels himself blush a little. Over the years he's inadvertently caught sight of hundreds and hundreds of bits of cabin crew underwear and every time he feels embarrassed. He can't understand why some women are so ungainly, so immodest. He pulls himself inside the galley thinking, if she's that desperate to pick up this old man I'm not going to get in her way, perplexed, perhaps even a little impressed, by some people's capacity to pursue so rigorously what they desire. He's always simply run away. His lack of anger for someone breaking the rules surprises him until he realises it must be a further manifestation of his mood today. Of this newfound energy. And yet unlike the other times when his mother has been ill he knows her current condition is much more serious. He knows she'll probably never fully recover. In fact he's sure the end is near this time, he can sense it. For a second she appears in his mind as he left her, propped in her bed almost drowned by the puffy eiderdown, her thinning grey hair flattened and askew. It wasn't so long ago that it was blonde and springy, making her recognisable a mile off on the front, or outside the café (which she still visited, despite no longer having anything to do with it). Seeing her out in the drizzle Nigel used to think of her as this beacon from another age. When he bent down to kiss her goodbye this morning he noticed how much life had drained from her eyes, leaving this vacancy, an unfathomable tiredness, an inability to focus on anything but the middle-distance. And yet, he thinks, he's still not particularly saddened, or dispirited.

Again he imagines home being empty, the small terrace house four streets from the seafront he's shared with his mother for nearly twenty years of his life. He imagines it being his. He'll sell it immediately. He'll move away from Worthing. But before he lets these thoughts gather momentum, before he feels this welling of excitement become uncontrollable and he does something really stupid (he suddenly realises he's felt like this once before) he tries to be rational. His mother won't have been carted off to hospital, she won't be dead. Had there been any chance of that the doctor would have told him so and he would have stayed at home of course. It's not as if she even wanted one of his sisters to come over – as it is, Sue's arriving this evening (first time she's been to Worthing for over a year). But trying not to think about Sue, or Christine, his other sister, for that matter now – he knows he spends much of his time not thinking about certain things (for a moment, in fact in the space of about two minutes, his mind picks up again on a distant echo of how he's feeling today – this uncontrollable excitement) though his siblings are one subject he feels fully justified in blanking out

– he wonders what present he can bring back for his mum. He thinks he'll get her something really special this time. When he was last in New York he bought her a fake Gucci handbag he came across when he was looking for his watch on Canal Street. She doesn't know it's fake of course and even he has trouble telling. He's seen so many real Gucci bags in First and Business, and quite a few which aren't, he knows he's got a good copy – plus it only cost $30. He puts a $30 ceiling on his mum's presents so he was delighted with the price, which is why he paid over the odds for his watch. He feels for the bezel and clicks it all the way round a couple of times.

Often he'll just get her something really cheap and touristy. A six-inch high plastic Empire State Building with King Kong clinging to the side, for instance. Or a model of the Golden Gate Bridge, or the White House, or Chicago's Sears Tower. It has occurred to him that his mother might prefer this stuff. His father certainly never gave her expensive presents and, despite her former flamboyance, she's always been embarrassed by overtly luxurious items (though she does love perfume). It's all right to act up a bit, she used to say, or something of this nature, to make the most of yourself, as long as you don't lose sight of where you come from, your roots. She keeps all this stuff on the glass shelves Nigel struggled to put up specially in the alcove to the right of the telly, away from the window so the light can't damage them. And like everything in the house she dusts them continually, carefully lifting them up, treating them as if they are made of something expensive and fragile. Since she stopped working at the café, cleaning's been her main occupation, or at least it was until earlier this week. She used to go through the house once a day, always starting and finishing with the lounge because she said the lounge deserved a double cleaning as that was where they entertained and it was important to make a good impression – except few people ever come over to appreciate all the effort that's gone into making the lounge pristine, or to admire the dustless and gleaming display of souvenirs which he's collected from around the world, America anyway. (Nigel's given up trying to get off the transatlantic routes – deemed within the company to be the least challenging and usually given to the least experienced crew.)

He has an odd relationship with these souvenirs his mum's so proud of – five smoked-glass and spot-lit shelves worth – these scaled down models of American landmarks. He can look at them and yet feel he was never really there, that he's never been to New York or San Fran, or Chicago. Because when he's in the stuffy, overheated lounge (sweating profusely so all the armpits of his shirts quickly accumulate a crispy yellow skin that even the best efforts of his mother and the washing machine can't seem to budge) going over his travels in his mind or with his mum, he feels no different to the last time he stood there and thought of New York say, or Washington DC or Miami for that matter. He once bought his mum a blow-up alligator from Miami International which sits on the spotless glass shelf semi-deflated. He sees it there now, next to a tiny Sombrero he picked up in LA, and this small, one-stem cut-glass vase they used to use to decorate the tables in First at meal times (they're plastic now). Occasionally he gives his mum things he helps himself to from the plane, like the vase, or more usually items from the toilets and the First class amenity packs – soaps, perfumes, shoe horns, combs, toothbrushes, sewing kits. He's sure she doesn't realise he's nicked the stuff (everybody helps themselves), though he tries to limit what he takes. Her favourite present is probably a life-size Oscar he found in the duty-free at LAX, though she's also very fond of a Statue of Liberty-shaped lighter. She's never smoked but his father did and he has often wondered whether the lighter reminds her of him somehow and not a distant city which she has never visited.

As his mind's eye floats over these objects from far-flung places, these little icons of another culture, he doesn't feel like he has left England at all. He doesn't think all the travelling he's done has particularly broadened his mind – he's the same slow, podgy person he's always been. He's never thought of himself as someone who stands out, more as someone you can't avoid – an awkward, lumpy

**53**

mass hovering in a corner. Without thinking he runs his hand down his front, straightening his tie and feeling the soft contours of his distended stomach – about this time into a flight he feels terrible wind building and the first urge to fart, but he holds on for the moment. He supposes he views his trips as simply a suspension of his time at home. As if once on board he enters into a sort of timeless dream world, where the earth disappears and the sky piles up – layer after layer of ever more complicated cloud formations, each with their peculiar Latin names and each smothering a little more of his home life, his past, his earthly desires and expectations. Somewhere quite untouchable and unreal. However, he knows it's not quite like that because thoughts, elements of his real life, are always getting through. Maybe, he thinks, there is no escape. Perhaps I've been conning myself all these years.

Sorry, Nige, says Wendy tripping into the galley from the sunny side of the plane so Nigel sees her coming at him in a flash of light like a shock, an aurora surrounding her, but working in First always makes me feel really frisky. Nigel watches her sort of shimmy on the spot as the curtain closes behind her shutting out the background brilliance. I can't seem to leave that old man alone, she says. He's got lovely ears, perfect for nibbling. Nige, I couldn't begin to tell you what I'd like to do with the rest of him. He's given me his card already. She waves it vigorously sending tiny blasts of stuffy galley air in Nigel's direction – he feels them hitting his face. Sean McPhee, she says.

Tell me the truth, Nigel says, is it their money or their bodies that turns you on? Come on, it can't be their bodies. He hates being called Nige.

I couldn't possibly divorce the two, Wendy says laughing. When you get to my age a bit of bad breath and saggy balls don't put you off – not if the owner's rich. Ooh, I'm going to ring him the minute I get to the hotel. Perhaps I can persuade him to take me out to dinner tonight. I haven't had a good shag for weeks.

And you're going to get one from him? Nigel says. You'll kill him. I don't understand you lot – how can anyone even think about sex while doing this job.

It's easy, Wendy says. What else is there to think about? What else matters — except money? She shimmies on the spot again but this time she thrusts out her tits, which Nigel thinks are ridiculously uplifted. He can't decide whether she's had a boob job or whether it's just the bra.

The meals, the service, whether the toilets are working properly, Nigel says. Have you checked them recently? The passengers, and not in that way. You know, what we're meant to be doing, what we get paid for.

Barely, she says. What we barely get paid for.

Are you telling me you're dissatisfied with your job? Nigel says. There are plenty of people who'd love to step into your shoes.

Oh sure, she says.

It's not easy joining an airline, Nigel says. He knows he's becoming irritated, that his patience with Wendy, already stretched, is finally running out — along with his unusual good mood. He hates it when people are disparaging about being cabin crew, the only job he's ever known and is now ever likely to know. Plus talking about sex in any context makes him feel uncomfortable. Brings him back down to earth (somewhere, he now realises, he might never have properly left). He reaches for an opened bottle of Evian and a glass. Most people just swig from the bottle but not him. He has manners.

Selina can't bear it any longer and gives herself a good scratch. She's slipped into the cabin manager's station and, hidden from the aisle behind a partition, she goes at her crotch, using her skirt as a sort of abrasive cloth, feeling it rub against her tights and her tights beginning to move against her stubbly skin underneath — first to the right of her knickers (which are far too small as usual) and then to the left, inadvertently edging her knickers uncomfortably up her. Sometimes she wishes she had the guts to just wear those huge things old women like her mum wear. Because she was on standby she thought she might get a Miami or a LA and she hates hanging around the pool with pubes sticking out everywhere, particularly as hers are not exactly fair – not as fair as her hair anyway. Instead she's landed New York in the middle of winter. Normally she gets her bikini line done at this salon in the centre of Epsom, Veronica's (where she also has her hair coloured – she gets it cut in London), but for some reason she forgot to book and they couldn't squeeze her in at the last minute so she tried to do it herself yesterday evening. She'd attacked her pubic hair with scissors – loose strands, the odd clump even (she finds as she gets older the stuff grows faster and faster) – but she'd never tried to shave herself there before. She started in the bath, though soon had to get out to perch on the edge of the toilet seat. Maybe her razor was a little blunt – she didn't cut herself so much as graze her skin – because it took ages and by the time she'd finished she had taken a lot more off than she had intended to. She's now virtually bald which she at first thought was quite funny – until it started itching like mad. Mike is always urging her to do something about her pubic hair, which she thinks is ironic because he wasn't even there to appreciate what she'd done. He says it's so he can know exactly what he's doing with his tongue, except she can't remember the last time he did anything with his tongue. In fact the only person who does anything down there, she thinks, is herself. Or maybe it's just the heat and the dryness that's making her itchy, she tells herself, looking at her watch to see they've been going for well over two hours, which surprises her. It's as if time has gone twice as quickly as normal. She wonders how far she's walked already up and down the aisles, checking the cabins and the galleys – that it's neither too hot or cold in the various temperature-controlled zones, that the entertainment systems are functioning properly, that none of the toilets are blocked or have run out of water, that all the passengers, and crew, are happy. She hasn't sat down once. She thinks she should be used to it by now but she isn't – the cabin pressure, the airlessness always gets to her, making any movement seem like such hard work. Still she stops scratching herself, vowing never to shave her pubes again herself (however much Mike insists) and taps on the top of the CM's work station, which is clear of paper and things to do for the moment, except for the cabin tech log that always sits there waiting for a problem and the duty record which she doesn't have to attend to until the flight's nearing the end. She knows she might not be the most confident CM, that her skills aren't necessarily best suited to people management (people can so easily unnerve her) but she's organised at least. Paperwork doesn't bother her – she's great with forms. She's certainly had enough experience at it in this business. She can handle the tech log and duty record, the duty-free inventory, even an accident report, though she sometimes stumbles when she has to do a crew assessment. They give you too much space to fill in, she thinks it's like practically writing an essay. Besides she's never sure what to say, she hates making judgments about people, particularly when so much depends on it. And she's meant to do three this trip – Becky's, Wendy's and Tim's.

Increasingly she finds herself wondering about what she might be doing if she'd never become a cabin crew. What she might be doing this minute for instance, with her feet firmly on the ground, in a place where there isn't this constant rushing noise, this trilling, this jarring, this overwhelming sense of unsteadiness. However, suddenly consumed with fear, she can only think of who she is and, more worryingly, where she is – this rapidly aging woman stuck in the middle of an aeroplane at some 37,000 feet or whatever it is exactly today (she wasn't listening when the captain made his announcement) above the Atlantic, glued to the counter of the CM's station, located just behind G2, David's galley, where she presumes he's still bossing around Angela and Karen. She wishes she could speak to people like that, well not quite so bossily but at least to be able to exert some sort of authority. Then Mike surely wouldn't behave the way he does. He might even respect her more. He might start treating her as a human being and not someone just to be walked all over. She feels a spasm shoot up her left side, from her bottom to her shoulder blade. Whether it's a further manifestation of her current anxiety, her fear of not just flying but of everything she thinks, or some stab of pain Mike's inflicted on her in the past finally catching up with her, she's not sure. Though she's beginning to realise that what might once have been simply mental – feelings, emotions, anguish – is somehow becoming physical. That her body is beginning to react to what's going on inside her head – these spasms of pain and heavy aching limbs. Perhaps, she thinks, it's not the thin, stale, highly pressurised cabin air that she finds so exhausting but the fact her life's not going anywhere.

Letting her eyes drift over the VSCU display panel, seeing that the video monitors for First, Business and Economy are showing running – the green and white lights being in the correct sequence – she tries to focus her mind once more on when she wasn't a cabin crew, to the three years between school and joining the company when she might have become anything – she laughs quietly to herself. She was mostly unemployed though she did stints in the bar of a small hotel and was a waitress at an American-themed burger and ribs restaurant for a short while. Though when it came to applying to the airline she managed to make it look as if she hadn't been unemployed at all and had gained valuable experience in the service industry – every cabin crew she's ever met has lied to get the job. When she advises friends of friends applying to be cabin crew she always tells them to say they've been managers of restaurants – that's what airlines are most impressed by. (There was a time when they favoured nurses but they now seem to think nurses are a little too removed from the commercial world, that they don't know how to relate to the passengers, particularly the First class passengers.) The fancier the restaurant the better of course. She made out where she worked – where she said she used to regularly stand in for the manager – was dead posh and specialised in steaks, not burgers, not ribs.

She suddenly remembers she used to fancy the manager, who in fact never let her stand in for him when he was off duty, who hardly paid her any attention at all. When he did it was usually to shout at her – he shouted at all the staff but particularly her. If she tried hard enough she thinks she could probably still hear his voice, telling her to hurry up with an order, or that she had got an order wrong, or hadn't cleared a table quickly enough. She wasn't overweight (she's never been overweight) or particularly ugly then, though she doesn't think she could have made the most of herself – she didn't have a clue. She had no one to guide her. She doesn't have an older sister and it's not the sort of thing her mother would have encouraged – her mum's always disapproved of women who wear lots of make-up. And her friends weren't much help. They were either clueless like her or, she has since suspected, they didn't want her to make the most of herself because underneath they knew she was much prettier than any of them. She supposes she chronically lacked confidence and an ability to trust what people said to her. She's not sure what exactly got her out of this state, what made her realise she wasn't ugly and that she had a head on her shoulders – what gave her a better sense of herself and how she could make the most of that. Donna probably.

Uncle Sam's with its car number plates (one from every state) tacked to the walls and the Stars and Stripes dripping from the ceiling, with its vast Wurlitzer and bright, multi-coloured spotlighting and individual booths which she invariably got hauled into by groups of drunken lads, and the manager shouting above the din of ancient rock music by people like The Eagles and Don McLean – she knew it was hell even then. But it took her longer to realise she only worked there because of him. There was no other possible reason to put up with it, the pay was a joke and it wasn't the sort of restaurant where people tipped much. She thinks of how people can do the most extraordinarily demeaning things just because they fancy someone, because they might have fallen in love. She thinks of Mike and how easy it is to let these patterns of behaviour re-emerge. That you think you've learnt something when you haven't or, if you have, you just ignore it the moment it comes around again. Your mind becomes immune to the warning signals. She imagines life as a series of looped and ever widening cycles – a bit like the Olympic symbol, or she thinks, oddly, the airline logo with its intertwining letters. She peers down at her name and status badge pinned to her breast with the company logo emblazoned on it in yet another combination of the corporate colours. And she wonders, in the same way that some people latch onto all sorts of symbols, whether this mark, these intertwining letters – the accepted and world-renowned abbreviation for the airline – is really a comment on how lives fall into inescapable patterns, an illustration of how weak people are. Then she hears Don McLean singing 'American Pie' and despite herself and under her breath she joins in the chorus, so this tune she absolutely loathed, more even than The Eagle's 'Hotel California' (the only person she's ever met who likes it is Mike, though she thinks he just plays it to annoy her), is getting louder and louder, eclipsing even the buzz of the air conditioning and the trilling whine of the engines. She always finds that's the way with songs she hates, once they get into your head and pick up momentum you can't get rid of them. She looks again at her badge, the dull symbol resting on her left tit, lifted a little higher than usual (but by no means outrageously so – she is the CM) by her new bra, which like her knickers is also from Knickerbox, Terminal One (where she seems to get all her lingerie nowadays), thinking meanwhile, just like men. Once they've slimed their way into your life, that's it. They hook you and go on reverberating forever.

Hearing 'American Pie' pouring from the giant speakers stuck at ear-level in every corner of Uncle Sam's she can almost feel herself walking between the rows of booths, smiling politely, this stupid grin fixed on her face (just how she walks down the aisles now) despite the patrons always being so fucking rude, desperately trying not to catch anyone's eye, making her way through this block of loathsome sound towards the back of the restaurant where the kitchen was located, as if she's walking down a tunnel – or along the aisle of an aircraft going into the orangey gloom of aft – as if all memory is like going down a tunnel (and for Selina the past is always dim), she can actually feel how memory can so quickly metamorphose into the present. Sensing the while people staring at her, particularly the manager – how he would glare. (She always feels that people are staring at her, picking her to pieces, when she's not looking.) It suddenly occurs to her that she can't remember the manager's name. She can't even picture him very clearly, this man who caused her so much grief – she wasn't very old. Though oddly she can almost feel his presence now, as if he's not very far away.

Perhaps it was him, she thinks, this experience that finally made her want to get away from Maidstone (when she thinks of Maidstone she thinks of being walled in) and her mother, of course, who was forever trying to make out that she should be content with what she had and not to expect too much in life, certainly not go about tarting yourself up and giving off the wrong impression. That that wasn't the way to get anywhere proper. 'Who the hell do you think you are?' her mother would say, seeing her slipping out of the house wearing nothing remotely out of the ordinary – even if she'd dared she wouldn't have known what to wear. Her mother was like this clamp, this thing that held her so tightly in place it hurt. She didn't even like her working in the restaurant because she thought she might meet the wrong sort of people. Even though she was told she had to earn some money as she had decided not to go to college. She felt she couldn't win. She used to think her mother behaved more like her friends' dads, that since her father died she assumed his role as well as her own in her upbringing, but more so to make doubly sure Selina never felt his void, or something, which of course she did.

No, she thinks, it probably wasn't him or her stint at Uncle Sam's which made her decide to become a hostie. Or even her mother who she used to hate but she's got over that – she has a better understanding now of what she must have gone through after her father died. Selina's often wondered whether she was in denial for much of her childhood, perhaps she still is and the impact of his death has still to hit her – she was very young when he died. Nevertheless she thinks her mother was appalling. She didn't even like the hotel job she had because she thought her daughter, her beloved only child, would be seduced all the time by strange men. If only, Selina thinks. She still can't believe her mother had a problem with the place. Okay, it was a little scruffy and stuck out of town a bit, on the A229 to Coxheath and Hastings eventually, and there were numerous couples who obviously shouldn't have been there together and the odd leery businessman who used to try to keep the bar open all night, and maybe there were a few times when she thought she might be in trouble, but shy and uncertain of herself as she was she always believed she could look after herself. Maybe it was simply the sort of strength that comes from being naive because she began to feel much more threatened later on. 'Get real,' she'd constantly tell her mother. 'I'm not stupid. I do know how to look after myself.' 'Well I don't know who taught you,' her mother would reply. Her mother was worried that she couldn't look after herself but was unwilling to show her how – she couldn't win.

It wasn't him, she thinks, or even the eventual realisation that she needed to get away from Maidstone and her mother, because she certainly didn't have the confidence then or really much sense of another world being out there that might have more to offer her, or at least which might entice her away because it was bigger and brighter, somehow otherworldly. (Her concept of glamour had yet to develop.) Nope. She was constantly angry with her mother but she wasn't so aware of how sheltered she was – this feeling of Maidstone having walled her in not coming to her until she'd left the place for good. Nor was it some aftershock of her father's death sliding into her consciousness. That again came later also, she thinks – if it's really come at all. Or her best friend Sally getting engaged. No, no, no, it was none of these things, and the more she thinks the more it occurs to her what it wasn't. She shuts her eyes – as if she's trying to clear her mind – seeing a wavy band of colours shifting across her blanked-out vision, the colour of thought. Her mind opened up.

It certainly wasn't this man whose name she can't even remember. Oddly, for an instant, she sees him more clearly and this new image makes her shudder because he looks a bit like David. Though she decides she must be muddling the two men up, with David still being high on her mind (she's always mistaking people anyway). However, a feeling of déjà vu begins to well inside her. And fighting it, because she hates the feeling, it spooks her, she decides her wanting to leave Maidstone had nothing to do with some unrequited teenage lust, but everything to do with Donna, her cousin. It was Donna who helped her begin to have some idea of who she was, some idea of her true self, her real ambitions and desires, and to understand that she wasn't plain or even ugly but pretty with long legs and a lovely, well-proportioned face, framed by thick, straight hair that could easily be styled into something striking. It was Donna who helped her gain confidence and to see that she was bright and had a good sense of humour. Donna was the inspiration, the key reason why she left what she knew – the stability of home, however claustrophobic it was, and her mum's over-protective zeal – to embark upon a career in cabin crewing. Yes, she thinks, it was Donna all right, her older cousin who she hadn't seen since she was five or something and who appeared from nowhere one Saturday afternoon in her uniform looking to Selina like she'd come from another world or at least a different continent – smelling of Chanel No 5, though Selina didn't know it was Chanel No 5 then of course.

Why people have to try to tidy up their meal trays Becky has no idea. She thinks it must be like a compulsion because they are always doing it, perhaps in the same way people are obsessed with tidying their houses, with tidying things away. The trouble is they usually stack things wrongly. They never know what to do with the miniatures or the foil lids or the empty water cartons, or the metal cutlery and it makes her job that much more unpleasant picking through this stuff, particularly digging out the cutlery, having to undo what they've done (they never had to bother until the airline changed its catering arrangements as part of yet another cost-cutting exercise). The significance of this idea of undoing what someone's just done momentarily distracts her. She wonders how easy it is to become unengaged.

Moving closer to the galley going backwards she has a clear view of the glare the seat-back video screens are throwing onto people's faces – like she's seeing the unfolding shadow of a film – and the harsher reflections in people's glasses and on the odd pieces of jewellery, while she stops and starts the trolley, stamping on the brake (she's endlessly stamping on the bloody brake), and she reaches for the used meal trays. It's once she's got hold of the trays that she has first to remove the cutlery and any glass bottles (which go into containers on the top of the trolley) and place the foil lid on the bottom of the tray and then squash all the other stuff as flat as possible (which is when left-over food tends to spurt everywhere) to get it to slide back into the trolley. And slowly moving closer to the galley and her first break of the flight she realises she also has a view of not exactly time standing still because she sees movement, at least movement on people's faces – this flickering light – but, perhaps because everyone's currently so abstracted, of time being somehow suspended. Like they've all, for the present anyway, been removed from real life and bracketed elsewhere. Like they're in a vacuum. (She's had similar thoughts before but never so strongly.) Really that they're untouchable – that everything thought or said on board only exists in this odd suspended time-frame. So whatever she thinks about Ben and her engagement is of no consequence to what happens when they land, that they're immune from the real world. Which makes her, in a way, free. At least temporarily.

Maybe she's thinking these things about time, about time being suspended, because she's last again – as if she can only operate at her own pace. She's always been useless at keeping time. She glances across the stuffed central row of seats to see no sign of Valerie, no sign of her sophisticated hair-do bobbing between the headrests, that peculiarly French way, Becky's decided, she carries herself. She can't see any remaining food trays on that side of the plane either. Shit, she says, managing to squirt some curry sauce onto her pinny (she always wears one for the clearing-in) and the arm of her blouse. The curry's practically impossible to get off, however hard you try it always leaves this bright, radioactive stain. She wipes the worst of it off with her hand, though she is wearing disposable plastic gloves. Some of the girls refuse to wear them but Becky would rather put up with the discomfort, with her hands getting really sweaty, than have to handle a hundred used meal trays with people's germs all over them. She's always amazed by the amount of food people seem to half chew and then spit out and how resourceful they are at hiding it. She finds it smeared on the bottom of the trays, stuck to upturned spoons, squashed into the narrow rim of the foil lid. Though some people don't seem to care where they leave it.

# gander

*Greg watches Dan pick up his headset, adjust it, flick a switch on the radio control panel, say, Gander – . He loses Dan as his stomach reminds him of just how hungry he is. Despite it being bloated with wind and flopping over his lap belt, making his shirt ripple horizontally, he still feels he could fit in a large lunch. He drank too much last night and whenever he's hungover he finds he has to eat a lot. He thinks about helping himself to another chocolate from the box lying on the ledge by the library but decides he should wait until he's had some proper food, he's already had half a dozen with his coffee. He tries to reassemble his concentration – hears Dan say into his headset mic, Position, five two north three zero west at one seven zero two, level three seven zero. Five two north four zero west at one seven four nine, five two north five zero west next. But he doesn't pick up Gander's reply because he's not wearing his headset, even one that's askew, and the flight deck speaker is on the blink, so trying to keep his mind from wandering too far from the cockpit, this great sweep of state-of-the-art avionics, the proper and safe functioning of which he's ultimately responsible for – Christ, he feels rough, not just physically but mentally, as if his brain's been liquidised – he turns to the CRTs, deciding he'll press on with the waypoint checks. There are times when he can look at the bank of screens – the PFD and ND, the upper and lower*

EICAS displays, the FMS – and nothing comes into focus, nothing registers, for what might be only two or three seconds but what seems like a frightening amount of time, as if nothing's connecting, and he'll simply see a pool of colours – the magentas and blues and greens and reds and oranges and yellows and browns, and dazzling whites like near stars on clear winter nights. The amber glow of the backgrounding panel lights. This flicker of static, of X-ray and ultraviolet radiation, of protons and electrons all tumbling over the glare shield.

He selects the log pages on the FMS and first up shows the equal-time point between Shannon and Gander still standing at 17.12, some nine minutes away – a figure that's been calculated to take into account the wind and the weather at the return and onward airports. He always thinks of the mid-way point in the Atlantic crossing – the point of no return if an emergency were suddenly to arise – as being somehow halfway to JFK (completely disregarding the nearly two hour run down the Atlantic seaboard). That the real journey is across the ocean and once over the halfway mark it's all downhill from there. He had a similar notion when he used to fly to South Africa. Then he regarded the main part of the flight as getting over the Sahara. It was as if this vast topographical hurdle had to be conquered before it seemed they were halfway there, regardless of the balance of nautical miles, of hours and minutes in the air before or after it. When he flew to Hong Kong it was the Himalayas, though technically it should have been some point above Uzbekistan. And years and years ago, when he was flying much smaller aircraft on short-haul European routes, it was the English Channel which provided this metaphorical midway point or barrier to cross, despite it being only fifteen or twenty minutes into, say, a one hour ten minute flight. He has often thought how geography can play odd games with your sense of time and space, and how flying can completely disorientate your sense of geography. Nothing ever joins up seamlessly because you are always on an outbound or an inbound. There's always a turnaround point, a return flight, not that he hasn't had the urge to keep on going forever or at least until he joined up with the ghost of his contrail. Besides, he thinks, the earth looks much less dramatic from 37,000 feet than people usually realise. Mostly it's pretty bland, just these shadowy bands of drab colours. He wonders whether he's grown bored with looking down at the earth –

he's always preferred watching the sky anyway. Sometimes, when he's feeling particularly fanciful, he thinks he only became a pilot because of his love of the sky, the openness, the scary, addictive vastness, this pull – and not because he was technically minded and wanted to travel. Not because he's always had a fear of being hemmed in, of being trapped.

The exhaust pressure ratios for each of the engines, with the compressor spool speeds and oil temperatures, are staring Greg in the face and without establishing whether anything's above or below normal, whether anything's out of sync or not he twiddles the instrument source selector switch and calls up the fuel feed and level synoptic data on the lower EICAS display and sees the tanks emerge as blocks of white – the centre, the larger and smaller mains, the stabiliser and the two reserve – and the feeding system linking them quickly unfold in purple and lilac, similar, he always thinks, to one of those back-lit maps you see in tourist information centres and which highlight different walks and places of particular interest along the way. But this time he makes a mental note of the levels, the total amount of kerosene left and cross refers this to the FMS, updating the flight log. Whereas a moment ago he felt quite lost with these panels of multi-coloured lights drifting in and out of focus, he finds his mind is suddenly agile and fully susceptible to what's at hand and that he can negotiate his tasks with ease, as if he's on automatic. Procedures, parameters, checklists – he slips between the folds of a pilot's working life as if they are cushions. Perhaps he always (eventually) reverts to the formalities of the flight deck when he finds he's becoming confused, when outside distractions, mostly frustrations and desires, begin to infiltrate the gently buzzing calm of the cockpit which he has often thought seems to hang in the sky independent of the rest of the aircraft, a seperate capsule. He needs the discipline, an order to negotiate. The confines and the constraints. He feels a rising flush of guilt again. For an instant he wonders how he'll cope when he's no longer flying. He's always sensed the disorder you get closer to earth – the blocked views and overcrowded airwaves. The chaos, the panic. The bouncing, muffled static. Maybe, he thinks, the flight deck is where he feels most at home, where he feels he truly belongs. The only place he knows that is both removed and regimented. It does seem to fit his psyche perfectly.

He's quite aware that there is no mystery to flying. That no great skill is required. That it's much easier than anyone could imagine. Stability can be achieved just by activating a few levers, though most trim arrangements nowadays are done automatically, of course. Still, he has the elevators on the tail for pitch, the ailerons on the wings for rolling and the rudder for yawing (or for taxiing or asymmetric flight in the case of an engine failure). Plus he's got the spoilers for extra steep turns and to use as brakes to decrease the speed of the aircraft or greatly increase its rate of descent. Instinctively he surveys the barely used control column in between his knees – the yoke with its electric trim switches and control wheel – and lifting up his legs a little, he catches sight of the clumpy rudder pedals and toe brakes, like something you might see on a tractor he has often thought. Each is linked to the various control surfaces on the outside of the aircraft by either hydraulic mechanisms or electronic pulses – there's no longer any direct connection between the control surfaces and the stick, not on this aircraft. In fact since Greg stopped flying a Piper in training he hasn't actually felt the air over the wings, the true pressure of trying to execute a ten degree left turn, or raise a speed brake at 200 knots. What he gets is artificial pressure supplied by independent power units linked proportionally to the movement of the control surface – made-up stresses to give the pilot some idea of the physical sensation of flying a wide-body. No, you don't need any special skill to be a pilot, he thinks again. You never even get to feel what it's really like. And yet he wouldn't have done anything else with his life. What else could he have done – been an accountant, as his father had suggested? He deftly works out the new ETA (they're now on target to arrive a few minutes ahead of schedule), amazed at how fast the flight seems to be going today. And he knows that once they are on the downhill run (despite being well short of the proper halfway point between Heathrow and Kennedy) things will only speed up further – he can almost smell landfall.

He thinks it's age. He's been noticing for some while that the older he gets the quicker time passes. He used to spend most of the flight itching to close in on the approach, feeling time drag, feeling every second between the waypoints, between main meals and snacks – which is probably why he started to flirt with the air hostesses (as they were called then and in his mind still should be). It relieved the boredom, it added some excitement – and he was continually searching for excitement (as an antidote to home, to Jeanette and the reality of having a small child? – he's often wondered). He was always in a hurry to land the aircraft, to get to the crew hotel and on with the evening, with whomever he had his eye on. It wasn't just him, every pilot his age was the same. How guilty is he? He thinks it simply went with the job. Jeanette knew what she was getting involved with, though he's never told her he's been unfaithful, not that he has ever really regarded his little indulgences, his dalliances as being particularly serious. Except for perhaps one, except for Paula. Now he finds he tries to slow down the flight, by postponing lunch, by waiting until the last possible moment before he completes a waypoint checklist, by letting his mind float free of his responsibilities on the flight deck so it can rest a while in slow moving, in perfectly still clear space – stalling the moment when it will all come to an end. It suddenly occurs to him whether after he's retired (after, most likely, he's been forced to retire two years early), time will start to trickle, leaving him marooned in the purgatory of Gerrards Cross with Jeanette and Emma (if his daughter is still living at home then) – without Paula, or any possibility of ever meeting anyone like Paula again. Maybe, he considers, it's because time has been rushing so fast, because the momentum of his life has gathered such an extraordinary pace that somewhere along the line he's left his family, his commitments, what should tether him to the ground, behind.

Time, he can almost feel it slip past. However, he's pleased he's only had one pee since Heathrow (perhaps he won't be kicked out before he's fifty-five after all) and he hasn't eaten anything more than a couple of chocolates, though he is starving. Not being able to decide whether to call a cabin crew now or wait until one next appears, which he reckons should be in about five minutes (and if he's lucky it will be Nicole – is it? – and not the other one with fat calves), he says, Fuck it, and flipping open his lap belt, because even he's not that big, he reaches across and behind the first officer's seat to the chocolates on the ledge by the glassed-in library containing the thick manuals that should supposedly help them rectify any problems and malfunctions which could conceivably arise. The manual that is not there, of course, but which Greg has always thought should be is the one on how to survive marriage, how to mend a broken home. What is there is largely superfluous, he thinks. Aeroplanes are so much more reliable than marriages. How many times has Greg slid open the case to retrieve the manual on, say, *Air Conditioning and Cabin Pressure Systems*? Once? Twice? How many in-flight emergencies has he had to deal with? In twenty-five years he reckons it can't have been more than half a dozen, and obviously none of which had proved insurmountable. In fact he can't think of one instant when he thought the aircraft was in real trouble – not even when an engine caught fire on take-off from O'Hare five years ago. The built-in fuel cut-off and extinguisher systems worked perfectly and after they'd been around they landed safely. The passengers were barely aware of what was going on. But as he bites into the chocolate, finding it has a coffee cream centre – he hates the soft centres, particularly the coffee or fruit ones – it occurs to him that perhaps he's due a real scare. Can he survive his whole flying career without a major incident – a rapid decompression at 37,000 feet for instance? Or an on board fire? The loss of two engines? Surely, he thinks, the idea growing in his mind, he's got it coming to him – not because he's been flying for a quarter of a century pretty much incident-free but because of all his indiscretions – that Jeanette and who knows how many other women are willing it upon him. He's always been a little superstitious, though flying's never bothered him before, he's never connected the performance of an aircraft he's piloting with how he might have hurt or deceived someone. He knows flying across the Atlantic is safer than driving to Budgens. He finds he's still holding half the chocolate with the remainder of the stuffing beginning to dribble out – he's swallowed the other half but it has left a nasty metallic taste in his mouth. He wonders what to do with what is left, seeing no tissues to hand and knowing he can't put it back in the now almost empty box, which is innocently sitting on the ledge by the how-to manuals (which could prove useful after all). Fuck it, he says, pulling his legs out of the way and flicking it forward into the rudder pedal well, but aiming to miss the pedals and the thick base of the control column (preset and armed to shake violently if the aircraft is on the verge of stalling). He doesn't see where it lands.

*Greg, are you married?* Dan says, making Greg jump.

*What?* says Greg, sitting up, instantly blushing because he's sure Dan must have noticed him throwing away the half-eaten chocolate. He's always blushed easily (which hasn't helped his withholding of the truth from Jeanette over the years) but is finding it's getting worse as he gets older – probably as his blood pressure increases. He can remain flushed for hours and it's not just a patchy reddening of the skin but an overall purpling. (Another reason, he thinks, why he can't continue to get into these uncompromising tangles – fifty fucking three). In fact he feels hot all over. His regulation short-sleeved white shirt with its epaulets each sporting four gold bands is beginning to stick to his back. He can feel the worn woolly seat-liner as if he's naked.

Are you married? Dan repeats.

Why? Greg says.

I don't know, Dan says. Something seems to be troubling you, you keep saying fuck it and shit, and in my experience if something's troubling a captain it's usually to do with his wife – or his lover. Something is getting in the way. He laughs. A sly, mocking laugh that instantly annoys Greg.

He looks at Dan, seeing this man in his early thirties, in his twenties perhaps (Greg's forgotten what the crew list said, presuming he even looked at the relevant column) who he hasn't flown with before, thinking he was never as cocky as this when he was his age. Quite as blunt and up front. As disrespectful. It surprises him, he finds most of the young pilots are like machines who move from one checklist to another without ever expressing an opinion, or coming up with a joke or some fancy opinion. Even on the ground they talk and seem to operate like machines, as if they're still connected to the flight deck, or at least a simulator. They talk about nothing else but flying, except occasionally their new cars or perhaps their latest computer game. Not that any of this seems to hinder their success with the girls – Greg's always been bemused by women's capacity to listen to bullshit, to be impressed by the most boring, mundane information, just because the person coming up with it has gold bands on his shirt and is called captain or first officer. He's even seen girls go for second officers – some twerp, he thinks, who might have an idea how the inertial navigation system works but you can bet hasn't a clue how to find his way around a woman's body. Flying is a piece of piss, Greg thinks yet again. It's not special, not anymore. He's nothing more than a bus driver with a fancy uniform – a yoke instead of a wheel. Yep, he says, I'm married. Just.

Dan says, I don't know what it is with you guys, you're always *getting yourselves into trouble thinking you can have everything. That once you're away from home you can behave how you like — right?*

*And you lot aren't? says Greg. He can't believe the cheek of this guy. He's never been spoken to like this by a first officer before.*

*I'm not married, says Dan. Not yet anyway.*

*So that makes you somehow superior, does it? says Greg.*

*It makes life less complicated, particularly in this job, says Dan. I get enough stress through landing one of these things.*

*You call that stress? says Greg. He reckons even being diverted to Newark in the middle of a snow storm at the height of the Friday evening rush hour isn't half as stressful as juggling Jeanette and Paula — particularly when Paula thinks she's not getting enough attention. He wonders how he'd be feeling if he'd never got involved with either woman, if he'd been celibate all his life (Jeanette is always saying he should have his dick cut off). Surely he'd be fitter, younger-looking, have lower blood pressure, and probably no problem with his prostate (Greg's sure most illnesses are psychosomatic). But what would be the point looking and feeling great if he were celibate? He might as well be fat and out of shape. He needs to pee again, badly. If you call that stress, he says, you're better off single.*

*I didn't say I was single, says Dan, just not married. Not yet.*

*So what does that mean — you've got a girlfriend? says Greg. Or perhaps it's a boyfriend. You never know in this business. He laughs.*

*I'm not gay, says Dan. Don't be ridiculous. I just don't believe in channelling all my energy into one person. I have a few things on the go. I don't promise anything to anyone. I'm non-exclusive.*

*Non-exclusive? Greg nods, feeling his age, suddenly feeling the emotional, the psychological, the generational gulf between himself and Dan. What the fuck does that mean? He knows in the past he's been antagonistic towards the younger guys, not simply because he doesn't understand where they're coming from but also out of jealousy for their youth, what they have lying ahead of them, but he decides he doesn't want to wind Dan up any more than he has. A month ago, last week even — if Dan had been on the San Fran — he might have let rip, but he feels too tired for all that now, plus he knows the kid's sharper than most. That he's not an automaton.*

*Essentially, I suppose, says Dan, that you play around a b*
*only do you not promise anything but you don't expect too much e*

*I was born too early, Greg says. My generation is still only interes*
*in exclusivity, despite the 'sixties, despite what we all once said about free*
*love. You fuck someone and it's like you owe them the rest of your life.*
*Wow, he says, thinking he sees exactly what Dan means, what I'd give*
*for a free fuck, a woman who's happy to get out of bed the next morning*
*and not expect to see me again, or at least not expect me to change my life*
*to accommodate her. Well, I'm a man just like you.*

*He's always believed the tangles he's got himself into were owing more*
*to his gender and the circumstances of his job than his own character. Is he*
*really guilty, personally? But part of him also knows he couldn't have just*
*let Paula (particularly) walk away. He knows he's partly to blame for at*
*least exacerbating some of the situations he's got himself into. Something*
*inside him craves emotional comfort too – exclusivity of a sort, he*
*presumes. He needs to be needed, to belong. He suddenly wonders*
*whether this is a womanly thought, whether he's not quite as tough, as*
*pig-headed, as thoughtless, as manly, as people (Jeanette and Paula*
*certainly) make him out to be. And something else occurs to him he's*
*never considered before. What if the aircraft were to blow up this second*
*and that when they eventually find the black box (lying largely*
*undamaged – he knows the impact these things can withstand – on*
*the ocean bed) and run through the CVRs the last thing anyone will hear*
*will be Dan and himself discussing marriage and free, non-exclusive sex.*
*How this would be played on radio and TV, every last word transcribed*
*in the newspapers. And this feeling comes over him again of Jeanette, and*
*all the other women he's been involved with, putting a spell on him and*
*the aircraft, and how justified they'll feel hearing the tapes – as if he'd*
*finally confessed to what they've always suspected. That he's a shit. A*
*non-caring, self-centred shit. There it would be in black and white – his*
*views on sex and marriage, monogamy and commitment, his full*
*adulterous history. The fact he was born in the wrong time, he can't*
*help thinking again. He should be Dan's age. Yes, of course he's jealous*
*of his co-pilot's youth. He vows to himself to try to keep his mouth shut*
*for the rest of the flight, definitely not to discuss anything of a sexual or an*
*adulterous nature, despite not having a clue what that'll leave them to talk*

*about.* Flight deck conversations always end up being about sex, about which cabin crew are the most shaggable and what they're going to do about it down route, and usually the laying of bets. *You know, Dan,* says Greg, *perhaps we should change the subject. I feel that I'm at a bit of a disadvantage here. You've got years on me. I'm an old man –* he suddenly senses the sharp pressure in his crotch. *Where do you live? What sort of a car do you drive? What computer games are you currently into? Don't tell me, I'm sure I can guess –*

*Hello guys,* Selina says, opening her eyes (she made it across the entire length of the upper cabin and onto the flight deck without looking – the only way she feels she could have got here today). She's instantly aware of the bad air, this mixture of farts and body odour, gingivitis and hair grease (a very male smell, she thinks) and how the flight deck seems to be on the wonk to her. At least not quite as balanced as the rest of the plane, as if it's even more precarious. It makes her feel giddy and she stumbles forward reaching for the back of the right-hand jump seat. *Phew,* she says, *it's stuffy in here.* She mock faints over the jump seat accidentally catching her skirt on the armrest so it rides up to where her tights start to darken making them appear to Greg anyway like stocking tops. Selina's often doing things like this in the cockpit, she used to think it was to break the ice, by giving the pilots something to laugh at as they usually look so bored, but she realises that it might be because the cockpit has always made her nervous – the way it seems so cut off from the rest of the plane, how you're so alone (and even more helpless) up here, out on a limb – and it's her way of coping with this. However she quickly realises she might be distracting the captain from doing something really important, like steering the thing out of the way of an oncoming plane – he's staring at her in an odd way, with these big droopy eyes, like a dog's – so she straightens herself as much as she can, making sure she doesn't bump into any of the switches on the overhead panel, pulls down her skirt and says, *Oops, I don't know what's come over me. Must be the lack of oxygen in here.*

Greg turns back to the flight panel but still fixed firmly on his mind is the image of this young woman's stocking tops – wow, it's turned him on. He didn't think air hostesses wore stockings anymore. He tries to imagine what sort of knickers she's wearing with them – black, white, frilly, a thong? Perhaps they're like the satiny ones Paula favours and which make her pubic area look so smooth, so taut. (He loves running his hand over them, pressing into the tautness, finding how easily it gives, feeling this growing warmth and maybe a slight dampness.) He looks over his shoulder, he can't help himself, wondering whether he'll be able to discern the outline of her knickers through her skirt (perhaps she's not even wearing any – the thought goes straight to his chest), but she's facing the wrong way as she's facing him and the skirt is not really tight enough anyway, though he finds when the girls are bending down, or stretching or striking a particular pose and he happens to be looking from just the right angle he can sometimes make out the impression. He decides the cabin manager is much more attractive than he first thought when he saw her in the crew briefing – despite whatever it is she's done to her face. He loves women with long legs and curvy hips and tits that look as if they could unbalance them if they were to walk too quickly.

Are Lynn and Nicole looking after you okay? says Selina – she's becoming more and more unnerved by the way the captain is still staring at her. She wishes he'd go back to doing whatever it is he has to do. Even though it's mid-flight Selina knows enough about piloting to know that at least one person has to keep a pretty close eye on the controls the whole time – the first officer barely looks old enough to even tell the time. She sees the screens behind the captain blinking away of their own accord. She imagines this spiral effect, how one unchecked piece of data could lead to complete catastrophe in a matter of minutes. How a particular malfunction could move through the various systems faster than a human might be able to react. She imagines she sees a row of switches beginning to light up scarlet and flash. I hope they're doing their job, she says, loudly, realising that neither pilot has yet said anything, that the captain is still staring at her with this odd fixed droopy look and the first officer hasn't even lifted his head from his comic or whatever it is he's reading.

Definitely, says Dan, finally folding his magazine, removing his headset and turning towards her – sorry I was listening for a weather report.

I didn't mean to interrupt, says Selina.

You can interrupt me whenever you like, says Dan, shifting further round in his seat.

*Shit*, says Greg, seeing the way Dan's looking at Selina, realising he's noticed her too and that he already feels threatened by him – these young guys. He also has an idea that she's obtainable (he's already forgotten about Nicole – is it?). He's not sure why he thinks this so soon – maybe it's her obvious nervousness, the way she seems so unconfident. In his experience they are always the easiest ones. (Why he picked on Paula he doesn't know – except perhaps she picked on him).

*Sorry?* says Selina.

*Sorry*, says Greg, feeling himself blush again, I forgot to input something in the tech log – it's not important. The girls? Impeccable service. Old Nicole and the other one. What's her name? He hasn't noticed much more than Nicole's tits and her toothy smile (she hasn't entirely slipped from his mind), or what's-her-name's ugly calves.

*Lynn*, Selina says, wondering what exactly he's forgotten to input in the tech log. Whether it is important, despite him saying it isn't. She knows how pilots like to downplay everything.

*Lynn, yeah, right*, says Greg. But how come we haven't seen you up here before now? (He thinks, I'm not too old to beat Dan at this game. I'm the one with the experience after all.) We're – he almost says over halfway already, but stops himself – we were beginning to wonder whether you'd got off at the last moment.

*It's been frantic*, says Selina. Surely you two boys can manage to amuse yourselves for a couple of hours with all these gadgets. She's not sure why she does it but the moment anyone starts flirting with her she always reciprocates. She supposes it's because life is easier that way, behaving how people expect you to. And also she knows it comes naturally to her – after twelve years in the job anyway. She's glad her mother has never taken up any of her numerous offers to come on a trip as her cling-on. Even now Selina would hate her to witness what she's really like at work. It's not that she's ashamed of the way she behaves, more that she's reached a sort of stand off with her mum which she doesn't want to unbalance. They've accepted each other, or at least aspects of each other. Perhaps it's simply that they've learnt not to look too hard at one another.

*We haven't worked together before, have we?* Greg says. He's sure she's his if only he can keep her attention away from Dan. *I would have noticed*, he says. Some girls stick in his mind for longer than others. He *can't believe he'd have missed this one — with those legs, those tits.*

*Oh yeah?* says Selina. She can't remember when or why but she recognised his name on the duty list and looking at him now close-up he does seem familiar, though there are plenty of pilots around his age who look just as bad. Still she must have flown with every pilot in the airline more than once.

*I'd definitely have remembered,* Greg says. He shuts his eyes for a moment, racking his brain, trying to picture recent cabin crews he's flown with, then more distant ones — an unfolding panorama of uniformed (and out of uniform) girls. But he can't stop them blending into each other. He can't place this CM, whose name he also can't seem to recall. *What the fuck is happening to my mind?* he thinks, presuming it's just another sign of his increasing decrepitude. That he's going senile as well.

Selina's suddenly worried that the captain, having stared at her solidly for the last five minutes, might now be dropping off. That the exertion of eyeing her up has been too much for him. *I haven't been a CM for long,* she says, wanting at least to get some reaction out of him, wanting him fully conscious and able to deal with any emergency that might arise — she thinks again of the thing he forgot to input in the tech log. *And before that for some reason,* she says, *I hardly ever got the upper deck galley.* She has found that unless you stick out a mile it's really only the CMs and the girls serving the flight deck who get the pilots' attention. Or even if you happen to make an impression out of uniform down route, back on board you're quickly lost. (Though she knows how most people on the inbound leg try to make themselves invisible anyway.)

*What a waste,* says Dan, *to have you stuck at the back of the aircraft all this time. I can hardly bear the thought.*

Selina quickly glances at the first officer before focusing on the centre console. He's definitely not her type either. She can usually tell instantly — it's like a gut reaction. Something that's probably got her more into trouble than not. (Her mother once said she never gives suitable men a chance.) She thinks he's too wimpy, too adolescent-looking. Plus she's never gone for men in glasses. She thinks the captain would be a better bet — if she were really desperate. She can't work out why but despite his heaviness, his large stomach and saggy face, he seems to have a certain strength, as if he could still hold you pretty tight. But she's not desperate

*(and even if she were in the market David is the person she'd go for —
what a body). However she doesn't want to consider anything of this
nature — part of her doesn't want to touch another man for the rest of her
life. She tries to make sense of the console, the mess of lights and switches,
the larger knobs and mini-levers, the numbers and letters and abbrevia-
tions. She spots SAT, SPKR, MKR, CREW REST, LEFT
WING DOWN, AUTOBRAKES, SLEW, RESET, TEST,
FLY DK DR, COMMAND and EVAC. Well, she says, I don't
want to distract you two anymore than I have already.*

*Don't worry about that, says Greg. We don't have enough to do as it
is. He laughs, feeling the ache in his crotch, a need to pee, and also,
oddly, his hunger. He feels both full and empty. And that he somehow
keeps slipping out of time. He's feeling increasingly disconcerted.*

*Can I ask the girls to bring you anything? Selina says, half wondering
whether she should stay to try to keep the captain focused on what he
should be doing — to keep prodding him into gear. But she doesn't want
to be on the flight deck any longer being continually reminded of the
captain's obvious inadequacy (maybe she should report him when they get
to New York — if they get to New York) and the mass of things that could
go wrong — the myriad switches and levers, which, if selected incorrectly
she's sure could tip the plane over, head over heels until it smashes into the
Atlantic. She looks back at the EVAC button and wonders how often
these things are pressed in real emergencies — whether she'll ever hear one
go off properly. Captain?*

*Greg, call me Greg, he says. Dan?*

*It's your choice, Dan says.*

*You go first, Greg says. Despite being almost weak with hunger and
obviously having the right to be served first as the captain, he doesn't want
to appear greedy in front of Selina. In fact he wants to appear considerate,
that he puts his fellow crew members before himself. I'm not that hungry,
he says.*

*Okay, says Dan, because I'm starving. Greg picks up this look from
Dan that he's sure means like fuck you aren't.*

*I'll pass on the message, Selina says. I don't know what you lot have
to eat today.*

*Great, thanks, says Dan.*

*See you both later, Selina says. She smiles at Greg but tries to avoid looking at the first officer. She knows how odd glances can be interpreted. She turns, and holding her breath – because she suddenly decides that if she doesn't breathe until she's out of the cockpit and into the cabin nothing will go wrong, there'll be no malfunction and the controls will be adhered to in strictly the right sequence – she stumbles quickly to the door, somehow knocking an opened box of chocolates onto the floor. Fuck she says to herself without so much as drawing in an ounce of breath and stooping down to pick up the box and the crumpled empty wrappers and a couple of chocolates which have spilled onto the smudged, fuzzy carpet, still holding her breath so hard she feels she's going to burst with the effort.*

*Wow, Greg thinks. Double wow. He's sitting in exactly the right place to see a clear outline of Selina's knickers, which appear startlingly brief. Again he feels his heart beat a little faster, his pulse quicken, a hotness sweep through him – and this pain between his legs. He sees no further indication that Selina is wearing stockings, no imprint of the telltale fasteners, but what he can see is quite enough and unable to say anything, he watches her put the box back on the ledge (as she stands the outline disappears, though remains clearly in his mind) and sort of fall towards the door and take three goes to get the door open, rattling it wildly – he can't imagine what the passengers on the other side think – and rush out without looking over her shoulder, flinging the door shut behind her so he sees only the briefest glimpse of the orange-hued cabin and a few stirring faces before the door snaps loudly into place.*

*Where does she come from? says Dan.*

Selina gasps a huge lungful of air and is surprised at how good it tastes. She deliberately looks straight ahead at Galley 6 as she begins walking through the upper deck cabin as calmly as possible. She feels a complete fool for spilling the chocolates and for not being able to open the door the first time, and angry with herself for letting the captain, and for that matter the first officer, flirt with her and letting herself play along with it. Idiot, she says to herself. It's as if however she's feeling, however scared and hopeless, however abused by Mike, she can't help behaving in a certain way once on board, once in uniform. That in this get up she's never really herself – or at least these clothes mask her, hiding her true self. She feels people looking at her, that the passengers are averting their sleepy gaze from the video screens. And she knows they'll be seeing what they want to see and not what is really there. Reaching the galley and Nicole and Lynn, who are sitting on trolley tops eating salad and sipping Evian, seemingly content and in control, happy to let the world go on around them, Selina suddenly feels this terrible vacancy, as if even she doesn't know what she's really made of. What is really there. Now she's not on the flight deck things might look a little straighter, a little less wonky, but the increased clarity is to Selina only more confusing. She's aware of being both apart and alone.

*Greg tries to get comfortable but the pain and the hunger make it impossible, plus the thought of Selina in these tiny knickers (taut black satin ones that give so happily when you press them in the right places, he bets) tipping about in his mind is making him even more fidgety. He thinks one last time. It can't do any more damage. He's always found it easy to rationalise his desires. Perhaps that's why he's a pilot, being so competent at rationalising the irrational – having learnt to cope with spatial disorientation for example. Having become used to overcoming the mental, the sensory conflict that arises when flying solely on instruments, when your brain is telling you that you are still banking when in fact you are horizontal, or that you are level when you are in a sustained turn, because your slow moving vestibular organ reacts to the in-flight forces before the force of gravity. What it ultimately amounts to, Greg learnt years ago, is having to disregard physical sensations, the sense of balance you grow up with, and to rely only on what the flight instruments tell you. It's putting your trust in the attitude indicator (these blocks of brown and a lump of blue), the turn and slip indicator (a flush of white and magenta – Greg has often thought that the true colour of flying is neither a perfect blue nor a cloudy white but brilliant magenta), the triple laser gyro which powers the inertial reference system, and to a lesser extent the air pressure driven altimeter. Greg might fail his next medical but he knows he'll be way up on his annual instrument rating test. He's become so much more attuned to the flicker of data, the swivel of a needle, the steady momentum of a spirit level, than what his body and his heart might be telling him. He regularly sees the flight panel in his sleep. Avionics stalk his dreams.*

*So, says Dan, fancy my chances?*

*Sorry? says Greg.*

*With Selina, the CM? says Dan.*

*No, says Greg. No way. He laughs, thinking what am I saying? What am I really going to do about it? He thinks there's nothing wrong with a little flirting, how it's just part of the job, what is expected, but he knows that, one last time or not, he's in enough of a mess at the moment. He can't get involved with someone else even if she knocked on his door (which he thinks is a distinct possibility given the way she was looking at him – a bottle of champagne outside her door notifying her of his room number would probably do it, it's worked countless times before). It's not Paula he feels particularly bad about but Jeanette. He can almost taste the guilt now, though it could just be the acids travelling up from his empty stomach. He doesn't know – he feels confused, unsure of himself, of quite who he is anymore. He used to be so self-aware, so confident in his betrayal (at least in the way his job, his sex dictated him to be).*

*A tenner? says Dan.*

*But he hates missing out on a challenge. And he'd hate to see Selina wasted on an inexperienced twenty-year-old with glasses (despite all his other ailments he still doesn't need glasses, not even for reading – he's always had perfect vision) and acne. I've got to have a pee, he says. (He also hates losing money and tries to never shake on a bet unless he's certain of the outcome.)*

*Again? says Dan. I'd cut down on the coffee if I were you.*

*You've got control, says Greg, unclipping his lap belt which immediately releases some of the pressure.*

Flicking the palm of her sticky hand (even though she wore gloves for the clear-in) across her hair, from left to right (it's always in that direction in the same way she always uses a clockwise motion – with her forefinger and second finger held tightly together – when wanking) feeling her crunchy hair (she's currently using a new hair spray which she thinks is dynamite) bounce back into shape as her hand passes, Becky contemplates whether to go for another ham sandwich or another forkful of chicken korma. She's poised for both with the tray of crew sandwiches on the counter next to this passenger meal she retrieved from her trolley and which is still warm. She can't decide so she takes a bite of sandwich, consuming most of it in one go, though it's not much more than a mouthful anyway, and while she's still chewing she picks up a fork and locates a chunk of chicken in the oily, fawn-coloured sauce which she stabs, trying to get as much sauce as possible to stick to it, and with her mouth still half full she sucks it off the fork. She thinks the ham sandwich and the chicken curry probably taste better together than they do separately. She often finds this, that by mixing things you're not supposed to mix – completely different types of food like Thai and Italian for instance – you can come up with some amazing flavours and consistencies. Not only can she normally never decide what to have, she quickly gets bored with too much of one thing. It occurs to her as she swallows – instinctively reaching for the remainder of the sandwich at the same time – that perhaps she isn't so keen on hot spicy food (even though the Economy chicken korma could hardly be called spicy). That maybe she's suddenly gone off Thai. The thought of chicken in green curry sauce with those strange little aubergines that taste so bitter makes her want to puke. She sees the remains of the meal Ben and she had shortly before her life changed for ever still spread out on the kitchen table. Becky swallows this latest mouthful of just sandwich, actually pleased it's so bland, pleased she hasn't complicated it, but she still feels hungry, or at least an urge to consume something else (when doesn't she? she thinks), maybe something sweet this time. She looks at the fruit cake Debbie brought and has just taken out of some Tupperware and is offering around but which she's already refused once because she was still tucking into the sandwiches and the puke-making chicken korma. Tim's having a slice but Valerie's declining, which doesn't surprise Becky one bit because people like Valerie don't eat cake, do they, baby.

84

Becky would like to become friends with Valerie, because she's sophisticated and funny and foreign-sounding, and full of good advice. But she finds it hard conversing with someone who looks quite so gorgeous. However friendly and natural they appear Becky always suspects they're really looking down on her, or at least they're feeling a tiny bit sorry for her and are making an effort to be nice out of pity. In these situations Becky finds she simply clams up more than usual. She wishes she were more up front with people like Valerie, with the majority of her work colleagues, despite whatever the reasons are they choose to talk to her, to acknowledge her. (Strangely she finds she's not so shy with men, particularly men she fancies. Perhaps it's when the possibility of sex comes into it she feels more confident. In her view most men are pathetically timid, a walkover.) She very much wants to make an impression on Valerie, wanting to stick close to her, because she's already helped her. She thinks she and Ben shouldn't rush into setting a date, that they should get used to the idea of being engaged for a while first. Hey, baby, what's the rush? Valerie said. Learn to live with each other. Wait until you know him better, what he's really like to live with. Maybe he's got all these disgusting habits. You've got the rest of your lives to think about. But baby, you're one lucky girl. I'd kill to be in your position – look at me, I'm single right now and nearly past it. Which made Becky realise – though of course Valerie doesn't look anything like past it – she hadn't properly considered how fortunate she is, so feeling happier, she found herself hunting around the galley for some food. It seems to work both ways – she eats when she's both happy and miserable.

She watches Valerie glide across the galley floor and help herself to a glass of Evian, which she begins sipping as if it's piping hot. Becky feels like an oaf next to her. Still she desperately wants Valerie to be her friend, besides she needs someone to go shopping with in New York. She reckons if anyone knows the cool new places to hang out it'll be Valerie. She's bored with Macy's and Canal Street and Tower Records and even Bloomingdale's. Everyone has to go to Macy's, or Bloomingdale's if they are short of time, but she'd love to see something new as well, some out of the way, funky little boutique. She finds she's stopped watching Valerie and is staring at Debbie's cake again and the crumbs Tim's spilt on the counter. She'd really love something sweet to nibble on. She suddenly needs to fart and moving towards the curtain on the sunny side of the plane (she can tell it's the sunny side by the light hitting the other side of the curtain) and tensing the muscles around her anus so she doesn't make any noise louder then the constant noise of the engines and the air conditioning and the hum of the galley electrics and the bev maker on brew, she gently lets it slip out, hoping it won't be smelly – they usually aren't at 37,000 feet, just hot air, though it goes on forever. Eventually rid of it, but with her bum itching slightly (she's never let anyone stick more than a couple of fingers up there though she's often thought of trying anal sex at least once – every man she's ever been with has had a go), she suddenly feels loads more room for cake. The crumbs under the intense galley lighting are sandy coloured and glistening slightly and have assumed a particular pattern which oddly reminds Becky of a stain on the kitchen counter at home which won't be her home when she gets back because she'll be moving into Ben's, or so it's presumed anyway. She thinks of Vicky and Kate, the girls she shares the house with but hardly ever sees as she's always with Ben, and how pleased they were when they found the place and the fun they imagined they would have living together (they first discussed it in Miami, or was it LA? – she can never remember what's happened where). She thinks of sitting on the sofa with Misty on her lap, watching Sky, enjoying a Cointreau and Coke. They moved onto Cointreau after their Campari phase, thinking it's even more sophisticated. She drinks it with Coke, 7-UP, orange juice, anything as long as there's plenty of ice.

Debbie says, Becky, are you sure you don't want any cake? Shouldn't you be celebrating?

At just hearing her name Becky feels embarrassed but because of her dark skin she knows she never goes puce and that it's hard for people to tell whether she's blushing or not – one thing she has her mother to thank for. Sorry? she says.

Or are you waiting until New York, Debbie says, to really let your hair down one last time? Cake?

Thanks, Becky says moving towards it. I don't think I'll be doing that, she says. I've spent the last three and a half years getting myself into trouble. Besides I don't really feel like celebrating. I'm a bit overwhelmed by it all.

Oh baby, says Valerie, baby, baby. We have to do something otherwise it's just like a normal stop-over. We must, we must go wild. Becky watches Valerie throw her arms into the air, but dead elegantly. With boys, she says. Tim?

Sure, Tim says, not that I'll be much use, darling.

Who else is on board? Valerie says.

There's David in Business, says Debbie. He's cute. And there is always Greg. He'd be up for anything – I've flown with him loads of times. Becky sees Debbie wink before she turns to the cake and helps herself to a handful of crumbs.

Greg? says Valerie.

The captain, says Debbie, licking the crumbs from around her mouth. She has a husky voice which Becky thinks makes her, in an older way, really quite sexy.

Him? says Valerie. Oh baby – I mean real men.

You'd be surprised, says Debbie. Becky didn't think Debbie looked the type to be taken in by flight crew but with her voice and what she's just said, and the confidence with which she seems to handle her well-rounded body – Debbie's not as fat as she is, but she's not far off – she's beginning to change her mind. Perhaps she's into sex as much as her. She can never quite tell with people who aren't her age.

There's a good-looking guy working in First, says Tim. Carlo or something foreign-sounding. But I can't decide whether he's gay or straight, which is like really unusual for me. And there's that other guy, the fat one, up there too – but who knows what he's in to. He looks like a real creep. He looks like a paedophile to me. Check out the size of his hands.

Nigel, says Debbie – he's harmless. I've worked with him before.

Becky looks down at her body, still encased in her clearing-in pinny, suddenly very conscious of her shape, the pinny emphasising her bulk. She might as well be wearing a sack. She wants to fart again already.

What about the first officer? says Valerie, smiling at Becky.

Spotty, says Tim.

Please, says Becky, trying to deflate the cheap drab material, trying to get it to hug her a little closer, no first officers, no pilots. I am going to spend the rest of my life with one. Perhaps we can have a pilot-free evening. She lets out another fart, shifting closer to the curtain again as she does so.

That'd be a shame, says Debbie. I mean we need a little frisson.

I'm staying out of it, Becky says. She's not sure what frisson means, she didn't do French at school.

Oh baby, says Valerie, you mean you're not going to celebrate your engagement with us?

No, no, of course I am, says Becky. She's beginning to warm to the idea of doing something this evening, particularly as the others seem to want to do something with her (and knowing that it's almost obligatory). How could she refuse? Normally she finds herself wandering around crew hotels desperately trying to latch onto some group or other. No one has ever organised an evening around her before. However, apart from Valerie, she's not sure she's had the reaction to her news which she expected. She thought everyone would be dead eager to find out all the details, like exactly where and when Ben proposed to her. (She told Valerie that he asked her in bed because she had been telling her that they have this great sex life and that he asked her after a session but she didn't want to admit they'd been doing it in the kitchen in front of the empty Thai takeaway cartons so she just said, He asked me in bed, on both his knees, and his elbows.) She thought they'd be talking about nothing else. She feels a little let down, almost winded, and despite the fact that they seem keen (Debbie anyway) to arrange something for tonight, she wonders whether they are really taking her engagement seriously, or whether they just want an excuse for a party. But should she expect anything else? So many girls say they are getting married and never do, there's always someone who's just got engaged – she supposes she's no exception. Why should they believe it's ever really going to happen to her? Perhaps it won't, she thinks, looking at her bare marriage finger and sensing for the first time a fluttering of relief – a feeling similar to waking after a terrible dream and realising that whatever it was that was so terrible is not happening after all. Yet despite their casualness, their ready acceptance of her news, Becky still feels different to all the other girls she's ever come across or heard about who were supposedly getting married. And despite this odd, momentary sense of relief, she can physically feel the weight, the pressure, the reality of her engagement, of this lifetime of commitment to Ben she's about to embark upon. The inevitability of it. She thinks back to the early days with Vicky and Kate, the Cinzano days, when all that commitment meant was going home with someone after they'd bought you a few drinks in a club. I don't mean that, she says, I mean you decide – I'll do anything.

That's the spirit, says Debbie.

Except with flight crew, baby, says Valerie.

I don't care, really, Becky says. With whoever.

As long as whatever you get up to, darling, doesn't get back to him, Tim says. Those flight decks are worse than the galleys for gossip. Probably because they don't have enough to do up there. Still I suppose talking about it is the closest most of them ever get to fulfilling their fantasies.

Steady on, says Debbie, they're not all useless.

Sorry, darling, you're not married to one are you? says Tim.

No, no, says Debbie, but I haven't been averse to the odd captain, or senior first officer in the past and, thinking about it, there may even have been a second officer or two. They really turn me on. It must have been the uniforms, the status. I've got pretty simple taste.

They've never done anything for me, says Tim. Besides they're all far too straight.

Excuse me, guys, I need a pee, Debbie says.

Over-excited at just the thought? says Tim. I don't know what this business is coming to.

What it's come to, says Debbie. Nothing's changed. It's always been about sex. Where have you been?

Still in school probably, Tim says.

Moving towards the curtain, Debbie brushes the rest of the cake crumbs into her hand, stops for a moment obviously thinking about what to do with them before slapping them into her mouth making a sucking sound – perhaps she's as greedy as me as well, Becky thinks. As long as there's a mixed crowd tonight, Debbie says, that's the most important thing. Not that we want to tempt Becky away from – what's his name?

Ben, Becky says.

Ben, Debbie says.

Becky watches the Economy purser finally fling aside the curtain and, as she does so, a shaft of clear sunlight hits her, highlighting the cheap pinny, making her feel that she's being singled out. Which she supposes she is at last – that people are no longer ignoring her or her news. And although she had to announce it publicly – Guess what? I'm getting married, was how she eventually put it to the galley (sick of the fact that everyone had been so slow to pick up on what she and Valerie had been discussing quite openly) – she supposes she does feel special. After all, everyone seems really keen to organise something for her tonight. This alone, she decides, is almost worth getting engaged for.

She wishes her mother had some idea of the fuss people are beginning to make over her, knowing she might even be proud of her daughter for once. And the thought creeps into her head that perhaps she orchestrated the whole thing with Ben, that she got him into the position where he'd feel compelled to ask her to marry him just so she could tell her mum someone wanted to marry her, that not just someone but Ben, a pilot, who even her mother has recently conceded is dead good-looking from the one time she'd met him. Quite in a different league to all Becky's other boyfriends. And this thought doesn't go away but starts inflating and twisting, wrenching inside her, until Becky questions (and not for the first time) whether she only ever does anything to either please or impress her mum.

Avoiding having to answer herself she looks at her watch, the face smeared with grease spat from opening sixty-two hot meals today, and sees that time hasn't dragged by as she thought it would, given the crew on board, but is actually going quicker than normal. She feels the need to fart yet again, her stomach solid with air, and an urge to try to slow things down for once. She wants to savour her moment (what there is of one), and keep from the time, once ensconced in the crew hotel, when she'll have to ring Ben – already she can't think what on earth she'll say to him. The galley might not be the most comfortable place in the world but it dawns on her that there's nowhere else she'd rather be right now. In transit. Where you can't even be reached by phone (not on this airline anyway).

It's the sense of movement, of the speed the aircraft is travelling at which Nigel finds so hard to ascertain from looking down upon the slowly, relentlessly unfolding vista of clouds and the odd tract of distant dark spangly sea, as if the atmosphere has opened up a giant sudden hole you could seemingly, if you're not careful, slip into and be lost forever. He fixes his gaze on a column of cloud rising quite distinctly from a solid deck of stratocumulus, as if by latching on to the one discrepancy, the one strident shape currently available in the sky (and he has no idea what it's doing there on its own), he'll be able to get an angle on their flight, the speed of their trajectory. But of course it's too far away for him to gain any meaningful notion of movement and after a while but more quickly than he anticipated the column becomes less distinct and less out of place – so he's thinking maybe it isn't that far away after all and that maybe it's simply isolated castellanus – and craning round, his face squashed flat against the faintly vibrating window, as flat as a well-rounded, fleshy face can get, he watches this column, this lone cumuliform cloud (if indeed that's what it is) sink back into the stratocumulus like a fountain being quietly shut off. And loath to lose his place, his nevertheless temporary and completely inaccurate hold on where they currently are – he imagines what the plane looks like from the outside, this glittering dot, a dot turning from silver to the palest shade of gold as they race towards the slowly dipping sun, somewhere in the upper reaches of the troposphere – he watches the stratocumulus appear to rise as if it's heaving itself over a mountain range and become less conformed with larger broken patches, deeper glittering holes, and a little more grey and white shading, and with definite waves beginning to define themselves amongst the spreading squat globular masses of water vapour and ice crystals, he watches the stratocumulus turn into altocumulus (which is still miles below them), probably because they are approaching a new, warm frontal system along the transition zone of the Arctic and polar air bands with the colder, denser air being displaced by the warmer, moister and less stable air. He thinks going this way in daylight is like glimpsing the future or witnessing weather undevelop itself and reach its very beginning as much as weather has a beginning – because he knows that about the time he gets home late on Sunday morning this area of low pressure will probably be waiting for him in Worthing, having been carried the 2000 odd miles by the prevailing westerly winds, unless of course it's displaced along the way by a more forceful front of high pressure, though at this time of the year that's not very likely.

He can imagine the rain slanting onto the kitchen window, which faces west, and trailing into tight diagonal smears of water like foil darts, with the kitchen light catching on the tiny drops on the other side of the glass so a bit of the kitchen is reflected again and again outside. He can hear the rain sprinkling against the glass in gust after gust. And despite the window being double-glazed he can feel the corresponding shivers of air which still somehow bounce around the room. The reaction of the swiftly changing air pressure between the interior and the exterior of the house, he wonders?

He often watches the sky from the kitchen window, a long thin patch he can see if he presses himself up against the sink, otherwise the creosoted wooden fence between their garden and their neighbour's garden (and his stomach) gets in the way. He thinks it's like seeing his world upside down. How it passes over him rather than he over it. The flappy underside of cumulus, the shady folds of cirrus and often impenetrable stratus as if the sky (and this life he's come to rely upon, where in many ways he feels he only begins to exist) has been sealed off, possibly forever. If there's some cirrostratus about sometimes he sees halos around the sun, one after the other radiating out, the result of the sunlight refracting and reflecting through this sheet of ice crystals. And sometimes he sees the beginning of a sunset, fiery colour seep into the sky, though the fence and the neighbour's kitchen extension (and his stomach) stop him from ever seeing the sun appear to close in on itself like the eye of a lens and suddenly disappear beneath the world – this final pinprick of flamey light he's caught so often from the air, and which once gone leaves him feeling slightly dizzy but awestruck so he usually remains by the window until the plane has shot further into the night and the sky's turned quite black, this blackness so quickly enclosing around the plane (if they are going from west to east) that it can feel as if they've flown into a tunnel.

He rubs at the mist he's created on the window and holds his face a little way away from it so the condensation doesn't instantly build up again and he has once more a clear-ish view (though the inner shield is a little scratched) of the rising altocumulus, the waves created by the ever predominant westerlies, the tops of the waves being whipped back in a fine spray, and numerous broader gaps in the cloud, these spangly, glittering, terrifying holes, and much further in the distance, almost hugging the horizon, heaps of cirrostratus piling into each other and eventually building to a fat band of smoky white that drifts and puffs into the stratosphere where it ultimately dissolves as, seemingly, the sheer vacuum of space becomes too great, with the stratosphere being superseded by the mesosphere, and mesosphere by the ionosphere and the

**93**

ionosphere by the exosphere. And Nigel thinks how this land-scape, this skyscape must have shaped him over the years – how he used to find it so consoling, the one place he began to feel himself. How, oddly, all this space used to fill him up. But pulling his head away from the window now (with pins and needles in his right leg because he's had it half-cocked on the emergency chute bulge), imagining again for a moment he's underneath looking up, that he's at the sink washing his mum's and his dirty dinner things (she cooks, he washes), he has this overwhelming sense of the true emptiness of the sky and that he's no more seeking fulfilment in it than he's simply escaping home. Escaping himself. That he's got everything the wrong way round.

The thought comes to him that maybe when he's next home he won't have to wash up after his mother, that he'll never have to wash up her things again. And that he won't, after a couple of days, have this huge urge to leave the house and to get back to work where it's impossible to get a measure on how near or far anything is, where everything exists slightly out of focus. How-ever, the realisation quickly arises that, because he'll no longer have his mum to worry about, because he'll be the only person at home (at least until he sells it), he'll have more time to think about himself. He can't carry on behaving as if he's on automatic, as if he's been slowly shut off – by the garden fence and the neighbour's extension and the clouds that relentlessly blanket Worthing. Has he simply been exchanging one shrouded view for another? He won't have to do exactly as she says. Or hide from her in his room (at forty-six, he thinks, for heaven's sake). Sometimes he feels so locked in, so shut off he's going to explode. No, he won't have this excuse, these constraints, however awful they are. He'll be free. He'll only have himself to confront.

He quickly looks over his shoulder to check no one has noticed him still awkwardly propped on the bulge of emergency door D1L, because he feels he's being watched, but the cabin is as dim and quiet as when he last looked, nobody has turned his way or stood up and the galley curtain is still firmly in place totally concealing Wendy and Carlo, though with the harsh galley lights boring through the material making it glow pale pink at the edges. He turns back to the window, seeing the sun on the wingtip and the wingtip glinting madly against deepening space, thinking at the age of forty-six he'll finally have some decisions to make. But he knows before he can actually make them he'll have to gain a clearer idea about who he is and wants to be, and exactly what he's kept hidden all these years (not just from his mum but himself too). He thinks it's as if he's smothered his past with layer after layer of these woolly jumpers his mother used to knit him (until a couple of years ago when the arthritis in her fingers became too debilitating) and which he dutifully wears at home but never down route – she was a terrible knitter and he knows they make him look even fatter than he is. He thinks it's as if he's at the bottom of this heap of woollies, which he's stuffed into the cupboard in his bedroom, fighting for air. And the thought of pulling away this mass of stifling wool, uncovering bits of him he's quite forgotten about – events and emotions, and even silly things which when all stuck together might point nowhere except they happened and because they happened they have to be worth something, simply just as an expression of himself – the thought of slowly unearthing his life, of discovering who he really is – makes him feel again this rising, almost uncontrollable sense of lightness, of excitement.

He finds his hands have gone clammy and that he's aware he's making moist imprints on the edge of the emergency chute bulge. He also senses an ache in his balls, that his penis is tingling and beginning to swell, so he has to adjust his trousers and shirt, which is bunched up and tucked into his underpants, and the way he's sitting to make room for it. He wonders whether anyone could tell if they were to walk past. He's sweating profusely now. He can't remember the last time he had an erection on board and he wonders whether in fact it's just because he needs to go to the toilet and that it has nothing to do with this feeling he's nowhere near to grasping fully, though knows he's getting a little closer to understanding.

Something's beginning to click. He concentrates so hard on what's going on out of the window, trying to ignore his erection, that he imagines he can see shadows of figures forming on the cloud banks. If only he could decipher these shapes, these clues, he thinks, and put a name to them. He wonders whether he's going mad, whether it's too late and he's completely lost touch with the real world. But he knows something's concrete all right. He can feel his penis getting wet and sticky at the end, as it does when he's very excited.

The sky starts to throb and he looks away from the window, shaking his head, knowing there's a limit to the amount of infinity even he can take in in one go. He considers leaving his perch but decides against it for the moment. His trousers are tight enough normally, plus the wetness might have seeped through his shirt and underpants and onto the creased grey cloth and be all too obvious a mile away, despite the dimmed, mid-flight cabin lighting. He has no jacket, no clearing-in pinny with which to shield himself (in a way he feels naked before he's even begun to try to remove this woolly jumble heaped over his past) but realises he could easily slip into the toilet – he can see it's free – and relieve himself (he's never done it on board before but knows people do – not that he's ever witnessed anything). He's so excited just two or three gentle strokes would do it. But no, he's not some dirty little galley chef, a foreigner who thinks he's too good for the job. He's the First class purser, he can't possibly do such a thing. He has status. He's in control. Besides he's not even interested in sex. So he doesn't budge, thinking he'll start clearing away some of this stuff clouding his head, his past instead. Why wait any longer? Why wait until his mother's dead, if that really is what's been holding him back all these years? Surely he's wasted enough time already and knows it doesn't matter if he might begin to no longer recognise himself, that people might not know who he is any more – he has no close friends. He can't just go into the toilet and get out his cock and play with himself until he ejaculates – with his shoulders hunched, he imagines, and his back arched and his knees pressed against the rim of the toilet, one hand on the soap ledge steadying himself – until he's splattered the back of the toilet bowl with hot spunk (which he then has to make sure all flushes away). He finds he's moved his hand onto his crotch, the palm lying across the rigid shaft of his penis. He's forty-six. He's in charge of First. He has status, a position to uphold. Traditions to adhere to. He doesn't have sexual urges.

Still not budging, he begins by trying to remember why he became an air steward, why he cut out this advertisement in the *Southern Daily Echo* twenty-two years ago, filled it in and sent it off with a passport-sized photograph of himself (he remembers sucking in his cheeks in the photo booth – he was conscious of being overweight even then). He'd only ever flown once before. He had wanted to be a hotelier. He had wanted to run his own place on the south coast – not a café like his parents, or a B&B, or a guest house, but a proper hotel with a reception desk and room service. He's always had a sense of grandeur, of propriety (he's not sure whether he gets this from his mother or his father). He has to stand up.

She remembers quite clearly saying, 'Mum, guess what? I'm going to be an air hostess.' Becky hadn't told her she was even applying for the job in case she didn't get it – her mum had already sapped enough of her confidence. And she can still picture this look of complete surprise that swept across her mother's face, as if she just didn't believe her. As if she were thinking, Becky understood, but you're too short, you're too fat, you're too ugly. She was standing in the kitchen, in front of the sink (which she hardly ever goes near) with the window behind her and this incredibly strong sunlight (this is how Becky remembers it anyway) dazzling the sink unit (which was always spotless because the cleaner used to come three times a week) and sort of exploding behind her mum, who seemed to be stuck to the spot with her eyes bulging (Becky knows where she gets her eyes from all right) and this grin twisting over her impeccably made-up mouth. It was ages, Becky recalls, before she came unstuck and rushed across the floor to hug her daughter. 'Darling,' she said, she's always saying darling, 'that's fantastic. I'm amazed. My own daughter, my little Becky is going to be an air hostess. Who'd have thought it. Why didn't you tell me anything about it before? How could you keep such a thing from me?' And Becky knows she replied, which in retrospect is one of the few times she's ever taken issue with her mother about her attitude towards her – the way she's always putting her down, neither believing in her nor exactly encouraging her – Becky said, 'I thought you'd laugh at the idea.' 'Whatever makes you think that?' her mother then said. Despite being so happy at getting the job (she was, she truly was at first), perhaps because of the heightened emotion it had brought on – the fact that maybe she wasn't quite so short and fat and ugly, and useless, that somebody believed in her, an airline, this supposedly glamorous organisation – she said, tearing herself away from her mother and rushing out of the ridiculously sunny kitchen, as if even the sun were in collusion with her mum and couldn't stop mocking her with its brilliance, she said, 'Because you hate me.'

Becky doesn't really think this and she's only ever said it to her a couple of times but there have been occasions when she's felt her mother would rather have had a different daughter, that the one she's been lumped with has thoroughly let her down. People only have to look at us together, she thinks. She's dumpy and misshapen and her mum's still got everything in the right place, and proportion except for perhaps her eyes but she's brilliant at disguising the fact with make-up – one of the reasons why Becky tries so hard with the stuff. Even though she's twenty years younger, she knows she reflects badly on her mum, that she's an embarrassment to her. She's sure her mum's always wondering how she could have given birth to such an ugly child. Such a mess. Her mum's always dead neat, as obsessed with her appearance as she is with her stars. She still has her hair done every other week and despite having the same dark colouring as Becky, she dyes it bright blonde. Yet Becky is always amazed when she sees her shortly after she's been to the salon (Heavenly

Thatch in the centre of Reading) because it does seem to work with her – maybe it's because the rest of her looks so made-up, Becky thinks, so fake. Though Becky knows that's not quite the right word for her. Her mum's not a fake, she's completely true to herself, it's just that there's this unreal sheen to her. So unreal in a way it's become real. She has her nails done almost as regularly as well, and her legs and her bikini line, which she's always talking about quite openly, as if because she's still concerned about things like this she must still be young. Though Becky knows she doesn't seem to care much about what she says – nothing's too private. She's as up front in her conversation as in her appearance. She'll happily tell Becky's friends about Becky's first boyfriends, about taking her to the doctor to be prescribed the pill when she was fifteen. How she once caught her in bed with her cousin. And, of course, how her daughter has always eaten too much. About the time she lived on nothing but Marmite and marmalade sandwiches and all her other peculiar fads. Plus she'll tell them how lazy her daughter is. In fact how she doesn't look after her body at all and how she really should follow her mother's example of working out for at least forty minutes every day. 'Feel my stomach,' her mum has said to her boyfriends (not Ben yet but Becky knows it's coming), feel my thighs, go on, they're as firm as anything.' And on her mother goes about how Becky should take greater care with her makeup (as if Becky doesn't try) and her nails because there's nothing more off-putting than dirty, badly chewed nails. She wishes Becky would stop chewing hers, just as she wishes she'd do something proper with her hair. Her mum can't understand why she has to have it quite so short, why she wants to look like a boy.

The fact her mother was never a hostie amazes Becky – she thinks she would have been perfect. She still would be. Everything about her, the way she never shuts up talking about herself, the way she's always looking in the mirror, especially this walk she has where she manages to make both her tits and arse wobble, as if she's modelling swimwear or lingerie. Becky can just see her coming down an aisle. Though Becky knows she would hate the actual work – the serving, the clearing-in, the duty-free. She couldn't possibly cope. She'd have to get her hands dirty for a start. She might think Becky's a slob but she doesn't do anything for anyone. She doesn't lift a finger. She's the lazy one. She stopped working as soon as she got married, three years before Becky was born. It's long surprised Becky how her dad seems so willing to let her mum do whatever she wants – he happily pays for all her beauty treatments, though she has an idea it suits him now. 'Darling,' her mum says – over the years Becky's noticed the way her voice has become more and more posh-sounding – 'work doesn't suit me. Besides your father doesn't like me working.' Becky thinks she gets her delusions of grandeur, her sense of superiority from sitting around watching telly all day, imagining she's whoever, and perhaps a little of it from the fact she is naturally attractive, even when her hair's in a mess and without make-up, or any clothes on for that matter (she's always wandering around the house naked – especially when they have guests staying). She often sees it at work, the really beautiful girls acting as if they're doing something beneath them. Though she thinks Valerie's turned out to be not too stuffy – she's friendly enough.

Recently Becky's started to suspect her mum's afraid of flying. She's offered to take her on a number of trips as her cling-on but she always comes up with some excuse why she can't go, which isn't like her because she normally jumps at any opportunity to see exactly what her daughter gets up to – to get in her way. Becky's not at all sure why she offers to take her, except perhaps to prove to her she really is a cabin crew, this supposedly glamorous person who flies all over the world (to America anyway) with tons of beautiful colleagues. To prove to her how she fits in, and how she's stuck at it for three and a half years too (she's up for promotion to a senior cabin crew post already). Because even though she's been to her parents straight off a flight in her uniform stinking of hot meals and jet fuel, and has so many stories to tell her mum about the foreign cities she's been to – LA, San Fran, Miami, Boston, Chicago, and New York of course –

how they're just like in the films (occasionally she might bring them a souvenir to add to the stuff she nicks on board, amenity packs or miniatures usually, especially if she's been working in Business) – there is still this look of disbelief on her mum's face when she walks through the door, as if she's still thinking how on earth can this be my daughter. Maybe her mum's expression of disbelief, at least to some degree, has always been on her face when she sees her daughter, though Becky never realised it until she left home, when people started reacting to her as if she were normal, taking her for what she is rather than some freak of nature. And, she thinks, her parents never take holidays abroad, they haven't for as long as she can remember (when she and her brother were growing up they used to go to Torquay), despite her mum loving the sun and putting on her bikini and prancing around. The more she thinks about it, particularly how her mum's always questioning her about her training and the emergency procedures and the safety equipment on board, the more it seems her mum must be shit scared of flying. (She doesn't think anything bothers her dad as long as he has an easy life.) Why this hasn't occurred to her quite so convincingly before she can't think – maybe because like so much else to do with her mum she tries not to contemplate it for long. When she does, one thing comes racing after another. However, she feels strangely satisfied now, as if she's actually got somewhere – the fact, the certainty that her mum is afraid of flying. That perhaps her amazement at Becky getting the job in the first place was not just to do with her regarding Becky as completely unsuitable (at least her appearance) but might also have been linked with her own horror of flying and wonder at how she could have bred someone who didn't share it, who is almost her exact opposite (except for the eyes and skin tone). Her own daughter who finally has one up on her.

Becky joined the airline because she wanted to impress her mum, through proving to her she wasn't as ugly and fat and useless as her mother seemed to think, not because she was trying to be brave or courageous or anything like that. She can't understand how people can be afraid of flying. Okay, she thinks, it's boring, you're in a confined space for hours on end, it's smelly, and airless, but it's not scary. You go up and you come down – perhaps she doesn't think about it enough, about what could go wrong (because it never does). Occasionally she's more aware of her environment, of being stuck in the cabin, like a little earlier today, which can set her mind wandering so for the odd moment she might feel slightly unsure, but that's largely because she hasn't a clue what makes these things fly. She has no idea how a jet engine works or how the navigation system operates, or why planes don't bump into each other all the time, or simply flip right over in bad turbulence. But she rarely thinks about things like this. The truly scary thing to Becky has always been landing. Returning to earth. To her family and now Ben.

She wishes she could have told her mum in person about her engagement – she would love to have seen her expression this time (quite what her mouth and eyes would have been doing) – but she couldn't wait, she had to phone her because she was working the next day, today. As it was, her mum said nothing for ages and then she said, 'Darling, that's fantastic news. I can't believe it. My very own daughter, my little Becky is getting married – Keith, Keith darling, quick come here, Becky's getting married. Keith?' And then Becky heard her sob, or at least force herself to sob. Her mother cries all the time. She can happily cry at will. 'To that good-looking young pilot?' she said, snuffling (she couldn't hear her dad in the background yet). 'The one with those lovely blue eyes? Ben, is it?' 'Yes, mum,' Becky said. 'Who else do you think it would be? We have been going out with each other only for ages.' 'Why didn't you say anything to me about it before? You must have known he was going to ask you. I tricked your dad into asking me – I told him I was pregnant. How could you keep it so secret? I hope you didn't say yes immediately,' her mother continued, snuffling still, this forced show of emotion. 'No,' said Becky, 'Of course not. He's been asking me for weeks.' Becky always lies to her mum, trying to tell her what she thinks she wants to hear – except ironically she didn't have to lie when she told her she'd got a job as an air hostess, or that she's getting married to a first officer who has lovely blue eyes and short brown wavy hair which she's always tugging playfully, who has a strong-looking face with a tiny cleft in his chin, and who's almost a foot taller than she is with these broad shoulders and a stomach she can punch as hard as she likes though she still can't get him to even flinch, not forgetting the muscles on his thighs that feel like rock when she's sitting on him, pushing down and leaning back, grabbing them for support, digging her nails in, manoeuvring herself into this angle that drives her crazy. Never mind the fact she finds him a bit boring already.

She's told Valerie that Ben's brilliant in bed and Valerie said, Of course he is, baby, otherwise you wouldn't be marrying him, right? But Becky knows that Valerie's probably heard this line a hundred times before. It's funny, she thinks, but all the girls who get married, who say they're getting married, make out their fiancés are brilliant in bed, while almost everyone else, those who actually are married and those who haven't even thought about it say their partners are crap and that they'd do anything for a good shag. The only hosties who she can think of who admit to having a half decent sex life are those who stick to the odd fling. However, Becky knows from past experience that you always make out a one night stand, or more likely a down route affair has been worth it, otherwise you feel used. We all lie about sex, she thinks. Every cabin crew.

Her mind switches to the prospect of this evening and the feeling that there she'll be in a groovy downtown bar, the centre of attention, surrounded by her Economy colleagues and perhaps some others, David from Business, Carlo (is it?) from First, the captain (Debbie's favourite), even the first officer, plus maybe one or two other people from different flights they've picked up in the crew hotel (there's always someone hanging about the lobby looking for some action) and there she'll be in this bar which is dimly lit with these gigantic mirrors and art on the walls which she doesn't understand (but thinks can't be that difficult to make) and perhaps velvet-covered booths and glass tables and the staff all in tight-fitting black clothes and this cool music blaring (just like this place she went to in Miami a month ago for someone's leaving), feeling sophisticated and sexy, on top of the world, with some guy – the first officer? (what's wrong with her?) – making a move and she'll be stuck in this awful dilemma, desperate for one last fling (she really has had some great casual sex) but knowing she's unable to do anything about it because she's now engaged and, as Tim says, it would get back to Ben quick as anything if she did. Will she never have sex with anyone apart from Ben again? The thought is far too depressing to contemplate so she wonders just how many people will show up tonight. Whether anyone will order champagne, or a cocktail she's never heard of (everyone drinks cocktails now). She wishes her mum knew that her colleagues, these people she's never met before today but already feels like she's known forever, are planning a party for her this evening in New York City. Where she went on her first trip as a cabin crew, and where her mother's never been – the chicken.

Nigel wipes his brow and face with a towelette, sensing the heat coming from his cheeks. It took him much longer than he anticipated and after he finished, finding himself sitting on the toilet seat, he realised he needed a shit – something he rarely does on board. He has a phobia about using public toilets and even though the toilets in First are comparatively clean and checked every twenty minutes (mostly by him) he still hates using them for anything more than a quick pee. He always presses the flush with his foot. He can't bear coming into direct contact with any surface. He particularly hates sitting on the seat so on the odd occasions when he needs to he lays out strips of toilet paper he can sandwich between himself and the seat first. But just now he was in such a rush he didn't bother and plonked himself down immediately, his legs being too shaky to stand, and grabbed his prick not thinking about anything except wanting to rid himself of this erection as quickly as possible, though while he was stroking himself images appeared in his mind (perhaps a clearer picture of what he had seen beginning to emerge on the clouds), images of someone who he hadn't thought about for years and which managed to excite him even more, though he wanted to hang onto this person, these images, suddenly clear as anything, for as long as possible so when he was about to come he stopped stroking himself and waited for the sensation to subside a little before he toyed with himself again. And he kept this up for a surprisingly long time for someone so unpractised, just reaching the brink and then pulling back (realising a little of what he's been missing), that when he finally came he felt as if his whole body was erupting, emptying itself of some poison, which he thinks is probably why he suddenly felt the urge to have a shit. Wanting to rid himself of everything inside him. As if he were turning his body inside out.

Flattening his tie against his stomach, he can definitely feel a difference in his belly's tautness, the way he can make it fold over his belt, and checking his hair's in place (as much as someone as bald as he is can ever get their hair into place – he's always tried to make the most of what he's got) one last time he turns in the tiny space, mindful not to let the backs of his trousers brush the toilet rim, clicks open the door and lets himself out, pulling shut the door behind him as quickly as possible, though it gets stuck on its runners, as always, and he has to kick it into place. He doesn't want any of the smell to escape of course and hopes it's a while before anyone uses the toilet again. He looks about him, happily seeing that no one seems to have noticed him leave the toilet. He would hate for one of his guests to walk in straight after him, or for Wendy or Carlo to for that matter and have them knowing for the rest of the flight who was responsible  for this terrible smell – the looks they'd give him. He always worries about this, leaving the toilet to find someone queuing outside, even if he's just had a pee. It's why he doesn't think he could ever work in Economy again. The idea of dealing with so many passengers, and all of them so unrefined, so unmannered. He's far too shy to begin with. Those days, he thinks, thank God, are definitely over. He wishes the flush could whisk away the smell as well, hearing from the other side of the toilet door the powerful sucking suddenly end.

Hovering in the aisle just in front of the curtain separating First from Business, trying to cool off further, he lets his gaze drift over to the vacant window in passenger door D1L (yet again), where he was looking out from when he was struck by this incredible urge that manifested itself in an erection he's sure wasn't at first particularly sexual, maybe the sort of erection he finds himself waking up with, but when he got to the toilet and took out his prick and this person suddenly, shockingly came to mind it certainly became so – but I don't have sexual urges, he thinks. And he sees from a few paces away – he can't spend any more time by the window just yet and goes no closer – the dipping sun. He sees this yellowing light smashing onto the glass or the Perspex (or whatever the outer transparent panel is made from – they are never told these things) and shattering into a million blinding fragments. Over and over. So quickly it's continuous.

Balls, thinks Selina, completely missing the line she so carefully drew this morning and smudging the stuff on her forehead because the plane jolted, just as she was applying her new eyebrow pencil, which is much softer than she's used to and comes off far too easily everywhere. She always has problems with her eyebrows anyway and she finds trying to apply make-up during the slightest bit of turbulence impossible. She's in the CM's station staring into the small mirror which has been sandwiched between the VSCUs and the library and she puts the pencil down on the ledge beside the as yet untouched cabin tech log (she doesn't know how she'll cope if she's faced with any malfunction today, even if it's simply a dicky bev maker) but which she always gets out ready just in case, and the voyage report folder and three crew assessment forms she's meant to fill in because two of the crew are up for promotion – Becky, the dumpy little one in Economy, and Wendy in First, who's almost old enough to be her mum, and Tim in Economy is coming to the end of his probation. She holds onto the ledge which acts as her desk, waiting for another bout of turbulence, grasping it tightly, but nothing happens (which she thinks is unusual because in her long career one jolt of turbulence normally leads to another and another before the bumpy air flattens out – you don't normally get just one jolt) so eventually she removes her hold, trying not to think about why the turbulence has so suddenly ceased, if indeed the jolt was turbulence, and picks up her eyebrow pencil with one hand and a tissue with the other and tries to sort out the mess she's created on her forehead, concentrating on making herself look particularly strong and confident today. Not she hopes too hard, not exactly tough but more executive-looking, indeed powerful (and quite different to the other hosties) now that she's in charge of the cabin. She's always thought that if you don't quite feel the part you can at least try to look it – CMs should always stand out.

Make-up amazes her – quite how easy it is to transform yourself. She knows she's not brilliant with it (especially when it comes to her eyebrows) but reckons she's had enough experience over the years and has watched enough people (everyone has a slightly different technique, each with their own tricks and shortcuts) to create pretty well whatever look she wants. She has just so much of the stuff, procured mostly in New York or LA. She gets discounts at numerous cosmetics counters, like most of the girls who've been around for a bit. She's always experimenting with new lines – Vincent Longo, Trish McEvoy, Smashbox at the moment. She loves Macy's cosmetics hall (she's never met a hostie who doesn't, at least not secretly) and maybe Bloomingdale's more so because it's never quite as crowded and the assistants are friendlier, plus it's a short walk from the crew hotel and if she's only got a morning it's perfect. She normally has coffee and a bagel at one of the diners on Lexington first.

She manages to remove the last trace of the misplaced dark brown eyebrow pencil, or Black Brown as it's technically called, with the flick of a finger and, trying not to frown, has another go at touching up her face, finding the pencil still far too soft for her liking but at least she doesn't get it everywhere this time with the plane steady as a rock once more. Quite pleased with the result, as pleased as she'll ever be (she might regard herself as pretty competent, even innovative when it comes to applying make-up yet somehow she's never a hundred per cent satisfied with the result, there's always something not right, apart from the eyebrows – she can't put her finger on it) she replaces the cap and hunts in her make-up bag (ancient Estée Lauder which she'll never replace however unhip Estée Lauder might be because it was a gift from Donna) for her Trish McEvoy eye shadow compact. It's matt black with two circles of this season's spring colours, Blue Eternity and Green Temptation, and a snap-in brush which she recently picked up in LA, with a fifteen per cent discount, because Paula's got one, and she usually buys everything her best friend (who she now hardly ever sees) has. She thinks Paula can look amazing considering she doesn't have the best bone structure in the world, or the best skin for that matter – though she does have this incredible body. Selina clicks open the case and extracts the brush and dabs it softly in the Blue Eternity. She gently applies the colour first to her left eyelid and then her right, while using a finger, the slightest touch, to smooth out the edges, blending it in with her eyeshadow. It's not that her make-up is in serious need of repair, more that she wants to maintain the freshness of what she created earlier in keeping with this urge to feel and indeed be perceived to be confident and strong, different from the others. How anyone might expect a cabin manager with twelve years' flying experience to be. She sees she's beginning to get crow's-feet and despite the make-up, how tired she really is.

While she's replacing the brush the plane jolts again, like they've hit a great rut in the sky, and Selina drops the compact and grasps the ledge with both hands. Again it didn't seem to her like a normal bit of turbulence – there was no warning it was coming, no trembling, just thump. The captain hasn't come on the intercom to say anything either (or informed her of the situation, whether it's up to her to make an announcement). She pictures him on the flight deck with his sleepy, dog-like face, probably tucking into his meal by now (maybe seconds, she knows how greedy these captains are, and how they like to hide the fact) and not paying the slightest bit of attention to the controls, or the warning lights which she can just imagine are beginning to flick away wildly in front of his food tray, with the first officer, with Dan not knowing what the hell to do (at his age, she thinks, how would he?). She can feel her heart beginning to pound and the palms of her hands grasping the ledge become sticky and less secure. Looking down she sees the compact open on the floor with the circles of Blue Eternity and Green Temptation staring up at her like two eyes belonging to two different people yet stuck in the same face. She daren't let go to pick it up, so she remains clasped to her work station, rapidly losing grip, waiting for another shock. Hoping no one's going to walk past and see her like this – the cabin manager, this confident-looking executive who should be out in the cabins checking everyone's all right, that the overheads are firmly secured. Who probably should have picked up the PA by now (despite having received no indication from the captain to do so – she suddenly can't think what the correct procedure is) and told everyone to return to their seats, but who is in fact hanging on for dear life, with her make-up spilled all over the floor. What the hell's he up to, she thinks. They were serious jolts. She should call him but she can't quite bring herself to yet because if it is something more serious than turbulence she doesn't want to know.

She looks out of her work station across the empty aisle (she's sure she still hasn't been observed) to passenger door D2L, seeing for a second this brilliant oval of light which she immediately looks away from, knowing the longer she looks at it, the longer she glimpses the outside, the worse the situation will be. Instead she focuses on the door mode panel nearby which is indicating, she can just tell by the amber light, that the door's in automatic (as it should be). The giant handle is slung fully forward and she sees the soft bulge that contains the emergency evacuation chute, which would deploy the second the door's opened, with its twin slide lanes and deceleration pads at the bottom and which doubles up as a fifty-six-person life raft incorporating a canopy, a sea anchor, locator lights and a survival pack. The survival pack alone contains water sachets, emergency food rations, a torch, a compass, the heliograph, two mini flares, four sea markers, six day/night distress signals. She can't see how it all fits in. Why it's even necessary. A pilot once told her that, whatever anyone might say, you wouldn't have a hope in hell of successfully ditching an aircraft this size in the sea. And though she knows the drill for such a ditching off by heart, of course – whether it's unplanned and the captain suddenly comes on the PA saying, This is the captain, this is an emergency, BRACE, BRACE, or it's planned (as would probably be the case now – they've a long way to fall) and she, as the most senior cabin crew, would be told to report to the flight deck immediately (this is the signal she realises she's expecting any second) where she'd be briefed on the exact nature of the emergency and how long they've got before attempting to ditch and then she'd have to go back into the cabin to inform the rest of the crew, should there be time, of what the problem is, what the pilot's intentions are, the time available, plus any other special instructions (she realises she knows these procedures all right) and then she'd turn up the cabin lighting and switch on the prerecorded ditching announcement and begin assisting the passengers with the fitting of their life jackets and distributing and securing the life cots for the babies and moving the most able-bodied into the relevant positions where they'll be instructed to help with the eventual evacuation (if anyone's still alive), and making sure the exit routes are understood, as is the Pax bracing position to be assumed, and all trolleys and equipment and hand baggage is properly secured, and the seats are in the upright with armrests down and tables stowed, and the galley electrics are turned off and she's finally dimmed the cabin lights (as if it's a normal landing – ha) and strapped herself into her crew seat and assumed the crew bracing position with her knees and feet together and her feet tucked slightly rearwards and pressed down firmly on the floor with her fingers interlocked behind her head while she forces her elbows as close together as possible, and she's begun praying like mad – she also knows, because this pilot told her so, that they'd have to catch the swell just right so you land running with the predominant wave pattern (she's surprised she's remembered this) and that visibility would obviously have to be pretty good, so forget it if it's night-time, and the wind would have to be coming from just the right direction, too. The chances are the plane would disintegrate on impact. It would be like slamming into to a wall of reinforced concrete. Even her safety and procedures manual which is gloriously optimistic about dealing with violent passengers and bomb threats and on board fires and sudden cabin depressurisation, says ditching at sea is catastrophic. She thinks she'll probably faint on the spot if the captain comes on the PA now and says, Will the cabin manager report to the flight deck immediately. She knows she'd be useless in a proper emergency. It's not just her either, half the girls she's ever worked with have admitted how crap they'd be. She wonders if anyone could do what they're meant to in such circumstances.

But the plane has remained perfectly steady since the last jolt and Greg's said nothing and she looks at her spilled Trish McEvoy make-up on the floor, knowing she's meant to be setting an example, that she was promoted to CM because she supposedly has what it takes, just the right levels of competence and initiative, and realising quite how pathetic she is (it makes no difference if most of the others are useless too), she lets go of the ledge and bends down to pick up the compact, finding it's actually broken, that the lid's become detached. She tries to fit it together as best she can before stuffing it in her knackered Estée Lauder make-up bag out of sight where it can miraculously mend itself. She frantically searches for her eyeliner, thinking if she behaves as if everything is normal and continues with what she was doing everything will be fine. She doesn't sense any worry or confusion coming from the cabin at least, no rising voices or ruffled air as people start to leave their seats and panic just when they shouldn't, so she rummages around but she can't find the eyeliner in there, because she's not thinking straight and keeps forgetting and reminding herself, forgetting and reminding herself, instant by instant, what it is she's looking for. She eventually extracts her mascara (one she's had for ages, called Black Immensity) knowing she's sort of on the right track. When she applies her make-up she always starts at the top and works downwards, from her eyebrows to her lips – after she's applied her foundation of course (she's just discovered this stuff called Water Canvas, or rather Paula's just recommended it to her, which is incredible, it completely evens out your skin, like plaster as Paula puts it). She's seen some girls dart from their eyes to their lips to their cheeks and back to their eyes again, all over the place. Though of course she doesn't always achieve a coordinated look. If she's being honest her make-up is often a complete mess. She's not totally convinced about it today, for instance. She tries, she really does – she just doesn't know where she goes wrong. Fuck it, she mouths, feeling this lump of dejection in her throat.

She pulls the loaded brush out and moves in on the mirror again and, bringing her hand up, she finds she's shaking. She tries to apply the stuff nevertheless but she's shaking too much so she lets her hand drop for a moment and looks at herself hard in the mirror, trying to see through the half-retouched make-up and the make-up that's already been crappily put there earlier today to what really lies underneath, to what makes her so useless. She pulls this childish expression, sticking out her bottom lip and her chin and opening her eyes as wide as they go, stretching every muscle, an expression she often makes when she's angry with herself. And as she strains to maintain this face, because it's hard to hold for long, the plane suddenly jolts again, a massive thump this time, and she bumps her head on the mirror, lightly but it's shocking enough, at least she's never done that before, and oddly she doesn't drop the mascara brush. She squeezes it, making the shaft ride up in her hand, so her hand's now in contact with the soft bristles sticky with mascara and the mascara's getting all over her hand, thinking this definitely isn't normal, no way, he's got to fucking say something now. And the plane jolts again and again, like it's stopping and starting and going up and down as well, and because she's convinced herself it's not turbulence (there was no warning in the crew briefing of any expected on route) but some major mechanical problem she really starts to panic and finding she's clung onto the ledge (again) with her free hand she leans out into the bucking aisle, instantly feeling seasick, but still she sees no one, which concerns her even more – what's happened to everybody? – and she thinks, seeing passenger door D2L again and its huge bright gaping window which she can't avoid, she thinks, what if they've forgotten to pack the survival bag, what if the emergency chute doesn't inflate, even after she's pulled the manual inflation handle, what if the swell's going in the wrong way? We're fucked. We're completely fucked anyway. She whimpers.

And the plane continues to twist and leap about, so much so she doesn't think she'll make it into the Business cabin in one piece, where at least she'll be with some of the others – she won't have to be alone. She's always hated being on her own. She hates living on her own, she hates waking up in the morning on her own (mostly). She hates her unmarried life and fucking Mike for helping her perpetuate this state. And not being able to remove herself from the CM's station, still squeezing the life out of the mascara, her fingers covered in it, with her face no longer pulling this ridiculous expression but simply pale and rigid with fear, the plane bouncing around as if it's a cork, she thinks if you get us out of this one, Greg, I'm yours baby. I'm all yours. And there, she finally hears the ping of the fasten seat belt sign and she knows what's coming next, she can almost hear it – will the cabin manager report to the flight deck immediately.

*Greg scans the ND he's overlaid with the weather but he sees nothing out of the ordinary – no red, not even much yellow and only a smattering of green, which he knows is in a weather system way below them anyway. He glances at the flight chart he had been preparing for the next leg after landfall and which is resting on his lap. Looks back at the right screen.*

*Says to Dan, C-A-T. Has any been reported earlier? I haven't heard anything.*

*No, says Dan.*

*He glances straight ahead, clear outside — something he often forgets to do for long stretches of time because he's been tucking into a meal or going through the charts, or daydreaming and not focusing on anything in particular, knowing the world will continue to slide safely by miles beneath them, all those bland earthy colours — as if he might actually spot a patch of clear air turbulence. He notices how golden the sky's becoming and that the horizon — he tries to get a fix on it despite the jolting — is strung with this thick, gluey-looking substance. He notices how stiller and softer than ever the sky seems. Fields of frozen air. Yet they're being tossed around in it seemingly inexplicably. And he thinks again how much flying, the experience of piloting an aircraft, involves discounting what you actually see, ignoring your senses, disbanding reason, and accepting the unexpected, the unusual, all manner of strange phenomena. The fact, for instance, the wind can suddenly change in strength from one band to another and flying through this transition zone, this windshear, even if the change is as little as four or five knots, will result in severe turbulence. And how difficult it is to forecast CAT because it's not picked up by the weather radar, which sees only water and ice. It can be possible to deduce imminent CAT from rapid changes in the outside air temperature but no one sits there studying the air temperature indicator for long enough or at exactly the right moment. And there are certain charts which attempt to map CAT but these have proved to be all but useless as jet streams are continually shifting and pockets of slower or faster moving air can pop up anywhere. He knows your only real warning comes from aircraft in the same track a few minutes ahead who happen to have experienced any and reported back on the pilots' channel. The Americans are particularly good at relaying such information, being so paranoid about turbulence because of the effect it has on the passengers (and any possible personal injury claims). It doesn't bother Greg much — he thinks of the passengers less and less. He usually forgets to turn on the fasten seat belt sign — he quickly glances at the centre console to check he's done so now, because, well, the turbulence is pretty strong. He hardly ever selects turbulence speed on the autopilot. He's been doing this job long*

114

*enough to be confident to trim the aircraft manually, to correct any control surface or system sent out of line by hand while still going at cruise. He might be old, he might have soaring blood pressure and a problem with his prostate but he's got all these years of experience. He's not going to wimp out now and slow down.*

*He suddenly feels this sense of power surge through him. A sense for the first time this flight that he's actually in control. That he's beyond any procedural restrictions and is no longer bound to the hundreds of checklists and strict flight deck parameters – with all his experience? He's the pilot who's flying the aircraft (on the outbound leg anyway) and he'll fly it how he wants. Besides he's the captain. He's in control, despite desperately needing to pee again – he thinks he probably needs a fucking catheter.*

*I guess we're in the right place for it, he says, seeing Dan's given up studying his route chart and is scanning the screens giving off this air, Greg's sure, of concern, the way his head is darting from screen to screen. I don't think we need to request another flight level yet, he says, this sort of turbulence never lasts long. He adjusts the mike on his headset he replaced a few moments earlier, reaches behind to flick the PA switch on the centre console. Urrgh, ladies and gentlemen, this is the captain, he says. As you've probably noticed we're experiencing a little turbulence at the moment. Please return to your seats and fasten your seat belts. There's absolutely nothing to be concerned about. You're in very capable hands. He turns off the PA, feeling his meal in his stomach slop about. He shouldn't have had a pudding but the treacle tart with white chocolate ice cream is his favourite.*

*And suddenly, as he knew it would and without having to request a new flight level and then go through all the rigmarole of getting there, without jeopardising the safety of his passengers (or crew), without having to slow down and hand over any more control to the computer by turning to turbulence speed, yet without really assuming any more control than he had before (it's always like this, there's only so much power a captain can exert before a situation stabilises, before the systems render you largely obsolete – however much you want to bend the rules a little just for the hell of it, just to remind yourself you are human and not some adjunct to a machine, albeit a very sophisticated one), the turbulence stops, as it always does. His stomach immediately begins to settle, gently flopping over the* lap belt, and the aircraft starts to sail once more through icy smooth air — air so thin it's left shattered and spinning behind them. No, he thinks, there's no skill to flying any more, not one of these things. Who have I been kidding otherwise? Jeanette, Paula? All those other impressionable young air hostesses? Myself?

Selina instantly comes to his mind, her glorious body, even more gorgeous than Paula's — Selina bending over, retrieving whatever it was from the floor (the box of chocolates, that was it) with the outline of her incredibly skimpy underwear showing through her uniform. He's just realised how he can orchestrate a down route rendezvous. He'll have a room party. Nobody ever refuses to come to a captain's room party, particularly not a career-minded CM. He rests his right foot on the edge of the centre console, this worn bar purposefully put there, sticks his arm on the ledge by the visors, lets his body sink further into the seat, knowing he's never going to get completely comfortable, but knowing nevertheless they're shortly to shift seamlessly from one air traffic control zone to another, from Gander to Moncton. That there are no physical boundaries in the sky, no earthly restrictions. Perhaps, it occurs to him, he's had too much freedom — that he's what happens if men are left unchecked.

# moncton

Come on, Nige, says Wendy, no one can be that abstemious. Carlo's out shagging every night, aren't you, darling? At least I hope you are, gorgeous, otherwise it would be a terrible waste. No, Nige, it's not possible. You'd have gone completely mad by now. That or you can't be human. I mean, where does it all go, all that goo you guys produce? It must start to leak out.

I think this conversation's gone far enough, says Nigel, looking down at his watch, the glinting dark blue face, having a flashback to his time in the toilet, wondering whether Wendy could possibly have an inkling of what he was doing in there. And yet despite what he's just said part of him doesn't want the conversation to stop, even if it might prove to be highly embarrassing for him. Wendy's loosening him up again, making him want to talk about things he wouldn't normally dream of mentioning – still he started the conversation, he swung it this way. When she asked him if he was married, giving him this knowing look, he said, No darling, only to my job, and put his hand on his hip and almost pouted. He never camps it up. And when she asked him whether he was seeing anyone at the moment he said, No, I haven't seen anyone for years. So she said, You must be joking. What on earth do you do for sex? And he said (and he never talks about sex either), I don't. Haven't done anything about it for years. As I said, I'm married to my job, and he made a big show of wiping some bits of wilted chervil and frisée off the counter. It's no big deal, he said, as one year moves into the next you slowly forget about it. I don't have sexual urges, not these days. (He's never admitted such a thing to anyone before.)

This is just beginning to get interesting, says Wendy. Come on, Nige, where does all that surplus energy go? I can't stand still for a second if I haven't had a shag for more than a few days. Look at Carlo, passive as anything, hasn't budged from that frigging counter all flight – I told you he's out shagging every night.

Perhaps I'm made differently, Nigel says.

I doubt it, says Wendy. We're all animals when it comes down to sex. It's in-built. And in this job, in this cauldron there's no one to stop you is there – except yourself I suppose. Have I got any self-control? You must be kidding. Carlo, darling, I'd take you now if you could get it up a woman.

I can't, says Carlo. Sorry.

Nigel looks at Carlo, his thick, dark, curly hair, his lovely olive complexion (as much as he finds Mediterranean types attractive he's also equally petrified of them), catching his eye, so he smiles what he thinks is an in league sort of smile, a smile that says, what the hell is she on? And despite sensing he's moving towards some place he might never be able to return from, heady with the moment, for the first time in a long while, for as long as he can remember he realises he's, if not exactly fitting in, at least joining in with the others. That he's one of the crew – chatting about sex. I've probably forgotten what to do, he says. He's certainly forgotten what it's like joining in, being part of something.

Have a word with Carlo, Wendy says, he'll be able to sort you out tonight.

I shouldn't think he's got the patience, says Nigel, knowingly camping it up a little now. He puts his hand on his hip again and smiles coyly, increasingly amazed with himself. This change so quickly.

I'm busy, Carlo says. Sorry.

Never mind, says Wendy, I'm sure we'll be able to find someone to help you. Isn't there anyone in Business or Economy?

Not for me if there is, Nigel says, putting on his clipped, finickety voice, as if he's talking to a passenger. They're far too rough back there, he says.

Ooh, says Wendy, but they're so much more eager, those young boys in Economy. Besides, Nige, I'm not sure whether you're in a position to be choosy. When was your last shag?

Nigel thinks for a moment, makes out he's thinking really hard raising his right hand to his forehead and scratching his temple – Urrrm, he says. But suddenly he feels his cheeks puff and fill with blood and more blood rush into his head and chest until he's throbbing with the stuff as this image of the boy comes back to him again – his young body, all bone and sharp angles, and soft fair hair and grey green eyes and pale smooth skin and sweet smoky breath (he was more awkward-looking than attractive. Vulnerable, Nigel supposes now – certainly easy to approach. He wasn't dark and difficult like Carlo.). He suddenly feels this indiscretion in talking so much, in laying himself open (in simply reacting in a way that's expected of an aged, overweight cabin crew during a galley chat about sex), catching up on him. He realises he's got a long way to go, that he's far from left behind the shy, difficult, pompous (and probably unfeeling – he's been accused of that) self he's always been. What was this blip, he thinks, this moment of lightness, of not being quite himself? An over-enthusiastic response to Wendy? He doesn't know why he should keep seeing the image of this boy again either, after almost twenty years. Those eyes, that hair, but most of all those bony limbs jutting everywhere asking to be grabbed hold of and contained.

It certainly looks like it was worth it, Wendy says. Carlo,

check out Nige, he's gone puce. You're not going to have a heart attack are you now, Nige? Frig-me, what the hell did you get up to? Some shag.

Nigel tries to cough, finding this constriction in his throat. He'd desperately like to just slip out of the galley, through the drab curtain and disappear into the dim plush cabin. He'd like all of him, all his great bulk to evaporate into the thin, stale air but he feels stuck and obtrusive, that he has to remain where he is, on display, otherwise it'll look even worse – like he's dodging something he's desperately ashamed of. He can't say anything and realises he's frantically turning the dial on his watch, feeling it click but not hearing it, waiting for an excuse, anything to get him out of this situation he's only got himself to blame for. Perhaps this is why he's always been so reserved, why he's never put himself on the line, why he's avoided so much – this fear of being caught out, this fear of his past catching up with him. This horror of humiliation. (But yet, he thinks, I don't have a past, I've never done anything wrong.) And like some sign from above (he's never thought of himself as religious, not like his mum, but he has an idea of there being some external, otherworldly power out there overlooking everyone, the world, holding it all together – how there must be something) he hears the passenger call chime go, sees the blue light appear on the panel next to the electrics, shouts, I've got it. His throat is suddenly loose, his voice surprisingly audible. He immediately pushes himself off the counter and makes for the curtain. Hearing Wendy shout, But it's mine. He's mine. Nigel doesn't give her a chance, not even looking back to see if the curtain falls snugly into place behind him, shutting out Wendy and Carlo and the reality of a cabin crew's life – this non-stop talk about people's sex lives, who's shagging who, in the sickening brightness of a galley – and he launches himself into the hushed First class cabin filling the short narrow aisle with his great sweaty bulk like someone who's just escaped one spotlight only to find themselves under another, except it's dim now and no one's looking at him – he just feels like he's still on show. And there on the overhead PSU strip he sees the corresponding passenger call light above seat 4K, Mr McPhee's seat. Mr McPhee, sir? Nigel says, approaching.

Arrgh, the old man says struggling to sit up, I don't normally get you, do I?

There are two of us looking after you today, sir, says Nigel crouching by the armrest. Wendy and myself, and there's Carlo, the galley chef, who's responsible for preparing all the food – but you won't be seeing much of him. We keep him chained to the galley.

I think I must have pressed the wrong button, Mr McPhee says. These seats are so damned complicated nowadays.

I'm sorry they're not to your liking, sir, Nigel says.

Oh, they're comfortable all right, Mr McPhee says, it's just that they're so damned complicated.

Would you like me to explain how everything works, sir? Nigel says.

I think it's too late for that, he says.

There are some instructions on a card in the side pocket there if you need them, Nigel says, pointing. Is there anything else I can do for you?

I don't think so, the old man says turning away and rummaging in the side pocket, perhaps for the seat instruction card. Wendy, uh, he says.

Nigel backs away, seeing that most of the other passengers are stretched out and dozing in front of dead screens. Two people appear to be working, however, and another reading a magazine. The sleepy calm atmosphere slowly overwhelms Nigel, making him realise that it's only ever in here, in the First class cabin that he feels at all in charge of his job, at peace with himself – pampering and comforting his guests, making sure they have everything they need. He used to believe that it was the little individual touches that made all the difference – addressing the guests by their full titles and names, crouching down towards them rather than looming over them, not insisting on showing them how everything works but rather pointing them in the right direction, letting them always think they know better, that they are obviously far more intelligent and richer than he is.

Though walking slowly towards the rear of the curtained-off cabin, in the dim blue light (the light in First always seems bluer for some reason than that in Business or Economy), a sort of perpetual twilight, looking to his left and right at these powerful people snoozing and skimming magazines, and wanting someone to flirt with (he thinks maybe he was wrong to chastise Wendy for spending so much time with Mr McPhee, that she was only doing what was required of her after all – pleasure in service), it occurs to him for the first time that he's never going to be able to satisfy all the passengers' demands – that they're as riddled with hopeless desires and frustrations as he is. He's never thought of them as being somehow like him before, that they might have anything in common except, obviously, that they are all stuck in the same cabin for a few hours or so.

Once through the curtain, in the bright white glow of the doorway lighting (which, according to company guidelines, is always left on the emergency setting), he glances at his watch, this great chunky fake with a midnight blue face and a fancy but quite useless dial which he picked up for a few dollars so he might, if he's being entirely honest with himself, appear to not just bear some resemblance to a pilot but perhaps more to be someone who's going places, someone who has money and power, someone who's significant. He sees it's 19.28 – if he were at home he'd be doing his mum's hot water bottle and making himself a Nescafé, which he usually spices up with lots of sugar (he has a very sweet tooth) and a couple of glugs of brandy. He finds there's just enough brandy in one miniature for two cups of coffee, unless he's feeling particularly restless when he'll tip in the lot. And having stepped out of the cosy confines of First, forever sunk in this dreamy twilight, he suddenly understands, perhaps he's always understood that money and power, that status cannot necessarily help you to suppress desire, however shameful and embarrassing you find it. Or help you wholly to overcome temptation, which he reckons is much the same thing. Or really change who or what you are, not underneath. Still looking at his watch he can't help catching sight of his stomach as well.

Wedged in the space between D1L and the galley, he feels just so big, so obvious.

You can't hide here, Nige, says Wendy, emerging from the galley through the curtain, getting it tangled up on her arm. There's nowhere to hide on this aircraft, she says.

Everybody hates the moment when the films end and the passengers head for the toilets or the galleys, demanding drinks and snacks en masse, as if it's a free-for-all. The passengers are meant to wait in their seats for the tea service which is due today – Becky looks at her watch – in only half-an-hour. Normally the crew time it better and barricade themselves in the galleys using the trolley tops, rubbish bags, whatever is to hand, for when the films end, but Becky finds herself stuck in an aisle with a fully laden duty-free trolley complete with a faulty swipe machine (they're always faulty) and she's shagged because it's her second time round. They're urged to sell as much duty-free as possible, despite everyone hating having to do it, even though the more they sell the more commission they get and she knows she could do with a bit of extra cash for this evening. She's broke, she's permanently broke, and she can't expect people to buy her drinks all night (seeing as she's going to get hammered), which is why she decided to go round again when she now realises she should have called it a day. She's not even halfway down the aisle and she's already blocked in. She'd been heading for service door D5R, her turnaround point. She notices the screens have gone blank or are only showing the sky map, except from where she is and because of all the other commotion going on around her she can't see it properly. They could be flying over Africa for all she can tell. People are flinging aside their headsets and standing up every-where, stumbling into the aisles, shoving her against the trolley, which has a tray of smartly packaged perfumes and the stupid swipe machine crammed on top. She's so squashed in she can't even fix the brake and is trying to hold the trolley from slipping backwards and banging into someone's shins. Excuse me, sir, Becky says, do you want to wait until that lady's got past? It amazes her how people insist on trying to get around a trolley when there's no possible way, particularly being as fat as these two are – unless they climb over the bloody thing. And even though she normally feels pretty fat herself, stuck in the aisle like this she actually feels small in comparison to most of the people around her who have somehow prised themselves from their seats. It's as if when one person breaks lose they all suddenly pop out – that they need each other to keep them in place.

Something sharp prods her bum and she quickly looks over her shoulder to face the man who she thought earlier looked a little like her dad smiling at her as if he hasn't done anything. She wonders whether he used his free hand or simply pushed the scrunched up amenity pack he's holding into her. She thinks that's exactly what her dad would do, pinch a hostie, squeeze some poor girl's bottom then pretend it wasn't him and probably point to someone else (she's caught him doing just this at parties – he's always attacking her friends). She doesn't see her dad much, of course, but when she does she's always slightly wary of him because she's never sure what he's thinking or where she is with him. It's not that he's unpredictable so much as he lives in a world of his own. He doesn't seem to care what anyone thinks about him. She knows her mum must drive him nuts doing nothing all day except spending his money, or lounging around reading horoscopes and watching telly, but she can understand how he would drive her nuts too – it's impossible to get through to him. They never talk to each other properly. They're always putting on these acts – her mum being over the top about everything, with her fake posh voice and false emotions, and her dad simply grunting at her, or else making some really cutting remark, like, 'What do you know about anything? Your head's been stuffed under a hair dryer for so long there's nothing left of your brain but hot air.' That's his favourite comment at the moment.

As far as she can remember they've always been like this, though Becky knows they can't have been quite so unloving when they first met, when they were just going out with each other, otherwise they wouldn't have got married, surely. Pressed in on all sides, with this man who looks like her dad, perhaps less so than she thought earlier after all – her dad's not quite so heavy round the face – with this man, who prodded her bum then pretended he didn't, only about an inch away, now leering at her like a complete perv, she wonders when her parents started to fall into this pattern of behaviour she's only ever known. When they started to not relate to each other. What sparked it. She wonders whether it's catching, whether all marriages go that way and pretty quickly. Or whether it's just in her genes. Because thinking about it, she can already see how Ben and she will become. There'll be Ben saying nothing, or worse boring her rigid about some new flight deck breakthrough and she'll be ignoring him, or maybe like her mum she'll have developed this weird voice and will be coming up with all these over the top things to say like, 'Darling, do shut up and fix me a Martini, extra dry.' Or, 'Oh, Ben, what's happened to the man of my dreams?', pretending to be who knows who off the telly, trying to get a reaction out of him. And this is when they'll see each other. For most of the time she'll be stuck at home with the kids, getting fatter and fatter, consoling herself with chocolate liqueurs, and he'll be off around the world taking advantage of all these girls as naive as she once was, getting shagged stupid. What the fuck have I done? she thinks, seeing her marriage, her future unfold disastrously before her.

Becky looks for support but there are no other crew about in this section of the Economy cabin unless they are completely hidden by passengers pouring into the aisle across the way. She can't see any sign of Valerie or Debbie, or Tim or Marissa even, though she is covering Zone D on the opposite side of the plane to her. She realises they've all got more sense than her, that they're not as greedy and are safely cocooned in the galley, probably tucking into the rest of Debbie's cake, perhaps making more plans for tonight. If only she hadn't set off for a second run – at the most she'd have made a couple of dollars. No one buys the expensive stuff in Economy, it's all fags and booze and tacky souvenirs – the snap-together plastic aeroplanes and teddy bears dressed up as pilots and logo-ed watches – stuff she nicks for her parents. No one's going anywhere until you get back into your seat first, sir, she says, exasperated. You're completely blocking the aisle. Now there's another man in front of her trying to squeeze around her trolley, dragging a small boy with him. You're not going to get past, she says, I'm telling you. She folds her arms on top of her breasts – just managing to ease them up from her sides – in a huffy, determined sort of way. Pushing out her breasts, pouting a little, edging onto tiptoes. Sometimes she finds men back off when she emphasises her sex in a confrontational way, but it doesn't seem to be working now. No one is budging and a feeling of being completely stuck swamps her. She feels not only stuck in the aisle, but stuck in Economy, stuck with this job which she's never had a real problem with until this minute though now realises she can't keep doing it indefinitely, not once she's married. It's not a job for married people – however happy Debbie might seem. She feels stuck with her parents. But most of all she feels stuck with Ben.

Giving up on trying to look so feminine and strong (the man with the young boy is still trying to get past the trolley in front of her and the perv's still at her back armed with his amenity pack) she scans the cabin yet again for any sign of help or at least a colleague across the way who's in the same boat as her so she won't feel quite so helpless and alone and that she can perhaps draw some strength from, plus she'll have someone to laugh about it with later. However, she sees no other hostie, no other trolley dolly, junior, senior, purser or even cabin manager in the same predicament as her. Checking the cabin one final time, before she feels she's really going to lose it, she suddenly spots Valerie poking her head out of the galley, her perfectly made-up face, her immaculately lopsided hair-do, and she wonders whether she would have said yes to Ben so quickly, whether she would have said yes at all if she looked anything like Valerie. If she were dead gorgeous.

Nigel thinks what's so odd is the fact he didn't join the airline because he had any idea he might actually enjoy the flying so much, this state of being above the clouds, yet it's become such an important aspect of the job to him, as if it's what he were always meant to do. However, he quickly shifts over to service door D1R and its naked window with a growing sense of trepidation. Not, he thinks, because he doesn't want Wendy, or Carlo for that matter to see him shirking off again (which he doesn't nevertheless) but because he's worried that the face, the full awkward figure of this boy he once knew and once did something very stupid with might start to emerge on a distant cloud bank again, thus signalling that this endlessly open view of the sky he's always relied upon, this sense of escape, this sanctity (probably the main reason why he's stuck with the job) has been ruined forever. Yet despite the trepidation there's something stronger urging him across the aisle into the service doorway with its non-slip rubber flooring. A need to confront his suddenly restless past? he wonders. Though he doubts it, not quite yet anyway – he's always been so weak. And closing in he realises it's something much simpler, something he usually feels about this far into a flight.

Before it's too late, glancing over his shoulder and seeing no sign of either Wendy (he doesn't think he's ever come across a woman as persistent as Wendy) or Carlo, Nigel steps up to the window of D1R, which is on the shady side of the plane, and resting his hand on the bulge – he's only going to take a quick look this time, really – he peers tentatively outside, over the shimmering clouds, the edges of which are now clearly fringed with late afternoon colour, tangerine turning to sanguine, to-wards cobalt space hanging just above the fading horizon. He doesn't wait to see if any image might form out of thin air, rapidly adjusting himself to get at the right angle to look directly downwards and as he just realised he probably would, as some intuition told him to do so, with his pulse quickening a little, he sees between soft ridges of altostratus and through a split in a lower sheet of bulbous stratocumulus a patch of cold grey earth. North America. He realises he's already missed the precise moment of landfall.

*Ladies and gentlemen, Greg says – he coughs trying to clear his throat – excuse me, good afternoon, this is the captain. We've finished our*

*Atlantic crossing and are currently flying over Newfoundland, which some of you might be able to see through the breaks in the clouds on the right of the aircraft. It doesn't look too hospitable down there right now I must say. We have a pretty direct routing to New York this afternoon, south along the Atlantic seaboard. We'll shortly be passing over the Gulf of St Lawrence then on to Prince Edward Island and crossing the Canadian US border just to the west of Fredericton in Nova Scotia. We'll be passing over Bangor in Maine and starting our descent just after Boston, coming in to Kennedy via Providence and Calverton in Connecticut. The weather at Kennedy hasn't changed, remaining overcast and two degrees Celsius, that's thirty-six degrees Fahrenheit, though a fall in temperature of some ten degrees Celsius and snow is forecast for later tonight. So those of you who are staying in the New York area and who are going out tonight do wrap up warmly. Presuming the weather doesn't deteriorate too soon, we're not expecting any major air traffic delays on our approach and should still be landing a few minutes ahead of schedule, though it is Friday evening and things do have a habit of clogging up a bit – I'll let you know should the picture change. I hope you're comfortable and trust that our excellent team of cabin crew are providing you with everything you need.*

Greg's feeling excited (he didn't think he had it in him any more) and when he's excited he can ramble on for longer than is necessary, becoming less formal too. But this is mostly because he's now in Canadian airspace and whenever he's in Canadian or American airspace (there's little distinction) he can't help being influenced by the pilots he hears on the open channel and the commercial lines. He's always thought they sound so much more relaxed than British pilots, who seem trapped within the stuffy limitations of standard 1950s RT phraseology. The British (and, but less so other Europeans) hardly ever deviate, unlike North American-trained pilots who could almost be chatting in some 2nd Avenue bar, where Greg hopes he might manage to slip out to tonight for a few beers before his room party. Even on the ATC frequencies he's always catching non-standard phrases such as *charlie* instead of *correct*, *out* instead of *leaving*, *repeat* instead of *say again*. Greg used to be renowned within the company for his lengthy announcements to the passengers, now he's often criticised by the CMs for not keeping the passengers well enough informed about the route and the weather and any expected delays. However, the fact he can visualise their passage to Kennedy – he's done it so many times he knows all the major rivers and mountain ranges, the cities and freeways they'll be passing over (on route 160 today) – and with the thought of his room party uppermost on his mind, he's excited, he truly is, and thus chatty in a way he hasn't felt like being for a long while. He no longer wants to prolong the flight, he no longer wishes it would all slow down. He's brimming with anticipation. He wants to be there, not plotting but acting, moving in on his prey – ah, Selina – just like in the old days.

He taps the glare shield, stares ahead smiling, because also the pain in his crotch seems to have subsided and his stomach is suddenly not as tight-feeling, and there's no hint of an ache in his left arm. Maybe he'd simply not had enough to think about earlier, or rather he was trying not to think about certain things and he'd dreamed up these problems, at least he'd let himself dwell on a couple of odd twinges, twisting them out of all proportion – he's always doing this. He feels whole, together, that there's nothing seriously wrong with him. Or if there is, he has second wind and for the moment he's happy enough with that. He knows he'll be able to last at least until tomorrow. And tomorrow? Seeing as Dan's flying the aircraft home and either it will or won't have happened with Selina – there's not going to be another chance – what does it matter how he's feeling? He might as well be on his way out, half-dead. Only tonight is what matters. (He thinks back to when he viewed the future as a series of stop-overs stretching to someplace beyond which he could imagine – he's never seriously contemplated retirement, his pension plan is in a complete mess, not to mention the whole question of his future with Jeanette – and it's come to this, one last night in New York. Wasn't New York his first transatlantic destination as a captain of a wide-body? Didn't he have a party that night too?)

He glances at Dan who's studiously going over the next leg of the route map, checking, Greg can see, the designated holding stacks on the approach, should any be necessary (it would be typical, Greg thinks, to have got this far so swiftly, against the wind, with Kennedy almost in their sights, to have to hold for forty minutes out in say Calverton, though it is Friday and they'll be lucky not to be lumped with some delay despite all ATC conversations so far indicating the contrary) and he realises he's going to have to ask Dan to his room party as well. He can't exactly ask Selina the next time she appears on the flight deck in front of Dan without Dan having been told about it first, otherwise Greg can see the kid will say something completely unsubtle which will make her realise she's being set up. Besides, he knows that to guarantee she does turns up he'll have to ask everyone anyway. She might have already arranged to do something with another crew member and if that's the case he needs to make sure this other person knows about it too so they'll both come to the conclusion that they might as well go to his room party because what they were going to do probably wouldn't be that much fun as it's what they always do in New York. Room parties are rare nowadays, particularly those given by a captain. And, perhaps more significantly, Greg knows he has a reputation which she might somehow have heard about – there are a few names and faces he recognises on board, Wendy in First and the Economy purser in particular – and that if all the crew are in on the party how can it possibly appear to Selina to be a set-up? However, it occurs to Greg that he might not see Selina until she reports to him just before landing – she has no reason to – and that even if he thinks most people will be only too willing to change whatever plans they might have made for tonight to come to his room party she and one or two of the others might just stick with whatever they've already organised. It would be just his luck. To be certain of her turning up he knows he has to ask her if possible before she's made any plans at all and that time is running out. Wow, he feels his mind is going round in circles today.

As the aircraft automatically begins executing an 18 degree left turn, lining itself up with route 160, they slowly face into the sun and the sun, not much higher in the sky than the aircraft – a burning ball an opened hand's width above the horizon from where they are currently positioned – flips straight into the flight deck, this great wash of light, rendering for an instant all the screens unreadable and turning everything to gold, themselves included, as if they've suddenly been set in amber, but still banking this solid ageless golden light quickly eases as they shift round some more and the sun begins shining for the first time on what was the shady side of the aircraft, leaving the formerly sunny side suddenly dimmed with shadow streaking down the fuselage, and cutting across the cockpit at a less intense, more oblique angle, and with the light now seemingly being sucked back outside, clearing the instruments, making every screen and dial distinct once more, Greg wonders how he can entice Selina onto the flight deck as soon as possible. He could call for her on the PA – will the cabin manager report to the flight deck immediately – which would certainly get her running. But it's hardly an emergency – yet. He doesn't want to scare the shit out of her before asking her to his room party. He reckons she's nervy enough as it is. He can't afford to blow it. Dan, he says, doing anything tonight?

I've got a couple of ideas. Why? Dan says.

It's just that I'm thinking of asking the crew up to my room for a few drinks, Greg says.

Who in particular? Dan says.

I don't know, Greg says, everyone I suppose, like an old-style room party.

Why? Dan says. It's not your birthday is it? You're not retiring just yet?

I've been under a lot of pressure recently, Greg says – domestic stuff – I just fancy letting my hair down. Besides we're not getting into Manhattan too late.

There's always another reason, Dan says. I've been flying long enough with you lot to know that. Captains don't just have room parties. So who is it? The CM? Are you trying to go behind my back? You don't stand a chance, mate. Look what I've got to offer – youth for a start. Plus I'm almost single. We've bet on it already anyway, haven't we? Let me give you a bit of advice, Greg. If I was your age, in your position, I'd forget it. She'll be too much trouble, apart from everything else the girl's bonkers. That's pretty apparent. There must be an easier proposition for you, someone nearer your own age. What about the Economy purser, or that bird working in First?

Thanks, says Greg. Thanks a lot. For fuck's sake, Dan, there's no hidden agenda. It's just a few drinks. I'm buying.

That'll be a first, says Dan. A captain buying the drinks. So let me get this straight – you're asking everyone, right, to guarantee she turns up? Selina, uh.

It's no big deal, Dan, Greg says, whatever you think. I'm sorry I asked you.

*Yeah, I'll come, Dan says, as long as that's what everyone else decides to do.*

*Great, says Greg, I'll enjoy your company, especially having spent all day with you.*

*But Friday night in Manhattan? Dan says. You'll be lucky.*

*We'll see won't we, Greg says. He doesn't know why he bothered to ask Dan. He wishes he hadn't because he seems to have wised up to his plan immediately. Still, Greg thinks, he's probably just jealous because he didn't have the initiative. But what choice did he have? He couldn't have not asked him. He doesn't care if Dan's guessed what he's up to as long as Selina remains in the dark. He knows he'll be able to ask her to the party in such a way she won't realise – he's experienced in these matters. He glances at the clock, sees they have just over an hour and a half left of normal time but they're currently running seven minutes ahead of schedule and, supposing they don't hit any ATC delays, they've actually got under an hour and a half left until touchdown. He'll ring her work station and if she doesn't answer he'll put out a call for her on the PA, fuck it. He can always ask her to ask everyone else (what else are CMs for?). He has every excuse to speak to her immediately.*

Hearing a couple of lo-hi chimes and seeing the pink light illuminate by the handset, Selina picks up the interphone, thinking whatever it is I'm not going anywhere. I'm not moving. She's only just managed to return to the CM's station. Hi, she says.

Selina, sweetie, hi, it's Debbie. I just wanted to let you know we're organising an evening for Becky, you know the dark-haired plump girl – she's just got engaged – and we wondered whether you might be up for doing something with us tonight. I'm not quite sure what exactly yet – a couple of the girls are suggesting going to this bar they know downtown. I think it's one of those trendy places where you can dance as well. It might be fun. But anyway I thought it would be nice to try to make the evening special for her, as long as we get enough people along – she seems a little depressed.

Oh, says Selina, yeah, sure. It hasn't even occurred to her what she might be doing tonight except, thinking about it, probably just collapsing on her bed and ringing Mike to tell him to fuck off (though she knows she won't do that, she doesn't have the balls). She'll just lie there wanting to and not being able to, feeling more and more pathetic. I'd love to go out, she says. She can't remember the last time she did so with a gang of the girls, when they all went to some trendy bar with dancing – it seems like it was in another life. Catching sight of her face in the small mirror sandwiched between the entertainment systems – this mirror seems to keep hooking her, perhaps because there's no one else about (she's always felt self-conscious looking in the galley mirrors in front of everyone, reapplying her make-up or whatever) – she forces herself to smile, even finding the ridiculous mess she's made of her make-up funny. Whatever was she trying to do? And peering at herself, despite this screen of messed-up make-up, she thinks she has an idea about who she really is, that it would take a lot more than make-up to disguise her true self. She's no different from any of the other hosties on board, she's definitely not above anyone. She loves to party just as much as everyone else. She feels this sense of how she used to be (in another life) coming through. Thinks tonight will be just like old times.

The thing is, says Debbie, we're a bit short of straight guys, as usual. I don't know whether you want to ask the captain and the first officer. You might have more chance of guaranteeing that they come than if I ask them. They always listen to you lot. I've already asked David, in Business. He thinks he'll come – have you checked him out? Fantastic body. And I'll ask the guys in First, not that they're going to be much use – she laughs. They probably won't come, she says, but I don't want anyone thinking this is an exclusive sort of thing and being bitchy about it all the way home. It is Becky's night after all. She's a sweet girl – too young to be getting married of course, but we've all been there.

Selina says, If you really want me to, sure I'll ask them. But I can't think they'll pay any more attention to me than you. She replaces the handset, suddenly aware that Debbie's manipulating her, getting her to do her dirty work. Maybe she thinks this because of her comment about David. So she's noticed him too, which is perhaps not surprising. He is the only decent-looking bloke on board who's obviously anything like straight. She quickly thinks back to what Debbie said just before the thing about Becky being too young to be getting married (she knows she would have got married like a shot at her age had anyone asked, that she most definitely hasn't been there) to her comment about it being Becky's night, and how it isn't an exclusive thing. Bollocks, Selina thinks, because in her experience, over the past twelve years, everyone only ever really thinks about themselves and setting themselves up with whoever for the stop-over, for the down route, orchestrating some encounter or another, however much they all like to make out otherwise. They just use each other. Cabin-crewing is as selfish a business as any other, she thinks, particularly as they are all stuck so close together for so long, when surely they should be a little more compassionate, a little more sensitive towards one another. Perhaps that's what makes them worse – this confinement inducing some appalling reaction. Still, she's not going to miss out on tonight and dancing, and David (whoever he is). She can play the same game – she knows how to get what she wants, she used to anyway. She sees herself in the mirror again, this stupid pale mess of a face she somehow manages to keep believing in. She winks, as if to say I know you better than you think. Maybe she's being too harsh on Debbie, on everyone. Nevertheless she is stuck with having to ask the sodding flight crew, Greg and Dan. She suddenly thinks of them as this comic duo, this joke, like what was that TV programme her mum used to love, Little and Large? Or was it Morecambe and Wise? They shouldn't be piloting an aircraft. They shouldn't be let anywhere near the controls.

# boston

Just as she's leaving the CM's station, with her back firmly to the mirror and her mind fixed on this idea of Greg and Dan being some comedy duo, chuckling to herself, the intercom chimes again, four low chimes, each one making her jump, while the pink light lights up once more. For a couple of seconds she thinks about leaving it but she's never been able to ignore a ringing phone (unlike Mike, who's forever saying, 'Leave the fucking thing, if it's important they'll ring back.' He never answers his mobile either, not when she's with him anyway.) and she swiftly returns, reaching for the illuminated handset. Hi, she says, Selina here.

*Is that all you girls ever do, Greg says, chat on the phone? I was about to put out a call on the PA for you.*

Sorry? she says.

*You've been busy for ages – never mind. He realises his attempt at trying to get a laugh out of her hasn't worked. For a second it occurs to him that maybe Dan's right (didn't he spot it too earlier?) and that she is bonkers. Still he thinks he's not going to let that get in his way, he can handle it, look at Paula, and thinking about Paula it strikes him that there's a certain similarity between the two women, though he can't put*

**135**

*his finger on what it is exactly. Perhaps Dan's right also when he says he should leave the CM alone and go for the Economy purser or Wendy in First – he knows he'd at least be guaranteed some success. But that's not him. It's not in his nature to go for the easy option, or to do what other people say he should do. Plus he thinks he's probably drawn to unstable women – beautiful but nutty. Even Jeanette has her moments. Something has calmed her down recently but there have been times over the last twenty years when he's thought she was really losing it. Still he finds himself saying, continuing with what was inevitable from the moment he saw Selina, he says, I was wondering whether you might pop up to the flight deck for a moment? Greg has decided he'll ask her in person rather than on the interphone, that way it'll be harder for her to say no. Besides he wants to see her again, the glorious outline of her skimpy underwear against her uniform which so fired him up. If only he can somehow get her to bend over again. He looks about for something to drop on the floor.*

Is there a problem? Selina says. A sinking feeling sweeps through her, as if her stomach suddenly has no bottom. As if there's nothing to hold her in.

*Not yet, he says. How simple it is to unnerve the nervous, he thinks – her voice clearly betraying considerable panic. He's relieved he didn't put out a call for her on the PA, realising that really would have distressed her. (He doesn't know how these girls get themselves into these positions, half of them shouldn't even be flying.) Still he's pleased with her reaction so far, knowing how much easier it is to manipulate people who are already anxious. When he was a first officer he witnessed numerous captains coming up with completely outrageous lies to get whoever they fancied onto the flight deck – making out they were being hijacked, that there was smoke on the flight deck, that the first officer had collapsed. No, he says, it's not an emergency, but something's cropped up that we need to discuss – as soon as you can. The only thing he has to hand is his flight plan and he can't drop that on the floor and wait however many minutes before Selina arrives to pick it up for him. He needs it right now as they've just past Fredericton and the ATC has changed from Moncton to Boston (Dan's already set up the squawk) and they are awaiting confirmation of their Kennebunk 4 standard arrival routing via the beacon at Bangor, and will any moment slip into US airspace. He sees Dan's shades resting on the edge of the centre console by the printer and thinks he'll probably be able to knock them onto the floor when Dan's not looking, pretending he's checking the TCAS. Failing that there's always his cup of water he could tip over – the oldest one in the book. Okay? he says, because Selina hasn't replied though he's sure he can hear her breathing, unless it's the static, see you shortly. He hears Selina replace her handset, still without having said anything further.*

Fuck, thinks Selina. Fuck fuck, she whispers – she can't get enough air inside her to shout. Even though she had to speak to Greg, and Dan, on behalf of sodding Debbie anyway, doing Debbie's dirty work for her (if it's not Debbie it's making excuses for Paula – she's always being used by someone), she didn't need this sort of reason, an emergency. Even though he's not saying it is an emergency she knows it is, otherwise he wouldn't have said, as soon as you can to get her onto the flight deck. She didn't expect to be summoned there. Only a few moments ago she was thinking there's no way she's moving anywhere. Still avoiding catching sight of herself in the mirror – she dreads to think what sort of expression has manifested itself across her face now – she brushes aside Wendy, Becky and Tim's crew assessment forms which she still hasn't touched (they'll have to wait until the inbound leg, she decides, when she'll just have to make up what she's forgotten) and takes a firm hold of the ledge. Some CMs insist on calling it a desk, no doubt to make themselves seem more important – that they actually have a desk to work at where they do paperwork and other such executive tasks – but it's not a desk, it's a small sloping ledge that's virtually impossible to write anything on anyway. She tightens her grip, as a parachutist might, she thinks, before launching herself out of an aircraft (it's not something she'd ever dream of doing, though lots of the girls are always going on these parachuting courses – it's become a bit of a fad), trying to breathe calmly, thinking, as she often does when she's panicking, of how her cousin Donna would react in similar circumstances.

There was a time when Paula eclipsed Donna as the embodiment of sophistication, when Selina wished she were just like her. They don't look dissimilar, though if anything Selina thinks she has a prettier face, she certainly has better skin (Paula claims she's ruined her complexion experimenting with too much make-up over the years). But as she's got to know her better, she's begun to realise Paula isn't quite so sophisticated, quite so cool. She has flaws much like her own. She's insecure, she lacks confidence, she always goes for the wrong men (well, who doesn't? Selina thinks, suddenly wondering whether Becky in Economy has made a sensible decision – she doubts it, she's never known a hostie to yet, presuming it all goes ahead anyway), which is probably why she and Paula have become such good friends. Not that they see very much of each other now, with them both operating out of different airports – Paula currently serving the Far East routes from Gatwick for a member of the alliance and herself still stuck out of Heathrow on the original transatlantic flights, where she's always been and where nothing much ever changes, even the destination weather's predictable. At least she knows exactly what to pack, unless she's on standby when she has to stuff everything in like today. She was craving some rays on her body, to lie on a sun-lounger covered in nothing but sultry air. She felt she needed warming up. She really wanted Miami – even LA would have done. Instead they're heading for New York and a freezing snow storm. She's always feeling she's been singled out and she just knows she was picked specially for this torture. Nine times out of ten you don't even go anywhere on standby, you simply have to hang around the company's Heathrow HQ drinking coffee for four hours or so until your window of operation runs out.

Suddenly all Selina can hear is the noise of the engines, this incredible throbbing, certain they must have changed pitch, as she becomes acutely aware of them for the first time in ages, and that they must be starting their descent already, or – she squeezes the ledge tighter and closes her eyes for a second screwing up her face so she can feel her recently touched-up make-up crack – that this is what the problem is, why she's been called to the flight deck. They're losing power, the engines are conking out. At least, she quickly thinks, they're over land and there must be an airport near. She knows in theory that these planes can glide for miles, for up to 300 or something, depending on the height, a pilot once told her. Boston can't be too far away – she's been diverted to Boston before, though only because of bad weather at Kennedy. For the same reason she's ended up in Montreal and Quebec City, and once in Cleveland instead of Boston. She tries to convince herself they'll be all right and that the problem, whatever it is, is hardly catastrophic – Greg didn't sound too concerned. He coped with the turbulence brilliantly (despite, in her opinion, not turning on the fasten seat belt sign nearly soon enough), which though it didn't last for long was some of the most violent she's experienced for ages. He'll get us out of this, she decides. She feels bad for having thought of him earlier as an incompetent joke – him and Dan as the Morecambe and Wise, was it?, of the airline world. She has every confidence in Greg now. She believes in him. He's all she's got to believe in, because she can feel them falling to earth, slowly, but surely. She stops breathing so she can listen better, trying to discern a further decline in the engine throb. It's almost as if she wants to hear the fan blades disintegrating, hear them lose their grip on the air, so she won't simply have imagined there's a problem and that her sense of doom, her fear is properly grounded. However, at last she has to breathe, a great tremulous gasp. Besides she can't be positive the engines are making an odd noise. They don't seem to be struggling. She eases her grip on the ledge though her legs feel quite unsteady.

She wonders whether she should take something to calm down, whether she should delve into the emergency medical kit and help herself to the Ativan, or a couple of Valium – she's got the keys. (Captains used to be in charge of the medical kit until it was decided an emergency – an emergency – could arise where the flight crew might be too busy to unlock and sign it out. She remembers the rules were changed after a plane on a transatlantic hit some severe turbulence and two passengers nearly died because they didn't receive medication quick enough.) Paula says Valium's fantastic. She took it for a while after her marriage broke up (despite always maintaining that the marriage was hell and that getting out of it was one of the best things she's ever done). Selina thinks if she finally manages to break up with Mike it won't be Valium she turns to but champagne. Just as Becky's celebrating her engagement, so she'll celebrate the end of her relationship in true cabin crew style – disengagement parties are usually more fun than engagement parties anyway. At engagement parties everyone tends to mope around being jealous. Not, of course, that she and Mike have ever been engaged. For the first two or three years of the relationship she thought it possible. She remembers lying on the sofa countless times with her head in his lap, with him stroking the hair away from her eyes, some music on the mini-disc or something on the telly neither of them were interested in, both realising it was only each other that mattered, and she remembers thinking, I don't need anything more than this, this'll do. She's not sure of the precise moment when she realised she wasn't ever going to marry Mike (long after they stopped lying on the sofa like that for sure) though, oddly, she seems to recall discussing it with Paula on a stop-over in New York (when they knew Wayne in admin and were able to rig the duty roster and occasionally fly together).

It occurs to Selina also that that must have been the last time she flew with Paula. She knows they are losing touch and this intimacy they once had – they used to tell each other everything. But she feels she really needs Paula now. She wishes more than anything she were on board. She's never needed Donna. Donna is like this untouchable figure, someone you can't discuss things with but simply look up to. Or if you do talk to her you only ever try to come across as dead interesting and sophisticated, you only ever try to emulate her. Selina thinks it's funny how this image she created of Donna when she was ten or whatever has endured so well – she can still see her in her cloak and hat, her uniform, setting off, immaculate. Then perhaps it's not funny, perhaps it's obvious because she's never got to know Donna well, unlike Paula. If she had, Donna too would probably start to crack. Everyone has flaws, she thinks, it's just that they're more visible the closer you get – that and the fact some people are better at hiding them than others. When Paula dropped her guard everything came pouring out. Where were they then, in Miami? Selina's sure it was somewhere hot. She remembers Paula crying and how her tears slid down her blotchy face, turning her Helena Rubinstein suntan lotion creamy (she threw the tube away after that and it had cost her a fortune even with a discount).

Aware she hasn't moved, acutely aware she's still stuck in the CM's station, with a ledge full of paperwork she hasn't even started to tackle (including of course Becky's crew assessment form – what's she going to say? She'll make a lovely wife?), Selina again tries to think how Donna would be reacting now, if she were feeling wobbly and frightened, on the verge of losing it completely. She tries to fix her mind on Donna like someone might concentrate on a mantra – Donna, Donna – as if it will help her to collect herself. But she can't. The pristine image is there all right – the beautiful blonde hair perfectly in place and those exquisitely made-up lips and eyebrows and cheekbones – though it's not pliable, it's not accommodating. She's not letting her in. And all she can think is, Donna wouldn't be in a similar situation because Donna's nothing like me. Paula's the person she needs to turn to, a kindred spirit. Both of them are pathetic and useless and cry like babies. She decides she must speak to her from New York, if they ever get there. She'll track her down in Singapore or Hong Kong or Tokyo, or Sudbury. Wherever she is.

Unable to hear any further decline in engine power, in fact any unusual sound at all when not breathing again, when not moving a muscle, Selina decides she really must head for the flight deck and her fate, unless she wants to be demoted already (or possibly even sacked – when a captain orders you to do something you do it). Stepping into the aisle with grim determination (she knows that even Paula wouldn't cower in the CM's station all day because she has a recklessness, a fatalistic streak that Selina doesn't have – she'd say fuck it and head straight for the worst) sun falls on her for the first time this flight, a warm, soft block of it pouring through the window in service door D2R, which though she avoids looking directly at she realises was previously in the shade, and instantly warmed, stunned a little by the natural light, this deep golden colour, like treacle, like treacle solidifying in the immediate space around her, she suddenly feels much better. Maybe it's because of the sun which she had previously been avoiding, any natural light, or, more likely, the thought of Paula charging ahead, willing to accept whatever is coming her way, saying fuck it, has given her resolve, a certain strength – much more so than any idea of Donna calmly going about her duty without so much as a smudge of misplaced make-up. She knew she needed Paula, though as she slips through the curtain separating Business from First on her way to the stairs and the upper deck and finally the cockpit, it occurs to her that perhaps Paula doesn't need her, that she's been avoiding her. She knows they're drifting apart, as people in this business eventually do when they no longer work the same routes, especially if they're not operating out of the same airports. She hasn't heard from her for months despite leaving numerous messages around the world. She wonders whether she's hiding something from her.

The scones are Becky's favourite, split in two and heaped with strawberry preserve and clotted cream, though she doesn't have time for the splitting and topping now and stuffs one in whole. It's a little dry but still beautifully sweet with that sour, doughy aftertaste. She very nearly reaches for another but decides against it as she knows she's never going to be able to squeeze into her dress tonight (she packed one specially in case something was arranged for her – the strapless black and sequined Kookaï which her mum gave her for her twenty-first and which was tight then, certainly too tight to wear any underwear with) and Debbie's just walked in and she doesn't want her to see her helping herself to the passengers' tea – she's already ransacked two trays – before she's been round with her trolley (though there are always teas over and the two she helped herself to had been slightly damaged in loading). She'll be last out of the galley again, tea always takes her longer to set-up than she imagines, and she can already see the looks she's going to get. It takes a while for the passengers to realise the other aisle in their section (in today's case Valerie's) is consistently being served much quicker than theirs but when they do they really let you know about it. There'll be row after row of sneering faces – people unwilling to help pass trays along, or hold their cups out for tea or coffee so she has to stretch across, risking being groped (not too mention spilling the stuff on someone), feeling completely vulnerable. It's as if they think they've waited long enough and aren't going to help you one little bit.

She finds tea's the worst meal to get out, with the passengers being tired and uncomfortable and often hungover, and bored stupid because the film has ended and they've bought their duty-free and finished their magazines and run out of things to bicker with each other about so the only person they have to take their frustration out on is the cabin crew. And particularly so if the cabin crew is taking forever with their next meal, their next distraction – plus of course she doesn't look a patch like the other hostie wandering serenely up and down the aisle across the way (Becky's noticed the men looking at Valerie). Becky knows it can't be pleasant being stared at continually by half-drunk slobs, but she thinks it would be nice to be noticed now and then, to know you had something people found worth looking at. She thinks what's really unfair about her body is the fact that, although she's dumpy, she has tiny breasts. Most people with her sort of build at least have decent-sized tits. Ben says he doesn't mind, he says he's more into arses, but she knows he does a bit. He never pays them much attention, a few twiddles with his fingers and a couple of sucks and he moves elsewhere. Still she supposes her bum is so large he's got plenty to be occupied with.

Debbie says, Here, let me give you a hand. I'm sure you've got other things on your mind today. Hey? She taps Becky's arm.

It's okay, Becky says, nearly spilling the teapot she's filling from the bev maker. I'm almost done, she says.

Sure? says Debbie.

Sure, says Becky. I'm just slower than everyone else, always have been.

Well it looks like you're going to beat most of the girls up the aisle, says Debbie. By the way the numbers are already looking good.

Sorry? says Becky.

For tonight, for your evening, sweetie. David in Business is coming – did I tell you? He's gorgeous. And the two girls in Business with him, Angela and Karen. Selina's asking the flight crew and if I know Greg he's not going to miss out on something like this. And I've sent Tim off to First – he's finished his tea run already, can you believe it? He must be on something, probably one of those designer drugs that keep you up all night. Becky watches Debbie pause to blow her nose, using a paper napkin from her trolley. I reckon if anyone's going to make an impression with those guys, she says, it'll be Tim. The older ones always go for boys like Tim. It's that innocent, naive look. Not my cup of tea, sweetie. I prefer my men to be more like Greg – you know, weathered. He might have a reputation but it's certainly not for being crap in bed. Who wants innocence? I want a man who knows what he's doing. The dirtier the better. She laughs, snivelling. The air on these things, she says, always gets my sinuses.

Becky says, That's it. I'm all set. She can see Debbie's point but she doesn't know why you have to be old and craggy to be experienced. She's slept with a couple of men who she thinks were pretty experienced and who certainly weren't ancient. And Ben's not that bad. A bit hasty sometimes (name a man who isn't? she thinks) but he's no prude. However, she suddenly remembers his surprise when he first came across her tattoo and she wonders whether she's confusing experience and lack of inhibition, a willingness to experiment, with vigour. With being over-eager.

Good luck, says Debbie. And try to conserve a little energy – it's going to be a long night. Though at this rate we might even have time for a nap before we start rocking.

See you shortly, says Becky reversing the trolley out of the galley, bending her knees and using all her strength to pull it over the hump and into the aisle as gently as possible though she still manages to make everything jingle alarmingly and spill a great slop of tea all over the trolley top (she's pleased she didn't try to squeeze on the coffee pot as well). She's meant to bring round the hot beverages after she's handed out the trays but she's so late and no one seems to mind whether you take a few shortcuts nowadays. Debbie's not going to say anything, Debbie's suddenly her best mate. Anyway if they stuck to every rule in the book – she has binders full of them at home – she thinks they'd have to fly to Australia and back before everyone was served the full complement of drinks and meals, along with being offered the duty-free etcetera. In fact, according to Ben, planes probably wouldn't take off at all. Flight crews are always fudging something. Skipping procedures here and there.

Lining herself up rearward she's struck by the sun coming through the few half-opened blinds, these fat wedges of golden light she feels she could almost grasp hold of – realising that the sun was previously on the other side of the plane and she's been wandering up and down in the shade until now, except for the odd rays that made it across the full width of the fuselage before everyone shut out the light so they could cut themselves off from the real world (in her opinion) and sit like zombies in front of their screens (not that Becky does anything different when she's a passenger – she gets stuck into the films like the rest of them). The odd thing is, she thinks, when she's crewing (and she hardly ever flies when she's not – her idea of a holiday is staying at home with Misty, despite the massive discounts she gets) she can look into the cabin and not see any passengers at all, not individuals, but simply a blurry mass of heads and bodies, which is roughly the same shape from one flight to the next and which has become in her mind part of the aeroplane, its physical layout. She's come to understand it's her way of avoiding, for as long as possible anyway, what's really out there – like looking at the day through steamed-up sunglasses. Sort of fixing onto nothing, or rather melding something into nothing – how she got through school (her teachers always said she could never concentrate). Of course when it comes to handing out the drinks and the meals and stuff, or when she's sandwiched in an aisle and people are pinching her bottom, there's nothing she can do to avoid them, people come glaringly into focus. She finds the really loathsome passengers stick in her mind far longer than any of the good-looking guys but even they pretty soon disappear and her memories of passengers on past flights slip into each other, becoming a bigger, multi-layered version of this ill-defined form she sees when she's trying not to look at a cabin full of people. Maybe it's her way of avoiding letting her work get to her too much – and she's only been doing it for three and a half years. She can't imagine what Valerie or Debbie see when they pop their heads out of the galley.

Turning round by service door D5R, just short of the narrow passageway that leads to toilets N and Q and the door to the crew rest area, in another flood of intense light (the blind in the door has been left up), as ready as she'll ever be for the trawl back to the galley, where she'll only have to reload the trolley with more trays of ham sandwiches, a few rotten grapes and the scones of course, and refill the teapot with hot water from the bev maker (if there's any left which there probably won't be because she's last so she'll have to refill it and wait for it to brew) and set out again, and in this thick golden light, like it's some special effect, as if she's in the spotlight (which she supposes she is), she remembers Ben only discovered her tattoo when they first did it in daylight, which was at least a couple of weeks after they started seeing each other. There's no way she's inhibited and in many respects she loves being able to see what's happening when she has sex but as she's got larger (and older – fuck it) she's come to prefer having sex in the dark – it gives her more confidence – certainly until she knows whoever it is well enough and reckons they're not going to piss off when they see the extent of her cellulite. She thinks the fact she didn't do it in daylight with Ben for so long means something – presumably that she wanted to hang onto him a little longer. A little longer? Now look, she thinks, I've got him forever.

'I thought it was a large spot,' Becky remembers Ben said, 'or a birthmark or something. I didn't want to mention it. It's really cool. What is it? A heart?' 'Course it is, stupid,' she said. 'It's even got a bloody arrow through it.' 'Oh, yeah,' he said, starting to lick it and lick around it – 'I'd been avoiding it.' He paused a moment before she felt his slimy tongue on her chilly flesh once more. She was lying on her stomach with Ben sort of on top of her but kneeling halfway down the bed so he wasn't really squashing her, and she lifted her bum a fraction spreading her legs some more (she loves this position) in an attempt to guide his tongue off her slobbered on left buttock and into the space between her legs, so he could run it around her bumhole, perhaps even lick it full on – that makes her shiver – and then sink it into her already soaking fanny, with his head pressed hard against her bum, pushing down and forcing her legs even wider apart, and with herself trying to raise her great big arse higher so he can probe deeper and she can feel his chin against her clit – the bristles of his two-day-old beard (he never shaves when he's not working). She can almost feel him now, that pressure, that friction – the blood rushing to her genitals. She crouches down to reach a tray in the bottom compartment of the trolley in such a way that her knickers dig into her, wanting to stop the feeling, wanting it to continue, and still crouching she clamps her legs together, and staring into the dark trolley her mind goes completely blank so she loses all sense of time, and picking up the steady vibration of the plane, the ever present trilling, she goes on staring at the racks of trays until she suddenly remembers what it is she's meant to be doing and with a start pulls out a couple of trays and stands and hands them to seats K and J in row 49, the occupants of which are looking at her as if they've never seen a tray of airline food before and have no idea what to do with it. Becky hands another tray to the woman in 49H and comes back with the tea. Tea, madam? she says.

Not if it's gone cold, dear, says the woman in the window seat.

**147**

Even though she didn't get it done that long ago, she's sure her tattoo has become distorted because her bum has got so much bigger. Vicky and Kate's of course are still perfect and instantly recognisable as tiny red hearts with purple arrows through them (none of them wanted to put any names anywhere). They keep pulling down their knickers and showing her and whoever else happens to be there, including Ben. What's so unfair, Becky thinks, is the fact that it was her idea for them all to get one in the first place. She chose the tattoo shop – somewhere in Staines she had spotted ages ago – the design (Vicky wanted this bird, this swallow-like thing, but Becky convinced her it was the sort of tattoo you see on skinheads' necks), she even made the booking. Despite it not hurting particularly and having had a couple of Sea Breezes first (it was during their Absolut phase) they all screamed like mad. Vicky's recently been suggesting they get their labia pierced, though Becky doesn't think she's being serious. Besides she keeps hearing these stories about cabin crew with various bits of them pierced who keep setting off the metal detectors at security. The company's constantly sending round memos re-minding everyone that only female crew are allowed to wear earrings, one in each ear, and that these must be studs – no other piercings are acceptable (not that that stops everyone of course). Could you just put your tray down, sir, she says. Thanks.

She manages to leave the flight deck without having a problem with the door, or having spilt anything inside (it was Greg who made a prune of himself this time, somehow knocking his water onto the floor behind his seat, narrowly missing the controls on the centre console, which she had to wipe up of course and which brought back to mind the idea that perhaps he is part of some comedy act, the guy's hopeless) and she walks through the calm upper deck Business class cabin full of passengers enjoying their tea (or at least consuming it), smiling ridiculously, this picture she thinks for once of someone utterly composed, of someone obviously on top of the situation, of what a CM should look like. Dead sophisticated, just how Donna would be. She

148

casually flicks some hair behind her right ear. There was no emergency. Nothing's gone tech. Greg was winding her up. All he wanted was to ask her to some sleazy room party he's concocting with Dan (who has room parties anymore?) and she was able to say, sorry, mate – well she didn't actually say sorry, mate, she said something a little more friendly like, sorry, Greg, but that was what she meant anyway – she was really pissed off with him for summoning her to the flight deck, scaring her to death, just to tell her about some fucking room party, though of course she was also incredibly relieved, she could have hugged him. She still feels light-headed, as if she's floating. She really enjoyed telling him about Debbie's do for Becky and how she was on her way to let him know about it anyway, as per Debbie's instructions, when he called her to the flight deck, and that she's so sorry he and Dan won't be able to come to Becky's do downtown. She said she hoped they would have a great time anyway, though she couldn't think who else might want to go to a room party, except maybe Wendy from First (the older ones will do anything down route to be with the flight crew). Greg didn't surprise her when he started back-tracking, like all men do if they're after something (not that she's a hundred per cent sure what it is yet, though she has her suspicions, she's not blind) and he said, thinking about it, maybe he could come to Becky's thing first – Dan was laughing by now – and that they could all go to his room party afterwards, once they were well tanked up (on someone else's booze, he might as well have said). Like at what, Selina remembers saying, four in the morning? Dan was still laughing, and Greg said, Yeah, why not? It's not as if we're leaving until Saturday evening, we've got the whole day to lie in, except I suppose you girls will want to be up first thing to go shopping. Sounding increasingly desperate – she discerned the tone in his voice all right – he then said, Surely it will be much better if we all stick together. He said he didn't see the point of half of them doing one thing and the other half doing something else. When he actually said, We are all part of the same team, she thought, yeah right, where have I heard that before. From only about a million other captains, though not usually until they're on the crew bus and it's fast becoming apparent no one wants to spend the evening with them, at least no one under forty.

David's in the upper deck galley chatting to Lynn and Nicole and, though Selina had promised herself only a moment or two ago that she would go straight back to the CM's station to at least begin her paperwork (now she feels that they might actually make it, she certainly doesn't want to spend the whole of the inbound stuck in her cubicle making things up), seeing David makes her change her mind and she finds herself drifting over to them.

Watch-ya, David says.

Hi, guys, Selina says.

I was just telling Lynn and Nicole about this thing being organised for tonight, David says. You're coming, aren't you?

Becky's? says Selina. Yeah, of course. I'd never miss a party. She thinks he looks different from how he appeared earlier, familiar yet removed somehow, as if part of him is missing – it disconcerts her. The captain's also organising something, she says, looking away, like a room party he wants us to pitch up at after.

It could be ten years ago, says David, with everyone going for it.

Maybe we're just one of those crews, Selina says. She suddenly feels as if she's this cog, or really a link connecting each of the crew. She suddenly feels necessary at last, more real. Plugged in to some greater being.

At first he thinks it's an unusually high band of cloud, an isolated whisper of cirrus catching the dying sun, but as the whisper becomes more pronounced, as it seems to split into two distinct fiery streaks (there's no face, no distantly familiar figure – with awkward bony limbs – however slight emerging anywhere, only what's really there), Nigel realises, even though he knows clouds can behave irregularly, that this isn't a cloud as such, it's a vapour trail and that they are following in someone else's footsteps. At the moment it appears directly so and that they're quickly catching up the aircraft ahead, however he knows this is probably an illusion and it will soon become clear they are on a higher course and the plane producing this vapour trail is some 1000 feet below them, or whatever the minimum vertical separation is in the US (he's not the pilot, he was never going to be a pilot, despite him leading his mother to believe otherwise – he doesn't know why he tried to impress her so much, why he led her to believe these things, except he supposes that he never wanted her to see who he really is, that it was another way of shielding himself from her). It's always the way with vapour trails, they're never quite where you think they are. He can go for weeks without seeing any at altitude, while sometimes it seems as if all they're doing is threading their way through others' paths – that there's nowhere left in the sky untouched. Untravelled. Leaning on the edge of the window, letting his right shoulder take his weight so he's facing aft and without thinking he reaches for the dial on his watch which he starts to turn, again and again, feeling each click.

*Just as Greg has learnt to desensitise himself from the physical sensations of flying in a pressurised cockpit and to orientate himself out of disorientation by using the instruments alone – these dials of seemingly contradictory information – so he's become accustomed to optical phenomena in the sky. To brilliant flashes and strange shadows, shimmering walls and distant blobs of quite artificial-seeming colours. Sparks of orange and pink and vermilion. Fragments of emerald, chartreuse and jade. Milliseconds of scarlet stretching far into the stratosphere. He's aware of the effects refraction, reflection and diffraction can have on the light scatter and the names given to the most common of these – halos, coronas and glories, blue jets, sprites and elves – though he can't always differentiate between halos and coronas, say, or sprites and elves. Things are forever appearing not quite how they should, or they're blending into something else. He's been in the game long enough to know nothing is concrete in the sky, of course, nothing is totally reliable, except perhaps the fact that during daylight the sky is always a shade of blue – because, as Greg was once taught, in the visual spectrum of light the blue photon has a shorter* wavelength than the red photon, with the energy of this shorter wavelength being dominant and thus creating the blue effect of the sky. Which indirectly, he thinks, is why beyond the earth's atmosphere everything is black, except for the sun, stars and illuminated planets. Simply, there are no air molecules for the photons to attach themselves to. Why, as you look up, the sky becomes darker as the air molecules slowly fade.

Greg loves to see vapour trails at sunset, the dying sun finding something to settle on, even if it's momentary. He knows he's about to be frantically busy. The STAR has been keyed into the FMS, the entry procedure for the stack at Calverton established (should it be needed). He's awaiting new weather and needs to initiate the descent and approach briefing as soon as possible (he's a little behind because he couldn't keep his eyes off Selina wiping up the water he'd spilt on purpose – it worked brilliantly). However, looking at these glowing trails he finds it hard not to feel the aircraft's hooked itself onto a ready-made path and they are simply being pulled towards their destination (and yet further away from his wife and his daughter, both of whom he's never paid as much attention to as he's beginning to recognise he should have). Still he knows he'll shortly have plenty of time to patch things up – if it's not too late. (He's had his suspicions about Jeanette and whether she's been having an affair for a while – she's just not behaving normally, she doesn't grill him anymore, she's too calm.) And he feels he's moving further and further away from Paula too (who should be landing in Singapore about now), which is partly his fault because he wanted her to transfer to Gatwick and the Far East routes, thinking he was going to be transferred too, until the rules were suddenly changed and the company decided they could only transfer flight crew to different airports and sectors if they had at least five years of their contract to run and he was up for retirement in two and half. Yet looking at these molten tracks, knowing that at the end lies Selina – she's not mad he's decided, just out of her depth – with her fantastic figure tucked into remarkably skimpy underwear which, if all goes to plan, he'll soon be peeling off (the evening's shaped up better than he could ever have planned himself, with this engagement party everyone will be able to get tanked up at first – he doesn't care about missing his drink in one of the tired old Irish bars on 2nd Avenue), he knows he's exactly where he *wants to be, that life is about grabbing hold of fleeting chances. Not letting them slide through your hands. He doesn't think he would have changed anything, whether he'd had it in him to do so or not.*

Nigel had hoped he'd be able to see Boston or at least a patch of the Massachusetts coastline, in the same way as he caught Newfoundland, despite the captain saying the weather in the New York area was likely to be overcast, though he never trusts what the pilots say. Even with all their sophisticated instruments and almost constant contact with air traffic control they are always getting things wrong. What annoys him most is the way they are usually so optimistic about everything, especially time – how they say they are ten minutes or whatever ahead of schedule, when they know full well delays are bound to occur on the approach and that the aircraft could well have to hold for thirty minutes or so and not just the five they might finally admit to – so you've been going round and round for ages before you even know it. It's as if they can never tell you everything. But all he can see looking down is the out of place contrail and much lower sheets of altostratus and the setting sun reflecting on this, with the rolls and swirls of impenetrable stratocumulus at the bottom of the sky – this place where everything finally collapses in on itself – sinking into ever deeper shade. He shivers as a shocking chill runs right through him, as he's increasingly aware he's been here before. He can't immediately place his present situation, his present state of mind with a former experience, some point in his past, but he suddenly knows his being here now is no accident. Nor is Tim's presence on board. Nor the fact that his mother is seriously, perhaps terminally ill and his life is about to change forever. That something out there has contrived to make all this happen at once.

A God? Some guiding spirit? Fate? For the second time today he finds he's thinking about religion, about spirituality, this idea that there's something out there. He's never thought of himself as being particularly religious, or of even coming from a religious family (his mum and him never go to church – the only weddings and funerals they attend are in registry offices and crematoriums), though over the years his mother seems to have formed stronger and stronger views on what she thinks is morally correct and acceptable. As she's never been properly educated nor having gone to church regularly, Nigel suspects she just muddles up and distorts things she hears and reads until they suit her, or at least her sense of propriety. She doesn't let him swear in the house, she believes in marriage (despite hers breaking up so suddenly and catastrophically, in his eyes), and was furious with Sue, the younger of his two sisters, for getting pregnant before she was married to John. She thinks as her only son it's his duty to get married and procreate, and she can't think why it's taking him so blinking long to find someone suitable. She's always wondering why he never invites any of his girlfriends round for tea. She hates it when she catches him lying. She used to send him to his room until eventually about ten years or so ago he refused to go upstairs (he doesn't know where he got the guts from) and just walked out of the house. He came back an hour later but she never sent him to his room again. She thinks hell is not unlike Brighton, though much hotter. She thinks homo-sexuals – queers as she always calls them – are the personification of evil, worse than paedophiles, and that they're beyond re-demption and should be kept locked up out of sight. He was with her in Brighton once when they came across two men strolling along King's Road hand in hand. She crossed the street, leading him with her, while in a loud voice saying, 'There've never been any queers in my family.' She said it in such a way he knew what she really meant was that if she ever discovered he were gay she would disown him. He would no longer have a mother, or a home. She would rip up his past.

He has often thought it odd how she should hate homosexuals as much and as overtly as she does because she used to be really quite theatrical, loud and showy and seemingly confident about herself. He knows – though he can't remember everything as if it were yesterday – that she and his dad used to be friendly with all sorts of strange, flamboyant people who worked in the theatres and hotels and restaurants and clubs down the road in Hove and Brighton, not all of whom, he's sure now, were straight. His dad's café, with this seized-up rusty mechanical dolphin outside (it was originally dark blue, Nigel can remember, though as the paint flecked off and rust took over it became a sad mottled rust colour) and a mirrored ball (the sort he's seen in nightclubs) incongruously hanging from the ceiling, and usually with someone like Demis Roussos or Barry Manilow or Elton John on the stereo (they were his dad's favourites, whom Nigel's grown to love but never dares listen to at home), was always full and raucous. But it all changed the moment his father suddenly left them and his mother took over the place. She swapped the dark blinds for net curtains, took down the disco ball, shortened the opening hours and banned most of the old regulars. She even got rid of the dolphin, which Nigel had always loved despite it never working properly and appearing increasingly neglected, replacing it with this plastic-looking dinosaur. However, she eventually had to sell the place when her debts, which she's always claimed were originally created by his father, became unmanageable.

Nigel thinks the thing about his mum is that she's always been able to shift her focus, to turn from one thing to another and steadfastly ignore what has gone before. In a way she sees what she wants to see. Plus she voices her opinions so forcefully, through this combination of blackmail and self-pity (she's always made him feel sorry for her, she's always making him feel guilty about one thing or another) that she manages to sweep you along with her until you become compliant with her intentions, how she wants you to be. Yet for all her presence Nigel doesn't think she's particularly perceptive. He's never understood why his father left, she's barely said a word about it (and his dad has never contacted him), but he knows it shocked her, that she didn't see it coming. And he knows also she's never had a clue about him and Paul (about what they did in this bedroom in this hotel in Hove, where Paul used to work) despite always going through his things when he was away, turning his bedroom upside down, saying she'd just cleaned it. Until very recently she'd check his pockets. But he also knows part of her could never believe it really did happen. That part of her will never accept he's gay. Her precious only son (who's already fat and over the hill). The future of the family name and reputation, as she puts it (somehow ignoring the fact the reputation, such as it was, disappeared with his dad years ago – Sue and Christine certainly haven't helped lift it since), being consigned to a queer? Nigel hates that word.

Seeing Tim in the galley, the living manifestation of the image he saw in the clouds (which he now understands was probably why he was seeing things, he'd obviously spotted Tim in the crew briefing but it had taken a while for the likeness to register in his subconscious) brought back Paul's name, a name he thought he'd forgotten. And here was this kid, this kid he felt he could so easily just reach over and wrap up tightly in his arms, saying something about them all being invited to an engagement party tonight and how he'd really like it if they came (even though he was only looking at Carlo when he said it, Nigel knew it was directed at him too) because otherwise he was going to be more than a little outnumbered by the girls. Carlo immediately said, Sure, baby, which surprised Nigel because he thought Carlo had already said he was busy tonight. Still it made him say he'd come as well. You can count me in, too, he said, trying to sound casual and chummy. Was he suddenly jealous of Carlo? He can't remember the last time he spent an evening down route with some crew. Not that he's interested in anyone except Tim, of course, and how he'll be able to get Tim on his own tonight – does he dare try? Does he really? His mind's racing with the possibility (shifting slowly but steadily out of control). Normally he stays in his hotel bedroom having room service and watching the weather channel or some terrible film. He stopped watching the pay-per-view movies years ago. He can't afford it, and it's always embarrassing because when it comes up on your extras bill (which might as well be public property) everyone thinks you've been watching the porn, even though everyone knows it's only the pilots who watch the porn.

**156**

Leaving the window at last and promising himself he won't sneak another look out until he's strapped into the crew seat for landing, he steps across to the galley and slips through the curtain, holding his breath, sucking in hard, trying not to be noticed, but inside he feels as if he's bursting. Letting out air in a great sigh he attempts to muffle by coughing and quickly drawing another breath, so it sounds as if he's almost choking, he smells stewed tea and egg and cress sandwiches and sweet sickly cakes and Wendy's tangy perfume and a trace of Carlo's aftershave, though he can't name the brand (there are so many new ones on the market nowadays he has no idea what's what). Wendy's still at the counter and either she hasn't noticed him or has decided to ignore him finally (because, as she said earlier, he's been no frigging use at all this flight) so he tries to regulate his breathing, not bothering to make himself invisible while he casts his eye over the tea preparations he's had nothing to do with yet. Normally it's the meal he enjoys most, not just because it reminds him of being small and stuffing his face at his dad's café (his father sneaking him one cake after another when his mother wasn't looking), or because it's the easiest meal to get ready (not that he's done anything today), but because he still loves cakes. He thinks he could live on cakes alone. His favourite is the orange and almond syrup cake they've been doing for almost a year – he always manages to pinch a couple (they're not much bigger than bite-size) – though he'll never refuse a baked real egg custard tart with a hint of cinnamon if he sees one unattended, or a Florentine, though he finds with the Florentines bits get stuck in his teeth, or a Viennese biscuit, which are best dunked. He's not so bothered about the sandwiches, though he liked the smoked salmon, sour cream and caviar when they did those, before the company pulled them, presumably because they were too expensive to produce.

# new york

Becky finally gets the trolley secured and stands feeling slightly unsteady – her back's aching badly – to see, incredibly, she's the first to get her stuff cleared away, though she supposes she didn't, like Tim or Valerie, have to hand out the landing cards, which is a total pain in the arse because no one ever has a pen or a clue how to fill them in, or even what form is applicable. It's worst in Economy, of course, everything's worst in Economy, she thinks, though because you are so much busier time tends to go that much more quickly (which is the old toss up between Economy or Business and First – you're either worked off your feet or spend hours hanging around doing nothing) and she reckons today has flown past, which nevertheless surprises her because the section is not totally full and she had thought it would be a real fucking drag. She's always getting things wrong, imagining something's going to be one way when it turns out to be the complete opposite. Still feeling unsteady and in pain and all blocked up too, searching for some water or something to suck on someone might have left out somewhere, she wonders whether her misgivings about marrying Ben are misplaced. Just her panicking over the most momentous thing to happen to her in her life so far and that she said yes not because she's desperate to get married or, as Debbie pointed out, because she wants to get married before anyone else her age (though she's seen what can happen to those left on the shelf) but because she really does love Ben, knowing he's perfect for her. And she should be blissfully happy (as her mum made very clear on the phone). Reaching for a boiled sweet (the basket's been put on the counter ready – she'd rather have stuffed down another scone but she thinks you can't have everything) she realises they're descending and that's why she's blocked up.

Normally it's like a blast of fresh air when she first realises they've started their descent and that they'll be on the ground in twenty minutes or so, but that's not what she feels now. She's full of trepidation again. Whichever way she looks at it, however hard she tries to convince herself otherwise, and her mind's seemingly been stuck on nothing else for the entire flight – going round and round in circles, sifting through the pros and cons – she knows she's not at all sure she wants to marry Ben. Why should she be so blissfully happy? In fact she's never been so unsure about anything and when she's confused and preoccupied she usually does something totally stupid. She dreads to think what she's going to get up to tonight – she doesn't trust herself. She needs Vicky and Kate to look after her. They're always stopping one another from saying something daft or drinking too much or flashing their tits in a wholly inappropriate place, or leaving with the wrong bloke (which nevertheless they've all done more than once). Valerie doesn't know her well enough. She's got no idea, Becky reckons, how she might behave and consequently how best to restrain her. (She remembers when Vicky rescued her from the flyover, not that she would ever have jumped – she doesn't think it's in her, she's too much of a coward.) And though, of course, she's grateful to Debbie and everyone for organising this thing tonight – being the first time anyone's made any effort with her since she joined the company – part of her still wishes it wasn't necessary and that it was going to be a normal stop-over and if she were doing anything tonight it would be popping out for a quick

**160**

Chinese with a few of the girls, so they could all moan about their boyfriends or lack of boyfriends and how they are dying to get married and have kids and stop flying. Becky knows she's always wanted what she doesn't have. She wanted a baby until she got pregnant, which was why she was on the flyover, and a few weeks later in an abortion clinic Vicky found for her in the phone book. However, she's fast learning that most things in life sound a lot better than they really are, that reality never quite lives up to expectation. In her dreams the man she's always marrying is nothing like Ben.

What's making her feel worse at this precise moment is that, even though they'll shortly be in America she senses she'll somehow be closer to Ben. At least he'll be on the end of the phone (he's not working this weekend) and she'll have to call him the moment she reaches the hotel (as she promised she would) to tell him they've landed safely and that she loves him and misses him and can't wait to get home so they can snuggle up together in bed. Except, she thinks, maybe she won't call him immediately, perhaps she'll leave it until tomorrow when her head might be a little clearer and her words a little more sincere (though she knows that's extremely unlikely, particularly as she'll probably get completely smashed tonight – she's aiming to all right). She can almost sense the angle at which they are slipping back to earth, like they're hurtling downhill – this terrible pressure of time. Right now she doesn't care whether they explode on impact.

That wasn't so bad, Selina says, entering the galley just by Becky. No serious incidents. Well done, gang. Though am I going to be glad to get off this aircraft. She laughs, the fact they've started their descent has gone to her head. She knows the descent, approach and landing are the most critical stages of the flight but still the relief at the thought of them shortly touching down is stronger than any sense of fear over what could finally go wrong. Can I have the figures for the duty-free bars? she says, trying to sound authoritative, trying at least to act the part of CM (she's still officially on duty until they reach the hotel).

Coming up, says Debbie, stretching behind Becky and handing Selina the document which she already had in her hand, they're all totted up. Hey, she says smiling at Becky, I think someone's in urgent need of a glass of champagne.

Becky smiles back but quickly looks down at the floor, knowing everyone else in the galley is staring at her as well – Tim and Valerie and Marissa, and the CM. She just hopes they can't read her mind because she doesn't want to disappoint anyone over tonight. She expects she'll feel better when she gets a drink or five inside her. She remembers feeling a bit like this on her first day with the company – a mixture of apprehension and excitement. And this overwhelming sense that she's very much on her own.

*Greg flicks the PA switch at the back of the centre console, says, Urrrgh ladies and gentlemen, this is the captain again – we have begun our descent into New York, though we have been informed of a ten-minute delay because of heavy traffic in the area. We estimate we'll now be on the ground in just under thirty minutes. However, this should still get us to the stand only five minutes behind schedule at four thirty-five. My apologies for the short delay. The local weather has actually improved a little with good visibility and a light wind, though it's a chilly minus two degrees Celsius, that's about twenty-eight degrees Fahrenheit. Those of you sitting on the left-hand side of the aircraft should be able to see Manhattan as we swing round for our final approach. I'd like to take this opportunity to thank you for flying with us today and we hope to see you again soon.*

*You didn't tell them about the new air miles offer, says Dan.*

*I can't remember everything, says Greg, scanning the green descent arc on the ND. He feels the first hint of a headache as he struggles to keep track of all that's rushing through his mind, juggling the technicalities of the descent, which despite the number of times he's landed an aircraft he still finds both challenging and exhilarating – he briefly settles on the thought that this could be the last time he executes such a manoeuvre, certainly coming into Kennedy, and for a second he has the very real sensation of falling, of becoming unattached – with this tingling antici-*

*pation about what's on offer tonight, what's surely his, this warmth, this naked comfort, and how exactly she'll end up in his bed. He's never felt happy being on his own (finding cheap hotel rooms particularly lonely). He's always needed someone to latch onto. He thinks it's his way of connecting, of feeling alive. His eyes race across the screens again, the rows of dials and faintly illuminated switches all playing their specific parts in keeping them on course (eventually) for runway 22L. He knows he has to reorder his thoughts, to shift his focus to the present. Noticing just in time that they're passing 18,000, the US transition level, he pushes the barometric pressure selector and checks the setting for New York of 29.50 on both servo altimeters, hears New York say, 'Await instructions once level at one six O.' Feels the aircraft hitting cloud, buffeting slightly, sees the four nacelle anti-icing lights illuminate green on the upper EICAS – a soft green light set against blocks of vibrant, flickering white. Shit, he says, suddenly needing to pee.*

Selina darts into the Business galley, reaching for the counter as the plane seems to lurch forward again. It's nothing like as bad as the turbulence earlier, though she finds it unsettling enough and that the light-headed confidence, the relief she felt a few moments ago when the plane began its descent, is fast evaporating. But the only person in the galley is David and she finds herself face to face with him, just a foot or so apart – she can almost feel him – looking straight into his deep blue eyes (they're so blue for a second she wonders whether he's wearing tinted contacts) and despite being suddenly breathless, and she's sure slightly flushed, she's determined to remain calm, to not reveal any sign of anxiety, or that she finds him attractive despite there being something very disconcerting about him – it's as if, she suddenly realises, she hasn't only met him before but she was in love with him. She says, Can I have your duty-free bar receipts, please? She coughs. The lack of air in these things always gets my throat after a while, she says, in an even fainter voice.

Is that all you want? he says, laughing. I thought I –

Thank you, she says, trying to sound stern and on top of the situation, holding out her hand. For an instant she imagines him taking her hand and pulling her to him, the past overtaking the present. At least her reinterpretation of the past. The fulfilling of old dreams. She looks away and for some reason she pictures her living room in its bright new yellow, but as the image becomes more vivid (she can even see the acacia in bloom through the back window) she feels that something is missing, that the room is really just as dull and empty as usual. And still holding out her hand for the duty-free bar receipts, she has this overwhelming sense that her life is slipping away from her, or rather that she's no longer engaging properly with it and that she needs to find something solid to cling onto pretty soon. Someone she can trust. At the age of thirty-two and after twelve years cabin crewing she knows she's been on her own for far too long. She believes people need each other, that they need to be comforted and cared for – not just abused. Mike's not a proper person, she thinks. And Roy, her boyfriend before him, was no more real. She's desperate to get Mike out of her system (desperate enough to chance old dreams), she can't believe she's remained faithful to him for all this time. You know, she says, maybe there is something else. (She wasn't being serious when she promised herself to the captain earlier, of course she wasn't. Besides, she thinks, the plane's about to land safely anyway, just as it always was.) She leans back against the counter, trying to be dead casual, casually arching her back a little.

Hot towels, hot towels? Nigel says. Where are the frigging hot towels?

You're beginning to sound like me, Nige, says Wendy. Don't lose your rag now. You know what's in the guidelines, what we're never meant to forget – that it's the last impressions the passengers take away with them.

I think you've already made your mark, says Nigel.

No need to be jealous Nige, says Wendy.

Of that old codger? he says, realising he's never normally rude about his passengers to other crew, however out of earshot they might be.

As I said I'm not too fussed about the physicalities, she says, it's what's in their bank account that turns me on. Still there's something about him – he's got nice ears. And I bet he has a pretty good idea about what to do in bed.

Maybe once a very long time ago, Nigel says.

Unlike some other people around here, she says. Though I saw the way you were looking at Tim when he was in here – as if you'd like to frig him senseless.

I don't know what you're talking about, he says. Besides you know I'm not into that sort of thing. Sex doesn't interest me.

Who are you still trying to kid? she says.

Don't believe me then, he says. He has this sudden desire to rush out of the galley and clamp himself to a window for the remaining minutes of the flight but he knows he can't keep rushing to a window the moment things become uncomfortable for him, not just because he realises it will surely compound his guilt in Wendy's eyes but because he's meant to be searching for the hot towels, and the landing cards, and the destination guides and should have completed the duty-free bar receipts ages ago. He's way behind.

Well, if you ask me Carlo's in there already, she says. Something's going on between those two, that's pretty obvious. I'm just sorry I won't be at this gathering tonight to witness it all.

Don't tell me, Nigel says, you've persuaded him to take you out to dinner.

Funnily enough, yes.

And he's going to ring you at the hotel this evening as soon as he's made a reservation?

Something like that.

I wonder where I've heard that before, Nigel says.

Come on, Nige, of course the guy means it, she says. He was drooling over me.

Wendy, Nigel says, suddenly more at ease, realising the ground's shifted and he now has the upper hand, don't count on it. Try not to be too disappointed if you never see him again. At least you know there's something happening tonight if he doesn't ring. Galley colleagues are always saying he behaves as if he's superior to them, sounding like he knows everything and he's aware he might be coming across this way now (he doesn't think he's been too bad this flight) but he suddenly feels sorry for Wendy – he thinks she looks so fragile – and he only said it for her own good. He's seen so many people being stood up. He can't believe she's been taken in by this man. He thinks she should know better by now. He can see he's hurt her. I'm just being realistic, he says.

If we were always so frigging realistic, she says, I don't think we'd be doing this job. If we accept it for what it really is.

And what's that? he says.

Shit mostly, she says. I can't even remember why I joined. To meet the man of my dreams probably, ha. Why else do people do anything? Two marriages down and I'm still looking.

I joined because I wanted to get away from home, to travel – that old cliché, Nigel says. But I don't feel I've really been anywhere. Nothing much has changed. I'm still living at home with my mum. He can't believe he's telling her this.

At your age? Wendy says. You're not being serious.

Yes, he says. Well, she's been ill.

Frig me, she says, that won't do at all, Nige. Can't you find a nice man to shack up with?

Where's Carlo? he says, thinking of Tim and this shimmering, sparkling sliver of an opportunity, this entry into a whole new world where he can lose his inhibitions, this sense of confinement that he feels he's always struggled with, where he can at last be himself, fulfilled, free, sliding past him. Just out of reach.

I don't think he's suitable, she says, shaking her head. Too much of a flirt – you can see it in his eyes.

No, no no. That's not what I meant, Nigel says. I mean (which he doesn't) he should be here helping to clean up this galley – he is the galley chef.

Where's he been all flight? Wendy says. I wouldn't be surprised if he's with that young boy, with Tim right now – doing things I don't even want to think about.

When the fasten seat belt signs are about to come on? Nigel says. He doesn't want to think about Carlo being with Tim already, having got there first, ruining any chance he might have had tonight. He knows it wasn't great but at least there was the possibility, a reason for attending this engagement party – something to hang on to. He wonders whether he should get the captain to put out a priority call for him, knowing that would really dump Carlo in it.

I suppose you haven't noticed but I have been running the galley single-handed, Wendy says. Carlo's been off wherever – with whomever, she laughs. And you've been staring out to space all day. What do you keep looking at through the window? When you've seen one cloud you've seen them all if you ask me.

Nigel feels his ears pop. He swallows, trying to even out the pressure. It's not quite like that, he says, knowing he can't seriously get a priority call put out for Carlo – it's not an emergency. I bet you've never looked at them properly, he says. Closely, he thinks. At the sheer variety of shapes. How they're never exactly the same. How they all pick up the light differently – the particular shading and level of transparency. How the light can change so suddenly and dramatically when you are travelling at 500 miles an hour into the sun or away from it (he thinks of the first flickering of dawn, this faint blue line, the slightest hint of a horizon which becomes rapidly brighter and deeper until the blue's been replaced by a band of fiery orange that suddenly spills across the sky), and how in any one moment there can be so many different weather systems all working against each other – this expanse of uncontrollable, conflicting forces. Just as his ears settle he finally locates the towels in the warming oven – the first place he should have looked. He knows his mind has been elsewhere today. He puts the towels on a tray, makes sure his tie is straight and picks up a spong ready to leave the galley but just as he's about to do so the cabin manager rushes through the curtain looking disturbingly pale despite her make-up, which he decides she's done something even worse to than

**167**

when he last saw her. He's not sure what exactly but her eyes, her eyebrows definitely look funny.

Watch-ya, Selina says. David kept her in Business far too long – or rather she couldn't bring herself to leave (her mind hooked on this idea of realising old dreams). She knows she's running out of time and has only done about half of what she should have done by now. Bar receipts? she says. Anything been entered in the tech log? No? Sorry I haven't seen much of you lot today – I've been stuck writing reports. Who's missing?

Excuse me, Nigel says, leaving the galley, these towels are getting cold. And Wendy, you'd better start thinking about returning the coats and jackets. He can't get involved with the CM now, his paperwork is in a complete mess and he has about a hundred other things to do before the crew have to take their seats for landing. He lets the curtain close behind him and seeing the window in D1L empty and just a couple of steps away, knowing this will probably be his last chance to have a look out of this side of the plane, and even though he could be a fraction too early to see Manhattan and he promised himself he wouldn't go anywhere near a window until he was strapped in, he can't resist and rushes over carefully holding the tray of steaming towels to his side, resting the spong on the emergency chute bulge. He's always breaking promises. And then pretending he never made them in the first place. He's always deceiving himself and those close to him.

*With the hold at Calverton some four minutes behind them Greg sees the fasten seat belt sign illuminate as they pass below 10,300 feet at 230 knots. He watches as the throttles retard so the aircraft can hit 9000 feet at 210 knots directly above Rober, Long Island, when Dan will ask for one degree of flap and they'll turn right onto a heading of 250 degrees which will take them directly to Kennedy some twenty nautical miles away. Cloud is hitting the windshield in waves and the ground is not yet visible. Looking out all Greg can see is white and patches of less white but mostly he keeps his head glued to the screens monitoring the preset progress, while listening to ATC clearing them for lower levels at less speed and Dan* intermittently calling for more flap, as the aircraft bumps around because of the increased surface area and the cloud and the cross winds. The engines are automatically being adjusted, along with the elevators, ailerons and speed brakes in a bid to keep the aircraft in trim and on the correct descent profile, in spite of the unstable conditions outside, which become more enhanced the closer to the ground and the aerodrome you are, with the wind starting to shear, coupled with wake turbulence from aircraft sequenced just ahead.

With so much else on his mind Greg is quite successfully not thinking about needing to pee but the moment his concentration lapses the pressure swamps him, as if there's a lump of lead in his lap, reminding him of his own mortality, the precariousness of life. Each wrong turn he's made and how he'll probably end up paying for it. This is what he's thinking now. He's always found landing an aircraft an almost spiritual experience, safely coming back down to earth, and the closer they are to striking the tarmac, so the stronger his superstitious streak becomes. He finds he's suddenly doubting the wisdom of pursuing Selina, orchestrating this room party. He doesn't understand why exactly, just that this time it's not right. But it's a fleeting moment and the feeling disappears as suddenly and strangely as it appeared. He looks up to see they've broken cloud and are flying over grey sand dunes and tracts of dull marsh and in the distance, slightly to his left, he spots Manhattan, glowing and numinous, with a thin shaft of sunlight, perhaps the very last rays of the day, somehow finding a passage through the clouds on the horizon – falling out of the sky at this extraordinarily acute angle – and almost striking the heaped skyscrapers square on as if the world has turned sideways. He can make out the Twin Towers, the Empire State Building, an aflame Chrysler Building, and for the first time in ages he feels humbled by a view, by this city and the force of nature lapping at its edges.

The door gives without a fuss and Selina slips inside, instantly fazed by the natural light, this chunk of sunset, and the crazy noise of ATC operators and the wonkiness – worse now than ever as she can actually see the ground beneath them (getting a sense of the true speed they are going) and the ground is rising and falling and dotted with houses which quickly become more concentrated, more suburban. It takes her a few seconds to feel steady enough to move further into the cockpit. She coughs trying to *get Greg's attention without making him jump and lose where he is, but he remains unaware of her, his head fixed on the controls. Greg? she says, waiting for some acknowledgement. She tries to avoid looking outside by concentrating on the back of Greg's head, his thinning grey hair – she wants to feel the wheels slam firmly onto the runway, not see land rush up towards them (this terrifying ground effect) – but she can't help noticing a clump of glistening buildings just to the left of his ear. This city, New York, rising like a mountain range ringed with fire, each peak strikingly familiar. She can no longer not look outside, at what's really there. And instantly she feels very calm, that time, having been pushed and pulled way out of proportion, has suddenly stopped and she's exactly where she should be. As if for once she's in place. Whether she likes it or not. Greg, she says, again, but much more assertively, the cabin's prepared for landing.*

✈ JFK–LHR

# new york

Each time she straps herself in she thinks she must be shrinking, there's always so much strap she has to tighten. And currently being forced forward against the straps (which is really back-wards) she thinks she can feel the full fragility of her thin, decrepit bones. Her knees are clamped together, with her feet a foot or so apart but with her toes turning inwards giving her a better grip with which to push herself back into the seat (otherwise she feels she could slip out from under the straps – except her tits would probably save her, in the bra she's wearing today anyway) and looking down she sees this ridiculous impression her skinny thighs are making under her revolting skirt. Why the company can't finally do something about its image she has no idea – the uniform might suit a few of the younger girls, the darker ones especially, but she thinks it just makes her look like an old hag. It's as if she doesn't really have proper legs – sort of shadows where they should be. Except in the knee area where bits are sticking up everywhere. She's always thought her knees were knobbly but as the flesh has fallen away from her they've become more and more hideous – particularly compared to the pair next to her.

She forces her head up against the hard padding of the double crew seat so she has to look straight ahead even though the plane is climbing sharply, wanting to take her mind off her physical deformities, made so much worse by the proximity of her colleague who she thinks has about as perfect a body as she's ever seen on a CM, and the fact she's probably half her age. She looks straight ahead at the toilet cubicle, at Toilet D, hearing the piercing whine of the engines, feeling her seat vibrating (because she's so thin she feels everything, every flutter, every bump), with passenger door D1L a creamy blur on her right and the aisle on her left trailing further and further aft and out of focus – a darkened haze, with just the slightest hint that there might be people back there, a well of murmuring and small movements because the cabin lights were dimmed for take off and will remain so until the plane reaches 6000 feet or whatever they deem the safety threshold to be. Wendy hasn't much of a clue about the technicalities, she might have been flying for twenty-one years but she's not the frigging pilot.

Because he's on the outboard seat on the right-hand side of the plane (though it's really his left as he's facing aft) and the plane is banking and climbing and slowing and climbing again (he doesn't know why it has to keep doing this, why it can't keep accelerating in a steady, controlled fashion – it's just how his mum drives) he's getting this incredible view of Long Island and Queens (is it? – his geography's not brilliant but he had a look at a map before he came), a quickly unravelling sweep of neat, brightly lit suburbia stretching as far as he can see. An ocean of lights. He struggles with the concept of all these homes and lives stuffed so closely together, not quite being able to grasp the enormity and the anonymity of it. Like how many nameless people there are in the world, none of whom he's ever going to come across, but how differently his life might be if he'd been born down there say, instead of in Crawley. He's also thinking how much prettier, how much more appealing it looks from this distance and at night than when he was on the crew bus travelling to the airport this afternoon. He remembers being surprised by how scruffy and dingy everything seemed, compared to where they were staying in Manhattan, as if the suburbs were coated with this thick film of grime. Then he thinks nowhere can compare with Manhattan. The moment he finally arrived was like stepping out of a dream, as if he suddenly came alive, and he knows everywhere else is going to seem dingy and boring from now on. (Even though he did something completely stupid last night which he'd rather not contemplate.)

He tries to sink a little further into his seat, not out of shame – he's too young to suffer from that – but so he can see more of the city, and perhaps because he'd just been thinking so longingly about Manhattan already (they only left the crew hotel at 16.30), or because the place is so infused with magic he suddenly spots the Twin Towers rising from this swelling ocean of lights and from this landmark he makes out the rest of Manhattan – the Empire State and the clump of midtown skyscrapers, with New Jersey (he presumes) in the background seemingly bleeding away forever. And as the plane seems to right itself while continuing to climb, he watches as the skyscrapers appear to subside until their outlines are lost and the sparkling lights merge, becoming a vast smattering of dimming glow and the sky outside the window in service door D4R gets blacker and blacker, except for the odd, isolated flickering of other planes' landing and navigation lights. He imagines all these aeroplanes buzzing around New York waiting to land, like everyone's drawn there – except he's going in the opposite direction, flying away from New York, back to where he came from. He doesn't feel particularly happy about it. He's always had a feeling of missing out, despite never being sure of what exactly, though he thinks he has a better idea now. He realises there are some places that can make you feel whole and a part of everything and New York is probably one of them – despite wishing to disregard a tiny slot of his time there, of course. Though maybe, he thinks, he did it, he did this stupid thing because he was so stuffed with a feeling for life, so giddy he couldn't help himself. Who knows?

The plane's being buffeted slightly and Tim grips the seat rim, feeling the security of the shoulder straps (he's half sitting on his hands so he doesn't think he's being obvious about it – he'd hate the people directly opposite to think he was scared or anything – he's just not totally used to the sensation of taking off yet). Nevertheless he also presses down harder on the floor, tensing his calf and thigh muscles (what he has of them) trying to wedge himself further into the seat as he still feels he could fly out at any moment. He has a slight headache and each time the engines power up or are throttled back it's like blood is being pumped into or sucked out of his head, as if his brain is swelling and shrinking in harmony. He doesn't think he can have had more than four hours sleep since he left home yesterday morning (yesterday? – it seems days ago, months ago, could almost be a different lifetime). He wasn't going to waste this afternoon napping like just about everyone else, he was far too excited. He slowly looks up to see the full cabin – row after row of heads looming out of the dimness, more and more the longer he looks. He senses the passengers becoming restless and agitated already. The way they appear to be rolling their heads and fighting for elbow room, making space for themselves, marking out their territory. He's found it's worse at night because people start to panic about not being able to sleep. He tries to focus on the middle distance, a blurry dimness, but one head or another keeps grabbing his attention. He can't understand what some people do to their hair, how they have so little idea. He thinks it must be the easiest thing in the world if you are a woman, certainly one of the most enjoyable – the possibilities, the extravagance. Dyeing, curling, playing around with extensions, wigs – he'd try every-thing (not that he hasn't anyway).

He keeps getting this impression of the passengers surging forward, in wave after wave, swamping the aisles, yet when he concentrates on what's really happening no one's moved beyond their seats – it's like a premonition of what will happen the moment the fasten seat belt sign is switched off. They are all squashed in there ready to pounce. He doesn't know how he's going to manage tonight. He feels totally fucked. If they didn't have such a short flight time, just five hours forty-five minutes, he doesn't think he would be able to cope. He'd have to make out he suddenly felt really sick so he could be sent to lie down in the crew rest area (which he had to do coming back from Miami). He's not used to this lifestyle yet – he's only been doing it for six months. Indeed, having so firmly rooted himself to the seat he's not sure he's even going to be able to stand up when the ping goes – he's coming over all shaky. He can see Angela next to him has her hands on the buckle ready. And he felt so keen on the outbound, so eager to impress Debbie and the CM (to make amends for the Miami fiasco) – he's not at all sure he's even going to get beyond his probation period. Letting go of the seat with his right hand, he quickly runs his fingers over his left breast outside his shirt, checking his nicotine patch is still in place (he always slaps it bang on top of his heart, because he reckons that's where it'll have most effect). Apart from everything else he could murder a ciggy.

*Dan watches the bug on the altitude tape rise through 10300 feet. The PFD is burning with colour – livid greens and blues, browns and pinks – and movement, with only the horizontal magenta flight director bar sitting perfectly steady and dead level because they've already hit their initial routing, which will take them east of Boston via Bridgeport and Worcester, over Rhode Island and out across the Gulf of Maine, heading straight for Halifax, Nova Scotia. The autopilot has been engaged, with the LNAV and VNAV systems (picking up signals from a series of on-the-ground radio beacons), in conjunction with the INS and the FMS, now controlling their progress. The room for error having been cut to a minimum, along with the pilots' workload, which Dan thinks is just as well.*

*Because Dan's flying this leg (as much as it's possible, though it's certainly enough for him to be getting on with at the moment – his head is only just beginning to clear) he's monitoring the instruments while Greg's responsible for dealing with ATC. Dan's only conscious of snippets of conversation between the captain and ATC. Such as Greg saying, Out of twelve heading for one six O, and New York saying, 'Recleared to flight level one eight O, maintain heading.' Dan leaves the PFD and scrolls down the FMS legs page, searching for an ETA for Gander and the start of their oceanic. Greg still has to get confirmation of their track, along with clearance of course, which Dan will have to pay attention to as well because there are some messages that are particularly important it's imperative they both listen together. This is besides the various checks they both have to acknowledge throughout the flight, particularly shortly after take-off and before landing. However much Dan likes to feel he's his own man – and he gets a particular thrill when he's flying a leg, a particular sense of his own worth (who doesn't? he thinks) – he nevertheless realises he couldn't quite do it on his own, and just how much he has to rely upon the co-pilot. That in reality he's wholly dependent on Greg. But vice versa too, he thinks.*

*Giving up trying to map a mental picture of the aircraft's position from the displays (as he's been relentlessly taught to do) and lifting his head and opening his eyes wide to see this blackness rushing at him, a blackness that's continually shifting in tone and apparent density, in the same way the sea is never still and is forever changing appearance the longer you stare at it, he knows at least it's his turn to make some sort of impression. Even though he does feel a little out of his depth – not that he'd ever admit it to anyone, least of all Greg.*

Finally managing to open the locker, having struggled with a paddle blade for at least five minutes (they're always getting frigging stuck, Wendy thinks), she stands back in relief, in the harsh brightness. She can sense the heat of the galley lights on her head and neck, and the heat of the bev maker having been switched to brew and oven 1 on high behind her, this heat bearing down on her. A feeling of familiarity suddenly over-whelms her. Stops her dead. It's as if she's never left the galley – that New York never happened. It's like she spends her whole life in here, confined by these four walls, or at least the banks of lockers and ovens and electrics, and strips of dull, lifeless curtain – preparing other people's drinks and meals, daydreaming, wishing she were somewhere else, almost anywhere (what cabin crew doesn't?). The thought comes to her that she only really exists on board, in the galley. But checking herself, her thoughts, realising she can't stand in the middle of the floor all night (like some sort of shop dummy – not that she has the figure for it, not anymore) and that she has a job to do (however boring), she knows New York isn't a figment of her imagination – it happened all right. She feels it in her bones, throughout her shrunken, aged body. She's actually stiff and slightly sore.

She moves back to the locker she had problems with opening and carefully pulls out a tray containing new packets of cocktail sticks and drip mats, placing it on the counter, wondering as usual where the hell the others are. For some reason she's always being left to it but she's frigged if she's going to do everything tonight even if it is a short flight and that most of the passengers will be flat out for the duration. Besides she knows just because it is a short flight doesn't mean it'll go quickly – night flights crewing First can be a real drag as there's hardly anything to do (not that she fancies Economy much – she's too old for Economy). She needs company, even if it is only Carlo and Nigel. She's not very good at being on her own (not that she knows of a cabin crew who is). It's as if she loses the thread somehow, that she becomes unstuck and simply wanders about aimlessly, her mind a complete muddle. Though of course most of her friends at home regard her life as being pretty aimless anyway. Joy's always going on at her, saying things like, 'Wendy, love, I just don't understand how you can keep doing that job – at your age. You're not twenty, love. You should be at home more, looking after the girls, making dinner for some nice young man – all right, a rich old one. It's not surprising you're always single, love. You're not home enough to conduct a proper relationship. Take it from me, men like to know where they are with women – they don't want to be worrying about someone who's always slipping off to the other side of the world, not sure when they are coming back. Besides, love, you must have learnt by now men can't be trusted. What's that saying? Out of sight out of mind?'

Wendy knows Joy can't understand why she didn't leave the

company years ago, why she's stuck with it. She thinks it's easy enough for anyone to see why you could be attracted to the job in the first place – because of the travel (ha) and the uniforms (ha bloody ha) and the pilots (she doesn't bother to laugh), especially coming from Chingford. But what no one can see is why even after you get married and have kids and get divorced and get married for a second time and divorced again (and your looks have gone and there's nowhere on earth you find exciting anymore), you still keep doing it. Why cabin crew never leave, not after the first two or three years. What she's come to realise (along with everyone else) is that once you've passed the three-year mark the likelihood is it's hooked you, you're in it until retirement – or a plane you happen to be on crashes (if only, she's often thought). 'Wendy, darling,' Joy says, 'You can't carry on living like this all over the place. It's not normal.' Joy's probably Wendy's best friend, the person she sees when she's at home even more than her daughters, though she does only live two doors away, while Gemma's now in Chelmsford attending a beauty course and Zoe's currently living with her photographer boyfriend in Bedford, doing a bit of modelling (so she says). And yet, Wendy thinks, Joy is no closer to understanding her despite the gin they've put away. Maybe she doesn't understand herself, quite why she's never chucked it in – except perhaps, like in most jobs, you end up being trapped before you know it. Though sometimes she has an inkling there's more to it than that. When it occasionally makes some sort of sense. Like now this minute. Because, regardless of just having had this feeling that her whole life seems to be solely contained in one galley or another, she's surprisingly full of hope for the future (or if not quite hope, contentment, a certain sort of peace). Her stiffness, her soreness perversely shaping this state of mind, reminding her her life might just have a happy ending. Where the frig are Carlo and Nigel, she thinks – she's dying to spill the beans. She's never been able to keep anything quiet about herself for long.

# boston

Please, says Tim. He's hemmed in already and someone's just rammed their trolley into his right ankle and it's fucking agony. He turns, rubbing it with his other foot, to see it's Becky. He thinks she looks about as rough as he feels so he says, Sorry, darling, I didn't mean to bark. I'm not quite with it yet. He smiles and she smiles back but she doesn't say anything – which he thinks isn't at all surprising after last night. He reckons she's probably got severe jaw ache and not just from talking, though what she was saying shocked him enough and nothing ever normally shocks him (except, he supposes, his own behaviour). It didn't take him long (like his first trip) to realise cabin crew can be pretty frank, though the detail this girl went into about her sex life has surpassed anything he's heard so far. He feels queasy just thinking about it and quickly turns back to the trolley top he's struggling to set up, reaching for the glasses and the mixers and the Worcester sauce and the ice bin and the water jug and the juice cartons (orange, grapefruit and tomato), the serviettes and the swizzle sticks and the drip mats and the nuts and the already sliced lemon – all this stuff which he has to cram on in a presentable fashion, and which he's started having nightmares about, honestly. He also has to make sure it's all secure so nothing falls off when he tries to manoeuvre the effing trolley out of the galley over the bump and into the aisle – which is virtually impossible. On the outbound he thought he'd finally mastered the knack (in fact he felt he was really flying the whole way) but he's not so certain now. He can't seem to fit on both the ice bin and the water jug and having no elbow room is not making things any easier. He thinks it's outrageous how they expect so many people to work in such a small, airless space. He's sure there must be some law against it. He could probably take the company to the United Nations or the European Court of Human Rights or whatever because it's torture. Battery chickens get more room. He manages to squash on the ice bin but gives up trying to squeeze on the water jug too and chucks it back on the counter – slopping some water over someone else's pile of drip mats (well what's he meant to do? There's no other place he could have put it) – so he can have a breather for a moment, wishing more than anything he could have a cig. He's feeling increasingly claustrophobic and panicky and his hands are still shaking violently.

It never occurred to him when he joined that flying (being cooped up in a galley for eight hours solid, more like) might make him feel claustrophobic. Perhaps he should have thought about it harder because occasionally he feels sort of trapped, especially in crowded clubs, and suddenly has to be outside (though normally he's so off his face he's immune from every-thing, nothing can touch him). However, in training – when they were learning what's what in mock-ups of galleys – he was fine. He even got through the smoke test okay, he's seen thicker dry ice. Thinking back, training was simply a bit of a scream, four weeks' worth. Nobody took it very seriously, least of all the girls, which he reckons doesn't particularly matter because the training is nothing compared to the real thing. There's no way you get any sense of what the heat is like, or the airlessness, in a hangar on the outskirts of Crawley (not a million miles from where he lives, though against his wishes). It suddenly occurs to him that perhaps it's not claustrophobia he suffers from at all but simply a lack of fresh air and how this starts him panicking as he simply can't breathe properly. Right now he feels as if he's slowly suffocating, that there's this constriction in his chest. He recently read some story in the cabin crew newsletter about how the planes aren't pumping out as much oxygen as they should do to save money – which would be typical of this company he thinks, the stingy bastards. And maybe he suffers from the lack of oxygen more than most people because he smokes so heavily his lungs, being clogged with tar (almost a decade's worth of Marlboro Lights), don't work as efficiently as they should. One of the reasons he wanted to become a trolley dolly in the first place was so he'd be forced to smoke less. If anything he probably smokes more now. When he's on the ground he has to make up for the fact he can't smoke in the air, and always over-compensates. Plus he's awake all the time and is never sure whether it's the middle of the day or the middle of the night, whether he should be smoking or snoozing. Since joining he feels his life has been turned completely upside down. He doesn't seem to have the stamina to keep up with his friends at home (when he's actually at home). He never realised this sort of work can take so much out of you. He honestly thought it would be a breeze, at least no more strenuous than working in a restaurant, yet with all these perks. That's what his best friends Stuart and Andy led him to believe anyway and they've been doing it for long enough. Maybe he still hasn't acclimatised.

Don't mind me, he says, feeling another trolley bumping into the backs of his legs but not quite so painfully this time, like it hasn't broken skin or crushed a bone or anything. He looks over his shoulder to see it's Becky again and he says, Darling, perhaps you shouldn't be in charge of that thing. I'd put it away if I were you.

Sorry, she says, breaking her silence. I'm all over the place tonight.

Unlike last night, darling, Tim says loudly. He can't resist having to play the joker (there's usually one on every trip).

Perhaps it's his age or the fact he's often the only male in the galley. Women have always made him nervous. He thinks they look down on him, that they find him impossible to take seriously (he knows being so thin and having a lopsided face and screwy-looking eyes doesn't help). He also knows there's something inside him that won't let him be quiet, that won't let him just get on with things, that there's this need to be noticed (how he was at school particularly). Maybe it's because he found behaving in this way meant he wasn't bullied so much, that people no longer tried to force him to play the fool, seeing as he looked so ridiculous and was really pretty shy. He became what they wanted him to be. Still, he thinks he's largely kept this side of him, this urge to play up under control until this flight (he doesn't think last night counts, he was off duty – same as in Miami) of all times, when his probation period is coming to an end and he really needs to be on his best behaviour or else he's out (Miami didn't exactly improve his chances of getting a full staff contract, with all the perks of course). He dreads to think how he's going to behave from now on, now he's started, because he's always been useless at controlling himself. It's as if he suddenly switches on to self-destruct, that his character has this one major flaw.

Not another word from you on that matter, thank you very much, Becky says.

I'll just leave you to be the spokesperson on what went on last night then, Tim says. No doubt you'll be able to describe it in a lot more detail than I can. From the corner of his eye he catches Debbie looking at him. He turns away so quickly he's not sure how to take her look, though he knows he has to shut up, somehow. (If you take any group of female cabin crew they're always going to gang up against someone like him sooner or later – he's never been a fag-haggy queen.) So despite still not being able to cram on the water jug – he doesn't know where he's gone wrong – he realises the best way to keep quiet will be to make a hasty exit from the galley and the only excuse he can see he's got at this precise moment is to take the trolley with him and act as if he's just getting on with the first bar service (as if he's still as keen and efficient as he was on the outbound). Besides he doesn't want to get too personal with Becky, he doesn't want to be too cruel (and he knows how spiteful some cabin crew can get) because if he were in her position – getting married and everything – he can't begin to imagine how he'd have behaved last night. As it was he was pretty disgraceful – not that too many people on board have much of an idea about that, thank God. Though he knows you can never be sure about who's said what. He certainly doesn't want this lot getting hold of any info which they feel compelled to bandy about (he's been working for the company long enough to have learnt that nothing stays quiet for long, particularly things of this nature) all because he was winding up Becky. He's certain she's a Cancer. He can normally tell what star sign someone is just by looking at them. But what she's said and done over the last twenty-four hours has only confirmed his first suspicions. Being ludicrously irrational and insecure and obviously desperate for company all the time (anyone's too), like she's this great sponge of emotion.

He deliberately doesn't look at the dates of birth column on the crew roster list before a trip because he likes to work out people's star signs for himself – he'll then check at the end of a trip how accurate his predictions are. He's barely been wrong once. Sometimes he even takes it further, if he's especially interested in a person (and if he manages to get a few necessary facts, such as exactly what time they were born and where) and will construct a birth chart, correlating what he's observed and the conclusions he's come to about them with what actually appears astrologically. Though his prior assessments of the ascendants are okay sometimes he finds he's a little patchy on the transits and their influence. Uranus normally foxes him. He uses his mum's charts and the Internet (the free Swiss site http://www.astro.ch in particular) because he hasn't got round to getting his own source material yet. He's not certain he even wants to. He has this really addictive side to him (being a typical Pisces) and doesn't want to become too hooked on it, so that he

**185**

can't get out of the bed in the morning unless he knows exactly where he is in the cosmos, the exact position of every effing planet, and what he can expect to happen on that particular day. So that it rules his life – like it does for some people he knows. He doesn't want to turn into his mother, not yet at least. He is only twenty-one, even though he feels ancient tonight. As if he's suddenly skipped a couple of decades. The terrible thought comes to him that maybe something of last night has rubbed off on him, that perhaps he caught something, some aging disease, in the same way that when he's with a group of people he starts acting like them without realising it, and then only more so because he wants to be noticed. He wonders whether he's now nearer fucking fifty than twenty. Bending down to make sure all the drawers are in place and standing again and starting to pull the trolley out fully from under the counter and fixing on the top properly and trying to turn the thing to get it out of the galley without tipping it over (it can happen) or bumping it into someone (and knackering their bloody ankles) he reckons he might as well be. Sorry darlings, he says, backs to the wall.

Haven't you forgotten something? Debbie says.

Forgotten something? Tim says. I don't think so. He stops just before the bump, facing into the galley but feeling semi-protected by the trolley and its loaded top and his skinniness, though knowing he must be looking guilty – there's enough of him still on display and he's useless when it comes to lying, once confronted he's never been able to get away with anything (that's having the moon in Aquarius for you, he thinks). He peers at the stuffed trolley top and then Debbie, pretending he doesn't have a clue what she's talking about. Sometimes people fall for his bemused, naive look he puts on and which is only enhanced by his lopsided face, though he can tell Debbie's no fool. She's seen it all before. She's not going to be taken in by a twenty-one-year-old from Crawley, even if he currently feels over twice that age. It occurs to him that maybe he didn't exactly catch something last night, but that some experiences simply age you – such as war, or your parents dying. It's not that you wise up exactly, he thinks, but that you lose a chunk of what made you appear so young. What made people assume you were so young and innocent anyway? He's not surprised Debbie's having none of it.

The water jug? Debbie says. Tut, tut.

He can just imagine what she's like at home, forever searching for things to complain about and not letting anyone have any time or space to themselves, even when everything is exactly how she wants it. He suddenly feels really sorry for her husband – he can imagine she's a nightmare in bed, demanding everything's done precisely her way. And he thinks she looks like she could go on all night. Oh, oh that, he says. It wouldn't fit on safely (he's found that if you mention the safety factor you can pretty much get away with most things). Besides I've got tons of canned mineral.

Yeah, she says, but you know what the new Economy service guidelines say, water jugs should be used in preference to individually packaged units of mineral water.

That's just them being mean, Tim says.

Who pays your wages? Debbie says.

What wages? Tim says. This strange feeling comes over him that the plane is suddenly slowing down. Almost as if it's coming to a stop in mid-air. He tightens his grip on the trolley, waiting for the thing to stall. He's not sure he's ever going to get used to the sensation of flying – whatever anyone says there are times when it seems pretty dodgy to him.

*Dan watches the thrust levers waver and finally retard as the initial cruise speed of Mach 0.84 is reached and then maintained. The airspeed indicator is steady at 295 knots with a heading of 127 magnetic showing on the compass arc at the bottom of the PFD. He shifts his gaze across to the ND, seeing their ground speed is actually 505 knots before scanning for the weather, double-checking their current track and the time and distance to the next waypoint and if there are any nearby aircraft (courtesy of TCAS and appearing as little white diamonds on the screen, coupled with arrows indicating whether they are climbing or descending) but there are none and his eyes are drawn in by the compass rose at the top of this screen too and then slowly down so he sees their current track in white and*

200 nm of the rest of their route in a gently zigzagging, vertically aligned magenta line completely undisturbed by any significant weather. It's as if he's looking through a long dark tunnel to a bright abstract neon sign at the end. The way the darkness at the edges of the screen envelops the information. He's always found the screens at night mesmerising but knows there's only so much information he can take in at once before his mind starts to play tricks on him – he has a problem segregating information, determining what is and isn't relevant. His hands are sticky and he can sense the wetness around his armpits already (despite having applied liberal amounts of deodorant earlier). He always sweats when he's concentrating hard (even though everyone knows it's often easier flying out of Kennedy, say, as opposed to London, with less ATC interference because of the greater dependence on radar and beacons and more recognised airways), whatever the temperature, and in the cockpit at the moment it certainly isn't too warm. He finds it only really becomes uncomfortable during the day when the sun's so strong it's as if he's working in a heat haze, with everything boiling and undefined – when he has trouble imagining the real outside air temperature. At night he can almost feel the frozen air slamming into the windscreen. The extreme wind chill. The coldness of space.

Ahead he sees again this tumbling black, though glancing to his right, through the side window and away from the glare of the flight panel, the night sky appears much brighter and he sees his first clear stars of the evening, looking east, and as his eyes slowly grow accustomed to the outside, he sees more stars and clusters, hints of constellations, as if he's watching the stars rise, as if the stars are only just beginning to arc over the aircraft and fill the sky and the sky is suddenly becoming another dimension, another world. He loves flying at night. The feeling of being sucked deeper and deeper into the Milky Way, seemingly having left the earth's atmosphere (because it sometimes appears as if they are zooming straight out into space, beating gravity), and everything to do with his former life – beginning to realise this sense of freedom, of boundless possibility. The real magnitude of what's out there. How quickly it is that you think you've spotted all there is to see, only for layer after layer to keep unravelling the longer you look – from one solar system to the next. This sense of infinity. It blows his mind every time.

*He knows it's a cliché but as a kid he wanted to be an astronaut – part of him probably still does. But he keeps quiet about this, knowing he doesn't exactly have the physical attributes for it or that he even possesses the requisite brain power – for instance he has a problem when faced with too much information in one go, of orientating himself through a mental overload. He's amazed he's managed to pass all the qualifications he has to get to where he is now (even though he did have to sit a number of papers more than once), the first officer of a wide-body jetliner stuffed with state-of-the-art avionics and nearly 400 people whose lives he's directly responsible for. Except he doesn't often think of the passengers, or their safety, once he's on the flight deck – he likes to imagine he's in his own capsule, that they've separated from the rest of the aircraft and are floating free. He supposes it's another way of engaging with his fantasy and of trying not to think of himself simply as a pilot of a commercial aircraft – though he is fiercely proud of what he's achieved so far (and is only too aware of the sheer slog it took). He doesn't think he suffers from delusions of grandeur particularly, it's just that sometimes he has a problem divorcing his imagination from reality, and at night especially he finds this blurring of fantasy and reality to be at its most potent. On the flight deck, awash with flickering screens and back-lit dials and softly glowing switches, with the starry blackness slowly unravelling through the windscreen, space stretching on forever, he finds he's able to live his childhood, his teenage dream a little. He doesn't think he's changed hugely in the last fifteen years – except of course he wasn't shagging then, much.*

*He quickly locates the Plough and from there finds the Sickle and, establishing the ecliptic line from Leo, he sees the constellations of Cancer (just), Gemini (more obviously) and twisting his head and looking up as far as the window will allow he's sure he sees Taurus too, with the variable star of Aldebaran being particularly luminous tonight. Although they no longer have to take a navigation paper in astronomy or know how to use a sextant, he's always reading around the subject (his parents first bought him a telescope when he was twelve) and unlike anything he was made to learn at school, or flying school for that matter, much of it has stuck in his mind – it's only when he's forced to learn something that he has difficulties. He drops his gaze, feeling slightly dizzy, feeling the strain on his neck ease, and lets his eyes rest on the cloud covering the Gulf of Maine and the gentle brightness of the stars falling on the cloud. He can't see any sign of the moon yet, which he knows is on the wane, to spoil the effect.*

*Standby, Dan, Greg says, for confirmation of our track. Come on, Dan, come on, lad, concentrate, concentrate. There's nothing out there.*

Nige, tell me, Wendy says, how come these people can drink so much hot chocolate? Even my kids could never drink as much as this lot do in one sitting. Have you tried this stuff? It's revolting.

It reminds them of being young, Nigel says. And it knocks them out.

The only thing that can put me to sleep is a few stiff gins and a handful of Valium – or a good shag I suppose, Wendy says. But that's increasingly rare these days.

Well they're not going to get that on board, Nigel says, are they?

I don't know, I'm sure I could accommodate them somehow. A hand job anyway – a blow job if I was quick. It's pretty dark in there. Once I've stuck my head under a blanket who's to know what I'm doing?

Do you ever think about anything else? Nigel says.

Money, she says.

Oh yes, I forgot, he says.

And more money, she says. Hey, Nige, what's that mark on your neck?

Where? he says.

She watches Nigel immediately cover this livid mark on his neck with his hand – she hadn't realised quite how large, and hairy his hands are before. Has someone scratched you or something?

No, he says, of course not. I must have caught myself getting dressed.

Or undressed, Wendy says – in a hurry. Have you seen this, Carlo? Nige has got like these red marks running down the side of his neck. They look like scratch marks to me.

I don't want to know, Carlo says.

She moves over to Nigel and tries to pull his hand away. Let's have a closer look, she says. She clings to him as he moves further down the counter, struggling to get free of her yet still keeping his hand clasped to his neck, but realising he's far too strong for her (she finds him almost frighteningly strong), she lets go. Come on, Nige, she says, what happened to you last night? Hey, are you wearing make-up? She's sure she can see foundation on his cheeks and neck too, this hint of powder. What else are you hiding? she says. You can tell, Wendy. It won't go any further than these four walls, I promise. I'll tell you what I got up to. She's still dying to talk about what happened to her (most of it anyway). She thinks it's such a hoot – at her age.

No, no, please don't, says Carlo. I've got food to prepare.

Hardly, says Wendy. How many are eating tonight? Two?

I still don't want to know, Carlo says. I don't want to know anything. You lot disgust me.

You're not much fun, you two, are you? Wendy says. She finds there's normally at least one person in the galley who she can have a laugh with but Carlo and Nigel are defeating her. In fact she's given up on Carlo completely (she finds the Mediterranean-looking types always act aloof, as if they're too frigging sophisticated to be doing the job). She thinks she nearly succeeded in getting Nigel to open up on the way over (enough to realise the guy's a complete weirdo anyway – he has to be to be still living with his mum), though she's suddenly not sure she's going to get anywhere with him this way round – even if that does mean she won't have anyone to confide in. She thinks she might have to start popping into the other galleys. Why should she stick here in silence, in purgatory all night? Where are you off to now? she says, watching Nigel scamper – as much as someone his size can scamper – out of the galley. (She realises she wouldn't want to bump into him on a dark night, even if he is gay.) They haven't been going more than forty-five minutes and already he's been in and out of the galley a dozen times or so when they're meant to be keeping as low a profile as possible, as it's a night flight and most of the cabin is tucked up on saccharin and tranquillisers. It's too frigging dark to see anything outside, she shouts. She turns back to Carlo and says, He has to keep looking out of the window for some reason. She points to the side of her head, screwing her hand.

Maybe he's missing his mummy, Carlo says.

Have you two fallen out over something? Wendy says.

Nothing you'd understand, Carlo says.

Want to bet? she says. I've seen everything in this business. There's nothing I wouldn't understand. Don't tell me, it's over that young boy in Economy, Tim?

I'm not saying anything, Carlo says, I'm above all this gossiping. Besides I've got more important things to be getting on with, like preparing this meal. Do you know how to make a cheese soufflé? I doubt it somehow. Why don't you get on with what you're meant to be doing – those drinks must be cold by now.

I don't think they should be encouraged to drink the stuff anyway, Wendy says. What is it with these people? When I first started the passengers used to sit back with a whisky and a carton of fags. You couldn't keep the noise down if you tried. Now all they ever worry about is how much sleep they're going to get. They hardly even smile at you, let alone bother to chat. We might as well not be here. It makes a mockery of all this frigging training we have to keep going through every time they decide on some new product. Carlo darling, don't you find it demeaning not getting a response, not being acknowledged. I suppose you wouldn't know, spending your life in here warming up all this fancy food nobody touches. (She doubts whether he has any more of an idea how to make a soufflé than she does – knowing that just about all the galley chefs have to do is set the oven timer.) She suddenly realises she's angry. She was feeling so up, almost contented, pleased to be where she is for once, until she started thinking about the passengers.

I thought they're always all over you? Carlo says. Like that old geezer on the outbound.

She quickly puts the two mugs of artificially sweetened hot

chocolate on a tray, managing not to spill any, which is something of a miracle for her (for any of them, she thinks). Who? she says, lifting the tray and starting to walk out of the galley, determined not to let this particular conversation go any further (she knows she's full of contradictions, but she doesn't want to attempt to explain quite what's going through her mind right now), feeling the stiffness in her back and pathetically spindly legs and this soreness deep inside her, which she's beginning to worry about because, although even by her standards it was a pretty vigorous session, she doesn't think she should still be feeling quite how she does in there (she can't remember having any pain quite like this before). She half wonders whether something might have ruptured, or that perhaps she's caught something and the infection's just taking hold. And at the time, she thinks, stupidly, it was him she was worried about. She's never seen anyone go so puce – this deep purple spread right across his chest. I can't think who you're talking about, she says. She parts the curtain with her foot and slips out of the galley into the dim cabin, waggling her bottom (over the years she's perfected this waggle that's as much come on as frig off). She might want to spill most of the beans (desperately), to let the guys know what she got up to last night and why she's feeling so breezy and full of it, or was until a moment or two ago, until she started thinking about the passengers and being demeaned by them, but she doesn't feel like revealing what she didn't get up to to the whole world. She doesn't think a girl, even a cabin crew, need necessarily reveal everything when it actually comes down to it (whatever she might encourage the others to do). Besides, she thinks, a girl has to maintain some element of mystery, if she possibly can, some intrigue, otherwise no one's going to be in the slightest bit interested in you (particularly if you are physically way past it anyway).

It takes her a moment to become accustomed to the light, and the peace, and the pitch and tremble of the plane. Though she finds stepping from the galley into the cabin is nothing compared to getting off the thing after a long-haul – she can spend a whole day down route (or at home for that matter) still feeling this sense of motion, in her legs, running right through her, which can unbalance her, make her reach out for the backs of chairs and handrails and people's arms. She's always grabbing hold of people's arms, though mostly they think it's Wendy just being Wendy. It's almost as if she finds it steadier on board, that her body has become so attuned to trotting around in a pressurised cabin five miles up it can't cope very well with solid ground, with fresh air. However, she slowly edges into the cabin tonight, carefully holding the tray in two hands because, although the plane has stopped climbing and appears to have settled into the cruise and there's no hint of turbulence whatsoever, she doesn't feel as well balanced as she normally does on board. (She's only ever spilled a drink on someone twice, in over twenty years – once when a man in the row behind the one she was serving pinched her bottom and the other being when the plane hit an air pocket and suddenly dropped 3000 feet, though it felt like forever.) She wonders whether it's because of her stiff aching limbs (she needs to take up yoga or something – Joy does this thing called t'ai chi), or the fact she only got about two hours sleep last night. She's never needed a lot sleep (which is one of the reasons why she reckons she's so thin, along with the fact she can never sit still, the fact she's full of this restlessness – as Joy puts it) but only two hours is pushing it even for her, and she didn't get much of a nap this afternoon either – she was too wide awake, thinking about the night before. It's not that something completely unexpected happened, more that she began seeing things from a different perspective. She can't quite put her finger on it, except she remembers initially (anyway) having this almost out of body experience. She could see herself straddling this man, as if she were watching from a safe distance, out of harm's way, somewhere high up, even though she could still feel everything, feel him inside her. In a way, she thinks, it was like she could (and maybe still can, though she's not so sure) see everything clearly for once, what's really going on, a sort of unbiased view, and that, whether you like what you see or not, there is a certain contentment to be gained from the clarity. That you don't have to chase any more lies and half-truths. Wow, she thinks, she's beginning to freak herself out – she never normally thinks about things for too long. Not things like this.

Slipping further into the dim cabin she finds Joy comes to mind again. She loves Joy, she loves running out of the house and leaping over the chain-link fence that divides their small scruffy front gardens (hers is a pit anyway – how can she be expected to look after it properly being away so often?) and up Joy's path to bang on her door (she never uses the bell – it's her way of letting Joy know she's back) to invite herself in for coffee or something stronger depending on the hour, and then the two of them settling down together in the kitchen to have a good natter – at least for her to rabbit on while Joy soaks it all up. She tells Joy everything, even the things she's most ashamed of. She knows she'll tell Joy exactly what did and didn't happen to her in New York when she sees her on Sunday – then Joy isn't cabin crew and what she tells her won't go any further than Chingford. While Joy's a great listener and she loves her, of course, Wendy believes she never has much to say because she doesn't do anything. It's often occurred to her that, unlike Joy who's always telling her she should be at home more (for the girls, for some gorgeous bloke to suddenly materialise out of thin air), that she's too old to be darting all over the world, that she's no longer twenty – 'Come on, darling, think of your skin, your complexion, what those air miles are doing to your body,' Joy says – she at least has plenty to talk about. Even if it does feel like she's been flying around in circles for the past twenty odd years. That however boring or uncommunicative some of the crew might be (thank you, Carlo and Greg) you'll always come across others elsewhere on the plane who'll make up for any galley shortfall. That most trips are extraordinarily intense experiences. How, in many ways, she only really feels alive away from home, away from her three-bedroom semi in a not so quiet close on the edge of Chingford. Standing in the centre of the cabin trying to recall who she's meant to be serving the hot chocolate to, she suddenly wonders whether she's been attempting to live two lives, to be two people – a Joy-like person who's firmly rooted to her home and family and someone else who's simply not grounded, who operates according to a completely different set of rules – and that she's never taken being a cabin crew for quite what it is, because it's not some part-time activity, it's a way of life. She can sense the relief that comes when you no longer have to pretend something's something else. When finally you accept things for what they really are – when you see what they really are. Perhaps, she thinks, she couldn't see her way clear because she was always trying to maintain some sort of hold on Gemma and Zoe, and now they're grown up and living elsewhere she's free again.

Excuse me, Mr Rubinstein, she says (with so much else going on in her mind she's amazed she's remembered his name, though he is the best looking man in the cabin by about a mile), your hot chocolate, sir.

Just put it there, will you, he says, moving a paper from the centre armrest drinks ledge.

Wendy thinks he must be in his early fifties, though she's useless at judging people's ages and finds it particularly difficult in First with everyone being a little more relaxed about their appearance and the message they are trying to get across (even when they're asleep) than in Business, where in her opinion everyone's desperately trying to prove something. He has thick dark brown hair and a strong, well-shaped face. He's wearing reading glasses, which might possibly be making him seem more friendly and approachable. From what she can see of his body now (and what she remembers of it, greeting him as he boarded) she knows there's nothing there to put her off. In fact, he's exactly the sort of man she'd dive on – if she'd had a few. She carefully places the drink on the ledge, having left the tray and the other chocolate – Mr Ford's, something beginning with F anyway – on the magazine and newspaper display cabinet, which also houses the fruit bowl, leaning over him in such a way that her blouse falls forward giving him, if he so wishes, a clear view of her cleavage (she doesn't look to see whether he takes advantage or not, not wanting to embarrass him). Over the years she's perfected the art of handing out drinks to passengers she fancies, and those she doesn't for that matter. She slowly stands back, imagining sliding her head under the blanket he has already tucked around him and undoing his flies and freeing his cock and quickly making him hard by running her tongue around the dry, circumcised tip. Is there anything else I can do for you, sir? she says. She's always coming up with mini-fantasies like this, which used to amaze her, seeing how unsexy she finds aeroplanes, though she's long realised they have little to do with her immediate environment and much more to do with her desires and frustrations and the fact she's so bored most of the time. Sex, she thinks, is like this thing that's always on her mind (more so the older she gets, though she was pretty terrible in her teens and twenties), mulling away in the background. When thoughts like these emerge, they often startle her with their vividness.

I'm fine for the moment, thanks, honey, the man says.

Okay, she says, surprised, mentally taking it all back about the passengers barely acknowledging cabin crew anymore, unwinding this conversation she's just had in the galley. Of course she knows it's not true, thinking she must have simply been in a bad mood brought on by Carlo and Nige being complete oafs. She loves the passengers really, particularly the Americans (she can't seem to resist them). She knows you'd never get some English guy calling her honey, or darling, not in First – maybe down the back, a few years ago when she didn't look about 102 anyway. If there's anything else you require, sir, she says, please press the buzzer and I'll be out right away. I hope you get a good night's sleep. She supposes it's a class thing, the fact that Americans aren't fussed about whether you are a cabin crew or a chief executive as long as you look like a good lay. That's not to say she hasn't been propositioned by any Brits over the years, because she has, though it's always in a different way – they don't even make any pretence about the fact they're using you. About presuming they can get something on the cheap. Not those travelling in

First. However, Sean McPhee comes to mind and she supposes it's all very well having someone suddenly being completely charming, making all sorts of promises, pretending there is more to a situation than there'll ever be, but when they don't come up with the goods you're left feeling totally stupid, and quite empty inside. Maybe, she thinks, it wasn't Carlo and Nige's fault, for being oafish, maybe she is pissed off with the passengers. She knows she's thinking about things for too long again but she can't seem to stop herself.

She begins to wonder what it would be like if everyone was completely straight about what they wanted, whether you really would get anywhere, or whether people need a certain amount of bullshit to get them going. She thinks she's probably too old for all this anyway – she's forty-three, for frig's sake. She's got two grown-up kids. And a three-bedroom semi in Chingford, which is not quite London or Essex – the place where she was born and has somehow managed to end up back in. For years she vowed she'd never return. Though she's not alone here. Most of the older hosties she gets talking to seem to be in similar positions, livingwise. It's as if when it comes to finding a proper home they all run out of energy and ideas and slump for the easiest, the most obvious option – where there's still some sort of back-up, an old network of friends or at least a few relatives who are always there when you need them.

*Since moving up to this type of aircraft eight months ago, which is technically the most advanced within the company, Dan keeps finding himself looking around the flight deck, the so-called glass cockpit, trying to work out what might have changed the least over the years, what any pilot could fathom. About the only things he can spot right now, looking directly at the main flight panel, are the standby attitude director indicator, airspeed indicator and altimeter dials – instruments which were once deemed pioneering (about a hundred years ago) and are now only used if a relevant system crashes (something he's never experienced, not on this aircraft outside training). And he thinks of the instruments that have had the most impact on modern aircraft (leaving the mechanical* age well behind) like the inertial reference system − the self-contained airborne positioning unit run by laser gyroscopes, initially developed to send men to the moon − or the microwave landing system that's just being introduced and that can guide an aircraft to within thirty metres of touchdown, or the ACARS communication and reporting system, using the global SATCOM satellite arrangement, which is already eradicating much air traffic control work and should one day enable track-free flight.

What really stuns him about this aircraft (he knows some people already view it as something of a dinosaur, certainly an aircraft that's no longer so suitable for UK-US East Coast destinations, though he prefers to dwell on the status it's accorded within the company and quite how well he's done to get into the driving seat), what really stuns him about this particular flight deck, and what makes him realise quite how far aviation has come, is the fact that there are exactly 365 switches, as opposed to the earlier models of this aircraft which had almost treble that number. He thinks it's as if the engineers and technicians not only had the power and the knowledge to reduce drastically a pilot's workload but they could also stick in a reference to the cyclical nature of life − a switch for every day of the year. As if, he thinks, they didn't want the pilots to forget their own mortality − and the eternal movement of the earth around the sun. (Though Dan's always looking for connections, trying to determine what's significant, trying to order his mind, because he knows he isn't naturally prone to order, to coherence, because he knows he doesn't always fit things together properly or pull out what's most important.) He's often wondered whether they added an extra couple of switches or removed something minor to arrive at this figure. As it is, without referencing his complete systems study guide he doesn't know what every switch does. He has no idea what could be missing, where they might have skimped, or what's superfluous. Though with the levels of redundancy built into the aircraft he reckons the thing could still fly quite happily on half the number of switches.

Suzi is always calling him a techno bore. He admits to being into new technology − avionics and communications especially. He supposes he wouldn't have become a pilot if he wasn't a little inclined that way. But he views it as means of advancement, a way of encapsulating the future, of seeing further. He doesn't think there's anything boring in that. He even *finds it sort of spiritual, being part of this quest. He's not into astrology or anything like that (unlike Suzi) but looking at the stars from 36,000 feet, or so, on a near moonless night always makes him think about what else is out there. It makes him want to know more. Such as where he comes from – not Swindon, but where exactly in the universe. And why. The more he thinks about it the more it blows his mind.*

*He tries to get Suzi interested in all this, reading things out to her from his specialist magazines (he subscribes to* Flight International, Pilot, Scientific Computing World, New Electronics), *showing her his new computer games and programmes and CD-Is, even letting her have a look through his telescope, but she just tells him he's being boring and why can't he fix the video or do something practical instead. He's sort of given up on Suzi, in his mind anyway. She still believes he's going to marry her. They haven't got engaged officially, though she's been calling him her fiancé for months, while he's been trying not to think about it. He's never told anyone at work. He mostly says he doesn't have a regular girlfriend, or that there are one or two people knocking about but he's non-exclusive. He found this phrase in one of Suzi's magazines which she threw at him – how some celebrity, he's forgotten who, viewed his relationships. He likes using the term, particularly on the flight deck. It always gets to the older captains, as if he's this young stud putting it about, having all this success with young women, when they're past it – he knows how jealous captains are and worried about getting older. He's not unsuccessful (he wasn't unsuccessful last night) but he's not exactly at it all the time down route either, whatever he makes out. He knows flying's not like that anymore anyway. It does happen (obviously), but certainly not all the time. And then, if he's being entirely honest with himself (something that he's becoming less and less good at – maybe it's just being less sure of things as he gets older), only when some girl pushes herself on him, usually someone he'd never normally consider. He's always been useless at picking up women he really fancies – being spotty and looking about twelve hasn't done much for his confidence over the years. Though he feels better in uniform, which is perhaps why he's able to sound more full of himself and behave more flirtatiously on board, or at least on the crew bus. Once in casuals down route he's pretty hopeless.*

**200**

*Sensing Greg is looking at him he turns to the FMS and scrolls down the legs page, trying to refocus his mind on what he's meant to be doing, half-expecting Greg to start shouting at him again. Still, he thinks, if anyone's been behaving unprofessionally on this trip it's Greg.*

# moncton

Serving his last row, Tim finally looks up, towards the rear of the plane (he tries not to do this before he knows he's almost at the end of his patch because he hates seeing how far he's still got to go if it's like rows and rows before he can nip back into the galley) and through the bright, yellow-tinged light – this light, with most of the blinds pulled down and complete darkness outside anyway, that he always thinks appears so tired, even at the beginning of a flight – past all these hundreds of people, almost all plugged into the in-flight entertainment system and trying to ignore their immediate environment, such as how cramped it is, or the fact they haven't been served a drink yet (though they'll come round to these matters shortly, they always do), he can see Becky. She's still near the rear bogs, like she's only just started, the poor love. And looking over his shoulder, the other way, wanting to locate Marissa who's coming down the adjacent aisle to him in Zone D, he quickly sees she's about ten rows behind him. Amazed he's managed to keep this lead (being completely shagged, nicotine-starved and unable to stop his hands shaking) he looks further round, half turning, to see just how far he's come so quickly, and craning this way he spots way in the distance, beyond Toilets H and J, almost two whole zones forward, the CM striding up Zone C. He knows it's her and not another cabin crew because of her hair, this thing she does to it which makes it stick out a mile, like she's got a spout, and he watches her, the back of her head and this ponytail thing swaying in the tired cabin air until she suddenly darts into the Business galley and he catches the briefest glimpse of her face.

He thinks Selina could be really gorgeous, she's got the body and the features, though she obviously doesn't have a clue about make-up, or what to do with her hair. He could certainly offer her a few tips, such as try a lighter lipstick, cut down on the eyebrow pencil and go easy on the blusher. He finds most women make the mistake of picking a too heavy blusher under the impression it'll enhance their cheekbones when in fact it just makes them look painfully withdrawn. He's not saying women shouldn't make the most of what they've got but that they have to understand their faces and attributes and should on the whole try to keep things as soft as possible, in his opinion, by avoiding too strong shades and harsh lines, unless they are a hundred per cent confident they know what they are doing, and have the face to carry it off. Someone with his sort of awkward looks could probably get away with it and, although he will always appreciate a distinctively well made-up face, something that really stands out – he simply loves Smashbox's spring line – he believes most women are better off sticking to deftly applied neutrals, whether their complexions are light, medium or dark. He's not sure what Selina's aiming at, though as far as he can tell most of the girls try too hard to be something they're not. He can't make her out. On the one hand she comes across as being really flirtatious and funny and sort of with it in an over-the-top-way (a bit how he behaves sometimes) and on the other she seems a complete mess, totally shy and nervous. Like she keeps losing it. He's certain she's a Libran – what with this duality of character. He's also pretty certain her moon must be in Pisces, if not Pisces, then Cancer.

It's already struck him how often both the air and water signs seem to show up among the crew he scrutinises. He knows air and water are yin and yang but thinking of them as elements it's like they both have this fluidity, these similar properties. In training he was told to think of the air as if it were water, that it's as stable and supporting as that, which took him a while to get his head around. He decides he's going to find out exactly where and when Selina was born because he wants to do her chart. She intrigues him – she's one of these people you are never quite sure where you are with. Not cagey, not at all, but just not very open or giving. For instance, she had all these men after her last night at Becky's do downtown – Greg and Dan and David (though Tim has an idea David's gay, at least bi) anyway – which he could see was pissing off the other girls, though she didn't seem very happy about it herself, she wasn't exactly making much of an effort with them. And he wasn't at Greg's room party afterwards for long so he doesn't know if she eventually brightened up, or who if anyone she left with for that matter. It suddenly occurs to Tim that actually no one seems particularly keen to talk about what happened at Greg's later – it's like it didn't happen. He might not have been flying for long but he's never been on a quieter crew bus at the end of a down route as the one that took them to the airport earlier this evening (through all these grimy suburbs going a sort of deep brown in the setting winter sun). Normally things dribble out, though he wasn't going to be the first person to start blabbing. In fact he pulled his knees up and slumped down in the seat not wanting to catch anyone's eye, wishing he were invisible. Hoping one person at least couldn't see him (which, he realises, is another reason he's so keen to get back into the galley – he doesn't want to be caught in an aisle, out in the open, so to speak).

Tim stands, unlocks the brake and lets the trolley begin to run forward, so as to build up momentum before he tries to swing it into the galley over the bump. But he gives it a little too much space and takes it too fast and the side of the trolley bangs against the entrance – or maybe it was because of a sudden tremble of turbulence unbalancing him for a second. He hopes anyone who noticed thinks that's the case because trolley dollies aren't allowed to let things get out of control. You're meant to maintain this façade of being completely unflappable, unfazed by anything – however nothing falls off the top despite it not all being packed on as tightly as when he set off (half of it having been used up, all the nuts anyway, the nuts always go first) and he brings the thing quickly to a standstill bang in front of Debbie, who obviously did notice, though he thinks she can't really complain about a minor bit of trolley mishandling because he is the first back and it's not as if he even ran it into her ankles. As far as she should be concerned, he's still showing the sort of form he did on the outbound – whizzing about like he's Mr Efficient, Mr Cabin Crew 2000. More than ready for a full time staff contract, with all the added perks (he didn't join for nothing). Of course she doesn't know he's nearly dying of sleep and nicotine deprivation (and the tiniest bit of shame – it's creeping in). Or the fact that he has no idea how he's going to deal with the meal service (it normally kills him anyway) but thank God that they're only doing one bar run this way, seeing as it's a night flight and a short one for a long-haul at that, though it's about ten times too long for him as it is. They still have to fit in the full complement of meals and chair-side duty-free services (they can never miss out the duty-free) in what will now be a really tight schedule.

The inflexibility within the company, like you always have to distribute a certain number and combination of products, amazes him. Everything has to be done in the prescribed way – despite them always going on and on about how, as cabin crew, you are meant to use your initiative, your individual flair. How you're meant to personalise the experience for the passengers. He thinks it must be like working for the civil service, or the government. Particularly as they are always saying one thing and expecting you to do the opposite. He stands back a foot or so and looks at Debbie, smiles at her, knowing of course she's exactly the sort of person who loves procedures and timetables and set ways of doing things and adhering to them straight down the line. And hates people making mistakes, however tiny – such as letting the trolley bump into the side of the galley entrance. He's not surprised one bit she's a purser. She should be a CM, she's old enough. Though he thinks she probably isn't attractive enough – they're always saying it's only the really pretty, flirtatious ones who make it to CM, whether they are any good or not. They need the hard workers like Debbie to stick around in Economy (where they won't be noticed by the all important First and Business Class passengers) because no normal person would want to kick about in Economy for longer than they have to.

Why Stuart and Andy didn't fully warn him about what he was letting himself in for he has no idea. Perhaps, it occurs to him, they were having a joke at his expense for once – the fuckers. Unless their experience is so completely different from his, which he doesn't see how it can be, though Andy is currently working for a member of the alliance on the Far East sector. However, he knows he can't blame them entirely, despite them continually going on about what's on offer down route – boys and more boys – and all these official perks that he's yet to experience because he hasn't passed his probationary period yet, and may never experience, of course. For more than any other reason he joined because he had to get away from home, and Crawley – no one, he thinks, should have to live in Crawley for all their life. And despite everything Stuart and Andy promised, he could see cabin crewing seemed like the easiest, the most convenient way of doing that. The company, with its worldwide headquarters just down the road at Gatwick, was recruiting and he didn't have the qualifications to do much else. Sure enough (though Stuart and Andy had prepared him for the interview) they gave him a job, or at least put him on probation for six months – which comes to an end the week after next. It's his first attempt at being a grown-up, at joining the real world. Though he can't help already feeling he's not very good at it.

Not purposefully looking, he spots himself in the mirror, pulling this startled, hopeless expression he seems to have perfected over the last few months, but which he doesn't think is him at all. Indeed sometimes now when he sees himself in the mirror he's under the distinct impression that he's looking at someone else entirely – this kid he's never seen before. Stuart and Andy always used to go on about how once you've become a cabin crew you start assuming this character, like you've just walked off a production line, like you've been cloned – and that once you've been cloned that's it, there's no going back, you're stuck with this personality for the rest of your life. Standing in the hot, stinking galley – he can smell the meals beginning to burn up – he wonders whether he's in fact turning into someone else. He might get out of control sometimes and be really loud and sort of over the top (how he's always been) but he's never ended up in a situation similar to the one he found himself in at two this morning. Because he's beginning to wonder whether it wasn't the effect of New York at all – being intoxicated by the spirit of the city (like the most glamorous place he's ever been) – but a sure sign of his cloning, his turning into a cabin crew proper, doing what's expected of him, in a way. Actually doing more than was expected – as is his wont.

That call button's going again, Debbie says, startling Tim – who quickly looks away from the mirror and this reflection of him that isn't him. It's turning into one of those nightmare flights, she says. I bet it's that woman in 28H who wants to be moved because of that baby near her. Could you deal with it, Tim, thanks. I keep telling her the plane's full and it's impossible. She's obviously one of these people who complain wherever they sit – and don't we know about them. I've got to give Becky a hand, I think she must be getting mauled at the back of Zone E. There's a love.

What, so this is my penance for being efficient and coming in first? says Tim. Dealing with the passengers no one else wants to touch.

Yep, Debbie says. Look, I'll put it in my crew report for the CM – helped to control a difficult passenger and maintain order in the cabin. It'll do your probation no end of good.

Thanks, Tim says. He secures his trolley and, wishing once more he were invisible, slowly moves towards the open aisle –

the curtains having remained pinned back since take off because of the rush they're in tonight, because at the best of times people are always getting themselves and their trolleys tangled up in them.

Come on, love, Debbie says, try to look a little keener. Show a sense of purpose. One day someone will help you out when you really need it. This job is all about team work, in case you've forgotten.

Yeah, right, Tim says. Like we're one big happy family.

You've got it, she says.

She steps over to the window in service door D1R feeling really foolish, knowing she's not going to see anything – she has only been doing this job for twenty-one years – but for some reason she suddenly has this urge at least to prove she's right and that Nigel's completely barking. She checks behind her again that neither Nigel nor Carlo, nor any of the passengers for that matter, are watching (not that she's exactly concerned about what the passengers think of her, even Mr Rubinstein, though he's asleep so he doesn't count at the moment anyway) before she presses herself against the door, sort of folding her body over the bulge the emergency chute makes (if she were ever in a proper evacuation she knows who'd be the first down it, shoes on or off – she's not going to be burnt alive waiting for the cabin to clear, waiting for a load of overweight businessmen to struggle out of their seats, she's looking after number one, for once) and shading her eyes from the bright doorway lighting and trying not to smudge the window with her coffee breath, feeling this breezy chill all around her, she slowly focuses on nothing, this great black nothing that's outside, and she thinks, thinking of Nigel, what a freak. Though something keeps her folded there and slowly stars begin to appear, then they sort of rush at her until she's never seen so many so clearly. It's not as if she hasn't looked out of the window at night before, but this lot keep on multi-plying the longer she stares, impossibly, so all she sees is not nothing at all but millions and millions of stars, twinkling away, as though it's snowing. She certainly doesn't see anything like this when she looks up on clear nights at home – there she just gets this yellow glow from the street lights in the close, unless one of them has bust and then she might see a few stars and possibly the moon, though it's always so faint and mushy. She tries to recall some names of stars and constellations she's come across and how they can be identified, but all she can remember is the Plough and the Pole star and she knows there's no way she's going to find these out there amongst this lot – she doesn't even attempt to.

Shifting her weight from one buttock to the other (because she's so bony she can't sit for long on anything that's not well padded) she gets closer to the window and is able to look down and see what she slowly realises is cloud and how the stars, this starry light, is reflecting on the cloud making it appear smoky. Maybe, she thinks, there's moonlight too brightening everything up a bit but she can't see the moon on this side of the plane and has no idea how full it's meant to be at the moment anyway (she never pays much attention to her surroundings, especially what goes on outside, especially nature). And like the stars, the longer she looks at the cloud the more depth and shape she sees to it, how it sort of keeps rolling, rolling away in the dark, and while thinking perhaps Nigel's not so nutty (she might give him another chance), because the view really is quite beautiful, she sees a break in the cloud and what she's sure is land beneath. It's definitely land, for she spots clusters of lights, small towns, and roads, and for the second time in twenty-four hours, she has this distinct feeling that she's seeing everything as it is, the complete picture for once – from some great vantage point. Though her bum is aching badly again already and there's no way she's going to sit here all night, whatever the view, whatever her vantage point. Besides she decides she's got the measure of it, this completeness already – she's always been realistic, she never tries to read too much into anything. She only needs the briefest of glances. Though it occurs to her that perhaps Nigel has to keep coming back to the window because he's still at it, still searching for this clarity, for this thing that has somehow clicked with her. Until Friday, until they set off from Heathrow she wasn't aware she was even looking for anything, certainly not a different perspective. She realises how much harder it must be actually to set out looking for something as abstract, as seemingly ungraspable as this, rather then just stumbling upon it. She can just imagine the complications and confusion that would arise – quite what happens when you go over too much stuff. When you read too much into things.

Being entirely honest with herself she knows she's never tried too hard at anything. She was pretty useless even with her kids when they were small. She never managed to get them into a proper routine and found she simply couldn't cope with their constant demands, their crying, with the way they never slept when they were meant to. Some of her old friends, friends she's had since school such as Jackie and Heather, just seemed to slip into motherhood, but she found it a constant battle – she knows she's not a natural. With Gemma it was bad enough but when Zoe came along she found she really struggled to keep everything together. She knows it was mean of her going back to work so soon for the second time, letting her mum look after them (when she wasn't fully capable, having chronic osteoporosis) but it wasn't entirely her fault, she needed the money, particularly as Mike had frigged off – before Zoe was even born, his own daughter. (As much as she found it a struggle she could never have just abandoned them, she always made sure they were all right – she thinks that's the difference between men and women.) She knows she could have tried to get another job which didn't involve being away so much but that wasn't very likely at the time, what with her qualifications and the recession. Plus there was this other thing that drove her back to cabin crewing and which she supposes she still feels a bit guilty about when she considers the kids. This urge to get away from Chingford once more. It was as though she needed work, she needed the company and all her colleagues to make her realise she had a place, a role outside of home. That she wasn't just this unemployed single mum, that she wasn't stuck. She wanted to make herself look good again, too, to feel attractive. (She used to turn heads walking down the aisles, strolling through immigration – she's always been too skinny but she was a little fuller then, at least her bum and tits didn't sag so much.) And the job was still sitting there for her. It amazes her to think how good the company used to be over maternity leave (she did have to squeeze in eight months between children, however) and all these other benefits they used to get, thinking about it – proper sick leave for instance and overtime pay as well as a day in lieu if a plane went tech, and two free uniforms each and a dry-cleaning and make-up allowance, and one return ticket for the whole family (for up to six members) anywhere in the world a year. (This was, however, before the union collapsed, a decade or so ago now.) She couldn't have not gone back after Zoe. She owed it to herself. Mike had destroyed enough of her ego. She never expected him to leave, not like that, not then.

However, she doesn't think Gemma and Zoe have suffered too much (there were times when she was worried about the effect Paul, her second husband, was having on them, Zoe in particular, though she did eventually get rid of him) because they haven't turned out badly. She knows they're sweet kids. Zoe's the more serious one, the quieter of the two. Wendy's always thought she takes more after her father, but that Gemma's just like her. She's constantly laughing and joking, egging people on – they even look alike. She loves them both equally of course. No question about that, she thinks, finding herself glancing out of the window but not focusing on anything particular outside, because her mum used to accuse her of favouritism, of leaving Zoe out. She knows that wasn't the case, and even if it had been how come Zoe's never shown any resentment towards her? She believes as a family they've always got along fine. They might see less of each other than in the past but that's because Zoe's in Bedford with her photographer boyfriend, modelling, and Gemma's in Chelmsford doing her beauty course – not because they don't get on, not because she was always leaving out her youngest, and idolising her eldest. It definitely wasn't like that. In fact despite her being away so much Wendy's always thought they are really close. They never get into serious fights. When they were all living at home she was either too knackered or was always trying to make up for the fact she was away such a lot – bringing them presents from around the world, letting them have exactly their way. If anything, she probably spoilt the girls too much, leading them to believe they could have whatever they wanted. Though she knows she didn't smother them at least, she wasn't overbearing – and as she's constantly reassuring herself she thinks they've both turned out okay. They seem happy enough right now, even though Gemma hasn't yet found a proper boyfriend and Zoe's sort of trundling along, saying she wants to be a model, having latched onto this photographer, who Wendy can see is dead gorgeous but knows is going to be real trouble. Then, they are only nineteen and seventeen and a half. When she was Zoe's age she hadn't a clue what she wanted to do. She didn't join the company until she was nearly twenty, after she'd failed at being a hairdresser and a waitress and was sacked from Boots for stealing a packet of tampons. She's always thought life's about luck, about stumbling upon answers – but not expecting too much either. When she went for her interview with the company and saw all these air hostesses wandering around this smart building (the place isn't quite so smart now) looking really glamorous in their dark skirts and lighter-coloured blouses, some having just come in wearing their capes and hats (she's changed her opinion about the uniform since then of course, and the corporate colours) and pulling these huge suitcases behind them as if they were going away for months (not just a few days), and overhearing snippets of conversations about these destinations – Miami and LA and Barbados (they did Barbados then) and New York – this life of travelling, of seeing the world, of getting away, it suddenly made so much sense.

She looks at her watch – this fake Gucci one of the girls persuaded her to buy an eon ago from this scummy stall on Canal Street she'd never have gone near on her own, though amazingly it still works even if some of the gold's beginning to flake off (she later bought Gemma one for her eighteenth – she loves it) – seeing it's 21.15 (New York time – she hasn't changed her watch back yet) and that they've already been going almost one hour and twenty minutes. She's barely done anything yet, except deliver a couple of hot chocolates – and flash her cleavage at Mr Rubinstein. She's surprised time is going so quickly, particularly as she hasn't exactly been engrossed in conversation with her galley colleagues. Then it always surprises her how when you think a flight is going to take forever (even if it's a shorter than normal night flight) it whips by – or vice versa. How hard it is to get any real measure of time on board, which is not helped by the fact you are always jet-lagged, and with the sun suddenly rising and setting at seemingly absurd hours, quite out of sync with your body clock, which is permanently out of sync anyway.

She suddenly leaps off the door, peering aft, spotting the CM as she does so because the curtains partitioning the Business cabin from the First galley area have been left open so the Business passengers know which toilets they're meant to use (according to the way this particular plane is currently config-ured). She sees Selina leave the Business galley and quickly dart into her work station (as if she doesn't want to be noticed doing so, Wendy can't help thinking), she sees her gorgeous figure, which is not that dissimilar she thinks – really – from how she herself used to look on better days years ago, when she was a little fuller, with these great long legs and a nice, shapely bum and decent-sized tits, though if Wendy were her she would go for a bra that was a bit more uplifting – in this world she knows you have to flaunt every inch you've got. She's always seeing aspects of herself in the younger girls, at least she's always looking for likenesses. She doesn't do it on purpose. It's as if she wants to make some connection with her past, her youth, despite it usually reminding her of just how old she is. She feels much older than forty-three (particularly now being so stiff and sore, still the pain inside her seems to be easing slightly. She doesn't think she can have caught anything because if she had it wouldn't

214

have come on so quickly, she was just being silly thinking that earlier, she was being paranoid). Maybe it's working with people who are mostly younger than her, or maybe Joy's right and flying's aged her – all the jet-lag, the terrible food, the cabin pressure, the cosmic radiation (she keeps reading about this in the cabin crew newsletter and how it can make you sterile – not that she especially cares about that). All these millions of air miles. She sometimes wonders whether she'd be looking any younger, any healthier if she'd stuck to being a hairdresser. Or if she hadn't nicked those tampons from Boots – though she was never going to stay there. She might not be ambitious but she at least likes to have the chance to look nice at work. To be in a position where people actually notice you, and not stuck behind a till in a white coat.

She thinks it's lucky she isn't ambitious because she's been a senior cabin crew for ever. She knows she's up for promotion to be a purser, again for about the fifth time and that Selina will be doing a crew assessment of her – though she hasn't a clue what she'll be able to put in it, she's hardly had any contact with her on board, on the outbound or this stretch and down route doesn't count, of course, (if it did she'd be doing okay because she thinks she was a great help to Selina last night). However, she's past caring about being made a purser – the extra money would be nice though she'd probably be stuck in Economy every flight and as much as she loves money she doesn't love it that much. It's virtually impossible not to be promoted eventually and people are always amazed that she hasn't been yet (seeing quite how long she's been with the company). She supposes she usually messes up the final interview with the sector manager. She has been caught out on board before, breaking some procedure when she's under final assessment, though everybody breaks procedures all the time and most decent CMs let you get away with it. She's just been unlucky, or perhaps she's actually been lucky – she doesn't care, really. She supposes she wouldn't mind leapfrogging to a CM's post if that were a possibility because then the financial rewards would be much more noticeable and as far as she can tell the workload wouldn't be too taxing either. Since the new service guidelines came into effect a couple of years ago she hasn't noticed the CMs being overworked exactly. It's largely customer relations nowadays (something she thinks she's had more than a little experience of). However, she knows she's never going to be made a CM, she's missed her chance – she's too old. Her figure and her complexion, and probably her health have gone. They only promote people who look like Selina. Had things been as they currently are when she was Selina's age she's sure she would have been promoted. She's beginning to see herself as this older version of Selina – though not too old to make the most of a down route. She suddenly wonders what happened to Selina at the end of last night. Who she sneaked off with. She realises no one's mentioned anything.

Hey, Tim, Becky says, don't you ever give it a rest? Come on, please. This is not the time – pick on someone else. I have just spent about the last hour dealing with these cretins at the back. First they wanted to know how you change channels, then they asked to have their duty-free now, oh and they all suddenly want the vegetarian meal despite none of them having pre-ordered it. One by one they kept coming up with this shit. They're all plastered too.

You should try the woman in 28H, Tim says, she's like screaming, this is the nightmare flight from hell, just because she's sitting behind a baby who's asleep as far as I can tell. I thought I was going to have to call for the restraints to keep her in her seat. She keeps demanding to be upgraded – Debbie's already told her she can't be – then she said she wanted to speak to the captain, like immediately, and when I said she couldn't at the moment but I'd pass on the message she said her brother-in-law works for the company, in the New York office – is there one? – and we are all going to be in big trouble when he gets to hear about it. Tim's always coming across passengers who say some relation works for the company in the hope they'll be upgraded or given this special treatment. He thinks everyone in the world must be related to someone who works for the company.

So then please, Becky says, have some sympathy – you know what it's like putting up with all this other crap when you're knackered. Don't keep laying into me. All right, I was drunk last night. I did something I shouldn't have. But who hasn't been in a similar situation? And Tim, I really don't want it getting around for obvious reasons. I know that's just about impossible in this business. That it's like asking everyone to change a habit of a lifetime.

Point taken, Tim says. Sorry. He really does wish he could control himself and stop cracking jokes at other people's expense, stop taking the piss out of them. How many times has he thought this recently? I've got that disease, he says, which means I can't control what I say. Things just come out.

Bollocks, Becky says. You just need to grow up.

He watches her turn away but the imprint of her big brown eyes stays on his mind, as if they're boring into him. He's not sure she isn't crying. Her eyes went all watery, like the surface was swimming before she turned away. He thinks, actually, Becky, I have grown up. I have changed. He does feel different. For a start he never used to even wish he could control himself. He has this strange feeling this trip has already affected him radically. He's like sensing how other people react to him and all his joking. How he's touching them – how he might be hurting them. And he's realising for the first time the effect people can have on each other. (Maybe it's because he feels he's beginning to get his come-uppance – or maybe it's the fact he actually is growing up. How some experiences can suddenly age you, he thinks again. Yeah.) He wants to say something else to Becky, to make up for his childish behaviour – for asking her whether she was on top controlling the tempo or whether she'd drunk too much and was lying back letting him do all the work (because last night she'd gone on and on about how she likes to be in control, how as a woman you have to dictate the tempo – she first used the word), but she's still turned away and he doesn't want to get her

**217**

attention if she is crying, though it appears as if she might now be eating something – there's this sudden, overpowering smell of an opened hot, too. He bets it's the braised beef in onion gravy. He hates onions. He hates the way they are always so slimy. He can't believe she's tucking into that.

Wendy thinks she first picked up on her affinity with Selina as long ago as yesterday in crew briefing, almost as soon as she first saw her – even though she was seated towards the back of the room and she couldn't see anything very clearly (her eyesight's definitely getting worse but the last thing she's going to do is start wearing glasses – she'd consider contacts but according to everyone they are useless on board because the air's too dry, particularly when you are so tired all the time, and she reckons she only needs glasses for working so it would be pointless having any). She remembers being struck by this odd thing Selina had done to her hair and which she'd obviously spent hours trying to get right though it still looked completely inappropriate (she's done it again today), and how awful her make-up was (and is again too), as if she'd tried too hard with that also, and how it was exactly the sort of thing she herself would attempt to do. Wendy's never known how to style her hair (despite training as a hairdresser for six months) or apply make-up properly. Actually, she thinks, it's not that she doesn't know how to apply it (she thinks she must have a fairly good idea after all these years watching others) but more she can never seem to achieve the result she's aiming for. When she has make-up in her hand and this image in her mind of how she wants to look, it's as if she suddenly loses all sense of coordination and style. She can't blend the colours. Or make marks that are either distinctive or subtle enough. She's sat in numerous briefings eyeing the rest of the crew – so many faces seemingly perfect and gleaming and framed by interesting-looking hairdos (though not all quite as elaborate as the French girl's, as Valerie's) – feeling how Selina must have felt yesterday, completely out of place. Wendy could tell she was nervous – even with her bad eyesight she could see her hands were shaking as she ran down the roster list. And then she started asking the test questions (including the one about where are the drop down oxygen masks located – you can almost guarantee this question's going to come up) in a terribly faint, warbling voice. Though thinking about it, Wendy's sure she and Selina aren't alone, that there are plenty of crew who at some time or another feel they don't fit in. She bets Becky for instance doesn't always feel totally at home on board, what with her colouring and short, boyish hair and plump little body (not that it stopped her from having a good time down route). That it's only natural. That maybe underneath it they are all pretty insecure about how they look, how they appear. It's just that some hide it better than others. She turns from the bright doorway lighting and pushes her way through the thick fireproof curtains back into the shelter of the baking galley.

# gander

*It's not that he wants to sit chatting to Greg for the next three hours solid, because the guy's hardly on his wavelength and the matter of last night is bound to come up sooner or later and though he's pretty sure he knows what happened to Greg – at least he knows what didn't happen to him – and that in a way it's no more embarrassing than what happened to himself, he's still not sure he wants it to be out in the open (though he's obviously not got as much to lose talking about it as she has, his partner in crime), but Dan hates it when he feels he's being ignored and Greg's said practically nothing to him that hasn't been procedural since JFK. With not long to go before they hook up with their oceanic he feels he might as well not be here at all, in this increasingly stuffy-feeling cockpit, and let Greg fly the bloody thing the rest of the way home on his own – which he seems so keen to do (despite him being up until God knows when last night, and drinking masses like the rest of them) given the amount of patronising instructions he's been shouting way out of line, especially seeing as it's not even his turn to be flying the aircraft – it's Dan's leg. (Although it's up to the captain, the unwritten company rules detail that the left seat flies the outbound and the right the inbound.) Dan decides Greg's been treating him as if he's a second officer on his first transatlantic and that as such he obviously has nothing interesting to say about*

**221**

anything other than what he's meant to come up with regarding the flight plan and the correct operating of various systems. In fact what really gets Dan is not so much being ignored (although he's used to that, he's always been ignored — Suzi says he has a lack of presence) but not being taken seriously. He thinks he can probably blame his looks for this, looking years younger than he really is. He hates his role being diminished, particularly as he's struggled so hard to get where he is. He's struggled against everyone, including in part himself.

He checks the ND (not that he supposes he really needs to but because it's the easiest screen to read, with its sparse, clearly defined colours), seeing they are well over the Cabot Strait heading directly for Grand Bank, Newfoundland, and then on to St John's, estimating to be overhead the St John's beacon in twenty-two minutes. From there they will turn right a few degrees and head out across the Atlantic at flight level 360 on track Bravo, which tonight starts along the 49th parallel at 50 degrees west heading to 51 degrees north at 40 west, and meeting 52 degrees north at 30 west, so as to take full advantage of the upper winds (which are expected to hit around 180 knots and which is why they have such a short flight time, though they've been warned it might get a little bumpy further out and, if they have to request a new flight level and cruise speed, time could easily be added on). The track then takes them on to 52 north by 20 west, finally meeting landfall just south-west of Killarney — a classic eastbound routing for this time of the year. Dan hears Greg making contact with Gander and in reply he can just hear, 'Good evening, flight — ' coming back from the controller on the ground, amid this tremendous crackle, realising they have just slipped into a new ATC zone and that he perhaps should have been monitoring the radio (and the ND) a little more closely — not that it's specifically his job right now. However, and despite all his training, he still finds the static extremely distracting. Half listening in tends to put him off concentrating on anything else and he can't afford to let his mind stray too far for too long (with his brain being the way it is). Even when he's meant to be monitoring the radio he occasionally has real problems trying to decipher exactly what ATC is saying. He supposes the ATC operators have similar problems, too, picking up these spurts of conversation coming from aircraft streaking across the sky way above them, entrapping these voices, grounding this information. Though the thought occurs to him that in a way air traffic controllers have more legitimacy than pilots, at least they have some sort of permanence, always speaking from the same places (proper places clearly marked on a map) despite many of them being pretty remote. Dan's been to Prestwick, home of Shanwick of course.

He waits until Greg's finished with Gander, surprising himself by actually hearing Greg get confirmation of their clearance straight through to the St John's beacon, before saying, I don't know about you, Greg, but I'm getting really hungry. I always need to stuff myself when I'm hungover. I should have asked Lynn for something when she was last in.

Well, we're not going to see her or Nicole for another fifteen minutes or so, says Greg. Why don't you buzz them if you're that desperate?

No, I can wait, says Dan. He doesn't want to appear greedy in front of the girls looking after them, no pilot does – most of them being particularly conscious of the fact they're overweight. Dan wants to appear as if he's just not fussed about the food. He wants to appear like any other captain – experienced, nonchalant, that he's seen it all a thousand times before. What do you reckon's on the menu tonight anyway? he says.

Same as we had last week on the inbound, and the week before, and the one before that, too, all the way back to the New Year, Greg says. They won't change it until Easter. I keep forgetting, this is your first go.

This is my first JFK, says Dan. I have been doing transatlantics for nearly a year in this aircraft, thanks – Boston, Miami, LA, San Fran. I just seem to have missed JFK. Though I've done New York more than once as a second officer. It's all there in my notes. Dan's now wondering whether Greg even bothered to glance at them yesterday.

Of course you have, says Greg. Sorry.

That's okay, says Dan. I can't imagine what it must feel like to be you – you know, with so many thousands of hours of flight time under your belt. He looks back at his idly flickering displays and up at the frozen air slamming silently into the windscreen and the stars filling the sky forever beyond. He suddenly picks out the north polar constellation Ursa Minor, the orange hue of Kochab some ninety-five light years away – sensing that Greg's just not taking him seriously again, that he's not regarding him as *a fully qualified pilot, as one of the boys. Though he knows he's probably not helping the situation himself being slightly impertinent, slightly sarcastic (he's been to numerous seminars on cockpit behaviour and how to cope with in-flight stress, which all mention how quickly things can get out of hand if one person on the flight deck is intent on winding up the other person and just how important it is to maintain a receptive, fully communicative atmosphere), but how's he meant to react?*

*Tell me, Greg, Dan says, do you ever get bored with it? The flying I mean, not the food. Dan doesn't actually intend this to sound facetious, or sarcastic, he really wants to know because, although he hasn't been flying the transatlantics for very long, he's beginning to find the repetition, the way everything is always done in exactly the same way, a little tiring (though he would never admit this to anyone, no one who isn't in the business, certainly not Suzi or his dad). Either that or he wonders whether the job is not quite living up to his expectations – well, he thinks, it's not like going to the moon. However, it occurs to him he might just be thinking this because he's not being taken seriously on this trip – he doesn't remember feeling at all bored on the Boston run last weekend, when he got on with the captain much better. Also he doesn't want to sound as if he might be mocking Greg now because he's suddenly feeling a little sorry for him – he's getting to his better nature (despite what Suzi says, Dan knows he has feelings, that he doesn't just think about himself all the time). He's beginning to realise there is something a bit desperate, a bit sad about Greg. Thinking about it he supposes he noticed this on the way over – how Greg was looking at the cabin crew, the CM in particular. Dan can see he's what Suzi would call a real lech but thinks he isn't – thinks he's just putting on the charm. (Dan's not certain it isn't an age thing, a generational thing, but knows that's no excuse, not in this business, not anymore.) He's also realised quite how unfit the guy is – the way he has to keep going to the toilet and how he wheezes all the time and looks so puce, as if he might keel over at any moment. And how he's got these really unsocial habits – he can't seem to stop farting or burping, or rearranging his balls, or swearing. Dan thinks he must have almost given up caring how he appears to others.*

*It didn't used to be boring, Greg says, not quite so predictable. Neither the flying nor the extra-curricular activities. He laughs. Nothing was as* controlled, as automated, he says. And the schedules weren't anything like as tight of course. We'd get five, six-day stop-overs on the West Coast – can you imagine? A ten-hour duty ceiling. On board relief pilots. Double days in lieu. We were our own bosses. We pretty much dictated our salaries, the perks. I don't know what you've let yourself in for. I'm glad my time's nearly up, I am. You still get that feeling when the air's over the wings and the aircraft lifts into the sky, as if it's being pulled away from the earth, that you're moving into this different world – I'll miss that of course. But the airline business is not what it used to be. It's not the same. They've made it too competitive. No one cares about us today, the people who actually fly for a living – the pilots, the cabin crew. We've become completely disposable. And I tell you what, you won't get any more nights like last night. Okay, everyone might be feeling a little sheepish today, it might not have gone according to everybody's plans, but that's the nature of these things. They get out of hand. I remember the room party I had the first time I flew into JFK. It was like the final indoctrination into this other world – from where I've since discovered there's no turning back. He laughs again. Are you listening, Dan? he says. There's a different mindset now. Last night was the end of an era.

Thank God, says Dan. I wouldn't want a repeat of that in a hurry.

It'll go down in company history, says Greg. People will be talking about it for years.

Christ, I hope not, says Dan.

Did something you already regret? Greg says. I can't believe it, coming from the man who's into being – what was it you said on the way out? – non-exclusive? Ha. What a load of bollocks. We used to have nights like that at least once every down route.

And always manage to get back on the aircraft in one piece? Dan says.

Always, says Greg. We had the constitution. Plus we used to write the rules, don't forget.

Maybe we're more professional nowadays, Dan says. A little more together. As pleased and surprised as he is that Greg suddenly seems to be making the effort to talk to him, to open up, Dan still can't get rid of this feeling that he's talking down to him, that he's lecturing him. He hates it when older people assume they know everything just because of their age. Okay, he thinks, maybe he does have a chip on his shoulder about people *not taking him seriously, he probably is hypersensitive about it, but he's finding Greg going on like this, making him out to be some shy, inexperienced teenager almost more uncomfortable than their previous silence. He can't get around the guy.*

*Not as desperate? How old are you? Greg says. Twenty-six, twenty-eight? I remember being your age – I remember being young and keen, having just qualified, thinking I had everything ahead of me. Thinking I was in control. Shall I tell you something else?*

*Oh, please go ahead, says Dan. I'm all ears. Not removing his headset he glances at the ND, then shifts his gaze out of the side window, waiting for Greg to come up with some other fantastic piece of patronising information. He sits up in the seat a little, taking his feet off the foot rests, stretching his legs either side of the stick before placing them on the floor, because he doesn't want to see the stars, the night sky for once, as if, subconsciously, he doesn't want to face his dreams, the future, but what's below them, the ground, the past, reality – as if he wants to connect with that. Immediately he sees scattered cloud, rolling, globular cloud, altostratus he thinks (though he's not as adept at defining cloud as he should be – he failed his meteorology paper the first time he took it, maybe because he couldn't get his head around the Latin with it already being stuffed full of so much Greek, all these names of stars and constellations – and if he's unsure of a specific cloud formation he generally picks on altostratus, finding it a pretty safe bet because it can incorporate so much), with the moonlight, with what little moonlight there is creating shadows on the cloud, and in the breaks he sees rough, snowy, inhospitable land and the lights of two small towns, perhaps Plancentia and Carbonear (he's studied the route map – realising something at least has stuck) and he knows St John's should be coming into view any moment dead ahead, depending on the cloud. St John's, the last aerodrome this side of the Atlantic, he thinks, the last place they can put down (between here and the equal time point anyway – which is just short of 32 degrees west tonight) if an emergency should arise (which of course it won't because they never do – and Dan thinks perhaps Greg's got a point about it all having become so predictable and he worries again about the job not quite living up to his expectations, something that really hasn't occurred to him before this flight).*

*It just goes so fast, Greg says. That's what's else. These last twenty-five years, ever since that first party in New York. Maybe it was because we were having so much fun, living life to the full, never being in one place for long, thinking it would go on forever, taking it all for granted – you still with me? As much as you think you're in control, once you've slipped into the frame there's nothing you can do to slow it down, to alter the course. When I catch myself in the mirror nowadays I don't always recognise who I'm looking at – I've got so fat, so red in the face. And I get these pains all over my body. My system's packing up. Spending so much time on a flight deck it's easy to lose touch with reality – to shut yourself off from the outside world. To forget what happens down there.*

*What does happen down there? Dan says, beginning to understand what Greg's saying, thinking about Suzi and his flat in East Grinstead and his parents in Swindon. And he realises what he did last night perhaps wasn't a mistake, that maybe it was meant to happen, the final indoctrination (as Greg would have it) into this new life. A way of simply putting yet more distance between himself and Suzi – the whole prospect of marrying her, of spending the rest of his life with her. She's never understood him or his job – his obsession with flying, with avionics, with new technology, with the cosmos, with seeing into the future.*

*I don't know, says Greg. I've never given it much of a chance.*

*But you're married, you've got a daughter, says Dan. A home in – where is it? – Gerrards Cross? He wants to know how Greg works all this into the equation, because he can't see how it fits. He's getting this very clear idea of these two separate existences – a life involved with home and family, a continuation of the past, and one that exists elsewhere. You must have made some effort, he says.*

*I suppose when I was younger I thought anything was possible, Greg says, if it even consciously occurred to me like that at the time. I imagine I was under the impression I could hold it all together – that the money, the perks would be enough to keep them happy anyway. Most families work on that premise, don't they? But I was away so much I didn't realise what was happening. I didn't realise how far apart we were growing, how completely different our lives were. And of course there were the odd dalliances, my one big weakness, which only enhanced the tension, the distance. I don't know. Maybe I was trying to live two lives, to be two* people. I know I wasn't being fair to my family – I can recognise that more clearly now. I don't know why – perhaps because I'm running out of time. Then I wasn't being honest or fair to myself either. I was living this pretence. I wonder, Dan, whether it's really possible to have anything like a normal home life, actually to be happily married and do this job – not long-haul. Is anyone happily married anyway? My wife doesn't understand me – she never has. That's part of the problem. When we got married I bought her this book on flying, with loads of pictures and diagrams explaining very basically how aircraft work. It might even have been one of those Ladybird books, you know, for children, but she's never even bothered to read it. She's just not interested. I would have done that at least. Had there been something she was really interested in I would have made the effort to learn about it, to understand it. She hates everything to do with flying, except the fact that it's a means of getting her to some fucking Caribbean beach – that's her passion, lolling around in the sun.

In my experience, Dan says, it doesn't matter what it is, flying or motor racing, computers, space exploration, whatever, if there's something you're really into you can bet your girlfriend won't be. It's always the way. Women think differently. They're like a different species. Dan thinks of Suzi and whether he's ever going to find someone who's right (he's thirty-one and already he feels all this pressure on him to get married, not just from Suzi but his parents, too, even the few friends he has left from growing up in Swindon – as if from where he comes from you have to be married before you're taken seriously). He thinks of last night and how although this girl he ended up with (who picked him up to be precise), is not exactly his type that there's something sort of sexy about her – she was certainly pretty wild when she eventually got her clothes off, like a breath of fresh air after Suzi (though they were both smashed) and how in many ways, increasingly, he's pleased it did happen. The more he thinks about it. Plus she made him laugh – he can tell there's something very natural about her. He's been avoiding her today, of course, which he feels a bit bad about, though what's he meant to do, with her being in her position? In the line checking out of the hotel he saw her and she smiled at him, he's sure, but he didn't sit with her on the crew bus. That would have been a dead give away. He tries to convince himself that he didn't sit

228

*next to her because he was only being considerate, he was only thinking of her interests and not because he was embarrassed.*

*I don't know, Greg says, where I've gone wrong – whether it's the flying or the women. You know, now you've mentioned it I could probably do with something to eat myself too. I wonder how busy those girls are.*

*I wonder how busy Selina is, says Dan. She hasn't been up yet. Although he doesn't particularly want to discuss last night in any more detail (what exactly he got up to and with whom) he can't help wondering what Greg has to say about Selina.*

*Hello, Gander, says Greg, this is flight –*

*He watches Greg adjusting his mike but Greg doesn't look his way, suddenly and conveniently having to relay their position to Gander (as Gander nevertheless stipulated they must do when over the St John's beacon) and ask for final clearance for their oceanic, so he turns to the side window again expecting to see the lights of St John's below, the capital of Newfoundland located on the northern tip of the Avalon Peninsula at 52 degrees west, and 47.5 north, but the cloud cover has thickened and he sees no sign of the town at all, only this faintly glowing cloud and he looks up into the starry blackness, at the imperceptibly slow moving suns of the celestial sphere, the mind-blowing deepness of space, sensing the aircraft leaving sight of land, pulling away into night proper. He realises he has butterflies in his stomach, but he's not sure why.*

Shifting a meal along the counter out of Carlo's way (the tagliatelle with wild porcini, pine nuts and sun dried tomatoes) so he can finish preparing Mr Jong's (for some reason Wendy has no difficulty remembering this passenger's name, even though technically he's not one of hers) watercress and chicory salad, which he's requested to have at the same time as the pasta and which she'll shortly have to serve him herself because, although Nigel took his order (as he's his passenger), he's disappeared again, she thinks, in the way she often thinks of things entirely unrelated to what she's actually doing, that it was so frigging cold this morning there was no way she was going to walk far (even if her limbs would have been able to carry her and she didn't have this frigging sore fanny). So as soon as she reached the corner of 50th and Lexington, where the wind really struck – it was blowing straight uptown – she immediately flung her hand in the air, like she was on automatic, and because it was a Saturday and midtown wasn't nearly as choked as she has seen it midweek she managed to get a cab within a couple of minutes (had there been one outside the hotel she probably would have leapt into that but there are never any cabs waiting outside the crew hotel – it's as if no one knows the place exists), for which she loudly thanked God as she slid onto the back seat, shivering.

She had arranged to go shopping with Debbie and Nicole (about the only two hosties who showed any interest in accompanying her) but when she finally got back to her room and had a bath (a good hour's worth of soaking) and did her hair and make-up (which took at least another hour) she couldn't reach them in their rooms and presumed they'd already gone. She half thought she might bump into them in Bloomingdale's (where they'd discussed going) but she didn't – she saw a few of the others though, who she wasn't expecting to see up and about, in the land of the living. Still she's getting used to shopping on her own. She used to do everything down route with someone or other but she's finding as she gets older (and her colleagues that much younger) it's harder assembling a group. It's not so much that people want to go to places she wouldn't dream of going to, that they don't have anything in common, because she'll give most things a try – all these supposedly funky shoe shops etcetera (if it's not make-up or lingerie it's shoes), even if it makes her feel about 102 because she's always thought the one area of clothing where you can't ignore your age is your footwear – it's more they don't seem particularly keen for her to accompany them, as if her very presence makes them feel older and more inhibited (when in fact, she should have the opposite effect, though she knows they'll change their views about this one day – as she eventually did).

Realising too late that Lexington goes downtown and Bloom-ingdale's is uptown (not that she wouldn't have got a cab but she might possibly have walked to 3rd rather than Lexington, though the hotel is that much nearer to Lexington) it took longer than she imagined to get there (the main entrance anyway, the one that leads straight into the beauty hall), seeing as the traffic wasn't too bad, however it was a gloriously bright winter day and steam was erupting from the middle of the road – one of the things she loves about NY in winter – and the pavements were sparkling and sun was pouring into the taxi, instantly warming her, so she soon forgot about the cold and her tingling fingers (she hadn't been able to bring her best gloves because Gemma's nicked them and she doesn't think her spares are suitable for New York – for shopping in Chingford certainly, but not Manhattan) and after spending so much of the day already in the hotel she didn't particularly mind the fact it took longer than it should have, being out in the open (albeit in the shelter of a cab), or that it cost $4.75 without tip.

She's surprised she remembers the weather so clearly because it's not something she normally notices much (being part of the natural world), unless she's on a beach or by a pool, or freezing her tits off waiting for a cab. When she's on board she notices the slightest changes in the temperature or the lighting or the oxygen level or the pressure, of course, but proper weather, what you get outside, largely passes her by, or so she's always thought. However, when she went out earlier today – suddenly being stunned by the cold and the brightness, the way the sun was angling onto the buildings, seemingly melting the glass, and the way the shade swept across the street, so darkly you could almost fall into it, this contrast – it was as though she were taking in everything afresh. She now realises, after last night, she was seeing things differently – in a way.

She should have been braver and stuck outside. She thinks she should have hobbled over to the ice rink in Central Park where they always used to go on bright winter days, when the guys running the skating knew exactly who they were and always put on Frank Sinatra's 'Come Fly With Me' and then appeared on the ice to show off and chat them up, asking for free flights to

Rio or Acapulco, or anywhere in the Caribbean – as if they could really do that – because as a group, Wendy thinks, not in uniform, they always looked stunning (even if their ice skating wasn't up to much, which perhaps was the point – they wanted assistance, they wanted to be helped around the rink, despite some of the guys being a little too liberal with their support). It suddenly occurs to her how much she loved being a part of that scene, as if they were just out to have fun, without ties, living for the moment, and how it doesn't seem to be like that anymore. Because, she presumes again, she's too old – she's too old to be having fun, to be living for the moment, to be included. Though she's not certain the younger ones even go ice skating anymore – maybe the crew around Selina's age, those in their thirties but not Becky's contemporaries, not the teenagers. She can't remember the last time she heard any of the juniors talking about it, which she thinks is a shame. And she wonders whether they still take the discounted helicopter rides around Manhattan either, or go to the top of the Empire State Building – the touristy stuff they all used to do again and again because they'd always done so. Because it was a laugh, because they enjoyed the familiarity. They were just following their peers. And yet she thinks there was still this great feeling of freedom. Maybe it comes from not having to think too hard, she wonders, from not being too conscious of what you are doing, from not having to plan too far ahead. The more she thinks about it the more she can see how the younger girls would regard all these things they used to do as naff. She finds attitudes change so fast nowadays she's never sure what's in and what isn't – what you're meant to be doing. (She's happy to tag along, of course, to be part of any new scene, though no one seems very keen to have her.)

However, not thinking at the time about Central Park or the ice skating, or even how alone she was, she simply got out of the cab, paid the extortionate fare and darted into the chequered cosmetics hall (a few years ago she did her kitchen floor at home in black and white lino to remind her of Bloomingdale's), which she's sure appeared a little brighter than normal, more full on.

But it suddenly occurs to her that she might have been under this impression she was seeing things differently, somehow afresh, because she'd had so little sleep and her head was ringing. She knows how distorted things can appear after a night of it.

If she actually needs to buy any cosmetics she heads for Macy's, she leaves Bloomingdale's for just looking, for wandering the aisles testing and sampling (very occasionally she might treat herself to something small – a beauty tool, or a lipstick). She's stopped seeing the point in spending a fortune on make-up, on any of these hot new brands the kids go nuts for (she's always having to bring back stuff for Gemma and Zoe), knowing she isn't skilled enough to be really adventurous (though that doesn't always stop her from experimenting with what she's got, or wishing she could look different). Plus if she's short of time, as she was today, she usually heads for Bloomingdale's, it being the nearer of the two, as the crew hotel is on East 50th Street between 3rd and Lexington, the same old dump they've been put up in forever (some things don't change, she thinks, except perhaps the hotel's got even dumpier – she's always finding pubic hair on the sheets and revolting stains around the toilet). On warmer days she often walks, joining this trail of cabin crew snaking up Lexington (going against the traffic of course). The girls always stick out a mile with their blonde hair having been specially let down for the day because they're in casuals and are flaunting themselves for all it's worth. No one eats breakfast in the hotel (if it does breakfast anymore). Most people tend to stop at the Broadway Diner, which is about halfway, for a freshly squeezed juice and a bagel (because bagels are almost fat-free but still fill you up, despite the fact they seem to give everyone constipation). Wendy normally just has coffee. It used to be coffee and a ciggy when that was allowed in the place and before she tried to limit her smoking to night-times only – not that she's always sure when that is, of course. She's never been big on breakfast. She's not really into eating at all. She thinks she probably starved herself for so long when she was younger she's simply lost her appetite. She never snacks on board. Just the smell

**233**

of aeroplane food makes her retch, though she does find working in First, with only fourteen passengers and this new system of serving food when it's requested (which on a night flight like tonight isn't exactly often) is so much more bearable than Economy, when you have to deal with hundreds of hots and a meal service can literally take hours – when the smell seems to cling to you like mud. (Wendy used to keep her uniform in the spare cupboard in Zoe's room because of the smell.)

She bumped into Becky by the MAC counter. She was with the French girl, Valerie, though she didn't recognise her at first because she hadn't done that incredible thing with her hair and she looked surprisingly plain. (Normally Wendy thinks the girls look better out of uniform than in it, with their hair down, how they obviously want to appear, but she thinks Valerie probably looks better, at least more sophisticated, all done up ready for work.) Becky's hair, of course, was exactly the same – short and crispy-looking. She was rubbing lipstick on her hand, laughing. The last time Wendy had seen her was about three in the morning being pulled out of Greg's room. She was pretending she didn't want to go but everyone knew she did. Indeed the way Wendy remembers it Becky had instigated the whole situation. A few of the girls from Economy were even cheering, Debbie and Marissa certainly, though she can't remember if Valerie was too. She has no idea what Becky and Valerie were laughing about in Bloomingdale's by the MAC counter but when she caught Becky's eye from the other side of the counter (by the skincare), Becky suddenly stopped laughing and said, 'Oh, hi,' in this clearly dismissive tone before shifting along a bit and hiding her face behind a mirror. Valerie didn't even say anything before joining Becky out of her view, as if they were in league. Feeling rebuffed Wendy wanted to say, well, she wasn't one of the people who'd been cheering her on last night, laughing at her as she left Greg's (she was already trapped herself by then, or at least on the way, she realises, to fulfilling what she'd set out to do after her earlier hiccup), instead she just said, 'See you on the bus.' That's what you always say when you bump into a cabin crew down route and don't feel it's appropriate to stop to chat, or indeed if you're trying to avoid someone. And as she turned away herself she saw Selina across the beauty hall, by the Trish McEvoy counter. She knew it was her right away but because she was wearing a hat and she couldn't see her ponytail thing, and she was with someone, a man she didn't recognise though initially thought might be David from Business, he certainly had that sort of build, she found herself drifting in her direction, just to make doubly sure (and to have a closer look at who she was with of course). Though not wanting to appear too nosy, or spoil things for her, she moved from pillar to pillar surreptitiously and just as she was approaching the counter, a couple of steps away – she could even hear Selina humming this tune, which she knows she knows, it got stuck in her head too for the rest of the afternoon, but she still can't think what it's frigging well called (as is the way with her and music) – Tim tapped her on the arm, saying, 'Fancy seeing you in here.' She's aware Selina left Greg's before Becky but she doesn't know who she left with. She thinks she must have been in the toilet at the time, touching up her make-up, pretending to decide whether to go for it or not (she'd made up her mind much earlier, of course). She's always talking to herself in the mirror. Telling herself to do something. Trying to work out what she really wants – who she really is. Pulling these ridiculous faces as if she just can't take herself seriously. And when she turned round, having chatted to Tim for a few minutes, they'd gone.

She leaves the galley, carefully balancing Mr Jong's two plates on her right arm, the salad and the pasta, so she can use her left arm to sweep aside the curtain, thinking maybe she's not seeing things differently at all today – from some great vantage point, or because everything's somehow out of kilter after last night – but that she's just seeing things how she used to. Before she started to blank stuff out, what she couldn't bear any more – all this feeling. Before she became so unreceptive, so hard. Before she went into some form of self-denial. (Zoe's always coming up with these phrases, telling her she needs therapy – her own daughter.)

*Dan quickly verifies their position – glancing at the map on the ND and cross referring this information with the FMC coordinates – waiting for the Selcal to respond, which Greg has just set up. The chime goes and Dan glances over his shoulder to the rear of the centre console where he sees the Selcal call sign on the radio selection box light up. He removes his headset, careful not to dislodge his glasses, scratches the top of his head, where the headset has been pressing, thinking at least he doesn't have to make any announcement to the passengers. Current company policy is to keep announcements from the flight deck to a minimum during night flights (until the final approach anyway). The CM is even meant to take responsibility for the turbulence announcements this way round, whether the fasten seat belt signs have been activated by him or not, having a better indication of how many people are strapped in already trying to sleep and if it's necessary to say anything at all, or in what zone something should be said (which usually turns out to be the rear of Economy, because there people are always getting up, clogging the aisles, not having paid the slightest bit of attention to the pre-flight safety announcements – Dan usually manages to avoid the passenger cabins in-flight, especially the zones at the back). Some slight turbulence is expected shortly, forecast in an earlier weather report, and Greg's just told Dan he's heard the pilot of an American Airlines heavy on their routing six minutes ahead of them request a new flight level – not that, Dan knows, this means very much.*

*Dan hates making announcements, either his mind goes blank and he struggles for words (despite having thought them through really carefully first – mapping out in his mind the flight details, the ground they'll be covering, the height, the speed, the air temperature, the estimated time of arrival, plus something witty, and usually ironic, about the cabin crew, or the duty-free, or the latest air miles package – so he can sound both experienced and nonchalant, as if he's said it all thousands of times before of course, just how the captains come across in his mind), or he becomes hugely embarrassed, sensing the captain is looking at him, laughing at him indeed because he sounds so incompetent, so unprofessional, which always makes him lose his place. He supposes it's this feeling of being on display, of being on air in a way, live. He knows he'll get used to it one day but for the moment he realises he needs more practice, he has to build his confidence, and feel less exposed. He thinks what he probably needs is to fly with younger captains who won't all look down on him, who won't be patronising. Though he's finding, oddly, that since Greg started to chat more freely about himself, since the old man's begun to open up (even though it has taken him almost a flight and a half – nine hours or so of flying time with them stuffed together in the same cockpit) he's not feeling as shy and incompetent as he was earlier, so out of his depth. (Not that he still fancies making any announcements.) What Dan is beginning to realise, despite Greg going on a bit (it's as if he now doesn't seem able to stop himself from talking) is that they have more in common than he first realised. Dan can see that in a way they are connecting, they are on a similar wavelength. The thought frightens him a little because this idea he had earlier about Greg being a bit desperate and sad, about Greg sort of having lost control of himself, is still with him too. If anything it's become more enhanced. He's beginning to think Greg's a complete mess – and yet he can see where he's coming from.*

*Pulling on the buckle Dan loosens his lap belt and stretches his back, his lower back, and shoulders, arching his back, feeling his muscles pull and his spine stretch while tipping his head further and further up until he's looking straight at the intricately illuminated overhead panel – this panel like a giant circuit board, like some ingenious but largely neglected map detailing the aircraft electrics, the air conditioning packs, the cabin altitude control settings, the hydraulic systems, the wing and nacelle anti-ice valves, the APU controls, the IRS mode selectors, the exterior light configurations (landing, runway, taxi, navigation, beacon, logo and emergency), the fuel feed pumps and jettison knobs, the equipment cooling overrides, the overheating test and detection panel, the ignition and stand-by power buttons, and most prominent of all the engine cut off and fire handles – things visitors to the flight deck are always bumping their heads on, which you pull down (to cut off the fuel) and then turn (to release the in-built and pre-armed extinguishers). He's only ever had to do this in training but he knows that there will come a time when he'll have to shut off an engine, most likely during start-up or take-off. He knows that despite the extraordinary reliability, the boring automated*

**237**

predictability (as Greg would probably have it) of flying today, occasionally things do malfunction and that the longer you're involved in the whole process obviously the greater the chance is that you'll encounter a serious problem. Most of the older pilots he's flown with have had a bird strike, or an engine blow on them. Or have had to cope with a rapid decompression, or a landing gear failure.

Part of him wishes something would happen now because he's suddenly feeling incredibly tired and needs waking up (but emergencies rarely occur at this stage of a flight, of course – nothing happens mid-flight). He's suddenly swamped by this feeling of over-familiarity, of sameness, of going round in circles. That he's hooked onto this great loop, with Greg simply going round twenty years or whatever ahead of him. He thinks he can almost see his own future. (He also knows that even if an emergency were to suddenly arise there's so much redundancy, so much back-up to cope with almost every conceivable malfunction, that it'll only be a matter of routine, of some preordained procedure or other – as Greg might put it also – to keep the aircraft flying and on course. These aircraft virtually never have to divert for technical reasons. Despite having so meticulously calculated the equal time point, he knows he won't be anywhere near St John's again until he's going the other way on his next transatlantic.)

You know, I think she's having an affair, Greg says, making Dan sit back in his seat properly, making Dan suddenly aware of where he is – the cosy dimness of the cockpit at night, the hush of cruise, and the part he has to play in keeping the aircraft bang on line, as per normal, without hoping for any unexpected hitches, without having to invoke any avionic trickery, because people's lives are at stake. Can you imagine what this means, Greg says, just when I'm about to retire – or let's face it, be retired?

Who? says Dan. He has no idea who Greg's talking about.

Now, after all these years, Greg says. He laughs, a mocking, feeble laugh. She's gone and done this. I've given her everything. Set her up in this dream house, done it just the way she wanted. You should see all this stuff she's put in it – the furniture, the fittings. Everything's top of the range. We've just had a new conservatory built, to her exact specifications, of course. And just when I might finally have some time to enjoy *the place — not that it's exactly how I'd have done it, I can only take so much — she's swiped the ground from under my feet.*

*Who? says Dan again. He still has no idea who Greg's talking about.*

*Jeanette, my wife, of course, says Greg.*

*How do you know? says Dan.*

*Intuition, mate, he says. Plus someone said something to me last night — this woman who I reckon's pretty canny, who obviously knows a thing or two about relationships. She helped me see the situation, my marriage for what it is. She brought home to me what's going on all right. Told me how women work.*

*How's that, then? says Dan.*

*Simple, says Greg, they operate out of revenge. Out of spite. They're always wanting to get their own back. And then I rang her, of course, not that precise moment but this morning, which is something I hardly ever do on a trip, and she didn't deny it, at least not very convincingly. Do you know, I've never asked her anything like that before. It was always the other way around. Her accusing me. I didn't push her but I could tell she was lying. And the strange thing was, rather than being really upset, though perhaps I'm beyond that now anyway, perhaps I'm too old for all that, I suddenly felt powerful. You see I'm in the right for once.*

*Well, I'm sorry, says Dan. He's not sure what else he should say but he says anyway, Are you sure she's having an affair? You're not just imagining it. It wasn't in this woman's interests to make you think that?*

*What, so I would feel better about sleeping with her? Greg says. Come on, we're grown-ups. No, I'm sure all right. I even know the guy — he runs the Lexus dealership, smooth little fucker. It all fits together, I can see that now. But that's beside the point. It's my fault, of course. She's just getting her own back — for all my dalliances. And you know, I don't think I would have minded a few years ago — a couple of months ago even. I've been seeing this gorgeous girl, Paula, she's with the company, though she's currently doing the Far East sector so I haven't seen much of her recently. But considering my job's about to come to an end — I've got a medical next week and I know I'm not going to pass it, I should think I'll fail on my blood pressure alone — it's thrown me. It's really thrown me. Okay, in many respects the marriage has been pretty dead for years — I can't say we have a great sex life any more — but I thought we'd reached a*

*sort of understanding, and there's Emma, the daughter, of course, though
she's not going to be at home much longer, not that she really cares
whether I'm there or not. Sometimes I wonder whether she knows who I
even am. Jeanette and I might have patched things up a bit, especially as
I'm going to be at home all the time. She's not so bad. She's still attractive
– the amount of money she spends on her appearance she certainly should
be. I did marry the woman in the first place. Now this comes along. What
really worries me is where the fuck am I going to live. After I accused her of
having an affair, do you know what she said? She said she no longer
wanted to live with me. She said there was no point in me turning up on
Sunday morning. And you ask me whether I'm sure she's having an
affair and she says something like that? For the first time in my life I'm
actually worrying about where I'm going to live. I won't have some crew
hotel to fall back on, a long-haul next week. Shit, I'm dying for a pee.*

*At the same time as Greg unclips his lap belt Dan hears the door click
open. He turns to see Lynn peering in. As she steps onto the flight deck he
glimpses the quietness of the upper deck Business cabin behind her –
people stretched out under logoed blankets, the emergency exit lighting,
the glow of the galley at the rear, perhaps Nicole, someone in a company
blouse anyway. He feels more tired and confused than ever and yawns,
trying to turn the yawn into a sigh in an attempt to hide the fact he is
yawning. He's in desperate need of oxygen.*

*Hi, guys, Lynn says.*

*I was beginning to think you'd got lost, says Greg, half out of his seat.
Come in, come in, we need some cheering up. I suppose you haven't got
Selina with you?*

*I've hardly seen her, says Lynn. She's been keeping out of everyone's
way for some reason.*

He can't believe he's back in the galley already. It's like he's been
switched onto motor drive tonight, despite feeling he's about to
drop, that he can't move another muscle. He looks at his watch,
sees it's just past 10.30, which means, he works out, it's 3.30 in
the morning UK time – and does it feel it. He's got no idea
where he's getting his energy from – maybe this reserve which
must have built up over all the time he was stuck in Crawley,

when he rarely budged an inch, spending years non-stop in his bedroom, so it seemed anyway. Though trying not to get carried away with this efficiency he reminds himself he is only halfway through the coffee run – he has another twelve rows to go. He tips the dregs from the coffee pot into the trash compactor, getting most of it all over the flap and the controls that no one understands properly anyway (he just presses the most obvious looking buttons) because someone's dumped a load of crap into the sink – meal cartons and burnt rolls etcetera – which they shouldn't have, of course, and which are blocking the plughole. Seeing the soggy rolls reminds him of talking to this really gorgeous-looking guy on what he realises must have been about his first transatlantic (it seems years ago already) who told him that there used to be this fad when everyone, the girls as well as the guys, held contests to see how many rolls they could get into their knickers in any one go, after they'd been warmed – the record stands at eight. This guy – Tim remembers him clearly because he had jet black hair and blue eyes and a trim body and was about five foot ten (exactly the type he goes for, though rarely ends up with) – also told him about this trolley dolly who'd been with the company for years and who, when working in First, used to stir martinis with his cock – to make them extra dry, apparently – and how this led onto a few of the guys having wanking competitions in the galleys and coming all over the canapés and the salad, the hors d'oeuvres, whatever they get to eat up there. So this guy said anyway. Tim's not sure whether he's looking forward to working in Business and First or not – he's definitely not getting his cock out in public. He's never been into that sort of thing, unlike Stuart and Andy who are always revealing themselves, being completely outrageous with each other in public. It's not that he feels inadequate, he just finds he can't get enthusiastic if other people are watching. Plus he's always been slightly squeamish about sex. He's not big into pain or other people's bodily fluids, however well protected they both are. He hates things that are slimy to touch.

What it really amounts to is the fact he's never been able to let himself go – until, he supposes, last night. He still hasn't worked out what came over him. He knows it wasn't just the alcohol, he's been drunker on numerous occasions. Or even the excitement at being in New York for the first time because, except for seeing the interior of this bar (okay, he thinks, it was a pretty swanky place with glass and steel everywhere and all the staff were dressed in an almost fluorescent white but it was no more special than the one he went to in Miami last week, where everyone always goes – the only difference he can recall is that the waiters in the Miami place were dressed in black whereas in New York they were in white), and a few dingy hotel rooms, it wasn't until Saturday morning that he got any real sense of the city. Even in the cab on the way to and from the bar he didn't have much of a view, of how high everything is, not being able to look up because both times he was stuck in the middle of the back seat as this person kept pushing him in there, saying as he was the skinniest (though he knows that that might have been a ploy so he could simply squash in beside him – he remembers this guy's huge, solid leg pressing against his and his arm behind him, keeping him in place, pinning him down). Fear? For some reason this suddenly occurs to him. Perhaps he was simply scared, or at least this rush that can grow out of fear, and suddenly overcome by the feeling, the adrenalin, forgot his inhibitions, being powerless to resist anyway. He's never been that close to a Scorpio before. To Tim being a Scorpio is all about power and emotional primitiveness, darkness and repression. Juggling this intensity of feeling.

Alone in the galley (he has no idea where Debbie can be) and thus, not feeling watched, he chucks some coffee bags into the pot and stuffs it on the bev maker, pulls down the clamping handle and presses brew. He waits for the sound of hot water to splutter through, for steam to rise and the smell of fresh coffee to hit him – anything to take away the stench of nearly three hundred hots which has been lingering poisonously in the galley for about the last hour. After much spluttering the brew lamp goes out and he unclamps the pot and carefully tries to lift it clear but because he's shaking so much, because his limbs don't seem to be doing exactly what he wants them to do, because they've been rendered almost useless by fatigue (he can feel the effects of last night now all right, every twinge reminding him of some aspect of what happened, of his shame, because uninhibited, being quite out of control really, he did something he vowed he'd never do, with someone he didn't even fancy and certainly hopes to never see again – he can't believe what he did, the situation he let himself get into), because he's not concentrating on what he's doing he manages to slop the coffee over the hot plate, some of it spilling onto the counter as well and on down the front of a parked trolley. It makes a loud hissing sound and he looks up, expecting Debbie to have suddenly materialised and witnessed yet another aspect of his incompetence, his unsuitability for promotion to the position of fully fledged junior cabin crew, his unsuitability for a full staff contract (wow, he thinks, big deal), but she hasn't appeared though there's this overpowering smell of burnt coffee, which he knows can still dump him in it but which at least completely negates the smell of old hots. He's always had a difficult relationship with food. He's never been fat, not remotely, but he knows how compulsive he can be, how addictive he finds things – with his free hand he slaps the nicotine patch on his breast, checking it hasn't come unstuck – so he either tries to avoid it altogether or, because he knows he's got to eat some times, he convinces himself he hates all these different things, like onions for a start, which are used liberally in just about everything his mum cooks (when he was younger his friends used to call her the witch because of these awful stews she made, and the fact she had long dark hair and wore hippy clothes, or at least these Eastern garments which she still occasionally squeezes into, especially if she's going out), or noodles because that's what everyone seems to be eating at the moment – stir fried noodles with pork, ginger and spring onion, or whatever. Stuart and Andy have got this thing about Thai food, as does every cabin crew he knows. It's become a fad, in the same way everyone's drinking Pernod and pineapple now. He hates spicy

243

food. He doesn't think he's anorexic, or bulimic for that matter – he only throws up when he's pissed and since he's been working he's found he's been too knackered to do any serious drinking, except last night of course and he wasn't exactly collapsing then, or the other week in Miami, thinking about it, when he was probably more out of it. But he hadn't been to Miami before, or New York. He had to celebrate somehow. Plus he finds being with a group of people he barely knows (despite them all having this thing in common, like being trolley dollies) makes him feel really shy and because he's so shy he reckons he drinks more than he should in the circumstances anyway – being so knackered and with people he hardly knows – and which is why he ends up putting on this act, becoming a sort of caricature of himself, not being able to behave properly. Why perhaps people take him for being someone he isn't. Why he does things he ends up regretting (as in Miami and now last night, of course).

Whereas Miami's still mostly a blur though, the later part of the evening anyway, after they moved on from the bar where all the staff were dressed in nothing but black (so at least he can't remember what he should be ashamed of), the whole of last night is steadily, painfully coming back into focus, from the time they all bundled into the taxis outside the crew hotel – when it was fucking freezing and all of them were shrieking with cold, dancing on the spot, and someone said, Becky he thinks, in fact he's sure it was Becky, 'You need thermal underwear in this frigging weather and I haven't even got any knickers on. The wind's going right up me,' and Greg, or if it wasn't Greg, the first officer, Dan (Tim thinks the pilots are all the same, whatever their age) said, 'Enjoy it,' and Becky said, 'I need more than a blast of freezing air between my legs to get me going,' and everybody laughed even though their teeth were chattering like mad, and he probably said, he's certain he said, 'Bless,' (he was always saying bless until Stuart and Andy told him he sounded like one of those girls who work behind the make-up counter at Boots, and still does when he drops his guard – well it was about minus 20 and he was feeling dead shy at this point) – to when he finally got back to his room at about six in the morning. It wasn't light, though looking out of his window, having struggled for about ten minutes to get the curtains and the blinds open (not realising they were all on this automated track system which you could only activate by using a master switch by the bed), he saw the first traces of dawn falling in the narrow gap between the hotel and the building opposite (which might have been more of the hotel – he found it completely confusing getting around the place, working out whose room was where and which lift you were meant to take to get there).

He supposes he must have conked out for an hour or two before he got back to his room because he remembers suddenly waking finding himself next to this hot, naked man, who was snoring like he's never heard anyone snore before – louder than reverse thrust. He was instantly wide awake – with the jet-lag kicking in, because it was really lunchtime – and he just knew he had to get out of there immediately. He pulled this great hand off his thigh and sort of fell out of the bed. He remembers struggling to get his balance. Indeed all morning he had a problem staying upright, getting his bearings. (He's sure it wasn't just because he was in a strange city. He thinks it was something more fundamental than that – that it had something to do with what was going on in his mind at the time, with coming to terms with what he'd just done. Which in a way he realises is all part of working out who he is, of growing up. Or not.) Though he did manage to pull his clothes on, sort of, and stumble out of the room without him waking up.

Shifting slowly over to the galley exit with the refilled (though not quite full) coffee pot – having put off for as long as possible the daunting reality of going back out into the cabin and serving the remaining rows, almost half a zone's worth – he ruffles his hair with his free hand thinking, ridiculously, that perhaps he can make himself look unrecognisable, at least from afar, from the other end of the cabin, as if he's this new cabin crew who's popped up all of a sudden (realising he's spent most of the day trying to look unrecognisable, trying not to be noticed, which isn't like him at all, despite his inherent shyness). As he reaches the exit he carefully pokes his head around the corner to check all's clear. The curtains are still pinned back and will remain so, under Debbie's orders, until the meal service is finished and everything's been cleared-in. Tim can't begin to imagine when that'll be – it all seems to be taking much longer than it usually does, even though the plane is full. A couple of passengers have already asked him whether he can do anything about the light coming from the galley and getting their meal trays cleared away because they would like to try to get some sleep. He didn't say, fat chance of that in this cabin, darling. He didn't say, either, sorry but the cabin crew aren't capable of moving any faster because we're all totally shagged after a night of it. He thinks, it's like everything is slowly slipping out of sync, that the company's precious Economy product (in the company bumpf, which they are always being bombarded with, everything's a product) is beginning to fall to pieces, that standards are collapsing every-where – he laughs. And looking aft he sees Becky five or so rows away, the back of her small, squat body precariously stretching across the centre section of seats, as if, he can't help thinking, she might be caught hold of and dragged down, among the soiled food trays and dim reflections of the in-flight entertainment system, forever. A cabin crew finally eaten up by her job. In Tim's nightmares about work he's usually invaded in the galley – he's by the bev maker or tending to the ovens when suddenly all these items he's already served start flying up the aisles and back into the galley – mixers and swizzle sticks, packets of nuts and drip mats, food trays and hots, duty-frees and landing cards – closely followed by the passengers, all irate, all demanding their things back, until he's slowly suffocated. Stuart and Andy have nightmares about work also. So does just about every cabin crew he's talked to. Like the job even takes over your subconscious, your dream world.

But Tim watches Becky pull herself clear of the row and as she straightens in the aisle, automatically brushing the front of her pinny (with this guy across the way, who Tim now realises was trying to look up her skirt as she was stretching over the centre seats, suddenly sitting up too – he's always catching men doing this), he sees her slowly, resignedly look over her shoulder, like she's sizing up how much further she has to go, until she's looking directly at him. He smiles, pleased it's Becky who's caught his eye and not this other person, not this person he's been avoiding all day, though he is looking aft and not forward where he's more likely to be coming from (unless the stupid man's snuck into the crew rest area for a quick nap, which Tim would dearly love to be doing right now – as long as the place is empty of course), and she smiles back though he's not sure she isn't grimacing also, that she's going like, help, get me out of here. He mouths need any help?, waving with his free hand, flapping his fingers open and shut as a small child might wave. He's still trying to make amends for being such a jerk earlier. For reducing her to tears in the galley, in front of Debbie, and Marissa and Valerie. And seeing her out there, dealing with the passengers, being groped and leered at, spot-lit in the aisle (that's how it always seems to him anyway with the lights running along the overheads bearing down on you, singling you out), swamped by the stale sweaty air (it always seems that much worse in the centre of a zone), he's suddenly overcome with this idea that she's really vulnerable. That she's stuck in this situation she doesn't want to be in – not just with the hot drinks service, or a few difficult passengers, but with the rest of her life, her life not on board. He decides he wants to help her. He wants to help her to make sense of what she did last night. Okay she was drunk but he doesn't think that's a big enough excuse (he was pretty smashed too but he still knew what he was doing – not that it made any difference). He could tell she was going for it before they'd got to the bar, before they'd even got in the taxi when she revealed to everyone on the pavement outside the hotel that she wasn't wearing any knickers (she was standing right next to the flight crew – she must have said it on purpose). He wants to help her understand why she got engaged to this guy, this first officer whose name he can't remember though Becky did tell him –

along with the fact that she had no idea why she's doing it. He wants her to see what's propelled her into this situation, why it's been preordained by the celestial bodies, the movement of the planetary cycles, the changing patterns of Divine Ideas, and what the future holds for her, what her blueprint foretells – whether she really will get married. (Personally he can't understand, however pressing your paradox might be, whatever the alignment to the Eternal, why anyone would actually go through with it. He can sort of understand why people become engaged, particularly in this business – for the party, to appear wanted, to inspire all this jealousy – he's seen it all. But to actually get married? To live with this other person forever? To deny all others? He doesn't think it's natural. Not anymore. Not today.)

Plus, besides the uncertainty she seems to have over her engagement, he thinks Becky needs to get on top of her relationship with her mother. He thinks she should tell her where to go, because this woman appears to be draining all her confidence – according to what Becky was telling them about her mum last night anyway. He knows his mum's got a lot to answer for – whose hasn't? he thinks – but at least she never puts him down, nor does she act like she's jealous of him or try to compete with him, or get overly protective of her own interests – such as when he started to become involved in astrology. She's only really encouraged him here, like they both have this thing which his dad hasn't a clue about (he doesn't think his dad has much of a clue about anything, except DIY, and he's useless at that) – this special bond, like they're on the same wavelength. His dad hates this. He's always having a go at his mum about how she spoils him, how she indulges him, how she's like trying to turn him against him, his own father. But Tim knows it's only her way of trying to hang on to him, of coping with Lawrence's disappearance – that she doesn't want to lose another son. Ever since his elder brother disappeared – that's how his mother describes it anyway, not that Tim's ever regarded it quite so dramatically, his brother went to America when he was nineteen with a friend and never came back (though he has stopped contacting them) – he's felt this huge pressure to be around, to be almost double the person he is. But despite all these demands from his mum, and his dad too in his strange way he's found he really does get a kick out of astrology. Also, he thinks, thinking back to Becky's situation with her mum, his mum's definitely never tried to pick up any of his boyfriends (not that she would get very far). He can't believe Becky told them her mother wanders around the house naked when she takes her boyfriends to stay at their place. For a start he'd never bring his boyfriends home. It's not that his parents particularly mind him being gay, at least they never mention it, (as if, he's thought, they daren't in case he does a Lawrence), but he'd be so embarrassed for anyone to see where he lives (the moment he passes his probation, if he passes, he's out of there). It's not so much that the house is tiny or that it's stuck in the middle of this ex-council estate (just off the Horsham Road), what really bothers him, after only a lifetime of putting up with it, is how it's decorated. For a start there's his mum's trinkets, all this mystic stuff everywhere (Tim knows she collects it because she thinks it makes her look more credible as an astrologer, in the same way she wears the clothes, that it adds a certain ambience to the house) – statues, pictures, carvings – shelves and shelves of it, most of which she's bought from advertisements she spots in the back of all these astrological magazines she subscribes to (he's amazed it hasn't put him off astrology), and then there's his dad's endless, half-finished DIY projects – like there's this constant battle between the celestial and the consumer durable. He's always working on some new kitchen unit or a car-port, or most recently, trying to replace the windows with these plastic Tudor-style frames (which he keeps proudly stating are guaranteed for ten years, as if that's forever).

Tim realised ages ago that there's a correlation between Lawrence's absence and his dad's DIY activity – the longer they hear nothing the more obsessed his dad becomes with it. It's like he's now on this quest to create the perfect house, which Tim thinks is really sad because however hard he tries he's never going to be able to erase the fact that it's a 1950s semi-detached ex-council house stuck in the middle of an ugly estate on the outskirts of Crawley, directly under the main flight path to Gatwick so it shakes madly every time a plane comes into land (as if, Tim thinks, he really needs to be reminded of work when he's off). He can imagine just how it'll be when he arrives home on Sunday. There'll be his dad's tools all over the place, wires trailing through every room, this noise of drilling, perhaps a couple of windows will be out so the place'll be freezing, and his mum will be shouting at his dad for creating this bloody mess when she's expecting clients and how's she meant to conduct her business when it's like the Arctic in here anyway (since his dad was made redundant last year she's had to work on the weekends as well), and his dad will suddenly stop drilling, as if some sixth sense has told him he's being shouted at – because despite the strength of his mum's voice there's no way he can possibly hear anything above the racket he's making (he's partially deaf as it is) – and shout something back like, 'Where am I meant to put them with every inch in the house taken up by all your weirdo stuff? You need help, Brenda,' – his dad's always saying this – 'it's not normal, there's a limit to how far you can take all this,' like he has a sense of moderation, like he knows when to stop.

On top of all this there's Lawrence's room which is never touched, having been left almost exactly how it was when he last slept there just over seven years ago now (though Tim has an idea his mum still changes the sheets), as if, he thinks, when he does reappear he's going to want to be reminded of just why he left in the first place, that all these memories will come flooding back and he'll be off again like a shot. Tim knows there are no decent CDs in there anyway, or clothes, nothing that's worth keeping – he's been through it all countless times just in case something might have come back into fashion, not that any of Lawrence's things were ever really in fashion in the first place. The only member of his family who has any sense of style is himself, though he's got no idea where he gets it from, not his mum and definitely not his dad – like he's this freak they've somehow managed to produce. Like he appeared from nowhere.

Becky's only a row away now and seeing her so close, seeing her short hair glisten, the dark fur on her neck between her hairline and the collar of her blouse, the tension across her wide shoulders, her surprisingly pale elbows, the way her tights are sagging around the backs of her ankles, the way she's supporting herself against the side of an aisle seat as she's pouring what must be her last cup of coffee, as if she just can't stand straight, clearly tired out, he's sure she must have been avoiding all these issues, that she's afraid of confrontation. That she doesn't really understand or hasn't yet come to terms with where she's coming from, which Tim thinks amounts to roughly the same thing. Because, he thinks, even if you are ashamed of your background, even if you find it so embarrassing you wouldn't dream of taking your friends there, you still can't erase it from your own mind, you can't deny it, not forever. He knows he might have various problems – his shyness and acting up because of it, this thing he has about food, and penetrative sex – but he doesn't think he's particularly avoiding anything. He's fully aware of who he is – he's certain about that.

He's going to suggest to Becky he'll do her chart – for free. This doesn't now mean he's not going to do Selina's as well, though suddenly he's really into the idea of working out Becky's. He's always found Cancerians more intriguing than Librans, with their vulnerability and neediness and irrationality, their un-fathomableness, plus the way they always have to be so much a part of whatever's going on, as well as so clearly representing the bonds that tie them to the past, their family, whether they like it or not. Though what really appeals to Tim is how obviously tied to the heavens Cancerians are, how you can read them like a book. He's itching to delve into her Imum Coeli, to get to her innermost self, the unconscious roots of her personality, all this stuff that's become blocked, or has been repressed. Until now he's always thought of his astrology as a means of getting something he wants, as a way of understanding people and the power this gives you over them, like he can know more about someone than they do themselves, and not really as a way

**251**

of helping people. As a way of helping them to see the shapes and patterns of their lives – their points of access to the Eternal – and understanding the past and what the future holds in store. How everything fits together. The great cycle of time.

If you stand there much longer that coffee's going to solidify, Becky says. You'll have to chip it out for breakfast.

At least I won't spill any, Tim says, oddly feeling a sudden, powerful jolt of turbulence, which knocks him against the side of the galley exit, where the curtain's bunched up, so he adds, when this is going on. I'm all over the place tonight as it is. He realises he'd almost forgotten where he is. He knew he wasn't on the ground but it wasn't as if he were conscious of being in a plane either. It was like – with the heat and constant lulling noise of the engines and air conditioning units, the dulled snatches of conversation, the odd, distant dinging of the passenger call signs – he'd been suspended somehow. Free of the ground but not exactly free to move wherever he wanted. Whoopsie, he says. Another bump hits and the plane begins to buck a bit and he puts his free arm out so Becky can catch hold of it as she stumbles into the galley with her empty coffee pot.

Thanks, she says. I can't say I'm in full control of myself tonight either.

Tim puts his coffee pot back on the counter, thinking if the turbulence keeps up he might get away without having to finish his hot drinks round (he finds the minute bad turbulence hits most Economy passengers forget where they are with the meal service, what they're supposedly waiting for – usually they just want their tables cleared). More turbulence shakes through the plane, as if the plane is suddenly made of rubber and Tim leans against the counter – with this jangling going on all around him and things coming loose and shifting precariously about the surface, such as the duty-free credit card machines which someone has got out early and a couple of rolls of plastic cups and a box of toilet care kits – trying to look completely steady, as if he's been doing this all his life, despite having said he was all over the place tonight (everyone's always putting themselves down, yet acting as if the opposite's true). He watches Becky trying to secure the loose items, quite unconcerned about the turbulence except for the fact that it's making her job that much harder. Tim thinks she looks pretty much in control of herself (despite what she said a moment ago too) and that it might be a good time to bring up the subject of him doing her chart, but all he can concentrate on is how much the plane is tossing him about and for the second time this flight he wonders whether he'll ever get totally used to flying, whether it will feel completely normal to him, the way it seems to appear to Becky. He hears the ping of the fasten seat belt sign, a couple of passenger call sign dings and the echoey crackle of someone switching on the PA.

Ladies and gentlemen, Selina says – Tim hears the CM trying to clear her throat, thinking she doesn't sound too great – we are experiencing some turbulence at the moment so can you please return to your seats and fasten your seat belts. While the seat belt sign remains on the toilets will not be in use. Thank you.

Wow, says Becky, she's actually said something. On the way out we didn't hear a squeak, did we. Nothing even about the duty-free or the new air miles programme. Normally you can't get the CMs off the PA.

She probably got a rocket from Greg, says Tim, particularly for not saying anything when she should have, like when we hit that really bad turbulence – you remember just over halfway through. It was much worse than this. (He feels a bit strange calling the captain by his first name, like he's one of these creeps who make out they're really chummy with the flight crew, but after last night he feels he can hardly call him captain, besides he's forgotten his surname.) Unless they've suddenly changed the rules about who makes the safety announcements and not told us, he says. Who knows, they change the rules so quickly I'm surprised anything gets done how it's meant to.

There's this rumour going round, says Becky, that she's cracked, that she's suddenly become afraid of flying. She sounded a bit nervous, didn't she? Angela in Business heard her scream yesterday. She's right next to the CM's office.

You're joking? says Tim. Whoopsie. He feels the plane drop yet again, though much more violently than before, like they've just gone over a cliff. He knows it's pointless for him to even try to look cool, to act calmly – he's never been able to mask what he's really feeling, his true emotions (one of the reasons why he believes he's so aware of who he is). But he'd hate for Stuart or Andy to see him now, beginning to get edgy over a little turbulence, despite the fact he's becoming less certain it is just a patch of turbulence and not something more catastrophic. He feels like he's being shaken to the core.

No, says Becky. That's what people are saying. It does happen, I've seen it before, particularly among the hosties who have been here forever. I imagine it's like they've gone as far as they can go. That they just can't take it anymore – all the travelling, the jet-lag, the lack of fresh air, the biliousness, being bumped around, the awful uniforms, not knowing who their partners have been screwing when they've been away. It builds up over the years, all this abuse and aggravation, until they finally crack. It'll probably happen to me one day. And you. When we've been here long enough. I expect it gets to us all in the end.

*Hang on, says Greg, let's stick it out for a bit longer. It'll pass. It always passes – how many times have I said this over the years? Christ, all I seem to do nowadays is repeat myself – well not for much longer. He laughs. We've got more resilience than those bloody Yanks, he says. I don't know, I used to enjoy chatting to them on the commercial channels. I liked their style, you know how relaxed they are, how unstuffy. Dan hears Greg laugh again. But they're all beginning to sound the same to me, Greg says. Boring. Bloody boring. Sure this and sure that, always wishing you to have a nice flight. All right, I might repeat myself, in fact I know I repeat myself, but I don't think I'm insincere. I'm not trying to hide anything by sounding totally compliant all the time, or by being overly friendly. I think what I have to say is mostly pretty straight forward. That lot never are – there's always some hidden agenda they're trying to push. You never know quite where you are with them. I used to think we'd been left in the dark ages with the way we have to adhere to*

*standard RT phraseology, this ridiculously formal way of saying things,
but I'm not so sure now, maybe we need certain guidelines, certain rules.
At least then there's no mistaking. Nothing can be misinterpreted.
Besides I don't think we're so backward. In fact, the more I think about it
the happier I am we're on the return. I've had enough of America for this
lifetime. Come on, Dan, this turb isn't anything compared to what we
had on the way over. This is peanuts.*

*Okay, Greg, says Dan, realising Greg's starting up again. Whatever
you say. He only mentioned the idea of requesting a new flight level
because he remembered hearing the American Airlines aircraft just ahead
of them doing so and he thinks the turbulence actually is getting worse,
even though they appear to be in a lull at this precise moment. He tightens
his lap belt waiting for the next wrench, tightening the muscles in his
stomach, which feels decidedly empty, considering he's just eaten his
meal, though it often feels this way during turbulence, whether he's
recently eaten or not. In fact he's just had the surprisingly tasty fillet steak
with ravigote butter, french beans and fondant potatoes, plus the rhubarb
crumble tart, which he downed in about two minutes flat without pausing
between courses (how all pilots eat) despite having plenty of time before
the next waypoint at five three north three zero west, which is when
they'll sign off with Gander and link up with Shanwick (the mid-point of
the Atlantic crossing as far as ATC is concerned, though tonight not quite
the equal time point between the aerodromes at St John's and Shannon,
this will occurg some five minutes earlier). Although Greg is currently
taking care of all the ATC of course Dan knows this is one of those reports
he should pay attention to as well.*

*He still wouldn't have minded changing flight level, slipping through
the jet stream in search of more solid air. When he thinks of the jet stream
he thinks of a hollow tube through which air passes at high speed and not
immediately of the World Meteorology Organisation definition which
was relentlessly drummed into him at flying school (given that he had to
sit his meteorology paper twice) and which states, if he can remember
correctly − a strong narrow current of air travelling at a speed of not less
than 60 knots and confined along a roughly horizontal axis in the upper
troposphere or stratosphere, characterised by strong vertical and lateral
windshears. When he thinks of windshear he knows technically that it*

**255**

occurs where bands of fast moving air meet slower moving air with the resulting sudden changes of wind speed (coupled with temperature and density) marking the specific boundaries, or shears, as they are more commonly known. But mostly he thinks of hitting windshear as falling off a cliff. It's so obviously felt that he can only really equate it with feeling, not theory, unlike a jet stream. To Dan a jet stream is this invisible, unfelt force that just so happens to be the key component determining the coordinates of the transatlantic airways. This chasing after the wind in the case of east west traffic (with the anti-clockwise direction of the spinning earth determining their westerly path) and going the other way the desperate attempts to avoid it (by either routing higher or lower latitudinally or occasionally in between individual streams, though typically a jet stream is some 200 nautical miles wide, 12,000 feet deep and around 1500 nautical miles long), which is why the specific coordinates of the tracks change with such regularity. And though Dan knows they have a pretty good idea of where the jet streams are (as they are detailed on the weather maps and constant pressure charts provided by dispatch), he finds in reality you still just drift into them, not being conscious, not physically, of any change in the aircraft's stability or cabin pressure or ultimately any change in speed (unless you're constantly observing the screens) and you are shot along regardless – this seemingly effortless gathering of ground speed, this free momentum (even the Mach read-out in the PFD remains steady). How in a way jet streams defy time and distance – the principal parameters of travel, to him.

He wouldn't have minded changing flight levels because it would have meant doing something to keep himself alert. With his stomach obviously full yet strangely empty-feeling (it's still trying to work out where it should be in relation to the now sudden lack of turbulence, though the aircraft is still wavering a little as if they're about to be struck by one really big last shock) and with Greg rambling on the moment he gets a chance (Dan can't seem to stop the guy) and the seemingly suffocating airlessness of the cockpit, with having to stare at these panels of warmly glowing switches and idly shimmering screens, though looking up every so often into the imperceptibly slow moving darkness, this infinite, glittering darkness – as if here lie all the answers, he thinks – while trying to work out whether he really has the guts to tell Suzi he's no longer interested in her as well as

*contemplating the idea of trying to get some message to the poor girl he
screwed last night and has completely ignored since (his feelings of guilt
over the matter seem to be growing in direct correlation with an urge to see
her again), with so much at stake, overwhelmed by indecision, he's
finding he really is struggling to keep on the ball tonight. He always tries
to avoid having to make decisions – having to face up to reality, as Suzi
puts it – which partly explains, so she also maintains, his obsession with
playing computer games or looking through his telescope all the fucking
time, why he never pays her any attention, why he never considers her
wishes and needs within their useless relationship.*

*He yawns yet again, turning away from Greg once more and shading his
mouth with his hand – a deep, shaky yawn, as if he's drawing in the last
gasp of air left in the cockpit. Although Dan knows Greg probably
wouldn't notice or care if he saw him yawning so expansively anyway.
What can he possibly say, he thinks, being only too conscious of the fact that
Greg hasn't exactly been the model of discipline and reliability, of
awareness and responsibility these last forty-eight hours. However, neither
has Greg been entirely consistent regarding his attitude towards his career
and position (as captain of a British airliner currently flying from New York
to London with 386 passengers and sixteen crew on board), or even his
domestic life, and although Dan's finding him increasingly irrational
(Suzi's always calling him irrational but he knows he's not irrational – he
might not be everything she wants him to be all the time but he's not
irrational, he's more solid than that), he can't quite decide whether Greg's
blaming himself or his job for what's gone wrong with his life, whether he's
really looking forward to early retirement or not, despite his problems with
his wife. He still thinks that somewhere, deep down, the old man cares
about things more than he's letting on. And that for some reason he's just
not being totally honest or up front with Dan (despite having just said that
what he has to say is mostly pretty straight forward – far from it, thinks
Dan). That he's putting on some sort of a show for him.*

*Fighting his drowsiness, this almost irrepressible feeling of drifting off –
as if he's suddenly flying through thick fog without any instruments,
without any indication of a horizon, which would quickly of course
become impossible – half-conscious, blinking, unable not to let his eyes
close for longer and longer stretches of time (exactly how he used to feel in*

*the afternoons at flying school when they were going through the technicalities of the fuel feed system or the intricacies of the inertial reference system, or how to interpret synoptic charts) he suddenly alights upon the idea that maybe Greg's simply trying (though rather hopelessly, because that's the way he is) to protect his job and the myths surrounding being a pilot, a pilot of the old school — belonging as he does almost to the first generation of pilots to make a whole career out of commercial flying, these men (because they were only men then) who came along in the late 1960s and early 1970s when jet travel started to boom, when the jumbo jet took to the skies and redrew the world, at least our sense of distance. That he needs, despite having these ambiguous feelings about it, to believe in it, to protect it, to promote it, because it's been the major factor in shaping his adult life. It's him through and through. Dan thinks he can understand this — in a way he feels it's where he's coming from too. Already he's finding he has to exaggerate what he does do at work for the benefit of his dad, for Suzi, his few friends who aren't in the business. He's finding he makes up stuff about how highly skilled you have to be, how knowledgeable, as well as greatly embellishing the glamour, and the danger — knowing, of course, how these stories will reflect on his own bearing, making him seem even more talented in the light of the fact that no one thought he'd ever do anything special. But he's not surprised they thought he was never going to make it. He didn't do well at school (not until it was almost too late), he was unsporty, unconfident, unpopular. He just didn't seem to fit in. He certainly never had girlfriends.*

*For a long while he knows he was this huge disappointment to his parents, to his father anyway, who had studied engineering at Oxford and had eventually set up his own software business, fulfilling his one dream in life — to run his own business, to be his own man, as he always says, and who still plays squash twice a week and looks as fit as he's successful, who drives to work in a BMW 7 series, always the latest model, which he leaves outside the house — this neo-Georgian villa they bought brand new when he was eight — rather than in the triple garage because he likes people to see it parked there, gleaming. Being the only son, and the only child, didn't help. He thinks he was always too tightly controlled. That his parents attempted to mould him into this perfect child that went with their perfect life style. He felt he could never just be himself,*

258

*that he wasn't allowed to develop at a pace natural to him. When he started to do badly at school, rather than try to help him, rather than try to understand why things weren't working out – in part because he was being bullied – his father became incredibly mean and was occasionally violent towards him. He was always being sent to his room, banned from watching TV, banned from going out, shouted at for being a failure, for letting the family down, slapped hard across the backs of his legs, shaken. He thinks he mostly hated growing up. The very thought of Swindon makes him feel ill, even today.*

*His loathing of the place (he can't divorce the town from his experiences of being brought up there) was another key reason why he became a pilot. He used to have this idea that flying was a way of extracting yourself from the world, from your home and transporting you to somewhere new and clear and free. Somewhere without a past, without echoes. When he was fifteen they went to Greece for a family holiday and on the plane his father asked if they could have a look at the cockpit. He remembers being amazed not by the controls, not by the technical wizardry of the flight deck (which is what most interested his father), but the view. He can clearly remember looking through the windshield and being overwhelmed by the sky, how vast and empty it appeared, and how appealing that seemed. Although by now he'd already started to dream about being an astronaut (this dream being fuelled by his interest in astronomy, his stargazing – which he's beginning to understand was probably another way of avoiding the reality of home), he suddenly realised that if he was never going to be an astronaut (even at that age, especially at that age, he had a very keen idea of his personal limitations, and that not all dreams come true) he could at least try to become a pilot. He started to work at school, amazing his dad in the process – which he found in a way was more satisfying than pissing him off (by under-achieving) because he couldn't understand it – and was eventually able to apply for a place at Prestwick Aeronautical College. He chose Prestwick because it was the UK flying school furthest away from Swindon.*

*And yet – having worked so hard to become a pilot, having done it on his own not only to prove everyone wrong but to give himself this power, this leverage so he could leave home and Swindon for good, having gained some confidence, some stature – he finds he's already beginning to struggle with*

**259**

*the frustrations and boredom of flying, the way everything is so procedural, so routine, the shocking sameness of it. The reality. Even the temptations, the down route dalliances as Greg calls them, obviously come with a price – he hasn't a clue how to handle the situation he's got himself in over last night. What he should do now. Despite always making out otherwise, he's never gone that far with a cabin crew before, he's never actually screwed one. In a way he thinks it's like he's lost his virginity all over again. And he can't seem to forget it. He keeps seeing her face, her dark brown eyes, the smoothness of the skin on her cheeks, her forehead becoming shiny with sweat. He can almost feel her body, which might not be as slim as some of the girls' on board but he found it quite sexy enough – he likes well rounded bottoms. He knows how easy it would be to let it go – it's not as if she's going to say anything to anyone – and to lie to Suzi and simply move onto the next thing, the next flight. That this would be normal flight crew behaviour, what's expected of him. But he can't help feeling he has to do something more, he wants to see her. Maybe, he thinks, he hasn't been here long enough, that he's getting himself wound up about it because as Greg's made only too clear, he's a novice. He's letting his conscience get the better of him (for once, as Suzi would no doubt add). He obviously needs more practice at letting things go. At being a shit.*

*He can suddenly see what his future is meant to be all right, he can see where he's heading. He's Greg waiting to happen. That in twenty, twenty-five years' time he'll be sitting on the left with four gold bands on his shoulders, a captain's badge on his breast pocket, his cheeks puffy and puce, his stomach flopping over the lap belt, farting non-stop, leering at the female cabin crew, spilling things so they have to bend down to clear them up, shoving their bums in his face while they do so, sounding confused and resentful, yet strangely proud and remorseful too, trying (and largely failing) to put on an act for a fresh-faced (Dan laughs to himself thinking of his own complexion as fresh – he still has acne) first officer, because he'll also have been sucked into a life that hasn't turned out to be quite what he expected, really anything like what he once dreamed of (this vast, clear space, this unconditional freedom). He'll be realising that in a way life will have betrayed him too, and like Greg he'll be too proud, too conscious of where he's come from to admit this failure to anyone he's really close to (not that there'll be anyone left he is close to, having grown further and further apart from his family, from anyone he might have married and set up a home with — Suzi crosses his mind — as he'll have always been either away or longing for the next trip, the next slice of action, the take-offs and approaches and landings, the easy sex). He sees this body again, brown and soft, sort of wonderful and comfy to hold naked, remembering how eager she was, how she lay on her front with him crawling on top of her, and how he started to kiss her all over, lightly licking her back, leaving a wet trail along her spine until she obligingly lifted her bum in the air a little, parting her legs — something, he thinks, Suzi never does (she never does anything obligingly) — which was when he noticed this funny mark on her right buttock, despite the dimness because she insisted on keeping the lights down.*

The seat belt signs have now been switched off and you are free to move about the cabin and use the toilets, Selina says, though we do advise you to keep your seat belt fastened at all times when seated. Thank you.

Did you hear that Tim? says Becky.

It didn't sound like someone shitting it to me this time, says Tim.

Maybe she's taken something, Becky says.

If there's anything going around I want some, Tim says.

*Not knowing what he wants any more, feeling completely disorientated, as if he's a teenager again, a fourteen-year-old, at his parents' house, in his bedroom stuffed with models of rockets and spacecraft, star charts and planispheres, waking from a dream which had gone on forever slowly turning into a nightmare, he opens his eyes half-expecting to see an alertness message posted on the upper EICAS screen. He hasn't touched a thing for he doesn't know how long and when no flight crew activity has been logged after a specific time (usually fifteen minutes, though he's not sure how the FMS on this particular aircraft has been programmed) a message will appear simply requiring you to erase it, so the system knows you are fully conscious. If you don't the message starts to flash and if that remains unattended to an aural cockpit alarm sounds. He flicks the ND over to weather (it's the first command that comes to mind), setting the parameters to 120 nm with an upper height of 40,000 and watches as a jagged patch of green, which means light cloud, appears to the left of their route. But there's nothing at all directly in their way and although Dan knows they're stuck in the thick of a 160 knot jet stream, with their ground speed pushing 615 knot (almost 130 knot faster than he recalls they were flying just a little south of here going in the opposite direction yesterday – or what's really the day before yesterday as they are back operating on London not New York time) he still thinks the aircraft is going too slowly, wishing it could pick up more pace.*

*Glancing over to Greg he realises he's fed up with the present – it's just not where he wants to be right now as it's continually reminding him of what he's tried to leave behind and what's in store. And although he doesn't exactly want the future to hurry up either, he'd rather that than this mid-Atlantic limbo he's sunk into and where his mind is getting tangled up on itself (trying to keep awake). But he knows they can't go any faster, that as ever they're bound by the flight plan, by air traffic control, the company rules over fuel economy and to a lesser degree the high speed buffet (though they've got plenty of room before they'll start to nudge that), so he looks at Greg yet again, longer this time, with the map light gently catching the side of Greg's face, creating shadows, bringing out his features, and the starkness of the night in the side windshield a whisper away behind him – as if he's that close to infinity – noticing how, despite the puffiness, the heavy bags and deep lines, his skin portraying that particular sheen of bad health all pilots eventually seem to acquire, he has a surprisingly strong face, a very manly face (Dan can see how some women might find him attractive) and that actually he doesn't appear so hopeless. That maybe he's not in such a bad position after all. He thinks at least he's probably done exactly what he's wanted, until now anyway. However, going back to the idea that he's Greg waiting to happen, Dan decides surely not everything has to follow such a set pattern. Why does he have to end up like Greg (whatever he's really like) just because he's a pilot too, working for the same airline?*

*He's suddenly certain he's been thinking so negatively, plundering the worst aspects of his upbringing, looking for Greg's dark side and how he's drifting that way as well (imagining the future's out of his hands), because he's knackered and it's about that time in a flight – over halfway but with a large chunk of time still to go. (He often thinks of time as something physical, as something you can pick up and hold, as three dimensional space, as airspace – moving from one jurisdiction to another.) He tries to shift his mind onto something more positive, more exciting, more pressing. What he can no longer ignore anyway. As last night, as Friday night becomes clearer in his mind, as he recalls it in ever greater detail (it wasn't until he saw the mark in daylight the next morning that he realised it was a heart and said anything about it, and she laughed replying, 'Most people think it's just a mole!'), the more he realises there was to it. He's sure it wasn't just a last fling for her. She was too passionate, too open with him. Too natural. He decides he has to get a message to Becky – Suzi can obviously wait, he can sort that problem out later. His first priority is Becky. If he leaves it much longer he'll be stuck preparing for the approach and then the landing and before he knows it she'll be slipping off the aircraft with the other cabin crew well before Greg and he have completed the logs and tidied everything up on the flight deck, and that'll be that, he'll lose sight of her forever, at least for a couple of years or so until they might be rostered together on another New York, or a Miami, or a San Fran. But she won't be, he thinks, because she'll be married by then, she'll be a mum, living in Bucks. Suddenly not feeling anything like as tired as he did a few moments ago, feeling as if this fog is beginning to lift (leaving once again crystal clear night sky) and instilling a new sense of urgency in him, a new sense of purpose, he spots a satellite rapidly traversing the eastern horizon, slipping between the bright, easily identifiable constellations of Lyra and Bootes, the herdsman and the harp. With a jerk he reaches for his flight plan realising Shanwick's just around the corner (and that time seems to have shot past notwithstanding).*

*Greg says, yawning loudly, Dan my lad, I need another pee. You have control.*

*Dan says, I've been in control since New York, if you haven't noticed.*

*Of course you have, says Greg, I'm just so used to saying it whenever I get up.*

*Dan can't understand why Becky wants to marry a pilot, watching Greg clamber out of his seat. Okay, he knows he's up here too, with three gold bands on his shoulders, presuming one day he'll get the fourth, but he's not your average flight crew. He's different. He's sure he is. He has a conscience for a start. Definitely.*

# shanwick

She can't believe she's doing this again – pressing herself against D1R, folding what's left of her body around the emergency chute bulge, sliding up the blind, getting as close to the window as possible without letting her breath smudge the view while shielding the ever bright doorway lighting from her eyes with her hands, cupping them, as if she's trying to look deep into the distance on a sunny day. Far from thinking she caught something last night she now thinks it's more likely she caught something from Nigel in the galley on the way over – from this part of him that obviously still needs to look for answers, that still needs to work out who he is. As if insecurity is contagious. Peering into the blackness, which quickly brightens to a milky dark (her mind is moving ahead of her eyes this time, picking up signals before they've been fully transmitted) and which rapidly begins to fill with stars, this echo of light, sprinkling after sprinkling, she thought she had all the answers she needed. Only a short while ago she thought she could see everything for what it is – a picture of completeness, of wholeness – as if she were looking from some privileged vantage point. And that what went on in New York had helped contrive this state, bringing it to the surface – and how it was all such a release. But she realises, with her hands acting like this buffer between her face and the cold, trilling plastic of the first layer of window (she doesn't know how many layers there are or indeed what they are made of – they don't tell you this sort of technical stuff in training, not that she can remember very much of what she was told in training all those years ago anyway) that it might have just been an illusion because she's increasingly unsure of herself, of everything. Why else would she be staring out of the window, again, doing a Nigel? She turns a little so she can look further backwards, moulding her hands to suit this new angle. She thinks perhaps she's trying to see where they've come from, the space they've just travelled through, the way you can when travelling by train or car, as if it might somehow clear up this growing feeling of uncertainty, of suddenly not having the right answers, of even bothering whether she has any answers or not. But all she sees is the flashing wingtip light, highlighting in these split seconds a small section of silver wing, the leading edge, and a sliver of night air. And the longer she's sucked in by its frantic flashing the more she has an idea that it's like a mirror of what's going on in her head, this growing alarm. Perhaps she's setting it off. Thanks, Nige, she says to herself. Thanks a lot.

Wendy finds all flights have a certain rhythm to them, with their periods of intense activity and stupefying lulls (how things can become hysterical in the galley one moment and then completely die down the next), with their spots of turbulence and great lengths of steadiness, the prolonged days and shortened nights, but she can't remember any as frigging disorientating as this one. She feels quite unbalanced, in need of support. Still, shifting back to the view she had a moment ago, clear of the wingtip light (she's noticed it on numerous occasions before of course, not that she has any idea how its flashing is interpreted by other planes, by outside observers – whether it means they are going up or down, forwards or sideways, backwards even), dragging her hands across the window, over the damp traces of her spent breath she couldn't avoid leaving, she suddenly believes everything is conspiring against her at once. That some terrible chemical reaction is taking place. She tries to concentrate on the stars, the way the longer you look at them the more impossible it is to get any sense of how far away they are, any sense of distance, and how they all seem to be moving slightly, jigging on the spot. But she finds her mind keeps coming back to the fact she's no longer completely comfortable with who she is, that she seems to have partly lost sight of herself, having really only just seen who she is and where she's coming from, somewhere between New York and here (wherever they now are). She thinks it's like watching the telly with the picture going in and out of focus and although she's got the remote, she's no longer sure of when to press the button to fix the image. She pulls her head away from the window, thinking of Zoe, pushes herself clear of the door, any hint of the outside, thinking of her daughter telling her she's in self-denial and needs to see a shrink. She wonders whether Zoe's right. That simply this wall she's built between experience and her real emotions, her real needs has finally collapsed. And this is what New York (as well as perhaps sharing a galley with Nigel) really triggered.

The ice rink in Central Park comes to mind again, and so too does Fisherman's Wharf in San Fran, Venice Beach in LA, South Beach in Miami, Boston's Sea World, all these places she used to visit again and again, as if she's flicking through an old photo album. But she finds it's not these places that particularly interest her now, these must-see attractions (except for a few key stores and boutiques, except Bloomingdale's) but the people they remind her of. The faces and hair-dos and wild, carefree characters they conjure up. The names they help her recall – Sara, Gail, Kelly, Lisa, Beverley, Jasmin, Sheena, Tracey, Paula. And how they always stuck together, how seemingly none of them had a worry in the world. How everything appeared to be so open, there for the taking. She's not quite sure when it all started to go wrong though she supposes it had something to do with reality catching up. With getting old. (With some of them being left behind and carrying on as if they were still in their early twenties.) She thinks everything that meant something about the job, about being an air hostess (she doesn't like thinking of herself as a cabin crew, she finds the term so bland, so unglamorous, so unsexy – she's never been a feminist, she doesn't believe in equality between the sexes, it sounds like too much frigging hard work to her) seems to have disappeared. Nothing seems the same anymore.

She feels this pressure behind her eyes, tears beginning to well. However, she knows she can't let herself cry because it plays havoc with your make-up and you only ever see proper tears in Galleys 5 and 6, coming from the new kids. (She imagines there might be plenty down the back tonight, especially as tiredness becomes overwhelming and the idea of landing, of going home to this other life, of facing up to all sorts of truths becomes that much closer, as the old mixture of remorse and resignation starts hitting the spot – she's been there.) She's too old to cry now, too experienced. She's been in the game too long. She knows just how to reveal the side of herself she wants to reveal, but she could never completely let go, not on board. Perhaps, she thinks, self-denial like so much else just becomes a part of the job, this way of life. She wipes the corners of her eyes, finding them surprisingly dry but itchy, as if she's been crying dry tears, as if the mechanism has seized up because of under-use, and moves away from the door area, stepping off the non-slip rubber matting and onto the drab cabin carpet with its indistinct pattern. Even if she needs to see a shrink, she decides, she's not going to because no one in Chingford does. It's unheard of there. She can't imagine what Joy would have to say about it, or where Zoe even got the idea from – from some modelling friend? Isn't this what models always go on about?

She looks at her watch, the fake Gucci with its peeling case despite which she knows it'll be completely accurate, that she can rely on it, seeing it's getting on for midnight New York time, which of course is really five in the morning UK time, and that there's little more than two hours to go. Two hours, she thinks, in which to find herself again, to come to some sort of idea about who she is and where she goes from here, to reach some sort of equilibrium, because she knows that once she's on the ground she'll lose all sense of perspective, not being able to see beyond the confines of Chingford. She'll be too busy trying to re-establish routines and contacts, letting the girls know she's home if they feel like coming over – picking up where she left off. Besides she'll be too frigging whacked.

Hey, hey, Tim says. Isn't there anything I can do? He puts his arm around her heaving shoulders, pulls her into him, surprised by how soft she feels, how cuddly.

No, Becky says, snivelling. It's all my fault.

You keep saying that, Tim says.

Well it is, she says.

Well there's nothing you can do about it now, Tim says. It's too late. I just hope you had a fab time. He laughs.

I'd rather not think about it, she says. Besides I was too smashed. But, Tim, everybody knows. They're all talking about it.

Here, he says reaching across the counter behind her with his free hand, have a chew on this. He passes her a roll from a basket that somebody's already got out in preparation to be warmed for the breakfast service – he bets it was Marissa because she's been completely out of step with what's meant to be happening when tonight, doing things either way too soon or too late (if anything she should be dealing with the duty-free right now), not that any of them is being particularly coordinated tonight. He realised on the way over that Becky must really love her food considering the amount of eating and picking she seems to be indulging in, which isn't the most unusual thing in the world. Most of the girls are the same, he's always spotting them stuffing things into their mouths. He can't understand how they manage it without putting on weight, except poor Becky of course. Though thinking about it he supposes they must all be rushing to the toilets to stick their fingers down their throats every five minutes or so. What did you expect? he says.

Oh, I don't know, she says, chewing, sniffing – that maybe people would be a little more understanding, given my situation.

You really thought they'd keep quiet about it? he says. About something like this? That's asking the impossible. You've been working here longer than me, you know no one can keep anything secret for more than about two seconds. Plus it's not as if you were particularly discreet about it. Sorry to say this, Becky, but you have sort of asked for it.

Thanks, she says. I was pissed.

We were all pissed, he says, but that doesn't mean we didn't see anything. Or do anything stupid ourselves, he thinks.

Valerie will keep her mouth shut, Becky says. She understands.

That's because she's French, he says. This sort of thing's nothing to them. They're always having flings and stuff – extramarital affairs. He laughs again, a short burst of his high-pitched nervous laugh, something he can't help himself doing.

What, and we're not? Becky says. We're all human.

Yeah, but we make a bigger deal about it than the French, Tim says.

So does that make us more or less human then? Becky says.

It makes us more stupid, he says. Who wants to feel guilty all the time – though fortunately it's not a particular situation I'm ever likely to find myself in.

And here was me thinking no one in this business ever feels guilty about anything, she says.

You were wrong, weren't you, he says. Look at you.

Yeah, she says. Dead wrong. Don't look at me like that.

Like what? he says, knowing exactly what she means. He feels more and more sorry for her, realising she's got everything the wrong way round, realising she's totally naive, worse than him – a typical Cancerian. He squeezes her tight into him again. He wishes he had a sister, even if his brother had stuck around he doesn't think they would have ever hit it off – apart from the age difference there was the fact Lawrence had absolutely no style. With a sister he feels he might at least have had more to talk to

270

her about. They could have discussed boys for a start, without any jealousy or bitchiness creeping in. He finds even with Stuart and Andy he never knows quite where he is, like who's being completely honest. There's always this urge to prove yourself, this competitiveness – everyone's always after something, if they are not going behind your back. He's not just thinking about sex of course. He's thinking about how it is with the men he knows well.

So what am I going to do, Tim? Becky says, when he's bound to find out.

Tim watches Becky put the rest of the unwarmed roll in her mouth and wipe her eyes with the back of her right hand. He realises she's been crying again. He eases his hold on her so she has more room to tidy herself up, so she doesn't have to worry about him noticing that she's been crying – he's never sure whether people want you to know or not. Deny it? he says. Tell him the truth? I don't know. It depends how serious you are about getting married. You're not talking to the best person here on this precise matter – I mean you're meant to be with this man for the rest of your life? No deviating? Marriage doesn't seem like a lot of fun to me. You can't really be serious.

Come on, Tim, she says, I haven't just got engaged for the fun of it, to please my mum or anything stupid like that. It's not some big joke, at least not to me Everyone else might be laughing about it right now but I'm not. I know this reputation we're meant to have, that we only get engaged for the attention, so someone can throw a party for us – ha, can you imagine that, like I got engaged just so last night could happen, just so I could sleep with another first officer and fuck everything up. What do you really think, Tim? I'm not just any other hostie who'll do anything to get out of this business. I love Ben. And he loves me. This isn't some fantasy, something I've dreamed up. It's for real.

Sure, Tim says.

What do you mean, sure? Becky says. Of course I'm fucking sure. I'm as sure as I've ever been about a boyfriend.

I don't think I've ever been sure about anyone, Tim says. Like how do you know?

Trust me, Becky says, you know.

So what, you've been with him for ages and stuff? he says. You know everything there is to know about him?

We haven't been going out for that long, actually, she says, but that's not the point. I believe it's either there or it isn't to begin with.

I doubt if I could tell, he says. What's it look like? Does it smell?

Don't be an arsehole, she says – any more of one than you are already that is. You know the thing about being serious with someone, about loving someone, about marriage I suppose, is that you have to be open to it in the first place. You have to want it. It doesn't just turn up out of the blue – at least not in my experience. I don't know why I'm getting this impression, Tim, but I reckon you're the sort of person who's always holding back. That when it comes to it you wimp out.

Oh yeah? he says. He moves further away from her, suddenly wondering whether he wants this conversation to continue. He thought she was the one who was having a hard time. The person who was crying because of the mess she's got herself into. The last thing he wants to do is to bring up what happened to him last night – not in the galley, not in front of everyone.

You've got to be up for it, she says. Hungry for it.

Perhaps that's my problem then, Tim says. I'm never hungry.

Could be, she says.

Could be you're a little too hungry, he says.

Steady, she says.

You started it, he says.

Well, you weren't going to, she says. I bet you never start anything.

I bet you never stop, he says.


Wendy walks into the galley but instead of seeing the banks of dry and wet lockers, the beaming electrics, the steaming bev

**272**

maker, the counter littered with bits of shrivelled chervil and browning pasta tubes, spots of crusty sauce and crumbs of roll, a sprinkling of chocoloate powder, half-drunk bottles of Evian – with Carlo and Nigel trying to look attentive but failing in separate corners, each sulking (she's noticed how they've hardly said a word to one another since boarding, not that they exactly hit it off on the way over – she's still not sure who's more pissed off with whom, though she has a pretty good idea, normally finding the boys much worse at hiding their true feelings than the girls), she sees her kitchen at home. As if it's later this morning and she's just got in because she can even smell the rank staleness that always greets her whenever she forgets to put out the rubbish and she's just remembered she didn't on Friday morning – she sees it sitting in the bin, overflowing, a couple of spent make-up pads on the floor, a shrunken apple core – partly because she woke up late and was in such a rush to get out of the house and to start making her way to Heathrow (which can take up to two hours depending on the traffic) and partly because she somehow always forgets to put it out. As if, subconsciously, she's punishing herself for her lifestyle, reminding herself of the fact she never has time to organise her domestic life properly, at least not since the cabin crew union collapsed and their maximum monthly flight time limits went to the wall, along with the respective rest period scheduling, so now it's like they're in the air all the frigging time. She scans the room in her head – the matching pine kitchen table and chairs which she bought years ago from the MFI on the outskirts of Chelmsford, along with the sink unit and cabinets (which Paul – who came after Mike, of course – fitted, when he was still trying to impress her and not the other way round), the fridge with her flight schedule for the next month and a load of takeaway menus and local taxi numbers stuck to its front with magnets made to look like half-size hamburgers and fried eggs, things she used to pick up for the girls in the States, the old school photos of Gemma and Zoe in their uniforms on the window sill above the sink. She loves the picture of Gemma particularly, which was taken when she was thirteen, because it reminds her of herself when she was that age, coming into her own, beginning to realise who she was and what her looks could do for her, this strange, new power. She was living with her mum, only down the road from where she lives now. It often occurs to her that despite all the travelling she's done over the last twenty or so years, the millions of air miles she's flown, she's still only managed to move a mile or so from where she grew up. And she sees the cooker looking almost new because she only ever uses the microwave – with the kids not being around much she doesn't see the point in making a big effort just for herself, or herself and Joy when Joy comes over (they're more interested in what they drink than what they eat). And above the cooker her mind's eye latches onto the extractor fan, which Paul fitted (badly) also and which is far too elaborate for the size of the cooker and the kitchen and looks completely out of place. It has a huge stainless steel hood (in a way, she thinks, it's rather phallic) and attached to the base there's a shelf and it's on this shelf that she's arranged the hundreds of tiny salt and pepper pots she's nicked from First over the years, a memento of each trip. She sees them now, coated with greasy dust but still able to reflect the light a little – like missing pieces from some board game.

They are all the same (except the pepper has three holes and the salt just one), about an inch high, made out of plastic but made to look like chrome. The moment you pick them up you know how cheap they must be to produce but from a distance Wendy thinks they could look pricey. She's not the only person who takes them, everyone helps themselves – crew and passengers alike. She started her collection the first time she was put in First. She remembers thinking of it as a reward, a prize for finally making it to the front of the plane (after everyone thought she was going to spend the rest of her life in Business, that Business was as far as she was ever going to get – people have always underrated her, never quite believing in her). And also because she had such a great time that trip she wanted something to remind her of it. It was a New York and there had been a party (she wonders what it is with New York and parties, why they always get more out of control there than anywhere else, except perhaps Miami). Plus when she got home and stuck them on the shelf – which follows the hood right the way round sticking out a good six inches – they looked so lonely. She never thought she'd fill it, not with just First salt and pepper pots and now there's hardly any room left. She's not certain she'll even be able to squeeze on the two she's about to pinch, which would be a shame because she knows they'll mean something particularly special. Although all the sets obviously look exactly the same she thinks each carries with it distinct memories of specific groups of people in specific places.

Everything's there, her life for the past decade or so, however long she's been crewing in First on and off (she doesn't want to put a figure on it), all held tightly within the miniature, chrome-effect vessels, despite the fact the different memories are obviously not immediately apparent and might need more than a little interpretation. In a way, she thinks, it's like recorded but unanalysed data – raw history. Diaries she's never quite got round to filling in. It occurs to her (as she pictures the stuffed shelf and wonders for a moment about this flight, and last night, quite how her mind and her affections seem to be jumping about, when normally she's not really conscious of contemplating anything too hard and simply drifts along quite happily with whatever's happening) the two she's about to pinch are really the summation of the lot, the crowning glory. Because before there was always a way to go, always so many more to collect, but now she's suddenly come to some sort of end. However, rather than finding a fitting conclusion, the final piece of a giant jigsaw, everything just seems to be so wide open. God, she thinks, this trip's really doing my head in. She shakes her head from side to side, as if to emphasise the fact, trying to determine whether she has a headache – hearing this sunken, whooshing noise, as if she can actually hear the cabin pressure – or whether something's simply fused up there and that things, her thought patterns aren't quite connecting as they should.

Are you okay? Nigel says.

Wendy looks up to see Nigel, his waxy, blubbery face blotchier than she remembers it being earlier, the scratches on his neck even more livid, making a move towards her, this huge hand held out, the thick dark hairs on his wrist clearly visible – for an instant she actually feels frightened, and dizzy, that she's going to be grabbed. She realises Carlo is no longer in the galley, is overly aware of the cabin pressure again, as if it's beginning to solidify and everything is slowing down to slow motion and that she can't get out of his way. She draws in a breath loudly, waveringly, wondering whether he often frightens people – she thought he was so harmless. Maybe large and powerful but completely harmless nevertheless.

Wendy? he says, again.

Nige, she thinks, it's only Nige and beyond his outstretched hand, almost as if he's pointing directly to them she notices a couple of sets of salt and pepper pots on the counter – Mr Jong's she presumes, with the other set probably having been used by the woman sitting in 1K who also had something to eat and whose name she can't remember, of course. She realises this is going to make things much easier because otherwise she would have had to search through the dry lockers (they're never kept in the same place) before deciding how best to get them into her bag without anyone noticing (despite everyone always nicking them no one actually wants to be caught doing so, not just because everyone likes to keep up this façade of being totally honest the whole time but also because no one likes to admit how cute the things are, given that they're actually produced by the company, which isn't exactly renowned for its style, not for the last few years anyway). Now she can simply make out she's putting them away. They're even on the same counter, by the bev maker, as her already opened handbag – except her handbag is overflowing with tissues and make-up and pantliners and she's going to have to do a little rearranging if she wants to hide them in there properly. Actually she's surprised no one's taken them already as she heard the other day the company was planning to phase them out in favour of throwaway packets, similar to what they already have in Economy and now Business.

Wendy? Nigel says, yet again. Knock knock, is anyone in there?

Hi, Nige, she says. She realises she can't ignore him any more than she can ignore herself – her reaction to him, to what's going on around her, her immediate environment.

Success, he says, someone's there, but is it you, Wendy?

I'm not sure, she says. I am feeling a bit strange.

Who isn't at this time, he says. What time is it exactly anyway?

Time I was in bed, that's for sure, she says. Time I wasn't here. She thinks she'd rather not know exactly (having only recently looked at her watch, thinking whatever time it is it won't have moved on quick enough) though she can see Nigel is not going to spare her the details. He's already stuck out his left arm in such a way she can't help but notice this massive dark blue and gold Rolex-like watch which has been clamped to his wrist. She knows it's not a real Rolex of course, she's never come across a cabin crew who wears a real watch.

It's gone midnight, he says. Twelve minutes past five in the morning to be precise.

She wonders whether it's just the jet-lag having finally caught up with her, twenty years' worth, the total collapse of her circadian rhythm. They always say it hits you harder when you are older and less fit, plus she knows that going east is that much worse than going west, which might be why she was okay on the way over (though they also say sex is a good antidote and she reckons she must have had enough last night to see her through to next month's schedule). She realises she's not feeling so sore any more, not in any specific place, just achy, that her whole body aches, like she's become dead weight. She was offered some melatonin capsules the other day (when she was on a Boston) by a girl who was recently in Australia though she declined, thinking she's managed for all this time without, believing she must have learnt to cope. I was all right when we left JFK, she says. I don't know what's happened since then.

Everything's gone a bit fuzzy. Perhaps it's just jet-lag. I'm sure I'm okay, really. She feels his hand reaching for her shoulder but she doesn't want it there, she wants him to remove it this second – he's still giving her the creeps. She ducks a little so he might get the hint, but he doesn't, he only increases the pressure, weighing her down even more. Honestly, Nige, I'm all right, she says. Please don't touch me. You're giving me the creeps. She can't help saying it because it's suddenly all she can think. She feels Nigel release her immediately as she pulls away, too, knowing, however, she shouldn't have said it. She's normally much more careful about what she says on board, about letting things slip, knowing how sensitive everyone is, though it's the second time in twenty-four hours when she's said something she shouldn't have. She sees this look of bewilderment spread across Nigel's large, soft face, a look of helplessness, childishness – almost a plea to be recognised she can't help thinking.

She remembers last night or is it now the night before (she doesn't know where she is this minute) when she said this thing to Greg about women being spiteful, how they operate out of revenge and that it's more than likely his wife (she can't remember her name except that it's something pretty, a bit like Gemma) is having an affair, seeing as he's been putting it about for years and not exactly hiding the fact, not within the company anyway (everyone's heard of Greg). She didn't say it just to make him feel less guilty about jumping into bed with her then, or to hurry him up even because she knew it was inevitable he'd get in eventually, that they'd end up together. In her experience there's always a certain inevitability about down route parties, however disparate-seeming the group, or lavish or inopportune the entertainment, whatever the precise occasion or, as was the case in New York occasions – Greg was never going to get anywhere with Selina, that was obvious from the moment she turned up at Becky's party downtown and saw Selina doing her best to avoid him. No, she said it because she believes it, because when she found out what Mike was up to it was the first thing she did – she went out and frigged someone else. If she were Greg's wife she'd be having affairs all over the place too, except she'd never be Greg's wife, definitely not, not in a million years. She's slept with too many pilots ever to trust one. And she remembers this look on Greg's face, this look of amazement, complete bewilderment, how his bloodshot eyes seemed to spring from their sunken, baggy depths, as if she couldn't be further from the truth, as if the thought had never crossed his mind and then the slow realisation that what she'd just said might actually have some substance to it (she never had the pleasure of telling Mike, as he fucked off before she had the opportunity, though she's often thought about how he would have reacted), that it might actually be the truth. She remembers Greg was standing there in only his vest with his cock and scraggy balls dangling hopelessly between his legs, looking like his world, everything he'd come to rely on and believe in had suddenly fallen to pieces. That he finally realised quite what he's lost over the years he's been flying, over all this time he's been playing around. She wonders now whether that was why he fucked her so hard (she never thought he would even be able to get it up) – that he was trying to grab something from the remains, to feel something. Not that she's complaining particularly, she enjoys vigorous sex. It's the only way she can come during intercourse and she came twice last night, or rather the night before. She looks at Nigel backing away, returning to his corner a lost, wounded man, too, and wonders how similar his story might be to Greg's, who he's abused over the years. She doesn't understand how she can have found him frightening a few moments ago. The guy's so obviously pathetic, like all men. She surprises herself thinking this, wondering whether she might be a feminist after all.

Sorry, Wendy, he says – she can clearly hear the hurt in his voice. I didn't mean to alarm you. Why are people always turning away from me, telling me to leave them alone, saying I frighten them? What's my problem? What do I do wrong, Wendy? I'm only me, for God's sake.

I might be a trolley dolly, darling, but I ain't ever shagged a pilot, Tim says. Cabin crew sure, but not flight crew.

**279**

It's not so bad, Becky says, if you pick the right one.

And how do you do that? he says. They all look the same to me.

Not when you get their clothes off, Becky says. Oh Tim, what have I done?

Not this again, please, Tim says.

Why did I do it? she says. I must be mad.

Probably because you just fancy flight crew too much, he says. Like I said, you're a little too greedy.

Don't be a bitch, she says.

I'm only trying to help, he says. Maybe you don't really want to get married.

Of course I do, she says. I'm just a bit confused right now.

I don't think we're getting very far, he says, thinking how this conversation is going round in circles, how he'd rather be doing a duty-free run or checking the toilets any day. However, he thinks at least she's being a little more honest with herself, that she's not still trying to hide all her feelings behind another mouthful of food, and that her true Cancerian vulnerability, her real emotional irrationality, is beginning to pour out. Like she's finally admitted to feeling confused. Despite expecting it, he's always amazed how accurately his predictions turn out to be, how closely people conform to their astrological make-up. One of the first things his mum ever told him about astrology is that the celestial forces are all-encompassing. That however much we ignore it or fight against it we're all part of the Eternal, governed by the cosmic order.

Where is there to get to? she says. Half of me doesn't even want this flight to end. I really wouldn't mind if it kept going on forever, at least then I'd never have to face Ben. I can't tell him about Dan, despite knowing he'll find out sooner or later, of course I can't, just as I can't break off this engagement, even if I came to the conclusion I no longer wanted to marry him – which definitely isn't the case. How can I not get married now my mum's expecting me to and everything? I can't imagine what she'd say. Oh Tim, what am I going to do? I'm just so confused. My head's going round and round.

All right, says Tim, there is something I might be able to do. However, he suddenly finds himself feeling really shy about suggesting he'll do her chart – as if he doesn't quite believe in it himself and it's simply been a front, another one of his fads to make himself seem more interesting, that there's a little more depth to him, like he used to be into Buddhism (even though Stuart and Andy discovered it) and before that he was a vegan (except he used to wear leather) – despite astrology running in the family. And although he's worked on a number of hosties' charts before, he's mostly done them surreptitiously, like he was just practising. Now with Becky he thinks it's as if his credibility is on the line, that he's about to be properly tested for the first time, who he really is. He knows he's not an expert, of course. His mum says it took her twenty years to develop her own style, her signature way of interpretation. He laughs nervously, unable to help himself. He also realises he has no idea whether Becky's into astrology. He knows most of the girls devour horoscopes like chocolate, fighting over relevant pages in the magazines and newspapers the passengers discard, that they can't live without their fix, but he hasn't seen Becky read anything at all. Plus his mum's always telling him that not everyone wants to know what forces have shaped them, quite where they are coming from. That some people want to stay in the dark.

How exactly? she says.

Still he knows he can't pull out of it now, that he can't keep hopping from one thing to the next the moment he's under pressure, that he has to persevere with something in his life. I can do your chart, if you like? he says, laughing again, though watching Becky carefully for her reaction. He sees her soft round face crease up, about the first time he's seen her smile since NY, noticing also for the first time what great eyes she has, so huge and brown and surprisingly honest-looking. Don't laugh, he says. You know, see how things line up, what your blueprint is, your potential. I can do Ben's and Dan's too and work out where there's any compatibility. I'll do it for free. It might help. He knows he's talking too fast.

Come again? says Becky.

See where the planets lie, he says. He's very conscious he's trying to sound jokey, that it's no big deal, as well as talking too fast – how he always starts to come across when he senses people aren't taking him seriously, all part of putting himself down (and acting up). You know, he says, your astrological chart.

Oh fuck, she says, my mum's into that. She can't get dressed without reading her horoscope. But I must be about the only hostie who finds it completely boring. I mean, I just don't get it. You're kidding anyway, aren't you? You don't really know how to do it?

Sort of, he says. My mum's like this astrologer so I understand a bit. He should have realised Becky might not be obsessed with her stars, seeing as she's about the only hostie he's come across (in this airline anyway) who isn't a blonde or a size eight – that she's bound to have different views to the others. But he's not going to just let it go now he's started. The thing is, he says, when you start looking into it, things do seem to fall into place – it's amazing really. My mum reckons we're all shaped by the heavens, what she calls the Eternal. She can read people like a book. Honestly. I've seen her do it.

Not me, she couldn't, says Becky.

I bet she could, he says. He can see Becky is looking around for something to nibble on. What's more it's great for working out whether relationships might be successful or not, he says. He doesn't want to come across as a complete flake. You just compare two people's charts, he says. It's a bit like looking at a graph with two lines on it and seeing where they merge. You only need to know a couple of things to get started – like when and where you were born, the exact time and location, that's all.

Tim, she says, thanks, but forget it. How can where I was born and at what time – five thirty in the morning, on the seventh of July, nineteen seventy eight, the Royal Berkshire, Reading, if you really want to know – possibly make any difference to whether I'm going to get married to Ben or not? Whether my marriage is going to work. Nothing's that simple, otherwise why isn't everyone getting their charts done or whatever you call it all the time?

They do, says Tim.

Well then, how come everyone still makes mistakes? she says, I might look like a hostie and a half –

You don't, actually, darling, Tim says. He realises she has a point – something he's never asked his mum.

- but I've got a bit more happening up here.

Of course you have, Tim says. He watches Becky gently tap her hair, as if she's testing it for bounce, something he's seen her do countless times, like it's a nervous tic.

I'm more sensible than that, she says, more down to earth.

That's why you did what you did the other night, says Tim.

That was just a mental lapse, she says, I am only human. Look, can't you just give me some normal advice? Tell me something that's going to have some effect, that will help me to see a way out of this mess.

He suddenly feels his world is turning upside down, that this thing he's clung onto ever since he stopped being a Buddhist is slipping away (for a second he wonders whether he got involved with astrology so he could get closer to his mum – and not the other way around – because his dad hardly ever talks to her and it's ages since Lawrence went and he was just feeling sorry for her). He wonders whether astrology does any good for anyone. He doesn't see how it's helped his mum, he thinks she's only retreated into herself further, that in a way she's become afraid to engage with reality, with real life, to reveal her true emotions. It occurs to him that what Becky's just said has hit some sort of chord with him because he's been thinking for the last few hours, ever since he got back on board in fact, that even if you know everything there is to know about yourself and your potential (as well as that of any present or future lovers) you still don't always act this way, or on this knowledge. That other urges and emotions can come tumbling into play. Nothing to do with the heavens, with the celestial bodies, but more physical, more down to earth (a phrase he realises Becky keeps using – as if he's now suddenly copying her) feelings like weakness, or lust. Or fear. This strange, almost uncontrollable sense of excitement that can come from fear. What's that? he says. What's normal advice? Nothing seems very normal to me, not in this business. Besides you're not the only one who's got herself into a situation. You're not that special. I reckon most of us fucked up one way or another last night. Whose idea was it to go for, what were those drinks called, Cosmopolitans? What the hell was in them?

Oh my God, she says. Don't tell me. Tim, you didn't?

Tim feels himself blush, feels the whole of his stupid, lopsided face turn puce. Like a day and a half's worth of being embarrassed, of silently blushing is beginning to pour out. He knows he couldn't have kept quiet about it the whole way back, he was always going to crack. The only reason no one ever found out about Miami was because he still doesn't know himself quite what happened, not after he left the bar, after he'd consumed about a dozen Bacardi and Cokes (he's never going to touch Bacardi again), and the fact there were no other members of the crew about, so even if he had tried to put some story together, however truthful, they would not have believed him – seeing as no one ever does. Like he was picked up by this gorgeous-looking guy called Jason, who he can picture all right – about five feet ten, well-toned, olive-skinned and with these beautiful deep brown eyes, sort of Becky's colour – who took him to this party in an apartment where everything was white and tidied-away so there was no clutter (like it was the exact opposite of his home), and it overlooked Ocean Drive. He can see the lights of the cars and the thick beams of the floodlights highlighting the buildings, picking out the pinks and blues and aquamarines, the swaying palms, the patches of dark empty beach, the sudden froth of the breakers fringing the shore, and beyond, in the unstirring dark, far out to sea, the lights of ships like distant stars. The place quickly filled with serious crumpet, as far as he was concerned, but they didn't stay long because he was having trouble standing, making sense (he thinks Jason must have been really embarrassed by him) before he took him to what must have been his own apartment, somewhere much dingier – Tim doesn't remember the view only the heat so perhaps it can't have been air-conditioned either – and this is where his mind goes blank. Still he thinks no one would believe him this far. He might have only been around for six months but he knows that unless you have witnesses in this business, unless someone actually sees something, you might as well not exist. I'm not saying a word, he says. I'm not going to incriminate myself.

I thought so, says Becky. But with him?

With who? says Tim.

Don't deny it, she says. I know exactly who. I saw how you two were behaving in the cab even before we got downtown. And then you were chasing each other around the room like a couple of kids. It was embarrassing.

Excuse me, Tim says, he was chasing me. He was like chasing me all night.

Which was why Carlo left in such a huff, says Becky. He's lovely. How could you let him go.

He wasn't interested in me, says Tim. People like that never are.

Could have fooled me, says Becky.

He was just playing a game, says Tim. You know, how some people need to know they can have whoever they want. It wouldn't have gone anywhere, or if it had, it would have been entirely on his terms and lasted for about two seconds flat – he thinks of Jason.

Yeah but, Tim, look who you ended up with, Becky says, of all people. Yuk. Did you really have to? Hey, what does that noise mean?

Don't ask me, says Tim. You're the one who's been here for like ever.

Just over three years actually, thank you. Maybe it's the CM.

Selina? says Tim. Wouldn't that be one chime, not four. He's sure he's just heard four low chimes.

They're changing the system all the time, says Becky. Who knows.

Surely she'd just wander down here if she wants anything, says Tim. It's not as if we're that far away. Have we seen her in this galley once tonight? No. You'd have thought she'd want to come by at some point just to check we're still here. Besides she could probably do with stretching those legs.

Maybe she's too scared to, says Becky.

She didn't sound too bad when she made her last announcement, he says.

Maybe she's having a relapse, she says.

Perhaps it's not her then, Tim says. Thinking about it he's becoming vaguely aware four chimes means something's up, that someone wants to get hold of them urgently. Isn't it a priority call? he says.

You tell me, says Becky. You're the one who's only just completed their training.

Yeah, right, he says. Like everything's stuck in my head. Like I'm the expert all of a sudden. He moves over to the curtain, slides it out of the way and immediately sees the pink call light illuminated on the interphone handset stowed on the inboard side of his and Angela's double crew seat – this pink light glaring on D4R's attendant panel. He knows the call is not necessarily for him, or Angela, not at this stage in the flight, but could be for any of the occupants of Galley 5, it being the handset used for this galley. You get it, he says, however, not moving any further. He suddenly can't help thinking that it might be for him, seeing as they're about to start the breakfast service and then the final clear-in and preparations for landing, that this is the last time between now and London when they're not going to be too frantic and if any crew member wants to get hold of another, for whatever reason, for a brief chat, say, to make some arrangement for when they are on the ground, this is the time. Especially, he thinks, as he hasn't heard a thing when he was expecting to be bombarded once he was on board. He can't believe he's going to be left alone quite so easily, not after he let himself out of the room without saying anything, when he was still asleep, snoring his head off. You don't do what they did and just leave, he thinks. Though by disappearing in that way he reckons he made his feelings pretty clear. Still he knows some people never get the hint, not if they're not looking for it, if they're under this illusion something completely different is going on. If it's for me I'm not here, he says.

So where are you then? Becky says. Out?

I don't know, in the toilet, Tim says. In the crew rest area.

On a six-hour flight? says Becky. The place hasn't even been unlocked. I know because I've got the key.

No one else knows that, says Tim. Anyway I spent almost the whole of an inbound from Miami in the crew rest area last week.

I bet that did your probation a lot of good, she says.

I didn't have much option, he says, I was really sick. I couldn't move. I think this guy spiked my drink the night before. Tim hears the chimes again, checks the attendant panel, too. The pink light is still burning brightly away.

Well I'm not getting it, Becky says. It could be him.

I'm sure it's a priority call, Tim says, four low chimes, and you are the most senior crew present, more senior than me anyway. Perhaps there's a real emergency. Maybe something's on fire. He knows this is more than extremely unlikely, that there's not even a remote chance. Nothing dramatic ever happens on board. Fires don't just break out. He doesn't know why he even said it – to convince himself of the absurdity of the idea? Nevertheless he finds himself trying to remember the fire drill, because he's still too new to the job to have become totally blasé (if indeed he's the sort of person who ever will be). He's sure it involves three people – the fire fighter, the communicator and the coordinator – though he's a little sketchy as to the exact roles of the communicator and the coordinator, who informs the captain and who informs the rest of the crew and the passengers, who controls them. He thinks the coordinator must be the CM, unless the CM discovers the fire, when she becomes the fire fighter or is number two on the scene and becomes the communicator (at least he thinks it works in this order). However, with Selina on board he reckons someone else would have to take the coordinator role anyway as she'd clearly be hopeless in a real emergency, not even being able to leave the CM's station. He doesn't much like the idea of tackling a fire himself either. He can't see himself locating a BCF extinguisher, grabbing a smoke hood and fire gloves from the bulkhead stowage, trying to get the smoke hood to fit securely, the neck seal as tight as possible, all in a real emergency – with the horn sounding in Toilet N or wherever the fire is and the bleeper starting to go in the galleys and call chimes repeating in the cabins and on every attendant panel, with people beginning to panic – then having to pull the red knob on the smoke hood to start the oxygen flow, knowing he only has fifteen minutes of air, fifteen minutes in which to put the fire out. Despite being armed with the BCF he still can't see himself trying to look for smoke around a toilet door (with the smoke hood beginning to steam up already – it always did in training), feeling the door with the back of his hand for heat, then slowly cracking it open, using the door as a shield and crouching a little before aiming and discharging all the BCF into the cubicle and then having to wait a few moments to decide whether another extinguisher is necessary, which he supposes would be brought to him by the coordinator, whoever that may be – Becky? – presuming, of course the fire is in a toilet. If the fire's not in a toilet (though they are the most common fires on board, usually being started by people throwing cigarette ends into the waste bin – even he hasn't been tempted to sneak a few puffs) it's likely to be an oven fire in a galley, or the auxiliary power unit blowing, or most alarmingly from somewhere un-detectable when the first you know about it would be when smoke suddenly floods the cabin, reducing visibility to a couple of feet in a matter of seconds, in which case the passengers would be instructed (by the communicator or coordinator, he's not sure who) to get down on the floor and cover their mouths and noses with a wet handkerchief or scarf or the headrest cover, what's closest to hand. He's amazed he's remembered so much. Having managed to wind himself up, for no reason except a few call chimes went off, it's all suddenly come back to him in a panic. Obviously this urge to survive kicks in, he thinks, making you concentrate (something he's never been great at), making you delve into the deep recesses of your mind. He can't believe it's all in his head. Maybe there's a fire in one of the forward toilets, he says, in Business or First (he wonders for a second how they'd be coping up there, who'd be the fire fighter – he can't imagine those big, clumsy hands would be any more use than his own weak, skinny ones, though he knows how strong the man is, how unrestrained). Maybe there's smoke on the flight deck, he says.

Oh, very likely, Becky says. Perhaps we're about to crash. Remember the procedure for ditching, Tim? I don't. I haven't got a fucking clue. I wouldn't even know how to inflate a life raft. She laughs. Isn't there some toggle you just pull? Look, the call light's not even flashing. It's static.

I don't think it has to flash in an emergency, does it? Tim says.

I don't smell anything, Becky says, beyond the usual smell of stuffy air and burnt hots. No one's running around in a panic. There's no sign of the others. Where are they anyway? Where's Debbie? Why can't she answer the phone? She's responsible for this end of the plane.

They're all probably working, Tim says. Doing what we should be doing, like patrolling the cabins, checking the toilets, finishing the duty-free service, handing out orange juice, collecting rubbish, thinking about breakfast. Attending to emergencies. Despite Becky putting his mind to rest with her nonchalance, he still tries to imagine what it would sound like – a sort of rising murmur, people beginning to scream, followed by this shocked silence. How quickly it would take for the plane to crash. At what moment people would realise they were going to die and whether time would then suddenly slow down, giving you just enough space for your life to flash through your mind – isn't that what happens, he thinks, to people who are about to die? He wishes he were more like Becky, that he could simply laugh at the idea of them crashing, be so flippant about it, but despite knowing nothing is wrong with the plane of course, that everything is functioning normally, part of him just can't help feeling anxious – someone obviously wants to talk to them urgently. And he wonders again, for about the fourth time since they left London, whether he's really cut out for this business. It's not doing his nerves any good at all, he's no Stuart or Andy – he feels for his nicotine patch, wondering whether he should change it. His dream of securing a permanent contract with the company and finding a place of his own (he had thought about moving to Brighton – until he discovered who else lives there, or too near for comfort anyway) seems to be fading. He's got no idea where he's going to go from here. He obviously won't be following his mum into professional astrology, if he can dismiss the whole notion so quickly, if he can see it from Becky's point of view just like that – ever since he started, his mum has doubted his conviction. Who's he trying to kid? He's not sure he's capable of believing in anything strongly enough. He wonders whether he's totally without conviction.

I'm not answering it, Becky says, no way. What am I meant to say? Sorry, Dan, the other night was a mistake. I can't see you again, not ever. Bad timing. My life's already sewn up. But he knows all that. Oh Tim, what can he possibly want?

What does anyone ever want? Tim says. Sex. And more sex.

*Why won't anyone answer? Dan says.*

*They probably don't know how to, Greg says. The kids they employ nowadays are all fucking useless. I expect they're standing around in that back galley working out what they're going to say to their boyfriends when they get home, how they're going to explain all these funny little bruises and scratches on their bodies, the fact they're so shagged. I can just see them leaning against the counters making up their excuses, these buzzers and pings going off everywhere, a tray of breakfast rolls being burned to bits in an oven, pots of tea turning stagnant, not knowing what this pink light on the interphone handset means. Who do you want to talk to so urgently anyway? You've been pressing that thing for about the last ten minutes solid.*

*It doesn't matter, Dan says, switching off the interphone, flicking away his mouthpiece on his headset. It can wait, he says.*

*Leave her alone, Dan, Greg says, whoever she is. She doesn't want you making things any more complicated. I should think you've done enough harm already.*

*Excuse me, says Dan. He suddenly feels he can't deny being with anyone, that he can't deny Becky, just as he knows he wasn't the one who initiated the thing. I'm not totally responsible for what happened, he says.*

*No, we never are, says Greg, but that doesn't mean we don't know any better. This thing with Paula, I should never have pursued it. I broke the cardinal rule. We can do what we like down route, what happens there is outside normal rules so to speak. But we have to forget all about it when we get back on board, certainly by the time we get to Heathrow. It's as if it never happened.*

*Since when was that the rule? says Dan.*

*It's always been the way, says Greg. Since we started. We wrote the rules don't forget. I'll tell you, you don't need to worry too much about your conscience in this business, not when it comes to the odd dalliance. Everyone plays the same game. I fucked up because I eventually let someone get to me. I just couldn't leave her alone. And look what's happened – she's run off to the Far East. I kidded myself for a long while that she took a job on that sector so we could actually spend more time together, on those long down routes, because I was meant to join her on it, too, that was the plan, though I think she knew all along I was never going to get a transfer – she has a friend high up in admin. And now Jeanette's got involved with this jerk who sells Lexus cars – I hate Lexus, I'm a BMW man – and doesn't want anything more to do with me. She had an idea about the others, of course she did, but she knew they weren't serious. I'm sure it wasn't until Paula came along that she even felt threatened – which was when she got involved with this bloke. Women act out of revenge, Dan, out of spite. That's so obvious to me now.*

*Yeah, says Dan, but if you hadn't got involved with Paula, with these other women, your wife probably wouldn't be having this affair. She wouldn't be chucking you out of your nice shiny home in Gerrards Cross.*

*Look, says Greg, I don't want to make excuses but in this business it's* hard to avoid the odd affair. I'm not saying it's not my fault, though I don't think I'm a hundred per cent to blame. These things come with the job. It's all part of getting involved in this business when I did. Still, I'm paying for it now all right. That must please you, Dan, your sense of schoolboy morality – God, the naivety. You'll grow out of it. One day you'll see that not everything is fair, that the world doesn't neatly divide into what's right and wrong. Most of us live in this sort of grey area, just trying to get by, trying not to make too many mistakes. The more I think about it the more I realise the price I've paid for simply joining the airline when I did, for thinking I was on the right track, and sticking with it. My health's gone. I won't be flying by the time I'm fifty-five. I won't be flying next week, not after my medical, not with the way my blood pressure is at the moment, plus I'm getting these pains in my arms all the time and I've obviously got a problem with my prostate – perhaps the cosmic radiation the girls keep going on about has finally got to me. Either way, Dan, it's early retirement for me. And what have I got to look forward to? Nothing. I won't even have a home. Just when I need the daft place the most it looks like I've lost it – and the wife, too, of course. Just when we could have had one last go at making it work. I've lost everything, mate.

Are you that surprised? says Dan. He can't help wondering why Becky decided to screw him, whether she was acting out of revenge for some reason, out of spite. That perhaps Ben or whatever his name is has been screwing around already, or she's just getting in there first because it's inevitable he will, when he's flying to America three times a fortnight and she's stuck at home bringing up the kids. Haven't you had it pretty much all your way until now, at least? he says.

Dan, Dan, Greg says, you still don't understand do you? Okay, I've had a certain amount of leeway, a bit of freedom if you like, I can't deny that, but that was just the way things are, or were anyway. There was nothing I could do about it. As I've said, it was all part of the package. What I want to know is why it's all suddenly come to end, why now. Why I'm being punished. What's happening to my life, Dan?

Don't ask me, Dan says. He feels confused again, that Greg's twisting things out of his mental grasp. All he can think is that, despite Greg maintaining otherwise, if indeed that's what he's doing, he's still paying *for screwing around, for the hurt he's inflicted. That whatever he says there is a right and a wrong way to behave. That Becky could easily have some hidden agenda, too. He's much more concerned about that than Greg this minute. He wonders whether he should try to forget about her after all. Maybe, Greg, he says, you've reached a different stage in your life, whether you like it or not.*

*Who knows, says Greg.*

*Maybe you've arrived at some place you don't want to be, says Dan. He wonders whether Becky's somehow pitched up at a place she doesn't want to be also and that actually she does need him, his help, his intervention. That he shouldn't just forget her. Of course she's not acting out of revenge or spite, he thinks, but desperation. He decides he'll try to reach her again, one more time. That the least he can do is let her know how he feels about her.*

*I wouldn't know, says Greg. I haven't much of a clue where I want to be, let alone not want to be. Maybe that's been the problem all along. I don't think I've ever felt I really belong anywhere. Or to anyone for that matter. I've simply let things carry on – as I've said, it's like I've been stuck on this track. I suppose I've needed to maintain some sort of momentum, a distance so I've never had to face this particular dilemma – where I belong. Where my place in the world really is.*

*Dan looks at Greg, waiting for him to say something else but he doesn't and he can't think what to add himself. He doesn't care about belonging or not belonging right now, he's just worried about reaching Becky. He watches Greg wipe something from the corner of his eye and shift uncomfortably in his seat, as if he's trying to shrink a little, Dan can't help thinking. As if he's trying to disappear. This great flabby bulk.*

*Hey, Greg says brightly, thinking about that lot back there makes me wonder what on earth would happen if there's an emergency. It would be solely up to you and me, mate, to bring this thing down safely – that's presuming we want to get home in one piece.*

*Dan looks away from the control panels and into the black that now almost instantly becomes less black, a sudden blurring of definition, a lessening of intensity. The stars appear no closer, fainter if anything, and he realises it won't be long before they slip silently into the dawn – the constellations of Pegasus, Aquarius and Aquila, the winged horse, the* water-bearer and the eagle, directly ahead as he's looking (as they're flying almost exactly due east) disappearing first, with Aquila taking with it Altair, one of the brightest, most easily identifiable stars in the sky (lying just below the blue-tinged Vega) and, seemingly, a soft, sticky chunk of Milky Way. He knows he could navigate by the stars alone, that he could cross oceans, continents, even hemispheres without having to rely upon the inertial navigation system – this box of accelerometers attached to gyro-stablised platforms that sense the slightest movement of the aircraft – and to a lesser degree the VOR, DME or IRS systems, that if he wished he could find his own way around the globe, except he suddenly has this feeling that it wouldn't be much use because he doesn't have any idea where he wants to get to, that despite this knowledge, this skill, he'll still be pretty lost. Like Greg. Like Greg already.

Dan realises he's missed any chance of seeing the aurora borealis tonight, when the northern sky becomes a shimmering neon blanket and which he often sees going this way at this time of year, or any distant lightning, when a corner of the sky looks like it's so charged it's begun to work lose and unravel, or any other night-time phenomena, and that soon he'll see a trace of blue emerging and then very quickly expanding along the eastern horizon – an indigo turning to cobalt to azure – while the cloud banks, the swathes of altostratus (it's always altostratus as far as he's concerned) assume a certain, puffy solidity as they spread behind them as well as in front of them, as if the aircraft has been cushioned all along and was never in any danger of falling back to earth – any more than it had risen clear of the tropopause and out of the earth's weather systems and gravitational pull. That some sort of equilibrium, a series of comple-mentary forces, has held them in check after all. He thinks he must simply have been under an illusion they had pulled free, free of his life with Suzi, his flat in East Grinstead, his parents in Swindon, his past, everything that had tethered him to home, to where he comes from (and that something could've happened with Becky in the future because her ties would be broken too). Unable to turn away from the soft, blurry blackness of outside, the last moments of night, he senses his mind is becoming too crowded again, that it's like the Milky Way, spiralling away forever. He senses how far everything seems to be from being resolved.

What are you saying, he says, that you wouldn't care if this thing blew *up in mid-air? He knows he wants to get back in one piece, however, to see whether anything has changed, whether he's capable of changing anything himself. Despite knowing it's been a short night, a short trip, he feels he's been away for ages and that something has to be different. Though surprisingly he finds himself thinking if nothing has changed, if everything's exactly how it was when he left he wouldn't mind getting back on board next week – putting up with all the procedures, the utter predictability of flying an airliner today, exactly what was depressing him only a couple of hours earlier – just so he experiences this illusion of freedom again, and has another chance to screw someone as lovely and eager as Becky, if he won't be able to see her when they're on the ground. To feel alive for once, engaged, wanted. He suddenly realises how addictive this might become, that previously he's been concentrating far too hard on the actual flying, on being professional – probably because it hasn't yet become second nature – and not enough on the life it encapsulates, what it's really about, the down routes. All these fleeting opportunities that obviously become more available, more pressing indeed the more senior you are. He's not surprised Greg's depressed seeing as it's all about to come to an end for him. Why he was being so difficult earlier, so condescending. So jealous. Sounding so fucked-up.*

*That's not what I'm saying, says Greg. What I want to know is how that lot would cope if there was a fire in a galley for instance, or a toilet, or if we suddenly lost cabin pressure. If I played around with the cabin altitude for instance. Can you imagine how Selina would react? Or that little Becky – after the amount she must have consumed on Friday night.*

*Don't be an idiot, says Dan watching Greg lift his right hand towards the cabin altitude control knob. He's sure Greg's not being serious though he also knows he doesn't exactly have that much to lose. What does he care if there's a rapid decompression, if they crash?*

*I'm just making a point, says Greg.*

*Emergencies don't occur on these aircraft mid-flight, says Dan. These things never come down, not through mechanical failure anyway. Pilot error sure, terrorism too and occasionally as a result of problems with ATC or approach signals, but not mechanical failure.*

*Oh no? says Greg. I can think of a few examples – there was that aircraft which hit some mountains near Tokyo after the rear pressure bulkhead failed, the one that came down in Taiwan after an engine fell off and, most obviously, the one that exploded just out of JFK when the centre fuel tank went up.*

*I wouldn't say they were mechanical failures as such, says Dan, more freak accidents – none of which were mid-flight or have been conclusively proved anyway. There are still questions to be answered about all of those incidents, except perhaps the one in Japan. Besides if you are talking about how many of these aircraft there are currently flying and how much they are used I think you can be pretty justified in saying they never crash, not of their own accord.*

*I'm not surprised you should say something stupid like that, says Greg. I was beginning to think you're the sort of guy who only sees what he wants to see, who's forever fudging facts, who's forever trying to fit everything neatly together, twisting things here and there. Don't laugh. I've seen plenty of guys up here just like you. People who need to be constantly reassured, who are always worrying about what other people think. How are you lot brought up? Did you all have unhappy, insecure childhoods or something? I can tell you're terrified of making the wrong move, of not behaving how people expect. You never take risks, or push yourself, do you? No, of course you don't. So what exactly happened to you in New York? Who dragged you back to their room, because you sure as hell didn't drag anyone back to yours? Come to think about it, didn't we have a bet? Isn't there a tenner at stake? Something to do with the lovely Selina?*

*I don't think we shook on anything, says Dan. He remembers offering to bet a tenner that if anyone was going to end up with Selina it would be him but he's sure Greg didn't rise to the challenge, that he made some excuse and went for a pee instead.*

*Shame, says Greg. I'd have been a tenner up, wouldn't I?*

*Possibly, says Dan, but I know for a fact you didn't get anywhere with her either.*

*For a fact? says Greg.*

*It was pretty obvious in that bar downtown that she wasn't even remotely interested in you, or me for that matter, says Dan.*

*Not that one should let that get in the way, says Greg. No one has any guts anymore. Though you're right. I'll be straight with you, just as I* have been all along – I didn't get anywhere with her. But, as I said earlier, these down routes don't always go according to plan. Still I have no regrets. I had a good time. Besides you can see Selina would be trouble, real trouble. She's one of these air hostesses who are always looking for more than they're ever going to get – in this job anyway. Who are completely unrealistic. Who never end up with anyone anyway. Poor girl, I should think she's been dying to leave the company for years. She'd probably much rather be at home with a couple of children and a steady bloke, though is fast convincing herself this will never happen and is consequently losing all her confidence – a bit like Paula, I suppose, not that Paula would ever admit it. If these girls don't get out after a couple of years they never do – you've heard that before. No, I'm glad I didn't get involved with all that on my last down route – I'm not very good at being sympathetic. As it was I spent a few hours with someone who knows exactly where she is and how to play the game – who's accepted what this life has got to offer her. And who's not going to expect me to start ringing her up the moment she gets home. All right, Wendy's a bit older than Selina – which is perhaps why she's come to terms with her lot – but she's not in bad shape. Slightly too thin, though that doesn't hold her back in bed. She can give as good as she gets.

Wendy? says Dan. The spindly one in First? Surprise, surprise. That was pretty inevitable I suppose, from the moment she turned up at Becky's late and drunk and kept asking for the captain. He laughs, reaching for what's left of a coffee tucked into the beaker slot on the window ledge moulding, just behind the ashtray which they're not allowed to use of course. 'Give me the captain,' she kept saying – don't you remember, Greg? Dan says. 'Where's Greg? I want Greg,' she kept shouting as she stumbled about in those ridiculous shoes. How old does she think she is?

I was there, says Greg.

You might have had your eye on Selina, or Lynn or Debbie for all I know, says Dan, on half the bloody crew, but thinking about it you were always going to end up in bed with Wendy just as I was always going to end up with Becky. He doesn't see the point in avoiding using her name any longer – Greg's admitted to sleeping with Wendy at last, even if it didn't come as a massive surprise. Not that he can understand how Greg could have missed him being pulled out of his room by Becky at four in the morning or whenever it was, with all this clapping and cheering going on. It was just meant to happen, Dan says. You know, how some things are. He's suddenly overwhelmed by this sense of being a tiny part in a giant scheme, just one element among the myriad aircraft systems. A variable star in the galaxy, with the galaxy obviously only being part of the bigger universe, consisting of numerous other galaxies and clusters of galaxies and galactic nebulae – the beautiful clouds of highly rarefied stuff stars are made from. (He can readily call to mind the famous photograph of the Great Nebula, M42, in Orion – this burst of white light dissolving into a broad drift of purple – which represents only the brightest part of a huge molecular cloud that covers much of the constellation, which in turn is the most splendid in the entire sky, incorporating Rigiel, some 60,000 times as luminous as the sun, and Betelgeux, a vast red supergiant, bigger even than the earth's orbit around the sun.) It blows his mind, every time he considers what's out there. I don't think there was anything we could have done about it, he says. He feels smaller and less powerful than ever, quite incapable of being able to determine his own future, his own path. Christ, the girl made a beeline for me as soon as we got to that bar, he says, ages before Wendy even showed up. In fact she was being pretty suggestive waiting for the cab downtown, standing next to me on the pavement saying she wasn't wearing any knickers.

Becky, hey, says Greg. How come I missed her saying that?

I don't know, you were standing there too, says Dan, next to me.

My mind must have been elsewhere, says Greg, because I would definitely have picked up on that. Wow, what a turn on. I always thought the girls who aren't stunning must make up for it in other ways. I should downgrade.

What about Wendy? says Dan. He can see she could once have been attractive but he doesn't think she's in anything like the same league as Becky. He's beginning to think Becky's the sexiest cabin crew he's ever come across – with her soft brown skin and shapely bum, her tattoo and the way she looks at you with these huge brown eyes, as if she's completely open, as if she can't possibly be hiding anything. The way she's so different from the others.

I need another pee, says Greg.

298

Dan watches him unclip his lap belt and reverse the seat. *So what about Wendy?* he says again. He's fed up with Greg going to the toilet whenever he doesn't want to answer a question. He's not going to let him get away with it this time.

*Well,* says Greg climbing out of the seat, *she's not quite Selina but she's still got plenty going for her – great legs, decent tits considering she's had two children. She acts young enough in bed all right. And I'll tell you something else, she talks more sense than anyone else on board, that's for sure. It's the Wendys of this world I'm going to miss. The people who've got their feet firmly on the ground.*

Dan waits until Greg's closed the toilet door behind him before he reaches for the interphone and taps in 24. He decides he might have more luck if he doesn't make this a priority call, that perhaps Becky knew it was him before, which is why she didn't pick the thing up, and now might think it's someone from First or Business just ringing to see if they can borrow some bread rolls or whatever. Despite understanding the cardinal rule a little better and knowing if everything fails he'll have more opportunities next week (he's scheduled in for a San Fran, which will give him two nights down route) he can't forget Becky. Trying to focus on the ND he sees her lying on her stomach, naked, raising her bum in the air a little, spreading her legs, revealing the tight curls of her thick pubic hair, the glistening folds of dark skin, inviting him in – even though it was almost pitch black in the room this is how he remembers it. He'll give it one more go, whether it's the right or the wrong move. He doesn't want to feel quite so small and powerless, so inconsequential for ever. Greg's got him totally wrong – he is prepared to take risks, to not always do what's expected of him. He's proved himself before, by becoming a pilot – he still remembers his father saying, 'You're never going to do anything with your life, Dan, you just don't have it in you.' He's not going to let Greg stick him in a mould, however much Greg needs him to be in one, however much Greg wants him to show some sign of behaving how he's behaved over all these years, so he can justify himself by blaming everything, his dalliances, his non-existent relationship with his daughter, the fucking-up of his marriage on the job, on the lifestyle, and not himself. Dan thinks he can see it now all right. Greg's just looking for excuses, a way out. Hearing the toilet door open, Dan finds himself

**299**

*turning off the interphone, deciding nevertheless he needs a little privacy if he is to speak to Becky.*

*So, says Greg, moving towards his seat, crouching and puce and wheezy, what did happen to Selina? Do we have any idea?*

*You'll have to ask either Lynn or Debbie, says Dan. They'll be in in a minute. They must know something by now.*

*Very strange this silence from her, says Greg. Maybe she's not feeling well. Perhaps she's gone to lie down. Though she should have told us.*

There was no one there, says Becky. I bother to answer the thing and the line's dead. Story of my life.

Oh, hello, says Tim, hearing another chime, a single one this time and seeing the blue call light illuminate on the attendant panel. I bet I know who that is. He looks towards the front of Zone D, no longer minding whether Nigel is up there, too, searching for him. Now the main ceiling and side wall wash lights are back on and the breakfast service has started (he sees Marissa's already nearing the end of her run) and passengers are moving about the cabin, trying to squeeze around Marissa's trolley (currently by row 36), queuing for Toilets J and H, he feels surprisingly safe. That too much time has passed. As with Miami – though he has no idea how he got out of that one – he feels he's escaped, that he's out of danger, even if some ugly repercussion on the medical front might still arise (but he's definitely not going to think about that at the moment). He spots the small white light on the PSU, exactly where he knew it would be. I wonder, he says, whether this constitutes unruly behaviour. He suddenly feels more lively, more himself than he has done the whole way so far. Like he doesn't have to bother to impress anyone. That he can be his old, shallow self.

It's that woman again, isn't it? says Becky.

Yep, says Tim. Do you think she's becoming a hazard? Perhaps it's time she was restrained.

Maybe, says Becky. In fact, why not?

Goody, says Tim, I've been dying to try these things out for real. He makes as if he's heading to the flight deck where the equipment is stowed, bounding up the aisle, trying to look every bit the reassuring but firm cabin crew, someone whose sympathetic handling of a situation, whose relentless attempts at placating an offending passenger (whose conduct has become prejudicial to the safety of the other passengers, crew and even the aircraft) have been exhausted without effect, thus leaving only one possible course of action. The bondage course was the only part of training he remembers paying any attention to. He knows he'd be able to immobilise a passenger within seconds – using the serrated straps around the wrists and feet and the tape around the arms and body – despite being so puny. I could have done with some cuffs the other night, he says, returning to the galley almost immediately. This guy was all over me.

Nigel? says Becky.

Who else could I be talking about? says Tim. I'm not ashamed. Well, I am, but I can live with it. I honestly thought he was going to kill me. Tim reaches for the Evian, suddenly feeling very hot, remembering how he scratched Nigel's face trying to protect himself, trying to get him to calm down. (Having avoided looking at him all day he has no idea what sort of damage he's inflicted.) I don't think he'd done it for like ages, he says.

Dan hadn't that's for sure, says Becky. He came in about two seconds flat. I'd hardly warmed up.

Perhaps you should give it another go then, says Tim.

You're wicked, says Becky.

# shannon

She can feel the pain moving up from her stomach and into her chest, as if the whole of her body is constricting, this terrible tightness. She's shocked by the suddenness with which it has come on and paralysed with uncertainty as to whether she can make it to the toilet in time to be sick or whether she will be better off staying where she is and trying to puke into the trash compactor in front of Carlo. She quickly looks at Carlo who's preparing a breakfast. Only one person has decided to have breakfast so far, not Mr Jong or Mr Ford or Mr Rubinstein (who've been the most demanding), but the woman in 1K. It always surprises Wendy that in First it's the women who eat breakfast, not the men, as though the men have to fit in as much sleep as possible – most request not to be woken until the last possible moment, until the plane has started its descent and the seat belts have to be fastened and the seats moved to upright. Seeing as they're so important, Wendy thinks, they need every minute they can get, not normally having much time for it on the ground. Carlo doesn't look up but she can tell from the way he's arranging the fruit salad, the way he's placing the sliced strawberries, that he's still in a mood, if anything his mood has worsened and he's just brimming with anger and silence, so she thinks he's hardly going to be sympathetic if she were to suddenly lean over, doubled up with pain and heaving, and splatter the trash compactor, which isn't exactly far away from where he's working (she's never come across a galley chef who takes quite as much time as Carlo to get a plate ready), plus she's bound to miss it a bit, getting specks of vomit everywhere – she's always missing the bin at home – and knows she doesn't really have much option.

She takes a deep breath, turns, sweeps the curtain across with one hand, while reaching for the edge of the galley for support with the other, and launches herself out of the galley and onto the non-slip rubber matting towards passenger door D1L and the adjacent toilet, Toilet D, feeling her stomach lurch with her but also independent of her, as if it's operating in a separate time zone, a few milliseconds ahead. She tastes sick but knows she can hang on a tiny bit longer – which is just as well because she can't get the toilet open, realising it's full, as is, she quickly discovers, the next door toilet, Toilet E. She looks over her shoulder to the galley, the curtain already having swung back into place, ima-gining Carlo still arranging strawberries around the bowl, won-dering whether she's eaten something on board that hasn't agreed with her, but she doesn't think she's eaten anything since leaving JFK. She hasn't had a crew sandwich or even picked at a First entrée. In fact the last thing she can remember consuming, apart from gallons of Evian, is a packet of crisps on the crew bus and she only had this because she wanted to appear to be doing what most of the others were doing, as if she didn't give a frig, with Greg sitting just two seats in front of her, except he didn't look round once, of course. Crew buses at the end of a down route are often pretty quiet but she doesn't think she's ever sat on a quieter one. The only people she can recall for some reason sitting together were Becky and the French girl, Valerie, who snubbed her in Bloomingdale's. She looks towards the Business section, where the lights have been switched on for the breakfast service, which she can see is well underway, wondering whether she would be able to make it to Toilet F or H in time, but there's a trolley in the middle of the aisle, David's – he's just stood up with a hot on the end of a spong. She thought he was gay when she first saw him in the crew briefing on Friday but she's changed her mind since then. She's decided he's the sort of person who appears differently every time you look at them – quite untrustworthy.

There's a clicking sound coming from Toilet D, the sound of someone trying to slide the lock across to open the door. She realises she's been supporting herself by leaning on the door with her forearms and she pulls away just as it folds in on itself and a large man comes out sideways, kicking the thing further open on its runners (the way you have to if you want to leave the cubicle without scraping your back, even people as thin as herself, because the doors are always getting stuck before they're fully open), straightening himself and his clothes, his clip-on tie. It's Nigel and he starts to say something like, Wendy, what are you doing here? You're not going in there are you? Wait a moment, there's something –. But she can't answer, she's not even hearing him properly. She's gagging, unable to keep the measly contents of her stomach down any longer (not that the packet of crisps feels so measly now), though he's standing in front of the toilet, blocking her path. She doesn't know why he won't let her in, why he won't budge, why he can't see how desperate she is. She closes her eyes and begins pushing him, feeling her hands sink into his stomach and her mouth fill with sick. Just as another spasm hits her Nigel shifts sideways saying, Sorry, sorry, I didn't realise, though she's not taking in what he's saying of course, she's hearing nothing now, not even the rushing sound of the air con, the steady whine of the engines, the woolliness of the cabin pressure, she's just stumbling into the cubicle, throwing her head, her upper body forward over the toilet. In the split second before she opens her mouth, before her mouth is involuntarily forced open, she notices, thank God, that the seat has been left up, and as she starts to be sick, as her stomach heaves into her chest (she can even feel her bra strap tighten, her tits pushing against the wire) and a rush of lumpy liquid splatters into the bowl, the force of it opening the flap at the bottom – this flap that she used to think was all there was between the inside of the aeroplane and space, because why else was there such a strong sucking sound when the toilet was flushed? – she thinks how frigging typical for a man to leave the seat up. Mike was always doing that, and Paul, both of whom used to pee all over the back of the toilet and the floor around it as well, creating these sticky yellow stains which she had to wipe up. (She thinks women are so much more pleasant to live with than men, so much cleaner, except possibly Gemma who leaves everywhere absolutely filthy and is forever flooding the bathroom. Though she can excuse her eldest, her favourite – of course she's her favourite, she looks just like her – anything.)

After Mike she's amazed she let another man move in, she's even more amazed she married him, especially as it was Paul. She's gone over it a thousand times and the conclusion she most often comes to is that she must simply have been really desperate – desperate to have some solidity in her life, to feel not quite so alone and insecure (though after Mike she thinks she's probably felt more insecure when she's in a relationship than when she's not in one). Okay, she had the girls and her mum down the road but she also wanted what Joy then had – a full-time bloke. Someone who would be there when she got in from a long-haul. Someone who would provide her with a reason for not simply wanting to set off again for LA or Miami four days later. Maybe that was it, she thinks, she just didn't want to feel left out any longer – she's always hated being left out. And in those days (though she thinks it's probably changed now) having a permanent man around gave you a certain status in Chingford, because you were part of an elite, and she liked that, just as she used to like walking down an aisle or through crew customs in her uniform when she was younger, when she was capable of turning heads. When she supposes the airline meant something, too.

She never loved Paul, not in the way she loved Mike, which makes it all the more surprising to her that she didn't notice what he was up to sooner – maybe it was because she was so uninterested in him that she just wasn't looking. With Mike (Mike had a thing about her uniform, the fact she was an air hostess – she presumes he's with one now, a younger model of herself, at least he's with her when it suits him) she only saw what she wanted to see. It took her about five years before she began to realise that Paul's interest in Gemma and Zoe, Zoe in particular, was beyond what you'd expect from a step-dad, that it was not entirely innocent. She knows he never raped the girls or anything as awful as that but he used to spy on them when they were getting dressed and in the bathroom. He used to make them play these weird games that always involved lots of physical contact – Zoe wasn't even a teenager. Wendy has thought that maybe she was just imagining it – Joy never believed there was a problem, her mum didn't either – but when she found a pair of Zoe's knickers in the pocket of his jeans which she's certain were covered in his wank (he once admitted he wanked into her own knickers when she was away, so she knew he did things like that) it finally came to her. She often regrets not informing the police though she didn't want to put the girls through all that, especially seeing as they didn't seem particularly disturbed by him, not Gemma anyway and Zoe was always fibbing (as she still is), so she never knew what to make of everything she said – Wendy thinks the girls were probably more troubled by her being away so much. And of course she couldn't be certain he did anything, that he actually molested anyone. It has occurred to her that maybe she was jealous of the attention he gave her children, the relationship he had with them, not even being their father, and that she imagined it, that she was looking for a problem, an excuse to get rid of him (and that he'd picked a pair of Zoe's knickers out of the dirty laundry basket mistaking them for hers – which would not have been impossible). She knows how frustrated she was then about being away quite so much. She honestly would have much rather been at home, particularly when Gemma and Zoe were slightly older, though not necessarily so she could have seen more of Paul. He was never part of

**307**

her long term plan, how she envisaged her future. Perhaps, she thinks, he lasted as long as he did, that he was there for all those years, because she wasn't. Had he been a bit more competent she might have felt differently. She might have been able to give up the airline for a start. But he was useless – he couldn't even put up her kitchen properly, considering he was meant to be a builder. Not that he ever had a huge amount of work – who was going to employ him?

One thing's for sure, she thinks, she's never been a great judge of character. She should have learnt something by now. However, she's always making the same mistakes, always screwing the wrong people. It's as if she's stuck on this cycle, which is, in fact, a downward spiral, because as she grows older everything seems to be getting more desperate, closing in – the men, her wish to be with someone for more than one night in some bland American hotel room (but if that's all that's on offer she knows it'll do, she'll settle for that). She can understand why she screwed Greg. After she'd been chatted up and then so coldly rejected by Sean frigging McPhee (she eventually tried ringing him, to be told by a young-sounding woman – his wife? – that he'd just come back from the UK and had already gone to bed) she didn't want to spend the night alone. She needed to feel needed, to have someone to hold on to for a few moments. And of all the potential crew members she knew Greg wouldn't reject her – with Dan being too young and not having quite worked out where David was coming from. But for the moment she doesn't want to think about Greg, her latest mistake, she's more interested in being sick. She's finding it oddly satisfying, as if she's somehow ridding herself of all this frustration and anger and misjudgment – Mike, Paul, Greg, she could go on and on. The constant rushing, the never being able to stop. She doesn't think she's ever felt properly settled (this thing that Joy's always talking about) or even remotely contented – not since she was about twenty-three anyway, before she married Mike (her time with Mike doesn't count because the nature of his departure has made her have to re-evaluate the whole relationship) when she had few responsibilities and nothing much was expected of her, when she thought life couldn't be much more fantastic, flying to America once a week, meeting all these gorgeous pilots – when she didn't want anything to stop, ever. (She's amazed Mike never became a pilot, being so obsessed with air hostesses, and stuck to selling secondhand cars. She doesn't think the training can be that difficult, not if half the pilots she knows well are anything to go by.)

She lifts her head a little, her stomach feeling empty but churning still, her eyes now watering badly (so she at least knows they haven't totally dried up), and reaches blindly for a paper towel, realising Nigel must have closed the door behind her, sealing her into this stinking, airless cubicle. At least she got to the toilet – unlike just about everyone else who's sick on board. Mostly being stationed in First she doesn't have to deal with it (no one's ever sick in First) but when she was in Economy she was forever clearing up vomit from the middle of the aisles, the backs of seats, people's laps. Wiping children down – their parents suddenly not being able to cope. How ironic, she thinks, to be the one doing the puking now – first time as far as she can remember in twenty-one years of service. She wipes her mouth and with another tissue (she managed to pull out about ten in one go, as usual) carefully dabs at her eyes, though the mascara's smudged anyway (despite it being waterproof), thinking, I have to get out of this job. I can't do this for the rest of my frigging life – it's destroying me. Is it really too late to start again?

Sorry, says Tim, I've run out of vegetarians. The normal breakfast only has a small bit of bacon with the scrambled egg and tomatoes. You could always just leave it to one side. That's what most people do.

I'd like a vegetarian, says the passenger. I don't want meat fat anywhere near my food, thank you.

You are meant to pre-book the vegetarians but I'll see what I can do in a minute, says Tim. Someone else might have a spare. He pushes his trolley forward (which is really aft) a row and clicks

on the brake. Crouching to retrieve this row's hots he's suddenly
sure he's being watched, that Nigel is up by Galley 3, the
beginning of Zone C, poking his large, scratched head through
the curtain that separates Business from Economy, spying on
him, wondering whether to wander down to say something (in
as casual a manner as possible), this thing he's been meaning to
say all flight but has only now plucked up the courage because it's
almost too late. Tim dares not look round in case this encourages
him. He stands, spongs a hot, places it on the outboard passenger's tray, despite shaking, spongs another despite shaking even
more. He feels strangely, shockingly excited again. Rather than
feeling apprehensive, or completely turned off, or disgusted, or
that he doesn't want to know, no way, he realises part of him
must want Nigel – that part of him must be attracted to his hairy
shoulders, his rippling sides, the way he's so overpowering, so
basic, like a Neanderthal, he thinks, so unlike anyone he's been
with before (he came all right, more than once). And in a way he
does want Nigel to wander aft in his large clumsy way to say
something about how maybe they should meet up soon, somewhere convenient, in Brighton perhaps. Because he's never
going to say anything. Not in front of Becky, not in case Stuart
or Andy get to hear about who he's been chasing – he can't begin
to imagine how embarrassing that would be. It's solely up to
Nigel. Well he's the Scorpio, Tim can't help thinking. (Whether
you believe in it or not he can see how astrology might still be
useful. How you're not completely responsible for yourself. Like
it's this get-out clause.)

With the light being so harsh she can't bear to spend too long
looking at herself in the toilet mirror (which she's always thought
must have some sort of magnifying effect built into it), redoing
her make-up, counting her wrinkles, being reminded of quite
how quickly she's aging. She feels weak but not sick still, as if
whatever it was has passed as quickly as it came on. She doesn't
think there's any need to inform the CM. She knows she'll be
able to hold out until London – she might be too skinny and

feeble-looking (someone once called her fragile) but she's pretty tough inside. Probably not tough enough to alter the course of her life (not that she has much idea where she wants it to go, in what direction – if only, she thinks) but tough enough to finish the breakfast service, for the one or two who want it, and wake up the rest of the passengers, Mr Rubinstein in particular (she's looking forward to that at least) and retrieve their expensive jackets and coats, or expensive-looking garments anyway (she has this idea that the passengers in First, certainly those in Business, buy almost as much fake gear as cabin crew do, trying to make themselves into people they aren't), and check the seats are in the upright position and all large items are properly stowed and the overheads shut, with the galley already having been tidied and secured. She's beginning to believe that something pretty un-expected will have to happen if her life is to change, if she's ever to find again any sense of security, of solidity, of calm, rather than just some short-lived illusion (she knows she's never going to orchestrate anything successfully herself, it's just not in her).

She looks at herself closely once more, leaning over the wet and soapy sink unit, the bottles of unused perfume and aftershave and moisturiser, at her bloodshot eyes, the thin brown line where her eyebrows used to be, her wrinkled forehead, her dull hair (dyed far too often), thinking who's going to want this in daylight? With all my baggage? Feeling her eyes beginning to water again (they haven't forgotten how to cry) she turns away from the mirror, still tasting sick, flips the toilet seat down with her foot, shoves the rest of the tissues she's still clasping into the waste unit (making sure there are no bits of tissue left poking up and that the flap closes properly, the way it's been drilled into her), pulls at the door, pulling the door towards her, getting it just so far and stepping back a bit, but trying not to graze the backs of her legs on the toilet, so she can kick the door the rest of the way open. Pleased no one appears to be queuing for the toilet and that the aisle is empty, she dashes out, heading for the galley, not exactly relishing going back in there and facing Nigel and Carlo, though knowing it's what's expected of her, knowing

**311**

there's nothing else she can really do at the moment – that it's all part of the routine, the endless cycle, the downward spiral she's stuck on, even if it has now started to make her sick. However, as she steps onto the non-slip rubber matting stretching between the toilet, the galley entrance and passenger door D1L (which always seems to her to get pretty slippery this far into a flight anyway, with people trailing spilt water and God-knows-what else from the galleys and the toilets over it – she can't imagine how it would hold up in an emergency evacuation, thinking people would be sliding all over the place) she hears someone call her name. And again.

# london

Wendy, Nigel says, for the third time, over here.

Wendy stops, sees Nigel by the door, leaning on the bulge, beckoning to her. She immediately thinks, I'm too tired for this, please, don't bother me now, intending to ignore him and slip back into the galley where Carlo's probably still preparing a fruit salad, replacing the sliced strawberries around the bowl because he just can't get it to look the way he wants it to (even though – she glances at her watch – they should have started clearing in the breakfast service) but she remembers being unkind to him earlier, accusing him of giving her the creeps. She recalls hearing the hurt in his voice and realises she perhaps could be a little more charitable, a little more understanding – her mother was always telling her that you get what you deserve in life, that people end up treating you they way you treat them – so she moves over to him, trying to smile, wondering quite what she's brought on herself over the years by being unpleasant to people. She doesn't think she's been too bad.

Hi, Nigel says. I'm sorry about being funny – outside the toilet – I've just got this weird thing – I don't like – never mind. I didn't realise what was going on. How are you feeling?

I'm okay, she says, noticing how nervous Nigel seems, not knowing quite what he's talking about. Whatever it was seems to have passed, she says. She's not tasting sick any more but the back of her throat is dry and burning a bit. I'll survive, she says.

Of course you will, Nigel says. That's the nature of this job, isn't it? We always survive.

Yeah, says Wendy, that's right. She watches him turn away from her so he's looking out of the window, sitting on the emergency chute staring into space, just how she kept catching him on the way over. What's out there now? she says, edging closer to him and the window, realising she can see more than just blackness between Nige's large head and the window casing, that the window has been smeared with a perfect deep blue, an almost electrical-looking colour, as if something outside, far away is shorting. A long, slow spark.

It's getting light, he says. And the cloud seems to be thinning. I don't know what's happening to the weather at the moment – it doesn't seem to be following any sort of pattern I can fathom. There should be more of a front than this. And New York was meant to be snowy when Saturday turned out to be a beautiful day. Look, there's the Irish Sea. Wales should be coming into view in a minute. Come on Wendy, why don't you take a peep?

You know it's not really my thing, she says, all this staring out the window, but she leans across anyway, putting her hands on the bulge for support, as Nigel shifts along slightly. What sea? she says. I can see a few clouds and sort of nothing. She thinks the sky looks cold and desolate with these blank, bottomless patches and she quickly pulls away because bending down like this is making her aware of the rawness, the emptiness in her stomach too.

Not far to go, he says.

Nope, says Wendy. We better get back to the galley, Nige. Carlo will be doing his nut. She steps away, turning towards the galley, though stops before she reaches the curtain, sensing Nigel hasn't budged, sensing an air of apprehension, of unease sur-rounding him. What's up? she says, looking over her shoulder, seeing him perched there (she's sure all that weight on the door can't be doing it any good) rubbing his right eye. For a second she thinks he's crying.

I get so carried away, he says.

Sorry? she says. She suddenly knows he wants to say something, that he's been storing whatever it is up for ages and now desperately wants to share it. She checks the time again, thinking why me, why do I always get people wanting to tell me their life stories, wanting to reveal some terrible episode of their past? But she decides she's going to listen this time because the thing her mum used to say to her about people getting what they deserved in life and not being charitable or considerate or supportive (she's not sure anyone's ever been that supportive of her, except maybe Joy but she always suspects Joy has ulterior motives, like she's incredibly nosy and really wants to know what she's been up to, everything down to the slightest details) is still at the forefront of her mind and she knows she hasn't given Nigel enough time yet. She wonders whether this is her new role in life, a sort of on board cabin crew counsellor. What are you trying to tell me, Nige? she says.

It's happened twice now, he says. After the first time I said never again because I knew I couldn't control myself and it frightened me. I hurt this boy. I didn't mean to, of course, but we just got tangled up the wrong way and I suppose I've never been fully aware of how strong I am. It felt like I was exploding inside. You see I'd never been with someone before, not in that way. It was incredible. I didn't have any idea it could be like that. Everything suddenly made sense and I messed it up by not being able to control myself. I can still see his face, see him lying there hugging himself, his dislocated arm, telling me to get away, that I gave him the creeps, that he never wanted to see me again. He looked so young but he wasn't. He wasn't totally innocent either. He picked me up in the first place. He went for me. Honestly – I wouldn't have had the nerve. He was called Paul. I thought it was all way in the past, something I never think about now but it's suddenly come back. I can remember everything – exactly what he looked like, even where we were. It was in a hotel on the front, the place he worked. He had keys to all the rooms, you see.

Steady on, says Wendy. You're going too quickly, you're losing me. She finds she's put her hand on Nigel's shoulder and that Nigel is starting to shake. Nige, she says, don't worry, nothing can be that bad. She crouches again so she's more or less at his height, manages to get half a buttock on the door, too. She slips her left arm the rest of the way around his shoulders and tries to pull him into her, comforting him because he's crying properly now. She feels awkward sitting with him, embarrassed. She doesn't want to be seen comforting a crying cabin crew, the First purser in particular (she's never had a purser cry on her before, she's never known anyone working in First to break down like this). But she knows she can't just leave him to it – she was forever breaking down on board after Mike left her (when she was still in Economy) and was always comforted by someone. She thinks the job's lonely enough as it is. If your fellow hosties don't even come to your aid when you need it most there can't be much point in living. (Maybe, she thinks, it's not some new role but her just being human for once.)

I've messed up again, he says, shaking and sobbing and sniffing and trying to draw breath all at the same time. I wanted him so badly – he looks a bit like Paul. I think that's what must have set it off. Wendy, I totally lost it. I don't think I hurt him particularly, not in the way I hurt Paul. He probably got the better of me in the end – you've seen the scratches on my face – but I must have freaked him out. He wasn't there when I woke up in the morning. He left without saying anything and he's been avoiding me ever since.

That's not so unusual, says Wendy.

I don't know what comes over me, he says. I don't think my mum being ill has helped. When we were in New York I spoke to my sister who's looking after her while I'm away. Apparently the doctor doesn't think she's got much longer, a week, maybe two. Do you have a tissue? I've just realised I've forgotten to buy her a present. The last present I'll probably have the chance to buy her – I had thought I might get her some perfume, from one of those places on Canal Street. I know they're fake but my mum can't tell the difference.

Sorry, says Wendy, I haven't any tissues on me. I can get you some from the toilet if you like?

It's all right, he says, I can use my arm for the moment. Wendy hears him trying to laugh but she thinks it sounds as if he's just gulping more air, steadying himself. The thing is, he says, as much as I don't want to live with my mum forever, I'm not sure how I'll cope with being on my own. Suddenly being able to do exactly what I want all the time – it frightens me. I'm not very good at organising myself. I need a routine, order. I need to know exactly where I am all the time – which is why I've stuck with this job for so long I suppose. Waiting on people, sorting out the cabins and galleys – always being on a schedule. He tries to laugh again. Also Wendy, he says, I like knowing there will be someone at home when I get back, letting myself in to hear Mum doing the Hoovering or watching telly. Having tea with her. Us both going over all the things I've brought back from America, repeating the stories I tell her about these places. Everything sitting on the shelves as normal – the diddy Empire State Building, the Statue of Liberty that's also a lighter, the blow-up alligator, the life-size Oscar I bought her in the duty-free at LAX. This is what I'm used to. On the outbound I was imagining how it would be without her. In a way I thought it would be exciting, as if I'd be embarking on a new life, but the more I think about it, the more I realise I don't want to be on my own. Maybe it's why I went for Tim in the way I did – you know, I was feeling particularly anxious. Sorry, Wendy, I don't normally talk about these sorts of things.

It's okay, she says. Maybe you just fancied him. There's nothing wrong with that. Not after all those years you've gone without, Nige. Look, we've all made mistakes, we've all slept with someone just because we want to grab hold of a bit of flesh and blood for a few minutes, to engage with another human being, to feel we're still alive and kicking.

I don't know, he says. I'm confused. Nothing's clear any more. I don't think I want things to change – not if it means I can't control myself. Not if it means I keep doing things like last night. I don't want to freak people out. I'm not ready for all this freedom, if that's what it is – I'm useless at it. I just want Mum to be there for me. I don't trust myself otherwise. I don't know myself.

Nige, Nige, Wendy says, we all want someone to be there for us, to be loved – please stop fiddling with your watch, she can't bear the clicking noise it's making. Ask any hostie on board, she says, and they'll all tell you it's not freedom we want but love. You know, love and a sense of security. A nice little home with a hubby who comes home every night and a couple of adoring kids. She finds she's trying to laugh herself – at this idea of home, of security, of everyone searching for this place, yet none of them getting anywhere near it, at least not for long. She wonders why this is, whether the job just attracts people prone to domestic failure – as if they are all really clones, all made from the same stuff – or whether the job simply induces it in them, whether it turns them into one another.

But I still can't stop thinking about him, he says. Part of me is desperate to see him again.

There'll be plenty more Tims, she says. There always are in this game. You have to get used to letting people slip from your grasp. But who am I to tell you all this. I thought I'd mastered it but I haven't. I'm no better off. I'd love for Greg to express some desire to see me again, and not simply as part of a sleazy assignation in a down route hotel. I know he's got this reputation and he's messed up his marriage and his health. But maybe he needs someone who understands him a bit better, someone who can see where he's coming from and why he's messed so much up. Now there's a confession.

There's land, Nigel says. Wales. And there's the Severn Estuary.

Great, says Wendy. I'm overjoyed to be nearly home. I don't know what's worse, being at work or stuck at home on your own – even my kids have left me. You know, Nige, I think I've been in this business too long – I've lost all sense of judgment. I need a change, a new life. I want something dramatic to happen for once.

Why don't you leave then? says Nigel. Get out for good.

Come on, says Wendy, you know it's not as easy as that. After all these years.

*Dan begins at the side wall, checking the EFIS source selectors. He quickly moves over to the PFD and ND screens, cross-referring each item of information. He then turns to the master control and display unit of the FMS. With this completed and while waiting for Greg to finish on the radio to London (he can hear Greg being given clearance straight through to meet flight level 180 by Baset, at pilot's discretion) so the captain can begin his descent and approach briefing, including, of course, the final check list, Dan yawns wildly, lifting his head and diverting his tired gaze away from the control panels, for about the first time in twenty minutes and out of the window. (Since they left their oceanic he's been too busy negotiating their way across Shannon and now London airspace to meet UK landfall by Strumble to not focus completely on the job at hand, fearing he might lose his place.) He's amazed to see how light it's become. To see this strip of intense, fiery orange running across the horizon, arcing in the middle slightly, a bit like a spot about to burst, he thinks, with a thin band of light blue running above the orange, though this blue quickly loses its luminosity, draining away into ever darker sky, into night still. Below he sees broken cloud catching what light there is – altostratus and more altostratus, though some might be cirrus and other patches stratus because of their clearly very different base levels and silky and flat grey appearances respectively – and the dimming street lights of Cardiff on his right and further away Bristol and the towns and villages hugging the Somerset and Devon coastlines, and rolling hills and fields, the drab English earth just beginning to assume colour as the daylight strengthens. Seeing land beneath them, how it passes so slowly, how it seems to realign the aircraft in the sky so the sky is no longer limitless but simply bound to the earth by the atmosphere, how in a sense it reaffirms*

*gravity, this incredible pull, makes him contemplate how much he,*
*Greg, Becky, all the crew have become bound to each other and that*
*whatever happens when they step off the aircraft (though he's at least a*
*little clearer on this front now he's managed to talk to Becky – when*
*Greg slipped out for yet another pee, which he claimed was definitely*
*going to be his last before landing) there'll always be this bond, that part*
*of them will always be flying. He can't think why this trip should have*
*proved to be so unusual, so memorable, compared to the hundreds of*
*others he's already experienced as a pilot, as a trainee, except by chance,*
*by some extraordinary fate that had them all rostered together, and that*
*this particular mix of people and personalities set off so many reactions.*
*He starts thinking of the solar system and spiralling nebulae, big bang*
*and the origin of the universe. The cyclical nature of astrophysics. Of*
*life. It blows his mind. It blows his mind how everything always seems*
*eventually to fit together.*

*Okay, Dan, says Greg, pulling on his shoulder straps, let's go.*

Tim pushes his trolley into the last available slot, locking it in
place with the paddle blades, which amazingly don't get stuck.
He turns, rubbing his dry, sticky hands, pleased with himself
that he's not the last to have packed up, despite being the last to
finish serving breakfast. He doesn't know what happened, he
was chatting with Becky one minute and the next everyone else
was out in the cabin sponging hots, apart from himself who
hadn't even loaded his breakfast meals. Excuse me, darling, he
says, trying to get around Valerie (who he reckons is finally
looking a little flustered – her hair seems to have come
unpinned on one side), trying to make it doubly clear to
Debbie, who's standing by the left exit, that he's all done –
he's even handed in his duty-free bar receipts. He gets past
Valerie and then Marissa and Becky (who he thinks has been a
changed person since she's made this arrangement to meet up
with Dan next week, which she couldn't keep quiet about for
more than two seconds – like she's just stepped on board, full of
beans) making for the exit by Debbie, who he steps around
now, beaming at her, but she's not looking at him, she's leaning

out of the galley staring up the aisle towards the front of the plane as if there's some sort of a problem, so Tim thinks he'll just wander up the aisle a little so she can't miss him and the fact he's finished already.

He was intending to go this way anyway – now Becky seems to have sorted herself out, or at least has come to some sort of decision, it's like he doesn't want to be left out. He doesn't want to be the one who's forever single because he's incapable of deciding what he wants or sticking with anything. He knows Nigel's old enough to be his father but he thinks at least they have something in common, that they're both chronically shy – and in an odd way inexperienced. For all Nigel's strength and eagerness Tim could tell he didn't really know what he was doing. And he doesn't care that Stuart and Andy might kill themselves laughing when they find out. He realises he should stop worrying about what other people think of him and do something for himself, initiate something. Maybe he just wants to prove Becky wrong. Or maybe it's because he'd never let anyone come inside him before, protected or unprotected (as far as he's aware – he doesn't think Jason could have screwed him in Miami but he's not totally sure he didn't) and not only did he really enjoy it but he thinks it's pretty significant, that it somehow marks a new stage in his life.

He sees the seat-back video screens have gone blank, emitting only the odd flicker of static, though the passengers are still staring at them as if the picture will return any second. He feels the plane slow and sort of lurch forward at the same time which makes him stop surveying the nearby rows of puzzled passengers (any moment now, he thinks, and they'll be madly pressing their call buttons, demanding the screens are turned back on) and look up, straight down the aisle which is clearly dropping. He sees David, the Business purser, appear through the curtains blocking off Business from Economy and rush towards him. As David pushes him aside Tim turns with him, immediately disconcerted by the expression on his face and the way he's rushing, to see him disappear into the Economy galley. He thinks he hears a scream coming from the Business section. Stuck in the middle of the tilting aisle he doesn't know which way to go, having suddenly forgotten where he was headed and why.

*Dan says, having taken a deep breath, having carefully thought about it, indeed having quickly rehearsed each word again and again in his head – he doesn't want to make a single mistake, imagining all that's riding on this announcement (puffing it quite out of proportion, as he does with just about everything) with Greg sitting next to him (even if he does appear distracted) and the passengers and crew in the back anxiously awaiting what he has to say, with Becky obviously wanting to know how competent he sounds or whether he comes across as a complete jerk, because now they've made this arrangement to meet (he didn't actually believe she'd say yes) she'll be working out whether she's done the right thing, looking for any excuse to change her mind, because he is, he's petrified about what he'll have to tell Suzi – Dan says, trying to steady his breathing, not wanting to sound in the slightest bit nervous, squeezing himself, he says finally, Ladies and gentlemen, good morning, this is the first officer. We have started our descent into London Heathrow. We've been informed of a small delay on the way but should be on the ground in twenty-five minutes – that's five past seven in the morning local time. The weather at Heathrow is clear with a light breeze, and the temperature's currently three degrees Celsius. Once out of our holding position our flight path this morning will take us just south-east of central London from where we'll be swinging back round and landing towards the west. I hope you've managed to get some sleep on the way over and that the cabin crew have done everything to make the flight as comfortable and enjoyable as possible. We've certainly enjoyed looking after you up here and hope to see you again soon. Dan turns to Greg, thinking, how about that, mate, not one mistake – it was informative, chatty, confident, I even breezed over the matter of the delay. You couldn't have done any better, despite all your experience. Though he can see Greg's talking into his mouthpiece and probably hasn't heard a word of it.*

*Greg says, switching off the interphone and swinging the mouthpiece away, Dan, we've got a problem.*

Where did they find her? says Wendy.

In the CM's station, says Nigel, slumped on the floor.

Where's she now? says Wendy.

She's still in there, says Nigel. David and Debbie didn't think they should move her, not in front of the passengers. She's in a bit of a mess. She's got sick all over her and – Nigel steps across the galley – apparently she's wet herself, he whispers. Worse than that actually.

Oh poor Selina, says Wendy. Poor baby. She must have the same thing I had. She'll be all right, I feel fine now.

No, says Nigel. I don't think so. He moves even closer, so Wendy can feel his breath on her face, so she can smell it, his rotten breath – she doesn't know why he's bothering to talk so quietly as there's only the two of them in the galley, Carlo having disappeared (not that there's any reason why he shouldn't be told, too), and knowing that there's no chance the passengers can hear a thing from here, most of them being still asleep anyway, regardless of the fact the main First cabin lighting has been turned on and Dan's made his announcement about landing (which she thinks went on too long for the time of the morning or maybe it was just that she hated the way he was so obviously trying to sound like Greg – all the first officers are the same in the way they copy the captains) – and says, still whispering, They think she's swallowed something on purpose, you know, that she's taken an overdose. Apparently she's gone through the medical kit. There are empty pill packets all over the place. They don't know quite what she's had – Valium, Temgesic, Ativan, Isordil, Buccastem, aspirin. Perhaps the lot.

No, says Wendy. No. The poor baby. How's she now? Is she conscious?

Yes, Nigel says, she's talking, though she's not making much sense. Debbie said fortunately Selina was violently sick almost immediately, probably some allergic reaction to one of the pills, and that it's very unlikely she's kept anything dangerous down.

Aren't they putting out a call for a doctor? Wendy says.

I don't think so, Nigel says. Debbie doesn't think it's necessary, seeing as we'll be landing so shortly – she used to be a nurse. They're getting a doctor to meet the plane though. You know how they are about passengers seeing things like this. They obviously want to keep it as quiet as possible. Debbie and David are trying to clean her up so they can at least get her strapped into a crew seat.

I must see her, Wendy says. I'm going to help.

I wouldn't, says Nigel. You'll only draw attention to what's going on, besides we haven't gone round with the hot towels yet, or handed the jackets and coats back. I can't do it all on my own.

You'll have to, says Wendy, and who cares if the passengers find out? Fuck this airline and its frigging reputation, which doesn't exactly amount to much nowadays anyway, does it? What do I owe it? I'm not going to start handing out hot towels which nobody wants anyway when a colleague's just tried to kill herself. Selina needs me. Oh Nige, why's she gone and done this? She pushes herself off the counter and towards the galley exit. Selina of all people, she says. She's so pretty and young still. She has everything going for her. All these men running after her – you saw them at Becky's. And she is the frigging CM. I'm not even a purser, after twenty-one years. If anyone should feel like topping themselves surely it should be me.

Maybe Selina has more guts than the rest of us, Nigel says. She saw what she thought was the only way out and went for it.

There are other ways, Wendy says. There have to be. She could just leave. Why couldn't she just leave?

It isn't that easy, is it? Nigel says. Isn't that what you told me earlier?

Wendy doesn't answer, she can't answer, thinking for the first time that perhaps there are some dead ends in life, these points you reach where everything closes in, leaving you no more room for escape, and hurries out of the galley not bothering to check herself in the mirror or to see if the curtain falls back into place properly (she doesn't care what impression she makes in front of the passengers, or how the cabin is presented, whatever's in the service guidelines, whether she says fuck instead of frig – not any longer) remembering for some reason that she still hasn't pinched her memento of the trip, the set of miniature, fake chrome salt and pepper pots, and that there were a couple on the counter right in front of her only an hour or two ago. She's forgotten what distracted her from slipping it into her bag, though she knows it's too late now, that they'll have been packed up and stowed in a dry locker, probably with the unused flower vases and the logoed napkin holders and any spare cutlery. That her collection at home, neatly lined up on the smoke hood shelf (which she noticed the other day is beginning to come away from the wall at the back) is never going to be complete, that it'll always be missing the one set that might have meant more than any of the others, the very last pair of salt and pepper pots she could have fitted on. (She would have squeezed them on somehow – she's had enough practice trying to get everything onto a trolley top.) But as she climbs towards the rear of the plane through Business – full of passengers frantically packing up their belongs before the fasten seat belt sign comes on – with her legs, the whole of her ridiculously thin body sensing quite how fast and steeply the plane is now descending, sensing the full force of gravity pulling her back down to earth (as she tries to walk against it), with her ears popping yet still with this incredible sound ringing in them, in waves, a sound she thinks she must have managed to blank out for most of the flight though realises was there all along – a whine, a terrible high pitched whine like a scream turning over and over itself – making voices so hard to hear you don't know who's talking, whether it's yourself or whether it's just in your mind, and as she pushes on through Business, struggling against gravity, passing people reaching into the overheads, people patting the creases out of their clothes, people she hasn't noticed before, as Tim, as odd-looking Tim, Tim the teenager who Nige obviously can't let go, comes running the other way, not even acknowledging her as he brushes past, as she nears the CM's station at the end of Business, just in front of Galley 2 and beneath the stairs to the upper deck, she realises she's pleased she forgot to nick the stupid salt and pepper pots, knowing it doesn't matter because she's going to bin her collection the moment she gets home anyway (along with the smoke hood). That she doesn't need to be reminded, however obliquely, of the sheer number of returns she's been on. Of all the dismal one night stands (the searching for a moment or two of comfort, of security, of steadiness). Of quite how much she's aged in the process. The price she's paid.

Though as the smell of sick hits her, immediately making her feel queasy again, as, amazingly above all this other noise, this whining scream, she hears the ping of the fasten seat belt sign (wondering for a second who will now make the announcement that goes with it about passengers having to return to their seats and the follow on rubbish about landing cards and code share transfers, car hire and partner hotels, now that the cabin manager is obviously out of action, whether indeed anyone will bother – she has no idea what the back-up procedures are), as she slowly, anxiously peers into the CM's station to see Selina sitting on the floor hugging her legs, her long, slender legs encased in laddered, sick-stained tights, with Debbie crouching by her and David dabbing at her blouse with a serviette, with bits of sick on her blouse and skirt too, and on the walls and all over the desk, where she can just make out the corner of a crew assessment form (she's seen enough of them in her time) and a few empty pill packets, she thinks, at least I have my kids. At least I have something to show for myself, to connect with outside this world. And suddenly feeling peculiarly maternal, as if she's responsible for not only Gemma and Zoe but also for Selina, and Nige and Carlo, and all the other cabin crew (she is the oldest hostie on board), she crouches alongside Debbie and David, trying to make space for herself, and says, Selina, darling, let me look at you. As Selina turns towards her, her eyes red and her face blotchy, her make-up having smudged and run badly, her ponytail thing having collapsed and partially come loose, Wendy says, putting her hands on Selina's shoulders, You still look beautiful. You're still lovely.

Selina coughs and says, No one else thinks so – her voice thin and quavering.

Of course they do, darling, says Wendy. Of course they do.

Why am I always being ignored then? Selina says. How come people are always leaving me in the lurch – forgetting about me completely?

I'm sure that's not true, says Wendy.

David says he never wants to see me again, Selina says.

That's not quite what I said, says David, stopping dabbing at Selina's blouse and looking up at Wendy, trying to look surprised, Wendy thinks, trying to look innocent. It's just that I can't, he says, not in the way you want me to see you, Selina. I live with someone. You know that. I haven't lied to you. I'm sorry. I didn't mean to upset you. I thought we were just having a bit of fun. Catching up. You know. We used to work together, he says, looking at Wendy again, as if, Wendy thinks, that explains everything. Ages ago, he says. In another life.

You've always been a shit, Selina says. I've always hated you.

David, Debbie says, I think it would be easier if you left us to it.

I was only trying to help, he says, standing. I don't know why she's done this. Nothing serious happened in New York, honestly. We were just having a laugh. We went to Bloomingdale's together. That's about it.

Look, says Debbie, don't worry, I'm sure it's not your fault. Wendy and I can manage. Just tell Greg we've got the situation under control. That'll be the most helpful thing you can do.

Wendy moves out of David's way as best she can, noticing as he steps over her he has sick on the tread of his left shoe, realising it was obviously him she saw with Selina in Bloomingdale's and not some mysterious hunk (she can't get over how every time she sees David he looks so completely different) and as he disappears into Business the name of the song Selina was humming and which got stuck on her mind for the rest of the day also comes to her as well – it was 'American Pie', by Don someone. Mike used to play it all the time in the car – My My Miss

American Pie, she remembers – it drove her nuts. She loathed it. Let's get you to a seat, she says, trying not to think of the song now, of Mike, of all those years ago, but the present, how best to deal with the situation at hand. We can't land with you sitting on the floor in here like this, she says, all messy. And it occurs to her that perhaps the best way to deal with anything, with life for instance – yeah, she thinks, with life – to not get stuck in a corner, in a dead end, is to focus on the present. That you mustn't let your thoughts stray too far into the past, or the future, where complications, where all sorts of dangers lurk.

I don't want to move, says Selina. I can't stand up. I'm frightened.

Come on, darling, says Wendy. Debbie and I are here. We're going to stay right by you.

You don't understand, says Selina. I don't want to go any-where. I don't want to go home – there's nothing for me there. Certainly not Mike – who have I been kidding? And I can't do this any more. It scares me. Don't make me move. Please don't make me move. I've got nowhere else to go. I've got no one.

Hush, hush, says Wendy. She finds she's stroking Selina's hair, combing it with her fingers, sweeping it here and there, trying to get the ponytail to do what it's meant to do. Wanting her to look nice and whole again, not because she's worried about the passengers seeing her in this state but because she needs to see her together, in one piece, as she first appeared in crew briefing (even though she was a little shaky then). She knows Selina's problems aren't that different from anyone else's. She knows how much in common they all have and that if one of them loses it they all might. That they are that close. She also knows that when it comes down to it they've only got each other to keep them sane, to hang on to. You've got us, darling, she says. You've always got us, Selina. We'll look after you. This is where you belong, with us.

Hearing the three pings and Greg or Dan say (how's he meant to tell the difference between them?), Cabin crew, two minutes to landing please, Tim pulls himself away (a little thankfully because he was becoming worried someone might spot them) still feeling the pressure of Nigel's fingers on his arm – like there was all this passion and relief in one quick touch. And not saying anything further because he's said all he has to say, he turns towards the rear of the plane where he knows he's going to be stuck for years (presuming he passes his probation – not that he's ever heard of anyone not passing), but what does he care, he thinks? What else is he going to do with his life? He has a much clearer idea how it really works. What Stuart and Andy see in it.

*London says, in the way London always says, thinks Dan, in this calm but slightly superior tone, 'Cleared for landing.' He was enjoying holding, flying this four minute right-hand racetrack above Swanley, not letting his mind stray too far, keeping everything in check.*

*Greg says, Gear down, flap twenty. He shifts in his seat, pulling against his shoulder straps – a heaviness, a chronic weariness to his movements, Dan can't help noticing. What did I say, he says, hey, Dan? I told you Selina would be trouble. The younger ones want so much attention nowadays – she should never have been put in that position. It was obvious from the start. You know something, I think I've been looking at everything the wrong way all these years, not seeing what really matters. The more I think about Wendy the more appealing the prospect seems. She could certainly brighten up my retirement – and she wouldn't be around all the time either. It's not as if she'll make me feel too hemmed in, too claustrophobic – you can't change everything that quickly. At least she understands me, the first woman I've ever met who understands me. Dan, I've just decided what I'm going to do as soon as we get this thing on the ground. When you get to my age you're entitled to break a few rules, hey son, especially if you made them in the first place.*

*Dan thinks Greg should shut up. That it's not exactly the time to start talking about retirement. He's now desperately scanning the screens, monitoring runway centre line and glide slope indications, the attitude, speed, heading, altitude, rate of descent, engine power setting and seconds to touch down. Checking the aircraft is in balance, the flight path perfectly stable. He wants the landing to be as smooth as possible of course, with*

*Becky in the back. He imagines he's flying the aircraft just for Becky, that this is what all his training has amounted to, the tremendous effort — he knew it would be worth it one day. He smiles to himself, feeling the aircraft begin to sway and lumber a bit as it hits denser air and probably some wake turbulence from the aircraft sequenced ahead, knowing it's all under his control at last (as much as a pilot is ever in control), sensing the power at his fingertips. However, he allows himself to look up (thinking it won't matter if it's just for a second or two — they are still in auto), way above the winding Thames and rapidly enlarging roads and estates and business parks of west London, the runway lights of Heathrow dead ahead, so he's staring at this clear, endless sky (this sky he saw as a child, with his dad on the way to Greece), he can almost feel it in his stomach like an ache, like nothing and everything, with the sun now rising behind them, with this fiery glow catching the forward rim of his side window and sprinkling the pane with sunrise, wanting this very moment to go on forever, endlessly also. Wanting everything to remain exactly how it is, with everything still possible. Never wanting to land. Numbed.*